IRON MAZE

Gordon Brook-Shepherd has written seventeen books previous to *Iron Maze*, mostly dealing with nineteenth- and twentieth-century European history, specializing in the Habsburg dynasty. Two exceptions arose when he was offered the chance to meet and question in depth all the major Soviet defectors to cross over to the West from the Stalin era to that of Gorbachev.

A historian by training (he gained a Double First in History at Cambridge) Gordon Brook-Shepherd served in military intelligence during the war, ending as Lieutenant-Colonel with the Allied Commission in Vienna. His first civil post-war post, as head of the *Daily Telegraph*'s Central South-East European Bureau during the Cold War years, brought him again in touch with the Western intelligence community. These contacts were renewed at intervals right down to the war in Afghanistan, which he covered on the spot when Deputy Editor of the *Sunday Telegraph*.

He was awarded the CBE in 1987.

Gordon Brook-Shepherd

IRON MAZE

*The Western Secret Services
and the Bolsheviks*

PAN BOOKS

First published 1998 by Macmillan

This edition published 1999 by Pan Books
an imprint of Macmillan Publishers Ltd
25 Eccleston Place, London SW1W 9NF
Basingstoke and Oxford
Associated companies throughout the world
www.macmillan.co.uk

ISBN 0 330 36877 X

1 3 5 7 9 8 6 4 2

A CIP catalogue record for this book is available from
the British Library.

Typeset by The Florence Group, Stoodleigh, Devon
Printed and bound in Great Britain by
Mackays of Chatham plc, Chatham, Kent

TO THE MEMORY OF

'HUBY' KÓS

(1929–1998)

AND WHAT HE STOOD FOR

Contents

[vii]

CONTENTS

CONTENTS

Part Six

End Game

List of Illustrations

RUSSIA

0   500   1000 Miles

U.K.

NORWAY

DENMARK

SWEDEN

Barents Sea

Murmansk

Stockholm

Gulf of Finland

FINLAND

Baltic Sea

W.
GERMANY

E.

Riga

Tallinn

Vyborg

Arkhangel'sk

EST.

RUSSIA

LITH.

LAT.

Pskov

St Petersburg

Vologda

POLAND

BELARUS

Kotlas

Minsk

THE
UKRAINE

Moscow

Kiev

Orel

Kursk

Ekaterinburg

Ural Mountains

ROMANIA

MOLDAVIA

Khar'kov

Voronez

Ufa

Tobol

R U

BULGARIA

Odessa

Kherson

Don

Saratov

Volga

Chelyabinsk

Tobolsk

Crimea

Sevastopol

Donetsk

Rostov-na-Donu

Omsk

Black Sea

*Sea of
Azov*

Novorossysk

Tsaritsyn

Ural

Irysh

Astrakhan

KAZAKHSTAN

TURKEY

Kuban

Terek

Tiflis

Caspian Sea

*Aral
Sea*

Lake Balkhash

SYRIA

UZBEKISTAN

IRAQ

TURKMENISTAN

KYRGYZSTAN

IRAN

TAJIKISTAN

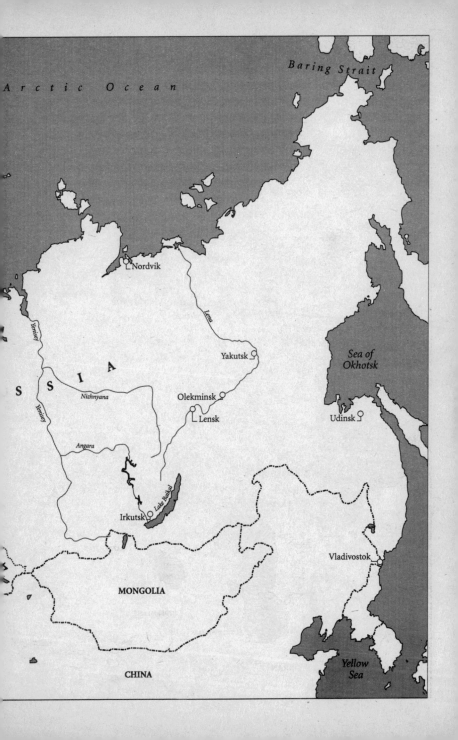

Foreword
(of necessity a lengthy one)

How on earth did the Bolsheviks manage to survive those first perilous and bloody months in power? After they signed their separate peace with Germany, in February 1918, they had the Western powers, as well as their domestic enemies, lined up against them; and, during the summer of 1918, both sets of opponents combined to hatch at least two *coups d'état* against Lenin's infant regime. One was botched; the other, the misnamed 'Lockhart plot', was penetrated before it could ever be launched. Yet, had push come to serious shove in either case, all that Lenin and Trotsky could have relied on to save them in Moscow was a few thousand Latvian mercenaries, hired as their 'Praetorian Guard'.

Then, in what I have called 'the war after the war' (once the Armistice with Germany had been signed), Britain, France and America abandoned thoughts of any internal putsch and pinned their hopes – as well as staking billions of their money – on the various White Russian armies trying to march on Moscow from east, south and north. This military threat grew so critical by July 1921 that, as we now know, Lenin secretly moved five million dollars (220 million in today's money) to Sweden so that he could abandon ship in Russia and carry on fighting the Bolshevik cause from abroad. Yet, within months, he was again triumphantly at the helm; how, and why?

These questions have intrigued me over the years whenever I was writing general histories about the closing stages of the Great War or the fall of the continental dynasties which that conflict had brought about. It was clear that part of the reason why the gap had never been filled was that some of the material needed to fill it was simply not available. Over the last thirty years, much of the relevant diplomatic and military archives of all three Western powers involved has been, at intervals, released. (In preparing this present volume, for example, I have been able to consult, at the Public Record Office, more than fifty volumes of the 371 Foreign Office series and the W/32 War Office series, *all* of which deal with one subject only: 'Russia 1918'.) Yet the parallel and complementary archives of the Allied secret services on the conflict, in particular those of Britain and France, were never available, although these services had played a prominent, and sometimes a leading, role in the failed attempts to unseat Lenin. They finally fell victim, in part at least, to the remarkable campaign launched by Lenin's successor, Stalin, to secure revenge on those who had tried to strangle the infant Bolshevik regime in its cradle.

These are the missing archives on which I have been given a series of 'special briefings' (to use Whitehall parlance) over the past three years. They revealed a mass of fascinating human detail which lights up the more formal records, and the background to this personal access is not without a certain fascination itself. The initial impetus to the work was given in London, but only after some twenty years of patient periodic prodding.

Back in the early 1970s, when I was preparing the first of two volumes on Soviet defectors to the West (a project also launched on my behalf by British intelligence), I enquired whether, one day, the files on our anti-Bolshevik activities might become available. The answer, was, regrettably, that that day might never dawn. There were seemingly insuperable political difficulties about revealing our attempts to assassinate Lenin while maintaining full diplomatic relations with the Soviet Union he had created. Then came the collapse of that Soviet Union and the ideological dethronement of its leaders, including Lenin himself. Surely, I politely but persistently enquired, the original objections were no longer valid, especially in view of the invitation of the then Chancellor of the Duchy of Lancaster, Mr William Waldegrave, to historians and researchers to identify specific closed government records to which they sought access.

Finally, after I had penned letters to two members of Mrs Thatcher's Cabinet (one of whom I knew well personally), the door opened when I was invited to call at a familiar mansion in London's clubland. There, over several lengthy sessions, I was briefed on everything that had survived in our closed archives on the subject I was dealing with: the struggle of Western Secret Services against the Bolsheviks in the early years of the regime. This included notably the first full and authoritative account of the doings of Sydney Reilly, Britain's so-called 'Ace of Spies' as given, partly, in his own *Diaries.*

I must confess that, at the time, I harboured doubts as to whether even this spread of hitherto undisclosed material really was the complete feast. Were not some very sensitive tidbits being held back in the vaults? There was not one single reference, for example, to Ernest Boyce, Reilly's station chief in Moscow during those critical months of 1918. Yet it had become clear that Boyce and, above him, Britain's 'special envoy' to the Bolsheviks, Robert Bruce Lockhart, were more involved in all the deadly hanky-panky than either of them pretended.

Over the three years of on-and-off research which followed, I came to the reluctant (but also somewhat apologetic) conclusion that my Whitehall friends and mentors were telling the truth. It became clear that our SIS files have simply been vandalized (speaking from the historian's point of view) by mass weeding, often carried out at random, to save time and money by drastically reducing space in the archives. The weeding process which accompanied any move of the department from one headquarter building to another seems to have been particularly savage. Thus a (to me) promising-looking file headed 'Anti-Bolshevik Activities in Russia' had been pruned to extinction. When opened it was found to be completely empty. This was true of later files whose contents would, in fact, have cast only unqualified credit on the SIS, thus showing how thoughtless much of this space-saving had been.

The reader (and any professional spy-writers interested) must therefore take my word for it that I have been able to draw on everything in the way of unpublished British secret intelligence which has survived on this period. The only possible exceptions would be references in the unpublished private diary of the first head of the service, the legendary 'C', or Captain Mansfield Cumming. But I am told there are likely to be few entries which would have interested me and the entire chronicle is anyway composed in 'C's' highly personal cypher code which nobody has so far managed properly to crack.

As to transatlantic help, an immediate back-up became available, though in contrast to American help over the defector books (which was also in the nature of 'special briefings') most of this was already on record in the National Archives. One of the important exceptions concerns the saga of Xenophon Dmitrivich Kalamatiano, the bizarrely named, and equally strangely destined, head of the American spy network in Moscow in 1918. In reality, he was a station chief like Boyce; but as Washington was not allowed officially to run a secret service in Russia, or anywhere else, he masqueraded as the head of a commercial intelligence organization. The only Western agent to fall into Soviet hands – and to go on filing reports from prison – he is the unsung hero of this story (in contrast to the much-trumpeted Sydney Reilly). I was indeed fortunate to be given unstinted help on him by Harry Thayer Mahoney, who has made Kalamatiano something of a lifetime study.

Some of my other American helpers are listed under Acknowledgements, but another must be cited especially here because meeting him led to one of the most unexpected and significant finds of the entire research effort. (Indeed, it is one of three very lucky finds which have come my way.) Some two years ago, I was contacted out of the blue by a Mr Edward P. Gazur whose son had recently sent him an American paperback copy of my book *The Storm Birds*, in which I had devoted two chapters to the highest-ranking Soviet intelligence officer ever to defect to the West – General Alexander Orlov.

Mr Gazur and his wife, Ruth, became the only truly close friends the Orlovs had during their more than thirty years of asylum in the United States – so much so that the general had made Mr Gazur his literary administrator and the legal guardian of all his personal papers. Was I interested in seeing these, asked Mr Gazur? He liked what I had written about the man he so admired and would be willing therefore to give me access to material which no outside eye had hitherto seen. When it turned out that the general (who died in 1973) had written extensively from his own experience on the early years of the Bolshevik regime, and that none of this material had appeared in his two published books, I expressed great interest. When it later transpired that, for example, no fewer than sixty-five pages dealt with the Soviet inside story of the rise and fall of 'Britain's Intelligence Ace, Sydney Reilly', my interest became compulsive. I soon found myself sitting under an apple tree in the sunlit garden of the Gazurs' hospitable Kentucky home with a fat typescript in my lap. It was the general's much rumoured but still unseen 'third book'.

Entitled 'The March of Time, Reminiscences by Alexander Orlov', it is 655 pages long and deals in twenty-nine chapters with episodes in his career as a soldier and Soviet secret service man, from those first years of Bolshevik rule down to his own break with Stalin in 1939 and his adventurous flight from his final post in Spain to North America. Much of that Spanish story and his escape from Stalin's clutches had already appeared in print. This account of the earlier period had never been published or even circulated. It covered half the book, much of it on that first decade of Bolshevik power with which I was concerned. (The whole of Chapter Five, for example, gives the real story, over seventy-six pages, of the entrapment of Boris Savinkov, the 'great conspirator', and the most dangerous of all the Bolsheviks' Russian foes.) I have quoted extensively from both of these sections, not only because of the fascinating human detail they provide, but because I came to regard them, after frequent counter-checks, as totally reliable. I ought to explain why, to the general reader and the intelligence buff alike.

There are four main reasons, apart from the circumstance that Orlov rose to be a KGB general. The first is that he was not involved himself in the events he was describing: there is no cause, therefore, to suspect him of exaggerating or of playing down (where things went wrong) his own part in any of the operations. He was, however (and this is the second reason), an irrepressibly curious man, always trying to get to the bottom of the major battles with the West which his department fought – and usually won. He was the ideal example of what, in the profession of journalism, would have been called 'the investigative reporter' (and, unlike some of that ilk, he was conscientious about getting his facts straight).

Moreover, and this is the third reason, he was in the right place at the right time and with the right connections. He was twice posted to the Moscow headquarters of the secret police during the years 1924–6, the very years when the Lubyanka was buzzing with excitement over the capture first of Boris Savinkov and then of Sydney Reilly. As a protégé of the police supremo, Felix Dzerzhinsky, Orlov was able to glean all the details of these successive triumphs from the colleagues responsible – either for the running of the deadly deception campaign or the interrogation of the famous prisoners (and sometimes both). Federov, Styrne, Puzitsky, Pilar and, above all, the chief's right-hand man in the operation, Artur Artuzov, are names which will occur frequently in this narrative. All were repeatedly questioned by the inquisitive Orlov and, in his chronicle of events, he usually names which of his colleagues had been the source for any event or anecdote related.

The fourth reason for believing in Orlov's account is, from the historian's point of view, perhaps the most important. His testimony, on these or other matters, has never been proven wrong when checked out over the years from other reputable sources. This held true when, soon after his death, I spent the best part of a week in Washington being briefed by his CIA case officers (above all the venerable and much-lamented Raymond Rocca) for those two chapters of *The Storm Birds* on his defection. It still holds true, so far as I can establish, today.

There is much, it must be stressed, that he did *not* tell his debriefers. Thus, there was no mention of the major role he is known to have played in the early 1930s as the OGPU's roving inspector of foreign intelligence assets – including, in Britain, Philby and the rest of the 'Cambridge Five'. On this he kept mum, though he seems to have been bursting to get it off his chest shortly before he died. But what he *did* state always stood up over the years and I have been able to confirm this again as regards 'The March of Time'. Whenever his account is compared with other objective versions, Western or Russian (and for non-objective Soviet revelations, see below), it squares up.

Now to special help from French intelligence sources. This is, in some ways, an even more remarkable story, inasmuch as, until fairly recently, they had hardly any of their own secret service material with which to help me. All their Deuxième Bureau archives, along with other special security and diplomatic files, were carted off to Berlin by the Germans after the fall of France in 1940. Those archives sat there for the next five years until, after the Red Army seized the German capital in 1945, they were transported to Moscow, where the Russians gave them a thorough working over in the period (close on forty years) they remained in Soviet hands. The collapse of the Communist regime and the arrival on the scene of *glasnost* and closer collaboration with the West opened the way for high-level negotiations about their return. An accord was duly signed between the French and Russian governments on 12 November 1992.

Then, between December 1993 and May 1994, seven deliveries of these French archives, each weighing some twenty tons, arrived in Paris and were deposited at Château de Vincennes, seat of the Historical Service of the French Army. The process came to an abrupt stop in June 1994 when President Yeltsin's opponents attacked him in the Duma for 'destroying the patrimony of Russia' (a ludicrous but effective charge). By then, 10,326 cartons of documents had arrived, for which no less than 7,000 linear feet of storage space had been made ready. (Some had arrived separately from the French Embassy in Stockholm.)

This mass of *documents repatriés* now had to be sorted out and catalogued. A dedicated team of four archivists under Claire Sibille managed to complete this task in three years and they were able to produce their fat catalogue in several volumes by June 1997. Having already been promised special access to such material by the French authorities, I arrived in Paris the following month and was among the first (and certainly the first foreigner) to have that catalogue in my hands. Like the trail which led to the Orlov papers, the timing, no less

than the material itself, was precious. It was, suitably, a French philoso-
pher who declared that 'The right moment is the sovereign of all things.'

There appear to be big gaps in these archives which still need
filling. The propagandist-spokesmen of the present-day Lubyanka have
assured Western enquirers that 'only about 5 per cent' of the French
intelligence material is now held in Moscow. The French, who still
have their old catalogues left to consult, beg to differ. They calculate
that more than 10,000 boxes still remain in Russian hands and that
these boxes contain three-quarters of the subject files (*dossiers théma-
tiques*) of their secret services. Some material may have been lost in
transit; but many of the most sensitive files are thought to have been
kept back for later release when they were caught by the 1994 ban.
From my point of view, Boris Savinkov may well be a case in point.
The most rigorous search in several archives has only uncovered one
returned file containing a single sheet. The file on Admiral Kolchak,
doomed hero of the Siberian campaign, also contains only one paper,
dealing with his tangled love life! However, whatever has survived and
been traced for the 1917–27 period has been made available to me,
and is of more than just rarity value.

Finally, there are the contributions from Russian sources, and
these are all the more cherished for having been made indirectly and
unwittingly by today's guardians of the Soviet intelligence archives.
These have latterly been specializing in 'co-production' with Western
authors, to whom much new and seemingly quite authentic material
has been provided. The actual selection of the material, however, has
been in the hands of the Russians, funnelled mainly through their
'co-author', Oleg Tsarev, the one-time public relations man of the
restructured department. It is no surprise that these, in themselves,
admirable additions to our knowledge deal, so far exclusively, with
past Soviet triumphs. They ignore Soviet failures, as symbolized, for
example, by every defector who figures in *The Storm Petrels* or *The
Storm Birds*. (They are, incidentally, attempting to rehabilitate Orlov
as being more anti-Stalinist than anti-Communist.)

The first of my unofficial providers of Soviet intelligence material
was an old family friend, George Vassiltchikov. Though the son of

a Russian prince of markedly anti-Bolshevik views, 'Georgi' often travelled to the Soviet Union as a bona fide representative of de Beers diamonds (which the KGB naturally regarded as a Western intelligence cover). On one visit soon after the collapse of the Communist regime, he called at the Lubyanka building and enquired whether he might see their police file on him. He was passed up and up a startled chain of officials, always treated with politeness, even deferential warmth. I never learned what he brought back for himself. But for me – knowing my long-standing interest in the subject – he brought photostats of everything being made ready on the Sydney Reilly affair.

I might add (and I have his permission to do so) that he is in fact 'Geoffrey Bailey', the author of that remarkable book *The Conspirators* – remarkable in that it revealed, back in 1961, so much about the anti-Bolshevik struggle of the 1920s and 1930s without the benefit of any access to archives. He has latterly been struck down with partial paralysis, after consuming a dubious oyster in Moscow. He assures me it was genuine bad luck, and anyway works on indefatigably. He has been greatly cheered by becoming the only émigré to be selected by an all-Russian panel of voters as their choice for a sort of good-will man-of-the-year.

He will forgive me for saying that the second contribution handed up to me from the bowels of the Lubyanka is of far greater historical importance than their tidbits on 'The Ace of Spies'. I am constrained not to reveal the identity of the person who provided me with this unexpected bonus, but I can indicate what it is. The 'History of Soviet State Security Organs' (of which I have read a full authenticated translation) is the only 'in-house' chronicle of the political police ever to be prepared. The specially appointed faculty of the Red Banner Higher School of the Committee of State Security (KGB) were instructed to record objectively and factually what had gone on in the secret intelligence world over a sixty-year span of Communist rule. The top secret study they came up with in 1973 does just that. It is a sober survey with no propaganda flourishes never intended for any outside eye, and I was glad to find that, wherever I compared it with Orlov's chronicle, finished independently in another continent ten years before, the general again checks out. He always elaborates events with fresh detail but the bare bones of each story are the same. I should add that all these special finds of material were quite new to my British helpers, so that a healthy cross-flow of information and analysis ensued over several months.

To sum up, what I have been able to do is to take the tapestry of this first East–West struggle (largely familiar as regards the military and political patterns) and work into it these threads of the accompanying secret intelligence war which have thus far remained hidden. I am aware that the picture is still not complete. The Russians may eventually come out with more authentic and non-ideological material on the lines of that 'in-house history'. And I am acutely aware that, even as I am writing these lines – composed after ending the book though they appear at the beginning – another telephone call or letter may arrive from Paris telling me that something else of great interest has just been discovered among those *documents repatriés*.

But, for the time being, what follows fills up the picture of this secret war as far as is possible, and stretches out to all four sides of the frame.

Gordon Brook-Shepherd
February 1998

London, SW1   Paziols (Languedoc)

Part One

Russia 1918 – Which Way?

1

The Man Carrying Diamonds

On 29 March 1918, the beleaguered British mission in Bolshevik Russia received the following telegram, sent by special secret service cypher from London. It was a requested repeat of an earlier message which had been corrupted in transmission.

> On 25 March, Sydney George Reilli [*sic*], Lieutenant Royal Flying Corps, leaves for Archangel from England. Jewish-Jap type, brown eyes very protruding, deeply lined sallow face, may be bearded, height five foot nine inches. He will report during April. Carries code message of identification. On arrival will go to Consul and ask for British Passport Officer. Ask him what his business is, he will answer 'Diamond buying'. He has sixteen diamonds value £640.7.2 as most useful currency. Should you be short of funds he has orders to divide with you. He will be at your disposal, utilise him to join up your organisation if necessary as he should travel freely. Return him to Stockholm if possible end of June. More to follow.

This is the first operational document in the hitherto undisclosed personal file of the man who was later to be dubbed the 'Ace of Spies'.[1] The telegram came directly from the head of Britain's nine-year-old secret service, the naval captain George Mansfield Smith-Cumming. The captain was already something of a legend himself under the pseudonym 'C', the green-ink initial with which he signed his personal messages, and by which all his successors were to be known.

There was 'more to follow' indeed after the arrival of this special British agent, described in such brutally unflattering terms; more than either the 'diamond buyer' or his Whitehall master had counted on. But before looking at the background of the two men, and before coming to the whirlwind which was to engulf both of them during that Russian spring and summer of 1918, it is worth dwelling first on the date of Lieutenant Reilly's despatch from England.

Twenty-fifth of March was only three weeks after Lenin's recently installed Bolshevik regime had signed the peace treaty of Brest-Litovsk with Germany and her Central Powers allies. In October 1917, Lenin had seized power from the nerveless fingers of his moderate rival Kerensky on the issue of ending Russia's fight alongside the Western powers. He was willing to pay the heavy price which the Germans had demanded[2] because he knew that the future of his regime and its revolutionary cause depended on bringing to an end a war of which both Russian soldiers and civilians had become sickened and weary. But for Russia's wartime allies, headed by Britain, France and the United States, Lenin's gamble represented a potentially lethal threat.

In the Great War (as in the Second World War to follow it) Russia, with its vast expanses and millions of men-at-arms, was the meat-grinder, capable of slowly draining the blood out of even the mighty German army. Now the meat-grinder had dismantled itself, giving new strength to that army as it went. The German High Command was able to transfer some forty divisions from the Russian battlefields to join in the so-called 'Emperor's battle' on the western front. It was, of course, pure coincidence that this final offensive, which was to sweep to the gates of Paris before being checked, had been unleashed on 21 March, only four days before Reilly's mission began. But the mission itself, like many another allied endeavour at the time, was directly linked to the military crisis. Could the Bolsheviks be somehow brow-beaten, bribed or cajoled into taking up arms again? If that should prove impossible, then how was this Bolshevik regime, which was now, in effect, a hostile force, to be weakened, destabilized, or actually overthrown?

And, as more immediate concerns, what could be done to stop the huge stockpiles of Allied war supplies falling into German hands, as well as those Soviet-controlled fleets now at anchor in Russian harbours? To find out some of those answers, and come up with some of the solutions, was a task beyond the capacity of any routine professional agent. It called for somebody out of the ordinary, and Reilly was certainly that.

Reilly's arrival in this world, like his departure from it (and much that lay in between), is blurred by misty trails of confusion, many of which were laid by Reilly himself. Indeed, it has been shown to be prudent not to take any of his own accounts of events at face value unless they can be corroborated from the surviving official documents on his own file, or backed up from other non-official sources. His birth and declared parentage are registered facts. Sigmund Georgievich Rosenblum, as 'Reilly' was really called, was born on 24 March 1874 near Odessa, the Black Sea port of southern Russia. His father, Grigory, was a well-to-do Polish Jewish merchant and landowner, though both he and his wife, Pauline, had converted to Catholicism in order to breathe and move more freely in the heavily anti-Semitic atmosphere of the time. The boy had a comfortable start to life, but soon developed into a youth who, though blessed with a remarkable talent for languages, was cursed with a violent temper and saddled with an unquenchable conviction that he, and he alone, was right about absolutely everything. Megalomania seems to have set in early.

It was not altogether surprising, therefore, that in his late teens he broke away from the restricted bourgeois life of a Jewish youth in Odessa. Versions differ, however, over the reasons for the sudden break. According to one explanation, derived from some unnamed surviving relatives of Reilly's in the 1980s[3] (and therefore quite possibly from the man himself), the young Rosenblum had left distraught when he was forbidden to marry his first cousin, with whom he had fallen violently in love. According to an earlier account,[4] seemingly relying on stories from his ex-colleagues (and therefore, again, ultimately on Reilly), he fled in rage and panic when it was disclosed to him that his real father was not Grigory Rosenblum but the family doctor, a Jewish physician based in Vienna, who had tended his mother for many years.

Of the two versions, the second seems the more plausible. As we shall see, Reilly was a man without a shred of moral scruples, especially where women were concerned. He would have been more likely to have eloped with the forbidden cousin, rather than tamely abandoning her. The taint of illegitimacy, on the other hand, was a smear he would have found hard to live with in his native town, whose middle classes were as sanctimonious as they were self-indulgent. Being a Jew, by whichever father, was something the young Rosenblum would have to live with. His race was, in any case, written in capital letters on his face, as that unkindly worded telegraph of 'C's' would emphasize some twenty years later. But to be called a 'dirty little Jewish bastard' (the denunciation thundered out by one of his uncles, disgusted at his nephew's left-wing views) would have been a brand-mark on the soul. The little Napoleon – who indeed eventually began to collect Napoleana – was confronted with something he had been quite wrong about, and which he was equally unable to put right.

Those misty trails get thicker and thicker, as well as more sinuous, when obscuring the next twenty years of his life, again because most of them were emitted by his own fantasies. He claimed, at various times, to have been a railway engineer in India and a docker, cook and brothel doorman in Brazil (where the first attempts were supposedly made to recruit him for British intelligence). There is no echo of all this feverish-sounding stuff on his official file. Here the earliest reference – perhaps appropriately, in view of all that was to come – concerns his first, and only legal, wife (he was to marry two others bigamously and to promise marriage to an unmeasured swarm of other victims).

We know that he landed up in London at the end of the century because a certificate at the Holborn Register Office shows that, on 22 August 1899, one Sigmund Georgievich Rosenblum, described as a 25-year-old 'Consulting Chemist', whose father had been 'a landed proprietor', was married on that day to the 24-year-old Margaret Thomas, a widow, whose father was given as Edward Reilly Callaghan, 'a Captain in the Navy' (the absence here of the defining word 'Royal' is disturbing). Margaret's late husband had been a comfortably-off Welsh non-conformist minister more than thirty years her senior whom Reilly is said to have run across while the ill-assorted pair were travelling as tourists in Russia. The minister had expired only five months previously in a Newhaven hotel where, it was later rumoured, the 'Consulting Chemist's' special concoctions had had something to do with precipitating the fatal heart attack.

That rumour might well have been nonsense. The facts remained that Rosenblum had acquired a pretty wife with a tidy sum of money and then the late minister's house at 8 Upper Westbourne Terrace in Paddington, into which the newly-weds moved. In addition to fast becoming one of the greatest liars of his time, it is possible that he had just married another liar. Margaret was said to have started off as the humble Irish maidservant at Westbourne Terrace. She herself, however, left a very different account of her life and romance in a typescript which resulted from an interview with one Captain Isaac of British Intelligence.[5] An extract from it reads:

> She first met R. in the summer of 1898 at her home, Kingsbury Manor, Middlesex. Introduced to her as Sigismund [sic] Georgievich Rosenblum. Told her that whilst at University in Russia he became mixed up in a political plot which on discovery forced him to fly [sic] the country. Described his father as landed proprietor. Completed his studies at a German University, taking a degree of Doctor of Chemistry. Came to England to perfect knowledge of English language. Employed as a chemist by a Company called 'Ozone'. Married woman quietly at Registers [sic] office Chancery Lane on 22.8.98. Connoisseur of objets d'art. He proceeded about a week after marriage to Spain. R. well supplied with money.

Mrs. R. apparently had money and during the absence of R. she liquidated Kingsbury Manor, selling her hunters for high prices etc. Apparently Mrs. R. financed the purchase of art treasures which, when sold at Christies, fetched little. R. then took up horse-racing which ended in disaster. Seemed then to suffer from homesickness and wished to return to Russia.

In 1901 they changed their name to Reilly. They then proceeded to China.

Rosenblum had chosen to call himself Reilly because it was one of the Christian names of Margaret's father, and though he looked most unlike anyone from the Emerald Isle, his behaviour often matched that of the Irish at their wildest. But, apart from the change of name and the marriage details, absolutely everything else in this officially recorded account is at odds with the various versions of events which have come down unsourced. It is entirely possible that Margaret (née Callaghan) had been a housemaid at Kingsbury Manor, and not the daughter and eventual mistress of the house. Nor does she even mention her first marriage, which we know took place. On the other hand, there is much in her account (Reilly's dabbling in fine art at other people's expense, for example, and his disastrous venture on the British turf) which exactly fits the man whom we shall come to know. At all events, if Margaret was a liar, she was a daring as well as a consummate one. It could easily have been possible for Captain Isaac to check on whether the family Callaghan had ever owned the manor house in Middlesex, but neither he nor anyone else in Whitehall seems to have bothered. The document stands alone and uncommented upon in Reilly's file.

Nor is there a line in that file about any contribution he may have made to British intelligence in the twenty years following his marriage. His main biographer[6] has him working under 'C's' direct orders at intervals throughout the period, beginning with the Boer War, then in Persia, Port Arthur and China (all at times before an independent British secret service, or 'C' himself, even existed). The epoch is said to have culminated in exploits in wartime Germany, where he posed as a German officer and, according to his own stories, met the Kaiser and joined in the councils of the High Command. Most of this can be written off as outrageous invention which would have left even Baron Münchhausen gasping. On the other hand, it seems quite likely that, like many another businessman-adventurer travelling the globe with extensive international contacts, a thirst for money and a nose for information, Reilly would have supplied British missions (and, doubtless, the missions of other powers when this seemed prudent and profitable) with information, even provided to order from the local authority. He was certainly in pre-war St Petersburg where he cut a flamboyant figure in what might be termed the *café-au-lait* society of the Tsarist capital. One of his many business activities there was as Russian agent for the Hamburg shipbuilding giant Blohm and Voss, which would have put him in a position to pass on details of German naval construction, invaluable in the context of the looming European war.

When that war came, Reilly is known to have established himself rapidly in New York with the first of his bigamous wives, Nadine Massino, whose *mari complaisant* had been a high official in the Russian Ministry of Marine. (The hapless Margaret, who had taken to drink, was bullied and bribed to return to England without him.) What Reilly now concentrated on, rather than those fictitious sorties into the Kaiser's Germany, was making another fortune for himself, this time in the torrid world of arms purchases. For reasons which are not quite clear, he left his business temporarily early in 1917 to go to Toronto. Here he enlisted in the Royal Canadian Flying Corps, receiving a commission as lieutenant before returning to Nadine and the arms trade.[7]

One thing needs disclosing as regards his recruitment by 'C' early the following year. Cumming may have heard a lot about Reilly's reputation as a resourceful international go-getter; but it was by repute only. This is made clear by a telegram which 'C' had sent to his New York station as early as 28 February 1918, asking exactly who this Reilly was; what precisely he was doing in New

York and what opinions were held about him in British official circles. None of these queries would have been needed had there been anything on file about Reilly's supposed exploits, or had 'C's' own people in America been urging the arms dealer to join the service for a special mission. The reply which the New York office sent back to London four days later was in fact blunt and damning: 'With reference to your telegram no. 206 of the 28th. SYDNEY REILLY is a BRITISH subject married to a Russian Jewess. He has made money since the beginning of the war through influence with corrupted members of the Russian purchasing commission. He is believed to have been in PORT ARTHUR in 1903 as spy for Japan. We kept him under observation 1916. We consider him untrustworthy and unsuitable to work suggested.'[8] It was signed, unusually, with the sender's initials, 'N.G.'

Further exchanges on the Reilly issue followed between London and New York for the next two and a half weeks. 'N.G.'s' final message to his chief was just as discouraging as the initial response. Quoting an American bank official, who had known Reilly over several years, it reported his verdict as follows:

R. is Greek [sic] Jew; very clever; entirely unscrupulous. Present war had made about 2 million dollars on Russian Contracts. Has connections in almost every country including Germany, Japan and Russia. ENDS.

In connection with above, may I point out there must be strong a [sic] motive for REILLY leaving profitable business here and wife, of whom he is said to be very jealous, to work for you.[9]

By the time (2.25 p.m. on 21 March) 'C' received that last dissuasive message, it was too late for him to change his mind even had he been so disposed. Lieutenant Reilly RCAF was already on his way to Archangel. His 'strong motive' for taking on the venture is not hard to divine. After all the posturing and pretence, here was the real thing at last – a mission from 'C' himself, the man he was claiming to have dealt directly with for years; and what a mission.

Russia, his native country, had just deserted her alliance with Reilly's adopted homelands, England and America. Could he help them to find out what was going on and what could be done about it? The little Napoleon from Odessa felt himself being tugged forward into history by his coat lapels.

Cumming's decision to put Reilly on his Russian team despite all the official warnings he had received about the man is harder to explain.[10] It can only be put down to a hunch, and the determination to follow his own instincts against any opposition, especially where, as now, a major crisis had arisen. This was entirely typical of the man, whose background needs sketching out, in view of the role he was to play from the wings in the drama now beginning to unfold.

'C' was then fifty-nine years old and was lucky to have had the secret service job put in his lap after the creation of Britain's first national intelligence organization in July 1909.[11] He was then a commander, but with seemingly little prospect of climbing higher up the career ladder. The truth was that the Admiralty scarcely knew what to do with him, for he was afflicted with the most disabling as well as embarrassing illness any professional sailor can suffer from: acute and incurable sea-sickness. This had repeatedly interrupted his early shipboard career which had taken him, in the 1870s and 1880s, to the East Indies, Egypt, South Africa and India; but from 1898 onwards, he became confined to shore bases and languished 'on special duties' in Southampton. He had made the best of this, especially when trying to improve the harbour's boom defences, but it was his knowledge of languages and his wide range of outside interests that caught the Admiralty's eye when they were asked to nominate an officer to head the foreign section[12] of the new secret service bureau and picked on their odd-man-out. He was to prove an inspired choice. All his successors in the post to this day have had to be measured against him.

'C' had an officer on his staff, H.F. Crowther Smith, who was an exceptionally talented artist and caricaturist. It is to him we owe the splendid full-length colour portrait of the chief in uniform which has been preserved in the service archives and is shown on the back cover. On top of the stocky, broad-shouldered body sits a head which is even more massive in proportion. It has a large chin and nose, a mouth set in very firm lines and a steady gaze from wide-open eyes, the right one sporting a cordless monocle. The expression is at once commanding and humorous. It is little wonder that he was held in affectionate respect by his subordinates, who were fiercely loyal towards him. The picture was done, incidentally, in 1918, the year when 'C' took his gamble on Reilly in the spring, and was to launch an even bigger gamble in the Baltic that same autumn.

The portrait shows one unusual feature. The captain is holding, and partly leaning on, a long walking-stick with what appears to be a soft tip at the bottom. The cane holds the key to a tragic incident in the first weeks of the war which had nothing to do with intelligence but a great deal to do with the legendary aura around 'C's' head. Compton Mackenzie, the novelist to whom we owe so many vivid cameos of his time, tells the story of what happened on 3 October 1914, when the intelligence chief was being driven by his son, a lieutenant in the Seaforth Highlanders, to a staff meeting:

> The car, going at full speed, crashed into a tree and over-turned, pinning C by the leg and flinging his son out on his head. The boy was fatally injured and his father, hearing him moan something about the cold, tried to extricate himself from the wreck of the car to put a coat over him; but, struggle as he might, he could not free his smashed leg. Thereupon, he had taken out a penknife and hacked away at the leg until he had cut it off, after which he had crawled over to his son and put a coat over him, being found later lying unconscious by the dead body.[13]

That the father escaped death from blood poisoning himself is something of a miracle. But, less than a week after the mangled foot had been amputated, he was on the way to recovery. From then on, he was to administer lesser shocks to people who did not know of the tragedy: to help his concentration, he would tap away with his stick at the wooden leg while in the middle of a conversation. Clearly, any man equipped with such ruthless courage and determination when tackling a life and death crisis was not going to be put off by subordinates questioning his wisdom in selecting a special agent for Russia.

That same determination served him and his fledgling service well when it was fighting for space and recognition in the Whitehall jungle, whose spruce appearance was deceptive. But 'C' needed patience and skill, as well as a firm purpose in his tussles with bureaucracy. To begin with, he was outranked in his own sphere: the Director of Naval Intelligence was traditionally a vice-admiral and from 1914 onwards this post was held by the formidable Reginald 'Blinker' Hall. To make matters more complicated, it was the Foreign Office whose budget funded the secret service (an arrangement which has persisted down the century) but, in 'C's' time, it was the War Office which actually distributed the money. This created the impression that the military were really in charge throughout and the confusion was compounded by the fact that many members of the SIS had been army officers. (The War Office, of course, had its own Directorate of Military Intelligence, headed by a major-general, whose arc of operations often intersected with 'C's'.)

Inevitably, therefore, the chief had many a tussle with the bureaucratic establishment. He forestalled these, wherever possible, by acting off his own bat and informing his Whitehall colleagues afterwards. As we shall see, this could lead to unholy confusion as well as great successes in the field. One minor battle much closer to home that he did lose with them concerned his own name. He had been born Mansfield George Smith but his second wife (there was a divorce from the first) had a maternal grandfather named Cumming who was a wealthy Scottish landowner. As far back as 1889, the year of his second marriage, he started to call himself Smith-Cumming, possibly to preserve an inheritance as well as to lend him more social lustre. But it was only after repeated official proddings that he formally assumed the surname Cumming in

1917. This could now properly be represented on paper in the form of that green-ink 'C' initial.

Needless to say, nothing with that mark on it had been given as credentials to Reilly, who appears to have journeyed out on a pass issued by Maxim Litvinoff, the Bolshevik government's representative in London. It contained the same error as in that advance warning telegram of 'C's': the surname was misspelt 'Reilli'. This, combined with his distinctly un-Irish appearance, landed him temporarily in a naval lock-up on arrival at Murmansk until he could establish his bona fides with a coded message. From that point forward, however, Reilly just surged ahead on his own propulsion: not so much a loose cannon on board a warship as a rogue warship breaking away from the fleet. Cumming had expected something special from his 'ST 1'. For the next six months he was to get more than he had bargained for.

After spending a few weeks in Petrograd, as St Petersburg had been renamed, Reilly turned up on the afternoon of 7 May in Moscow, which Lenin had made into the Russian capital.[14] What he did immediately on his arrival sounds like one of his colourful tales but is, in fact, fully documented. The first act of ST 1, who was supposed to be on a highly secret mission, was to walk up to the Kremlin gates, announce his identity and demand to see Lenin. He told the bemused sentry that he was the personal envoy of the British Prime Minister, who was dissatisfied with the reports he had been getting from Britain's official representatives in Russia and had therefore instructed him to find out what was really going on in the minds of the government's leaders. The Bolsheviks were more receptive than most to the concept of special messengers wielding considerable influence under the cover of modest credentials and wild appearance. Instead of being sent packing, therefore, Reilly was let in and though he never got to see the great man himself, he was interviewed by one of Lenin's closest advisers, Commissar Vladimir Bonch-Brouevich. The incident was reported the next day to the British consulate-general, with the polite enquiry as to whether the unexpected visitor had been an impostor or not.

This introduces the third figure in that trio of Englishmen ('C' and Reilly being the others) who were both to experience and to cause such mayhem in Russia over the next five months. The official who received the news from the Kremlin was the thirty-one-year-old Scot, Robert Bruce Lockhart, who had moved down to Moscow from his consular post in Petrograd on a special assignment which further complicated the general reshuffle described. His new task, as we shall see, was already fraught with difficulties, including that of defining his own authority; the last thing he needed now was an apparent challenge to it out of the blue. Here, as so often, the problem of different channels came into play, for 'C's' cyphers, like his whole organization, were separate from those of the Foreign Office. Lockhart knew nothing about that cable of 29 March announcing the mystery man's arrival. But he summoned the one man who would know the answer, Lieutenant (later Commander) Ernest Boyce, the former naval officer who had recently taken over as the head of SIS in Moscow.[15] Sure enough, Boyce confirmed that the man 'Reilli' was indeed a new British agent sent out by 'C'.[16]

The next day Reilly was wheeled in himself to offer some explanation to the highly indignant Lockhart, who found his anger slowly ebbing under the excuses put forward, which were humorous as well as ingenious.[17]

Lockhart's grudging admiration may have had something to do with the fact that, in some ways, Reilly was a caricature of himself, however distorted, debased and exaggerated the parallels were. Lockhart also had a wild, even unbridled side to his character, expressed in the abandon with which he plunged into a succession of love affairs. So far from conducting these with discretion, he positively flaunted them in public – very much in the Reilly style – seemingly indifferent to any effect this might have on his career. Already before the war, when a young planter in Malaya, he had been obliged to return to England through a combination of ill-health and scandal. The latter had arisen from his infatuation with Amai, the lovely ward of a deposed sultan. Ignoring all advice – official and private – not to 'go native', especially with such a resplendent product of the blood royal, he installed the young girl in his own bungalow and lived with her there openly, until the day he was put on the boat for home. Such was his obsession that he had contemplated becoming a Moslem if this change of faith might lessen the fury of her outraged family. Amai remained as fatalistic as she was devoted. The girl did not utter one word of farewell as he left, even moving to a back room so as not to witness his departure.

Lockhart's next ill-fated obsession abroad arose in wartime Moscow where he had been posted as a junior vice-consul in January 1912, after passing first the previous year in the Foreign Office entrance examination. After 1914, he witnessed the ups and downs of the Russian army's campaigns; the fall of the Tsar; and the febrile existence of the provisional governments which followed. Only his flagrant love-life prevented him from witnessing the final drama. During the summer before the October Revolution he had become involved with a Russian Jewess, a Madame Vermeille, whom he had met casually at the theatre. Despite various admonitory nudges, he persisted openly with the affair. The lady was far from being of royal blood and there were no religious complications attached. But Lockhart was now a British diplomat and also a married man. His wife, a long-suffering Australian woman, was with him in 'en poste' Moscow and as Lockhart himself grimly admitted: 'My marriage was a contract from which I alone reaped any benefit.'[18]

It was to bring him no benefit at the moment, however. The scandal reached the ears of the ambassador in St Petersburg, Sir George Buchanan, the quintessence of the old-style diplomat, who summoned him up to the embassy for a show-down. An alarming instability in Lockhart's character, a crack in the confident façade, now came to the surface. The elderly gentleman gave the young hothead such a sympathetic and, at times, emotional hearing that Lockhart returned to Moscow a chastened man, pledging to put country before self by breaking off the attachment. But he held out only until he heard his inamorata's voice over the telephone three weeks later. He went back to her immediately and the scandal flared up with redoubled force. This time Sir George was less sympathetic. For him, a broken word was an even graver matter than a broken marriage. Lockhart was quietly packed off home. As in Malaya, illness was given as the sole reason for his repatriation. He was, Sir George informed the Foreign Office, 'on the verge of a nervous breakdown due to over-work'.

Lockhart got back to London just six weeks before Lenin seized power; but it was that revolution which propelled him back to Russia only three months later. Whatever the 'provenance' of Reilly's mission had been, there is no doubt that Lockhart was despatched on the personal orders of his Prime Minister. Lloyd George had read and heard a lot about the young Scotsman, who had been cruising around official circles in London, airing his views as to what should be done about the new Bolshevik regime. After a meeting at Downing Street, he was now given the chance to put those forthright views to the test. It was a complete changing of the diplomatic guard, and an ironic one. Lockhart sailed out on the same Royal Navy cruiser which was to bring the recalled Sir George Buchanan home.

The old sea-dog, sitting with his wooden leg and his pile of secrets in the flat at Whitehall Court; the ambitious and impulsive young Scot, now snatched back from obscurity and presented with, not just a second chance, but the greatest chance he would ever have to achieve some glory; and the bastard Jew from Odessa, transmogrified into a Canadian Air Force officer and a British special agent with ideas of his own about glory ... all three ill-assorted men were now in place. Each had before him that by now familiar conundrum which was puzzling the Western alliance as a whole: was it possible to turn the Bolshevik revolution to any advantage for the Allies, and, if so, how should they set about it?

2

Options

On 23 February 1918, Lord Robert Cecil, the head of the special Russia Committee at the Foreign Office, circulated a memorandum to the War Cabinet. His theme was how the Alliance could most effectively react to the challenge posed by the Bolshevik revolution of the previous autumn. The likelihood that the new regime would take Russia out of the war had been looming ever larger for weeks. Nonetheless, Cecil wrote his paper eight days before the treaty of Brest-Litovsk was actually signed. It shows that, though there had already been much head-scratching over the matter among the loftiest brows in the Alliance, no firm decision had been taken. Lord Robert's memorandum is a document of some significance. It is the first survey on official record which not only sets out the options available over grand strategy but comes down with a firm smack on the choice to be made.[1]

He begins by referring back to a decision taken by the British Cabinet as early as 3 December (less than a month after Lenin's seizure of power) which, 'after some hesitation', had decided to provide financial help to movements in Russia which were 'anti-Bolshevik and pro-Entente'. Nothing of substance had been done, however, until a top-level conference held on 23 December in Paris, where Clemenceau, who had become Prime Minister only three weeks before, approved a policy which seemed for the near future to look both ways at once: 'Though we should continue to have unofficial relations with the Bolshevik government at Petrograd, we should do everything we could to support the [anti-Bolshevik] movements in the South and South-East of Russia, and elsewhere if they should develop, and it was distinctly agreed that if the result of such action was to produce a rupture with the Bolsheviks we should not be deterred by that happening.'[2]

Then, Cecil's résumé continues, at a Cabinet meeting summoned by Lloyd George on 25 January, the question of Japan's role was debated. Though a member of the Alliance (and indeed destined to become one of its 'Big Five'), Japan had contributed little to the common conflict effort; now, it was felt, her moment had come. The Foreign Secretary, Arthur Balfour, approved an attempt to 'promote Japanese intervention in Siberia' and undertook to sound out Britain's principal allies on the idea. At this point, there broke to the surface again that major split in the Alliance which was to befuddle all the options to be considered over Soviet Russia and all future actions to be taken there. France and Italy both agreed to the British proposal. However, 'The State Department in the United States gave an unfavourable reply, but at the same time the President privately intimated that if we pressed the matter strongly he might consent.' (The Japanese were to come round readily enough to the idea, while trying to ensure that, if they did take action, it would be done on their own.)

Cecil then addressed another issue which was to divide Allied policy-makers throughout the year ahead, and beyond: would the popular reaction inside Russia to Allied intervention be favourable or hostile? (In the latter case, of course, it could only serve to strengthen the Bolsheviks' hand.)

Cecil came down strongly in favour of the first prognosis, provided any action 'were carried through with vigour'. He ended by stressing the 'enormous importance of a speedy decision' on intervention, adding that, had such a policy been implemented six weeks or even a month ago, he was personally 'very doubtful whether any separate peace would have been made by Russia'.

That was a large and unquantifiable assertion as regards the past, but Cecil had set out clear parameters which enclosed the future: the hesitancy of President Wilson who, as we shall see, had to be dragged kicking into the idea of direct American involvement; the unknown quantity and quality of any home-made armed resistance to the regime; and, equally unknown, the reaction which any foreign intervention might provoke. Indeed, on that final point, Balfour was about to receive contradictory assessment from two of his top Russian experts in the Political Intelligence Department of his Foreign Office: one, from the future ambassador Rex Leeper, saying that the Allies should not intervene without the Bolsheviks' consent, and the other from the distinguished academic, Professor Simpson, declaring that intervention should be launched whatever they might feel. It was typical of what, later in the century, was to become known as the battle of 'hawks' versus 'doves' in Western attitudes towards that same Soviet Union.

Balfour, with the backing of Lloyd George, was emerging as a mixture of the two, though with hawkish arguments advanced only for practical and pragmatic reasons.[3] President Wilson was the man they all had to convince, on both sides of the Atlantic, and with this in mind on 19 April Balfour sent a crucial telegram[4] to Lord Reading, his ambassador in Washington which he wanted directing to the White House via Robert Lansing, the American Secretary of State. It was basically a military-strategic document and started off where all minds were concentrated that springtime: the western front and the great German offensive there which was still steam-rollering forward. More and more German divisions were being transferred from east to west to give the steam-roller added power, and it was estimated that another fifteen could still be brought across. The only way to meet the crisis, Balfour's paper argued, was to bring about 'German anxiety in regard to the East'. Here, an effective Allied front had to be created. In the north, at the ports of Murmansk and Archangel (both major depositories of war material), a 'naval demonstration' should be conducted, to secure both bases.

But it was on the Far East that Balfour concentrated his fire, knowing that this was the area where Wilson might more easily be persuaded to cooperate. The Japanese should provide most of the military strength in any Allied action there, followed in numbers by an American force consisting of one division plus technical units. If that happened, the British would certainly contribute something, probably followed by the French and the Italians. This was in no sense an 'alternative to the sending of American infantry to Europe ... It is complementary to it.' (There was one aspect of the plan which Balfour failed to stress, because it would have done his argument no good at all with Wilson. In trying to erect an Allied bulwark of some sort in central Russia and Siberia, Britain was hoping to protect India from the infiltration of Bolshevik propaganda.)

The proposals thus far were concrete enough. It was when Balfour moved across to the political scene that the familiar muddle over options re-emerged. The Allies, it seemed, were to intervene but without actually interfering. The 'de facto government of Russia' was to be offered their help 'in order to fight the Germans and so enable the Russian people to recover their independence'. But the Allies would avoid 'taking sides in Russia'. Indeed, the object of the exercise was stated to be Russia's resuscitation: 'If we could bring about a national revival in Russia such as freed Russia from the despotism of Napoleon, very great results might ensue.' This touched on another riddle: could a Russian nation by now be said to exist any more? But before following the exiguous train of thought – and indeed the outcome of the British appeal – we must return to Sydney Reilly for, almost simultaneously, another of these surveys of Allied options had been produced by ST 1 himself.

This was the only long report[5] (at any rate the only one to survive in the archives) which Reilly sent back to 'C' before going underground and substituting deeds for words. It is in total contrast to the lofty discussions on grand strategy which were going on between the statesmen in Washington, London and Paris. Reilly does not even mention the campaign raging in the West or the military possibilities opening up for Japan and the rest of the alliance in the Far East. In fact, he does not mention the war at all. After some three weeks mulling over the situation, he produced the outlines of a purely home-made solution to the problem, with ST 1 at the centre of the action. His approach develops that agreed by Clemenceau just before Christmas: not to hesitate between the passive and the active options but to pursue both at the same time. He begins:

> Every source of information leads to definite conclusions that today BOLSHEVIKS only real power in RUSSIA. At the same time opposition in country constantly growing and if suitably supported will finally lead to overthrow of BOLSHEVIKS. Our action must therefore be in two parallel directions. Firstly with the BOLSHEVIKS for accomplishment of immediate practical objects [sic]; secondly with the opposition for gradual re-establishment of order and national defence.
>
> Immediate definite aims are safeguarding MURMAN; securing ARCHANGEL; evacuation of enormous quantities of metals, ammunition and artillery from PETROGRAD which liable to fall to Germans within month; preventing Baltic Fleet from passing to Germans by their [sic] destruction or rendering it unserviceable; and possibly substitution of moratorium for final repudiation of foreign loans. All above objects can be accomplished only by immediate agreement with BOLSHEVIKS. For minor ones, such as MURMAN-ARCHANGEL a sort of semi-acknowledgement of their Government, better treatment of their ambassadors in Allied countries may be sufficient . . .

Reilly then gets down to hard business, in the literal sense of the words, when he moves to the question of destabilization:

> For the other objects [sic] only equivalent is money which positively is most potent factor with BOLSHEVIK leaders and explains all German successes. This may mean an expenditure of possibly one million pounds[6] and part of this may have to be expended without any real guarantee of ultimate success. Work must be commenced in this direction immediately and it is possibly already too late. If outlined policy should be agreed to, you must be prepared to meet obligations at any

moment and at shortest notice. As regards opposition, imminent question is whether support to them comes from the Germans or from us.

Reilly presumably expected 'C' to advance this enormous sum of money to him, but without any indication as to who in the 'opposition' (which, as we shall see, was both fractured and fractious) had been singled out to receive such largesse. He was offering only vague hopes of success but presenting the huge bill in advance. Provision had already been made for some of the money ('expended without any guarantee' etc.) to dribble away in the gutters, or perhaps never leave some safes. It was indeed an extravagant proposition and too close to the familiar Reilly pattern of fortune-hunting to be comfortable. In the event, ST 1 was to receive, later in Moscow, money from 'C's' coffers; but these sums, though substantial, never approached the figure he was demanding so soon after arrival. Moreover, they were handed out for a quite specific purpose.

To do him justice, his proposals in April did include one more modest request for a stated target: £100,000 to establish two anti-Bolshevik newspapers, the *Noyoe Vremia* [*sic*] and the *Vetcherni*. Immediately, he told 'C', these would become 'the most effective rallying centre of pro-Ally sentiment and the trumpets of national resistance'. The trumpets do not, in the end, appear to have sounded. (Indeed, though his long telegram was marked for distribution inside the London Centre, no comments are recorded on it, much less any record of action taken.)

It is the final paragraph of Reilly's message which has the real ring of ST 1 and his mission: 'In any case, we have arrived at critical moment when we must either act immediately and effectively or abandon entire position for good and all.'

This was the language of the *beau sabreur*, the identity which Reilly now began to assume. Before trying to follow him in that role, two other assessments, both made in Moscow at the time, need to be mentioned. The first was from Boyce, 'C's' head of station in the new Russian capital, and the man to whom Reilly was supposed to answer. The second was by Sir Oliver Wardrop, the British consul-general in Moscow, under whose aegis Lockhart was functioning, though in this case the link was even more tenuous.

Boyce's report to 'C', sent at the end of May, was headed 'Affairs in Russia'.[7] The vague title was an appropriate label for the tangled bundle of information and advice tied on to it.

'While it is generally admitted that the position of the Government is precarious and that both Workmen and Peasants are almost all hostile to the Soviet ... it is nevertheless equally generally admitted that at present no other party or combination of parties has sufficient force at its disposal to enable it to overthrow the Bolsheviks ... and retain power for any length of time.'

There was, Boyce alleged, 'an appreciable increase in the volume of Monarchist sympathy', and, despite the fact that no party existed[8] with the set programme of restoring the crown, 'masses of nebulous opinion in all strata of society are crystallising to constitute a Monarchist formation'. Though Boyce could scarcely be blamed for such vagueness (see note 8) this did not give the policy-makers at home much to get hold of. Nor did the three alternative scenarios he set out (three was to be a favourite number in such surveys). The anti-Bolsheviks, he said, had the following choices to pursue their aim: first, Allied intervention; second, just waiting until 'the nation's wrath burst all bounds'; and lastly, an entente with Germany. Of the three, number one seemed to be emerging among them as the most promising solution, though it was accepted that it might take any Allied force 'the best part of a year' before it could reach any national centre, especially as both Petrograd and Moscow were liable to be occupied by the German army in reaction to an Allied landing.

In the whole document there was only one firm judgement: namely that Boris Savinkov, who had been Minister of War in the Kerensky government, stood out from the squabbling pack of anti-Bolsheviks as being the only man who might conceivably bring the regime down. Savinkov, like Reilly, with whom his fate was to become fatally linked, will stay with us on and off to the end of this story. Suffice it to say here that he was that rarest of revolutionaries, the man who would conspire and murder in the name of human freedom against any regime which threatened it. Before the war, he had been responsible for organizing such acts as the assassination, among others, of the Grand Duke Serge, uncle of the Tsar and therefore a symbol of Tsarist oppression. After the Bolsheviks seized power, Savinkov saw the same evil features of tyranny in them and immediately resumed his all-out campaign, this time directed at a regime which was supposed to be ruling in the name of liberty. Boyce comments: 'The only fighting organisation is that of Savinkov who, thanks to his organising ability and, it is stated, to Allied support, has been able to gather around him 2,000 men.' Even here there seemed to be muddle. Boyce's report continues: 'However, it is freely stated that this body is in ignorance of the fact that Savinkov is at its head; otherwise it would not support him.' This sort of comment illustrates the problem – for Allied intelligence agents and diplomats alike – of sticking a firm political label on Savinkov, or indeed any other figure in the anti-Bolshevik mêlée.

Officially, Savinkov was the leader of the left wing of the Socialist Revolutionaries, whose main aim was to create a democratic republic which would distribute Russia's land among the peasants while continuing the fight against the Germans. But by the spring of 1918 Savinkov had grown so embittered by the squabbles among the SRs that he had formed an underground movement of his own, the so-called 'Union for the Defence of Fatherland and Freedom', and it was under this banner that he had collected the band of army officers and men to which Boyce had referred. What the British agent either did not know or did not report was that Savinkov was already making plans for his armed *coup* against the regime and he also had his eye on the Latvian or Lettish regiments, who were the Bolsheviks' most trusted mercenaries. Other eyes were to follow his, in the same direction.

Mention must lastly be made of Consul-General Wardrop's own attempt to peer into the future since it contains, in a paper which was printed for the War Cabinet,[9] one howling misjudgement and one prophetic forecast. The misjudgement, which, it is to be hoped, the War Cabinet did not take too seriously, was his paragraph thirteen: 'That the overwhelming majority of the peoples who formed the old Russian Empire will reunite in a new federated Russian democratic state can hardly be open to doubt.'

In his prophecy, he stood almost alone among Allied observers at the time in stressing the ideological dangers which Lenin's victory posed for the West: 'Bolshevism will spread in some form or other to all European countries. It is highly infectious and almost as full of proselytising power as was, at its inception, that Christian Communism which Lenin and his associates despise ... It is only speedy, practical measures, consonant with early Christian ideals, which will save us from violent social disturbances.'

We have noted the ironic coincidence in January 1918 when Lockhart had travelled back in triumph to Russia on the same warship which was due to bring back the exhausted ambassador, Sir George Buchanan. But there had been a similar game of musical chairs when Lockhart was packed off home the previous summer. At the Norwegian seaport of Bergen, the young man on his way out met up and had a depressing talk with the elderly gentleman on his way in. Wardrop was Lockhart's replacement in Moscow: a scholarly bureaucrat, the personification of Foreign Office caution and Christian ideals. Whitehall was taking no more chances with Madame Vermeille and her ilk.

Now the two men had come together again and, though it was this time as colleagues, relations between them became just as uncomfortable, though without fault on either side.

The main problem was the terms of the assignment on which Lockhart had been sent: 'Mr Lockhart,' Wardrop was informed by Balfour when Lloyd George's emissary, coming from Petrograd, was about to join up with the consulate-general, 'will on arrival in Moscow continue to act as unofficial British agent to the Bolshevist government and will, as before, maintain direct though informal relations with them.

'I feel sure you will render him all the assistance he may require in carrying out his mission.'[10]

'Unofficial British agent', 'direct though informal relations': all the ambiguities expressed in each of the surveys listed above (except that of Wardrop) were compressed into those two phrases, which meant nothing for the plain reason that they could signify anything. Lockhart was a walking token of Western ambivalence, one leg resting on each of the opposing options of recognition or rejection. If any action he took turned out to be successful, or even promising, it could be backed by the West as the fulfilment of his mission. If that action faltered or led to trouble (let alone disaster), it could be repudiated as having had no official sanction.[11] Whitehall was spinning its traditional double-headed penny. Whatever criticism was to be levelled at Lockhart afterwards and wherever he did indeed stumble into errors, his fault should be weighed against the fact that he stepped out on to this fateful assignment with hobbled ankles.

He, of course, was the main victim of all this; but the wretched consul-general also suffered. For two months Wardrop had endured an increasingly awkward situation in silence. Then he erupted in what, for such a mild and seasoned bureaucrat, can only be termed an explosion. Though his personal relations with Lockhart were described as 'pleasant' it was clear that the official relationship was becoming unworkable.

'Position of Lockhart is unique. He is variously described in official and inspired Press as "Ambassador", "Envoy", "Official Representative", "Consul General" and so on ... He has a cypher of his own ... He has a staff of some six persons, exact nature of whose duties I am unaware but nevertheless with my ready consent uses my staff for cyphering and decyphering.'

What was particularly irksome was that Lockhart had gone far beyond his remit of 'informal relations' with the Bolsheviks. Thus, when a leader of the anti-Bolshevik Cadet Party[12] had asked

Wardrop for guidance, 'I was unable to give him any satisfactory answer but Lockhart was in a position to tell him that Allied intervention would certainly happen at an early date.'

Am I, or am I not, Wardrop asked, the 'Senior British official in what used to be Russia' (a country, he pointed out, of which his own experience went back to 'beyond the date of Lockhart's birth'). Unless the position could be regularized, perhaps it were best if he applied for leave of absence?

A combination of Lockhart's ill-defined authority and his own restless ambition had created a bureaucratic chaos which somehow matched the political chaos around him. Though the old embassy in Petrograd was still occupied, there did exist a new acting ambassador, the chargé d'affaires, Mr Findley, who functioned mainly from the Allies' temporary refuge at Vologda.[13] Above all, there was a fully accredited consul-general in Moscow, and that official was indeed Sir Oliver Wardrop. So he had to be sent a reassuring reply from London stressing appreciation for his 'loyal attitude' and urging him to remain at his post. But the accompanying promise to 'regularise the situation' was not properly fulfilled because it never could be. Lockhart had become the most influential official in Moscow, not only of Britain but of the Entente as a whole. He was the only person charged, not just with maintaining contact but with negotiating with the Bolsheviks – and Moscow, not Petrograd or Vologda, was their capital, where all the action was.[14]

There was to be action a-plenty over the next six months and it is best followed mainly through the fate of Lockhart's mission. Until his departure in the autumn nearly all the political threads were to pass into, be seized by, or slip through, his hands. Moreover, as the intelligence archives can now be added to the diplomatic ones, it is possible to provide a fuller account of what was really going on during this period when the fate of the Bolshevik regime seemed to hang in the balance, and much else with it.

3

'Eyes and Ears'

It is worthwhile, first of all, to try to establish what intelligence resources were available to Lockhart, and to his French and American colleagues in the spring of 1918, before conflict was joined with the Bolsheviks over the fate of Russia. This struggle was to end three years later in a great clash of arms; but it began with a battle of wits in which the three Western intelligence forces were pitted against Lenin's newly formed political police, the Cheka. The Allied combined effort (for it was in theory a joint one) has a certain historical significance as the first such operation of its kind, and it must be admitted straight away that this opening round in the Cold War did not go too well for the West. The main reason, apart from a shortage of trained manpower, was the woeful lack of coordination, not only between the three Allied services, but between rival elements within the national intelligence communities themselves.

If we begin with the British, Lockhart was already despairing by the end of April 1918 over the 'lack of cohesion and cooperation' between officers of various British missions in Petrograd and Moscow.[1] He had brought out with him, as part of his modest team, a Captain W.L. Hicks, who was later joined on his staff by a cavalry officer of the same rank, Denis Garstin. These two men made up the military element of Lockhart's mission, though each had a limited experience of Russia and an even scantier background in intelligence.[2] Lockhart noted that there were more than a dozen other British officers on the scene, all vaguely involved in supplying intelligence to various masters and all with the same rank of captain.

His attempts to get Hicks promoted to major and confirmed as 'Senior British Officer in Russia' were turned down by the authorities in London.

Their refusal was partly due to a new complication looming on the horizon – the appointment of Major-General F.E. Poole with the initial title of 'Commander of the British Military Equipment Section in Russia'. Poole, of whom much will be heard later, had tried to inflate this post into one of supremo over all British commercial, diplomatic, military and naval affairs in Russia, which would have also given him automatic overall control of intelligence operations.[3] The government could not dispute his argument that each of these departments was 'at work on different lines, each entirely ignorant of the work and scope of its neighbouring missions'. But though he was eventually to end up as Commander-in-Chief of Allied Forces in Northern Russia, the Foreign Office predictably threw right out of its Whitehall windows his bid to control diplomatic affairs. There was no love lost over policy-making between it and the War Office, which would occasionally put out a General Staff memorandum straying on its preserves.

The channel of independence which 'C' had dug out for his secret service always had to run between the high banks of War Office and Foreign Office, towering above it. This caused problems also in Russia. But the main handicap which the SIS faced in Moscow was a lack of resources. Boyce, the naval officer who ran the station, was, to begin with, the only fully fledged SIS man in the office though he was joined in April by one Lieutenant Reid, bearing the curious title of military control officer, who was more concerned with administration than fieldwork.[4] As a result, Boyce was short of high-level informants on the ground outside. That political survey of his, already quoted, which was sent back to 'C' at the end of May, was largely based, for example, on conversations with a trio of Russian professors, sources which were so non-sensitive that he actually named all three of them. His field-work appears to have consisted largely of going around the capital himself openly quizzing people.[5]

Sydney Reilly, on the other hand, though only a 'contract agent' assigned to Boyce, rapidly built up a network of his own. This consisted partly of helpers provided by or shared with the other Western services but also of his own intimates from pre-revolution Petrograd. The closest Reilly ever got to the routine business of collecting information was a series of talks he had during April and May 1918 with General Bonch-Brouevich, the brother of Lenin's aide whom Reilly, on the evening of his arrival in Moscow, had roused up after hammering on the Kremlin gates. Some CX telegrams from ST 1 on these meetings passed on to the War Office have survived but they are accurately described only as 'Interviews'. The general, who was supervising the creation of the new Red Army, was seeing officers of all three Western powers at a time when a degree of cooperation with the Bolsheviks was still in force. Most visitors therefore went openly and in uniform.

The truth is that the 'Ace of Spies' was never really interested in espionage as such. As we shall see, his game, apart from the insatiable desire to make money, was to carve out his own niche in history by toppling the Bolsheviks and replacing them with a regime made up largely of his own cronies. The lawyer Alexander Ivanovich Grammatikoff, a boon companion since the pre-war Tsarist days, was a prime example: for 'Sasha' he had pencilled in the key post of Minister of the Interior in the Reilly government of his dreams.

There were, evidently, plenty of reasons why British secret intelligence work based in Bolshevik Moscow should be pulling in different directions. But there was at least one example of them pulling steadily together and, somewhat surprisingly, it involved that solo buccaneer, Sydney Reilly. The close partnership and friendship between 'C's' ST 1 and Captain George Hill, the chief agent of British Military Intelligence in the Soviet capital, remained firm throughout the vicissitudes which lay ahead, and was to survive all their Moscow adventures. Hill, an officer of the 4th Manchester Regiment, who worked initially under the War Office, had none of Reilly's braggadocio or political ambitions but, as a solid and reliable field operator, he made the perfect working partner.[6] Before linking up with Reilly he had spent several months in southern and central Russia aiding the Bolsheviks in doing whatever they could to weaken the German army. This involved blowing bridges and ammunition dumps and evacuating out of German reach everything they could lay their hands on – including large stores of steel and ammunition and no fewer than twenty-two squadrons of Russian planes, complete with spares. It should not be forgotten that this policy of denying all available assets to the Germans was the prime task allotted at the time to Allied intelligence officers, whether military, naval or civilian. Hill's was one of many contributions to that policy.

From May onwards, as Allied relations with the Lenin regime grew increasingly tense, Hill turned his attention to recruiting anti-Bolshevik cells and he soon merged with the Boyce–Reilly operation, pooling resources and sharing the same cyphers.[7] By midsummer of 1918, apart from derailing trains (now directed against the Red Army), establishing nine safe houses in and around the capital and setting up a small unit to produce forged Bolshevik documents, he had organized a courier service linking Moscow with Saratov, Rostov and Kiev in southern Russia and with Petrograd, Vologda and Archangel to the north. It was costly and hazardous and it occasionally failed; but in a country where the telegraph system had broken down and was highly insecure even when it worked, Hill's couriers were invaluable in passing information inside the network and, ultimately, on to London.

The British government, in common with its Allies, needed far more information than everything that Lockhart's telegrams, General Poole's reports and Captain Hill's courier messages could furnish. Moreover, once the great dividing line between the Bolsheviks and the West had been drawn by Lenin's conclusion of a separate peace with Germany, official representation needed to be expanded throughout the Soviet Union, to serve also as an additional chain of listening posts. Thus, already in April 1918, a 'Memorandum in connection with Intelligence Work in Russia'[8] was circulating in London. Its author was Sir Arthur Steel-Maitland who, apart from being a baronet and an MP, bestrode Whitehall like a colossus: he was not only joint parliamentary secretary at the Foreign Office but also parliamentary secretary to the Board of Trade. He now proposed establishing new British Consulates in ten towns of European Russia and eight in Siberia. Each would be allocated a number of British 'helpers' who would be recruited from a pool of 'between 200 and 300 men who know Russia and who could be utilised for this purpose'. They would all be required to supply a mixture of political, commercial and military intelligence.

In June, the Foreign Secretary went even further than the Steel-Maitland blueprint. He appointed two new vice-consuls at Vladivostok and Omsk and set up an additional vice-consulate at seven other Siberian towns. European Russia and Turkestan were similarly treated. With one anxious eye on the Treasury, Mr Balfour emphasized that all these new posts would be 'purely provisional and temporary'. Thus, by midsummer of 1918, the Russia Department of the Foreign Office had to digest information coming from more than twenty new consular outposts, in addition to everything that 'C' and the existing diplomatic, military and naval networks furnished as a matter of routine. Not surprisingly, these Russian experts in Whitehall often found it hard to come to a collective verdict as to what was really going on in the Soviet Union.

Details of the French secret service network in Bolshevik Russia were very sketchy until the re-emergence, described in the Introduction, of the Deuxième Bureau's own files which had lain for half a century in Moscow. Even though these *documents repatriés* still give only a fragmentary picture, most of the fragments are new, and some correct mistakes which, for want of an authentic source, have been repeated down the years in countless books, articles and professional manuals on the subject. Thus the head of the French secret service in Moscow during the crisis months of 1918 has always been given as Colonel Henri de Vertemont (or Vertement). Not only are the spellings and arm of service wrong; so, quite possibly, is the role attributed to him. The mysterious person concerned was called Martial-Marie-Henri de Verthamon. He had nothing to do with the military but was a 47-year-old career officer in the French Navy with the rank of *capitaine de corvette* (roughly equal to commandant or major). Most important of all, he does not appear to have been a career member of the Deuxième Bureau at all, but rather a special agent of the French Ministry of Marine, despatched to Russia not to collect intelligence but to carry out a mission of sabotage.

This is the clear impression given by a series of telegrams sent back to Paris from Vologda in May and June 1918 by the resolutely anti-Bolshevik French ambassador, Joseph Noulens. These telegrams, which are among the diplomatic documents dealing with intelligence in the French archives, show the envoy progressing from a mood of concern over the forthcoming de Verthamon mission to one of tetchy protest once he had turned up. The first two telegrams, both sent on 30 May, while the officer was still en route, are from Noulens and his naval attaché at the embassy, Commandant Gallaud.[9] The attaché, noting that Verthamon was due to arrive expecting a sum of two million roubles to be put at his disposal, made it evident that the embassy had been left completely in the dark as to what the mission was all about. Had it anything to do with their own reports or had it been conceived for other reasons in Paris? In any case, the attaché added, it was vital that the newcomer 'should only act in accord with me, as I am familiar with the various intelligence networks of the embassy and the Military Mission and, being in touch with the situation here, can point him in the right direction'.

The ambassador rammed home this request, turning it into a demand. He appealed directly to his Foreign Minister to 'insist' with the Minister of Marine that 'M. Verthamon should be placed under the orders of our naval attaché'. And he reminded Paris how important it was for French intelligence services to be placed under one centralized control, to avoid unnecessary expense and wasted efforts (*déperditions d'activité*). The same plea was being heard in London and Washington, and to equally little effect. Certainly the matter had not been cleared up in Vologda when de Verthamon arrived there on 7 June.[10] Noulens, still awaiting clarification, merely complained that the 300,000 roubles already advanced in Paris had been drawn at far too high a rate.

A fortnight later, however, when there was still no reply to his earlier queries, the envoy sent off an extraordinary message which (perhaps fortunately for him) was despatched by courier and did not reach his masters at the Quai d'Orsay until October 1918 (!). In this he expressed some sarcasm over the code-name – admittedly a woefully transparent one – of 'Henri', under which de Verthamon was operating. Such an unconvincing rig-out (*affublement*), he declared, could not fail to draw attention to the mysterious nature of the mission. But then, in repeating his demand that de Verthamon's operations should be coordinated with those that had already been carried out under cover from the embassy, he spelled out which these clandestine activities were: 'Since last April, our military attachés with my approval, have succeeded in preventing supplies from reaching the Germans by destroying war material and provisions intended for them.' Among the 'important results' achieved under this heading over the past few weeks, the ambassador cited the destruction or crippling of one park of aircraft, an electricity plant, several dumps of shells and petrol as well as the blowing-up of three railway bridges. De Verthamon should join in this effort, Noulens urged, for the operations he had been sent out to fulfil were 'analogous'.[11]

The naval officer was therefore a specialist saboteur[12] and in no way comparable with a professional intelligence station chief like Boyce. The fact that 'Henri' has gone down in the records as the head of the French secret service in Moscow is understandable since sabotage always figured at or near the top of clandestine Allied plans. It can also be explained by the fact that no other figure has been identified as filling the post. As with the English and the Americans, the left hand of French intelligence often did not know what the right hand was up to. But at least the other Allies knew where that right hand was.

In the early months of the Bolshevik regime, the most influential figure for France on the intelligence scene was certainly Captain Jacques Sadoul, a well-known Paris lawyer and former French Socialist deputy. He was an old friend of Trotsky's and had been attached to the French Military Mission in Moscow to maintain liaison with the Bolsheviks. But, unlike Lockhart, he had no power to negotiate with them and was in no way a representative of his government. That status belonged unequivocally to Noulens, and the ambassador was as fiercely right wing and anti-Bolshevik as Sadoul was ardently left wing and instinctively pro-Bolshevik. The rift between the two men was unbridgeable. For a while, Sadoul could fight his own corner, supported by Lockhart in Moscow and the firebrand Socialist Minister of War, Albert Thomas, in Paris. But once the Allies, in a shift of grand strategy, gave up wooing the Lenin regime and began undermining it, Sadoul's cause was lost. Lockhart, hoping to become a career diplomat, trimmed his sails and set his wheel for the new course. Sadoul, the idealist and politician, simply jumped ship. He joined up with the Bolsheviks, even fighting in the ranks of the Red Army.[13]

With his defection, the French Military Mission in Moscow, headed by General Lavergne, lost its most important source of information on Bolshevik affairs – however ideologically coloured the source had been. The general was to become a key figure in the anti-Bolshevik campaign which started to unfold from the summer of 1918 onwards and, as with all such French military missions, his staff included a section of the Deuxième Bureau. The intelligence archives returned to Paris include reports on that bureau's activities in the missions set up in Siberia and, later, in Warsaw (which are drawn on in their context below). But there are only fragments on the Lavergne mission and on the general himself.[14] The full archives may have been withheld in Moscow. They may have been lost, weeded out, even destroyed at some point in Paris. As is clear from other sources, the high degree of French involvement in Allied conspiracies against the Lenin regime could have been politically embarrassing for those governments who embraced its successors. Whatever the reasons, the identity of the head of the Deuxième Bureau in Moscow in 1918, who would presumably have been the official head of the French secret service in the capital at the time, remains uncertain.[15] (It could, conceivably, have been Charles Faux-Pas Bidet, on whom an interesting file exists in the archives of the Paris Préfecture de Police. On 30 June 1917, when serving as Commissioner of Police in the capital, he was transferred to the Ministry of War, given the rank of captain and sent on a special mission to Russia, to serve as 'chief of the intelligence bureau' under General Lavergne.)

When we move across, finally, to the American component of this Allied intelligence operation, the situation is confusingly reversed. We know the identity of the man who functioned in Bolshevik Moscow as Boyce's opposite number and both his life and family background have been exhaustively researched. To all this, the present work can now add some unpublished data about the resources set up for him, details which are lacking about both the British and French networks. Yet paradoxically he was not a secret service officer for the plain reason that, unlike the SIS and the Deuxième Bureau, an American secret service did not exist in 1918, and was not indeed to be created for almost another thirty years.[16] Before looking at the fascinating figure who controlled the core of Washington's spy operations against the Bolsheviks it is worth sketching the penumbra of ad hoc sources which circled around him.

There was, for example, the American Red Cross Commission under Raymond Robins (he was addressed as 'Colonel', a title the New York financier appeared to have acquired on the transatlantic crossing). The work of the Red Cross was at the starved grass roots of the Russian nation and their chief soon demonstrated that compassion was not the best basis for politics. All his reports and representations argued in support of the Lenin regime, which, he maintained, could be turned into a reliable ally of the West. Robins had his own extensive information network which, in the early months of Bolshevik power, amounted to the best civil intelligence service operating in Russia. But supplying information was one thing; trying to tell Washington what to do about it was quite another. It was a campaign which not only took him far beyond the proper boundaries of his task but led to a headlong collision with the diplomats whose territory he was invading. The view held both by the United States embassy in Petrograd and by its consulate-general in Moscow went through some alarming gyrations. But the final verdict was that, whether or not the Bolsheviks were allies of the Germans, they could never be transformed into partners of the Western democracies. Robins stuck obstinately to his guns throughout the spring of 1918, only to be blown up by them in May when, after strong pressure from the State Department, he was recalled to Washington 'for consultations'.[17]

In common with its allies, the United States also received a steady flow of information on Russian affairs from its diplomatic and consular offices who had to act as intelligence listening-posts. Attempts were made to collate this information in a series of papers entitled 'Periodical report on matters relating to Russia', which, even if they drew no conclusions, at least gave the picture from a variety of viewpoints spread throughout the Soviet Union.[18] On top of all this came subjective and often misleading information supplied by a variegated horde of American businessmen and carpet-baggers: prospectors for gold and other minerals, bankers, agents of shipping companies, grain and timber merchants and, at the semi-official level, emissaries like the eight-man American Railway Delegation which arrived in Siberia in March 1918 to 'assist in reorganising Russian railways according to the latest American standards'. (In fact it produced much valuable data; railway intelligence was invariably the most detailed and accurate, especially on military matters.) Whether or not confirmation of this sort was received by the American Military Mission in Russia, much less collated by them, is unclear. Indeed, this mission, headed by Lieutenant-Colonel A. Ruggles, seemed as much interested in anti-Bolshevik political groups as in the balance of armed strength.

At the centre of these swirling trails of information stood the extraordinary figure who, secret service or not, had been hired and paid by Washington as a full-time spy, the first to be designated for Europe. Xenophon Dmitrivich Kalamatiano – whose adventures were to be just as extraordinary as his name – was born in imperial Austria on 14 July 1882.[19] At least, that is the assumption; the actual place of birth, entered almost illegibly as Vilomar on the certificate produced by his family, does not appear to exist on any map of the old Habsburg monarchy. There are similar problems about his pedigree. His mother Verra had it put about when she came to America that she was of noble birth, even related to the Romanovs. Though certainly a cultured woman who spoke several languages, no basis has been established for this sort of claim, which came fairly frequently from Russian émigrés once they had crossed the Atlantic.

There is also some mystery about his father who was of mixed Russian-Greek extraction and was sometimes described as a wealthy Greek merchant. He is more likely to have been of peasant origin, but he anyway disappeared from the scene in 1894, when he was reportedly killed in a street brawl. Later that same year, the widow met and married a young Jewish St Petersburg lawyer, Constantine Paul Blumenthal, who, also in 1894, emigrated to America, eventually adding a 'de', the prefix of minor nobility, to his name, in order to impress the natives.[20] These family obscurities, pretensions to nobility and dramatic changes of fortune and domicile put one in mind of the early life of the man who was destined one day to be young Kalamatiano's espionage partner in Moscow, George Rosenblum, a.k.a. Sydney Reilly. But unlike all the fiction and fantasies spun round Reilly's entry into the world of espionage, Kalamatiano's path is clearly marked and documented.

The fifteen-year-old first studied at the Military Academy where his father was working and then, on a scholarship, entered the University of Chicago, an institution which was to play an unexpected role in his career. After graduating in 1902 (now using the surname of de Blumenthal Kalamatiano) he worked for a while as a language teacher before switching to industry to earn more money. It was as a representative of the agricultural machinery manufacturer J.I. Case that he returned in 1908 to his Russian homeland. There he remained for the next seven years, taking on new United States dealerships and eventually being nominated as American representative of the Russian Association of Commerce and Industry in Moscow. He had always kept in touch with Professor Samuel N. Harper at his old alma mater of Chicago University and it was to Harper that he wrote this latest news in a letter of 21 April 1915, using the stationery of the association. That letter changed his life. Unbeknown to Kalamatiano at the time, the Professor was an unofficial recruiting agent for America's unofficial secret service.

The shiftiness of the Wilson administration's attitude to espionage stemmed from the President's own illusions that a new world order could be created after the war based on 'open covenants openly arrived at'. The very word 'secrecy' thus became a brandmark of Europe's effete imperial order which he was resolved to throw into the dustbin of history. His rhetoric was to collapse under the weight of that history. The old-style secret diplomacy, which he affected to despise, enmeshed him, and often tripped him up, when he attempted to conduct peace-making without it. The same illusion, futile but damaging, was applied to intelligence work. Espionage, he pontificated to Congress in his keynote address of 2 April 1917, was a thing of the past. It had been used by monarchies and aristocracies to guard their privileged existence and had no place in the new democratic order where the people were entitled to know everything. 'Self-governed nations,' the presidential fantasy continued, 'do not fill their neighbour states with spies.'

It is worth noting in passing that this posture had been contradicted by Wilson himself who, during his first term of office, had despatched a series of spies and saboteurs into neighbouring Mexico, on missions which included an attempt to assassinate the revolutionary leader Pancho Villa. The pretence became even more strained after the United States entered the Great War in the spring of 1917. Washington's need to know what was really going on inside Russia had emerged in Tsarist times – if only to pinpoint areas which American finance, commerce and industry could penetrate. Kalamatiano, the experienced and respected businessman, was an ideal candidate to collect such information and he appears to have been recruited by Harper for this purpose while on a visit to America in the spring of 1915. The office for which the professor was talent-spotting was not an independent organization within the Washington bureaucracy but an integral section, the so-called Russian Bureau, of the State Department. This system was reflected in how Kalamatiano operated for nearly three years after his return to Russia. In Petrograd, he was under the control of the commercial attaché, Chapin Huntingdon, while in Moscow his supervisor was the vice-consul, later to become acting consul-general, de Witt Clinton Poole, of whom much more will be heard. It is not clear whether these diplomats had any special status within the Russian Bureau but in common espionage parlance they functioned as Kalamatiano's 'case officers'. However, what they collected was always described as 'information', rather than intelligence.[21] Whatever the labels used, Kalamatiano had no independence of action in organizing his work and no separate network to collect his data.

This situation was turned upside down – together with almost every other aspect of Allied policy towards Russia – by the signing on 3 March 1918 of the separate peace between the Lenin regime and the Central Powers. The document has been traced,[22] showing precisely how the repercussions of the Brest-Litovsk treaty put the work of Kalamatiano on to another plane. It transpires that on 20 March, little more than a fortnight after the conclusion of the separate peace, the State Department instructed the consulate-general in Moscow to 'spare no reasonable expense to keep the Department regularly and fully informed of facts in different parts of Russia'. On 26 July Poole, who was now in charge of the office,[23] described how the new network, still known as the 'Information Service', had been set up.

Two officers in Moscow, a consul and a vice-consul, had been placed in day-to-day charge of the organization. They had under them three separate groups of informants spread throughout the country. The first was a group of seven consular officers now assigned to discovering the required 'facts in different parts of Russia'. They were evidently having a hard time travelling, let alone reporting. Consul Thomson, for example, who had been ordered to make his way from Omsk to the temporary Allied capital of Vologda, had been 'last heard from in the Chelyabinsk region, trying to get through to Ekaterinburg'. Consul Tredwell was 'endeavouring to reach Omsk' from his former base at Tashkent. Vice-Consul Doolittle was starting out on an 'observation trip through Western Siberia' and was hoping eventually to send some full surveys back to Moscow from Irkutsk. No reports from these intrepid travellers have survived. They are, in any case, less interesting than the two other groups listed in Poole's memorandum.

The first of these is described as 'Especially appointed Vice-Consuls'. Eight names are given together with the Russian towns to which they had been despatched but the intriguing thing is how they were enrolled. Most were 'former members of the Young Men's Christian Association' and the top recruits were to be paid 'an annual salary of $2,400 with a daily subsistence allowance of $40'.[24] The third group of Poole's informants brings us unashamedly, though still unofficially, into the regular espionage world. It is headed 'Observers and Special Agents' and assigns the one-time representative of 'Case Agricultural Machinery' in Russia to his new role. The consulate-general, Washington was informed, 'is now employing 27 observers, 19 of whom are under the immediate supervision of Mr X.B. Kalamatiano, an American citizen'.[25]

None of these observers was named but their input was described: they were submitting written reports on 'political, agricultural, commercial, financial and economic conditions, and frequently furnish important military information'. Poole added that it might prove necessary to organize 'a separate branch of this service for military observations only'. In the meantime, two of these special agents were being trained to replace Kalamatiano 'should the Americans have to leave Moscow'. As we shall see, they had to leave but he had to stay, thanks largely to the evidence found on him of the extensive intelligence network he controlled. It seems likely that some, if not most, of the nineteen 'observers' allotted to Kalamatiano were Russians, as the YMCA and the consular pools had already been drained. In any case, by the time this 26 July report was sent, he had already added to the covert list one Russian staff colonel working at the Moscow military headquarters, one Red Army major-general and one former staff colonel. Some were shared with the British and French networks, who had nothing comparable on their books.

Such was the sprawling and largely uncoordinated miscellany of sources – covert, semi-covert, military, diplomatic, academic, amateur and unofficial – which made up the Allied intelligence nexus in Bolshevik Russia when the battle of wits was engaged. What had Lenin to put in the field against this motley army? The answer was a political police force much leaner and meaner and also, on the whole, far more effective.

The history of the Vecheka or Cheka, as it was more often called,[26] is an open book when compared with the hitherto sealed archives of the Western secret services. We therefore need only a summary of the published facts to point the contrast.[27] The Cheka had sprung into existence as recently as December 1917, largely as the brainchild of the man who was to lead it for the rest of his life, Felix Edmunovich Dzerzhinsky. 'Iron Felix', as he came to be called by his cronies, was the most terrifying figure among all the dedicated monsters to be thrown up by the revolution. Utterly ruthless, and without any scruples about bathing the landscape in blood if it would serve the Bolshevik cause – this can all be seen in the eyes, the gaze of a basilisk which can freeze even when looked at today. Yet this chief executioner of the regime was neither a Russian nor a member of Lenin's prized proletariat. Dzerzhinsky was the son of a minor Polish nobleman, brought up in a patriotic and devoutly religious home. Indeed, his childhood dream – ironic in view of the nightmare which he embraced – was to become a Roman Catholic priest. The youth rejected the child and the church and family with it, for the Marxist creed which he worshipped with the passion only a renegade can muster. By the time the revolution released him from jail, on 1 March 1917, he had spent more than eleven years of his life in Siberian exile or Tsarist prisons.

The organization which he set up was, to begin with, tiny compared with the combined resources of Western intelligence which opposed him. Even by the end of 1917 he still had fewer than two dozen people on his staff, though this had probably risen to about a thousand by the time Consul Poole and his colleagues had built up the expanded Allied networks described. There was, of course, no shortage of potential recruits for the Chekist rank and file: the Okhranya, the Tsarist secret police whom Dzerzhinsky knew only too well, had had thousands of informers and agents provocateurs on its books and many were only too willing, after its disbandment, to switch over to the new brand of political police. But how many of these turncoats could be trusted at a time when turning coats still seemed an uncertain business?

On the other hand there was no questioning the loyalty of his principal lieutenants. The problem here was that there were so few of them with the necessary experience to choose from. What is interesting, when the list of his twenty top Chekists is analysed,[28] is how many of them reflected the origins and background of the chief. At least twelve of the twenty came from the bourgeoisie so despised and hounded by the regime, while only seven were of pure Russian stock. The remainder were either Poles (like Dzerzhinsky) or Latvians, with the odd Armenian or Ukrainian thrown in. Like Himmler's Gestapo in a later reign of terror, Lenin's political police relied heavily on foreigners for its brains and brawn.

We shall meet with several of these chief henchmen later – notably the two Latvians, Peters and Latsis. All that needs emphasizing here is the immense advantages Dzerzhinsky enjoyed in having such a small but select body of lieutenants around him – all of whom had a single undivided loyalty to the same regime and

shared the same blind faith in a common philosophy. The contrast
with the political splits and divisions both inside and between the
three Allied camps and the miscellany of intelligence resources they
had assembled to serve them leaps to the eye. As in the armed
conflict which lay ahead, so in the espionage tussle which was now
opening, the Bolsheviks enjoyed the supreme advantage of concentration along their inner lines of battle. They also, at one critical
point in the tussle, enjoyed the direct personal guidance of one of
the greatest brains of the century, that belonging to Vladimir Ilich
Lenin himself.

4

Maelstrom

In one dimension, events in Russia during the summer of 1918 did unfold roughly as the Anglo-French policy-makers and their favoured options had hoped at the start of the year. The northern bases of Murmansk and Archangel were secured by Allied forces, with both the idle Russian fleets in the harbours and the vast stockpiles of war materials in the ports being kept out of German hands. Furthermore, American troops did, in the end, contribute to the Allied contingents, both in the north and, on a larger scale, in the far eastern theatre of Siberia. These landings were, in the end, imposed on the Bolshevik authorities, whether they liked it or not. But, important though they were, these were happenings on the periphery.

In another dimension, the internal one, events erupted that had only vaguely, if at all, been forecast by intelligence agents and whose effects took Allied observers and officials equally by surprise. All such Western experts during these months were like travellers moving cautiously together along winding unfamiliar paths. Suddenly, an open gate would appear; then, when they passed through it, it would just as suddenly close behind them. The confusing thing was that they did not know whether they now stood on the right or wrong side of it. Sometimes it was not just paths which became free or barred, but the entire landscape around them which, without any action on their part, was transformed. This unpredictability, as well as the complexity and the scale of the Russian conflict, should be borne in mind before criticism is levelled at Allied forecasts. (That their actions were often at fault is beyond dispute.)

The first months of the year saw a relative honeymoon period in Allied relations with the Bolsheviks and this is reflected in Lockhart's own experience. From mid-February onwards, he was seeing Trotsky (still the head of the Foreign Office before moving over to become Minister of War) several times a week. As it was Lockhart and not the British chargé d'affaires, Francis Lindley (formerly counsellor at the embassy), who was charged with the negotiating, it was his reports that mattered.

For a while, Trotsky seemed to be bearing out the opinion held about him in the West, namely that, compared with Lenin, he was the pragmatist in the Bolshevik camp, the man one might do business with. Indeed, to begin with, the young Scotsman got quite carried away at the prospect and swallowed almost everything he was offered. These were the weeks when the Japanese were edging towards their first landing at Vladivostok; clearly the Bolshevik aim was to try to block the move. Thus, on 14 March, Lockhart reported[1] that though he had been received 'very kindly', Trotsky had appealed to Britain to realize that 'the only country that could possibly benefit by Japanese intervention must be Germany', into whose hands the British had been playing for two years by their policy in Russia. The brusque comment in London on all this was that Lockhart 'was just plugging Trotsky's line'.

Indeed, their special envoy had already raised Whitehall eyebrows by a telegram which had arrived the week before. It contained the starry-eyed speculation that the Bolsheviks might, in the end, turn out to be everyone's salvation: 'The humiliating peace [of Brest-Litovsk] is the beginning of a national revival in Russia ... The Bolsheviks may help in this revival ... They may simply be the nucleus of a real national resistance [to the Germans] which would necessarily be a broadening of the political platform ... It should be our business to foster this revival whatever form it should take. The peace is not the end of Russia. It is the beginning of a strong Russia.'

Exotic, airy-fairy stuff indeed and a long way off the mark, both in fact and in prophecy. (In other messages sent over the same period, Lockhart was urging London to oppose intervention – he had in mind the looming Siberian action – because this had to be 'invited and not forced'.) To the hawks in the Allied camp, this was insufferable. One of the most influential of their number, Major-General Sir Alfred Knox, head of the British Military Mission in Siberia, positively exploded. On 19 March, he circulated a memorandum which went far beyond the usual war of words over the issue. It was the most virulent attack imaginable by one British official against another.

Quoting Lockhart's early reports to London, with their note of high optimism and faith in the regime's future, Knox commented:

> Lockhart, like a very courageous bluebottle, proposed to play with the Bolsheviks. He was already deeply entangled in their webs but the worst of it is that he continued persistently to buzz and people here listened to his buzzing . . .
>
> I have tried in these extracts to show that Lockhart's advice has been in a political sense unsound and in a military sense criminally misleading. Why is he retained in Russia?[2]

The general was regarded in London as one of Britain's foremost experts on Russian affairs, and not simply in the military field. A damning report like that could not fail to take effect, especially in the Foreign Office, whose mandarins still resented the fact that the 'special envoy' had been appointed not by their department but by the Prime Minister in person.

Their comments on the Knox memorandum display tart satisfaction. Thus Lord Robert Cecil: 'This paper is violent, but contains much truth. But although Mr Lockhart's advice may be bad we cannot be accused of having followed it!'

Worse was to come from the deputy under-secretary, Lord Hardinge. His great abilities, social connections and steely ambition had already carried him before the war to the very peak of power within the empire, a six-year spell as viceroy of India. His annotations, initialled with the lordly 'H' acquired from that post, often give one the feeling that Hardinge had never got used to leaving Viceregal Lodge in Delhi. In this case, they were blistering: 'I cannot say that we have so far extracted much good from Mr Lockhart's mission. All his forecasts have proved wrong and we do not know whether he presses our views. He is hysterical and has achieved nothing.' It was fortunate for Lockhart that the Foreign Secretary himself had an indulgent spot for him. Balfour was a kindly intellectual, much interested in philosophical problems. He confessed that he always found the young Scotsman's reports 'amusing'.

The piece of advice which had particularly irritated the mandarins, and made the general incandescent, was Lockhart's insistence that, in order to keep good relations with the Bolsheviks (i.e. Trotsky), Japanese intervention in Siberia should be held off. Before long, all such annoyance was to become out of date when the Japanese went ahead, off their own bat, with a small-scale landing at Vladivostok. But the circumstances of that event gave much greater cause for concern. Hitherto, the argument between America and her allies over intervention had been conducted in secret exchanges. Now it was to be displayed in public, with the Americans, predictably, as the odd men out.[3]

At the end of March, when the situation in Russia's great far eastern port was becoming tense after increasing Bolshevik activity, three of the Allies had warships in the harbour: the Japanese with two cruisers, the Americans with the USS *Brooklyn*, and the British with the cruiser *Suffolk*. They were there primarily to keep an eye on the vast amount of Allied war material stored in the port but also to play a game of naval peekaboo with each other. This remained a harmonious affair until a crisis was reached on 4 April, the first of a series of Siberian incidents which nobody could have predicted. On that morning, Red Army soldiers raided a Japanese shop in the city to demand money and, in the ensuing brawl, three of the shopkeepers were killed. Thus, though the safety of Allied arms dumps had always been the main Allied concern, it was this criminal hold-up which provided the flashpoint. The Japanese commander, Admiral Kato, promptly put 500 of his marines on shore to safeguard his country's property. Captain Payne on the *Suffolk* responded on a more modest scale by landing 50 men to guard the British consulate.

The Americans, however, refused to participate in the joint action, despite appeals made in Washington by Lord Reading to the American Secretary of State. Lansing told the President that the Anglo-Japanese action ought not to affect their country's 'hands-off' stand over intervention and the President, predictably, agreed. The American government then got itself into a tangle over explaining its attitude: on the one hand claiming (untruthfully) that there was 'a thorough understanding among the Allies concerning their intervention in Russia'; and on the other hand admitting (truthfully) that the situation at Vladivostok 'unquestionably demonstrates that the landing is not a concerted action between the Allies'.

The fountain of American policy towards Russia, now and later, was the White House and this is a good moment to ask what it was which drove the President to act as he did. All the mounds of diplomatic documents available do not give the whole story unless one looks at the character and temperament of the policy makers themselves. In the spring of 1918, Woodrow Wilson was fast emerging as the leader of the Western world. It was a role to which this austere philosopher-academic was to prove disastrously ill-suited. Nonetheless it was thrust upon him, first, by the enormous undrained economic strength of his country as compared with an exhausted Europe, and second, by its equally vast and untapped reserves of military manpower. There had been muddle and delay in turning these reserves into fighting formations[4] but plans were afoot in the spring of 1918 to bring them over at the rate of a division a week by the autumn. Each was three times the size of a German division and, for that matter, a French or British one. Wilson was thus like a man who, whatever his condition had been at the beginning of 1918, was bound to put on muscle without ever exerting himself as the months passed.

On to this growing physical framework, the President had already grafted his own personal spiritual dimension. His famous

Fourteen Points, declared at the beginning of the year, had proclaimed a new world order of peace, and a new world organization,
the League of Nations, to maintain that peace. All this was remote
from the situation of Bolshevik Russia in 1918. But another of
Wilson's most cherished principles, the rights of all nations to self-
determination, had a powerful, if indirect, bearing on that situation
– above all, as things turned out, in Siberia. Behind the call for self-
determination (which was to be applied most drastically in the
dismemberment of the multi-national Austro-Hungarian empire)
lay his revulsion against empires as a whole. He could not apply this
principle to the empire of his British ally (though he was doubtless
itching to) but he could and did apply it to the former realm of the
Romanovs. He was opposed to intervention from the very start of
Lenin's regime, not merely because the military strategy involved
was quite beyond his ken. He resisted it also because weakening the
Bolsheviks implied strengthening the monarchists. That was the top
end of the long line of command which had kept Admiral Knight's
marines on board the USS *Brooklyn* in the first week of April 1918.

The President's stand was consistent. Less than a month before,
Wilson had sent the following greetings telegram to the Bolshevik
regime, via the American consulate in Moscow: 'The whole heart
of the people of the United States is with the people of Russia in
the attempt to free themselves for ever from an autocratic government and to become the masters of their own fate.'[5]

Ten days later,[6] the Congress of Soviets replied to this effusion by
expressing their gratitude for the statement. But this gratitude more
or less bypassed the White House. It was extended 'above all to the
labouring and exploited classes of the United States . . . looking to
the happy time not far distant when the labour masses of all
countries will throw off the yoke of capitalism'. The head of the
world's proudest capitalist country seems to have taken the rebuff
placidly: the professor hoping that an unruly pupil would learn good
manners. Months would pass before he would finally yield to the
pleas of his allies over intervention. It would be longer yet before he
would bring himself to see the true nature of the Bolshevik beast.

Ironically, the Soviet regime did not give Wilson any credit for his failure to support the Allied action at Vladivostok; on the contrary, there were suspicions that the White House had engineered the entire operation as a preliminary exercise in 'American imperialism' on Russian soil.[7] The initial reaction in Moscow to the landings was one of anger and concern, as Lockhart had safely predicted. This abated somewhat when the puny scale of the Anglo-Japanese marine forces involved became apparent. But Lenin feared that there was much more to come. A message he fired off immediately to the Bolshevik commanders at Vladivostok contained the warning: 'It is probable, in fact almost inevitable, that the Japanese will advance. Undoubtedly the Allies will help them. We must prepare ourselves immediately, straining all our energies to this end.'[8]

Lenin's forecast was to be only partly borne out by events. A very substantial build-up of Allied troops did develop in Vladivostok; but, as we shall see, it was other and even larger forces which were to march westwards on Moscow.

That April, both the Bolsheviks and the Allies soon had something quite different to preoccupy their minds and further complicate all their calculations. Following upon the peace treaty which Trotsky had concluded with the Central Powers, diplomatic relations between Boshevik Russia and imperial Germany could be opened up; and so, on 24 April, the ill-fated Count Wilhelm von Mirbach arrived as the Kaiser's envoy to the Soviet capital. The incongruity of the situation was pounced on with gusto by the official organ of the Bolshevik press, the grossly misnamed *Pravda* ('Truth').

'The German ambassador,' its leading article observed, 'has arrived in the revolutionary capital not as the representative . . . of a friendly nation but as the plenipotentiary of a military gang who, with boundless insolence, are killing, violating and robbing wherever they can penetrate with their bloody imperialistic bayonet.'[9]

It was the rebuff to the Wilson overture once again, but this time played *fortissimo*, and surely unique in the diplomatic annals of the century as a greeting extended to a fully accredited envoy.

For a few weeks, the count really did behave like a would-be viceroy in Moscow. He was performing as the representative not so much of his emperor as of Hindenburg and Ludendorff, masters of that great German army which was still consolidating its hold on Russian soil while pushing ever nearer to Paris on the western front. He also started off by indulging in political intrigues against the Bolsheviks. He was said, for example, to be courting the centre-right of the Cadet party with a proposal to reinstate the Romanovs in a constitutional monarchy and to revise the Brest-Litovsk treaty in Russia's favour. (This was one of several rumours of German plans for restoration derived from secret sources at the time.)

Then, in mid-May, Mirbach altered course completely. At least, that was what Lockhart became convinced of, and it caused Britain's 'unofficial envoy' to change tack accordingly. The Germans, he reported,[10] had now decided that it was in their best interests to work with the Bolsheviks. This was partly because their offensive on the western front was faltering, so that they would no longer have the strength to impose their will on Russia by military means, but also because they had come to the conclusion that the Bolsheviks, despite all their problems, were the only real power in the country.

The West, Lockhart argued, could only respond to their new situation in one of two opposite ways (on this occasion, the familiar third option was missing). One was to trump the German cards by recognizing the Bolsheviks immediately and offering them substantial economic aid. The alternative was 'Allied intervention on a large scale, preferably with the consent of the Russian government but if not without it'. As (Lockhart now admitted) that consent was unlikely to be forthcoming, 'intervention should be prepared as speedily and secretly as possible', to be launched simultaneously at Murmansk, Archangel and the Far East, after issuing the Bolsheviks with a twenty-four-hour ultimatum over compliance.

From then on, Lockhart's calls for immediate intervention became even shriller: 'Hour has come when Allies must decide on intervention or be prepared to risk complete collapse of all our policy in Russia' was one follow-up message. At the suggestion of General Lavergne, head of the French Military Mission, he also paid a visit, accompanied by the general, to the Allied emergency 'capital' up at Vologda[11] to get his new policy on intervention approved by the French ambassador, M. Noulens. On returning to Moscow, he reported on the ambassador's enthusiastic endorsement.[12]

What both men agreed on from the start was that the cause of complete Allied unity was unlikely to be enhanced at the White House as long as their American colleague, Ambassador David Francis, remained at his post. Francis was as anti-Bolshevik as they came in the Allied camp but he was elderly; frail, he was just recovering from a severe illness; and too uncertain about Russian politics[13] to do anything but follow his President's lead. In fact, this dreamlike sojourn in Vologda – whose atmosphere seems to have been more like Chekov's *Month in the Country* than that of an Allied diplomatic centre – suited Francis down to the ground. By day, he could play golf of a sort over holes marked out with wooden stakes on a field under the walls of the town monastery. In the evenings, there were hands of bridge or poker, or else he reminisced over his days as mayor of St Louis back in the 1880s. When that palled, he could listen to his Brazilian and Siamese colleagues (most of the Allied countries were represented in this sleepy town) debating such arcane matters as which of their countries had the largest snakes. At times, it must have felt as far removed from Moscow as Timbuktoo.

The real world hit Lockhart with a vengeance as soon as he got back to Moscow. On 26 May, the eve of his departure to Vologda to discuss his pet framework for Allied intervention, fighting broke out along the Siberian railway line in central Russia between the Bolsheviks and the troops of what was later to be called the Czech Legion. This one event threw that entire framework out of joint. Paradoxically, at the same time, it offered hope that an agreed policy could at last be clamped into place.

The legion had its origins in an entire army corps, commanded largely by Russian officers, which had fought alongside the Russian army since 1916. Its first recruits had been drawn from Czechs and Slovaks residing or colonized in Russia when war began. Reinforcements soon arrived from the enemy ranks of the Austro-Hungarian army, which had spent the first months of the campaign in a fruitless battle to hold on to the key Galician fortress of Przemsyl. Thousands of prisoners were taken then, and in later actions; thousands more, unwilling to fight for a Habsburg monarchy which, in their eyes, was the supreme oppressor, simply deserted. The fall of the Tsar, followed eventually by the triumph of the Bolsheviks and their separate peace with the enemy, plunged the future of the corps into confusion.

To try to sort matters out, the Czech émigré leader (and future President of the post-war Czechoslovak Republic) Dr Thomas Masaryk left his base in America in May 1917 and spent the best part of a year in Russia to determine a future for his legion, as we may now call it. In December, he secured agreement that, together with Czech soldiers drawn from Western countries, the legion in Russia should be recognized as a regular fighting force, placed under the control of the French High Command. The ultimate aim was to evacuate them to France. This brought some potentially useful reinforcements into the Allied camp. It also brought incalculable (though well calculated!) benefits to Masaryk and his independence movement.[14] From now on, they ranked among the 'co-belligerents' in the Western camp, marking their stake for political recognition.

However, despite all these distant arrangements, the soldiers on the ground in central Russia remained in a confused situation. The legion was now under the command of the Red Army. Relations were never harmonious and friction increased in the spring when some Bolshevik commanders tried to block the legion's passage eastwards along the line to Vladivostok and freedom. Then, on 14 May, at the railway station at Chelyabinsk, just east of the Urals, came the fluke incident which was to set the revolt in motion. As chance would have it, two military trains were drawn up on parallel tracks, waiting to pull off in opposite directions along this enormous line, the sole direct link between European and Asian Russia. One was full of Hungarians, released from their Siberian prisoner-of-war camps and heading west for home. The other was a trainload of Czechs and Slovaks, members of the legion which had begun to battle its way eastward to the Pacific coast and so, by a very different route, back to Europe.

As both were waiting to pull out, a Hungarian soldier suddenly picked up a piece of scrap iron and hurled it at the train alongside. It hit and mortally wounded one of the Czechs, whereupon his enraged comrades scrambled out on the track, seized the culprit and lynched him on the spot. The local Soviet authorities then arrested several men on the Czech train as witnesses and also a delegation sent to secure their release. By a further coincidence, a 'Congress of the Czechoslovak Revolutionary Army' was meeting in that very town to decide how best to organize their move eastwards. The news from the railway station only strengthened the hand of those urging a resolution that they should break away and get out by force. When Trotsky heard of this in Moscow, he issued one of his firebrand directives to all local Soviets in Siberia: all Czechoslovaks were to be disarmed immediately and any of them found anywhere along the line still with his weapons was to be shot on the spot. This order arrived on 25 May. On 26 May, the Czechs rebelled to a man, and fighting broke out. That bit of iron was like the nail in the shoe of the war-horse which swayed the outcome of the battle.

The saga of the Czechs' two-month struggle east along the line all the way to Vladivostok, which they entered by capturing it on 29 June, does not need retelling here. In any event, the main effect of these heroics was not felt in the military sphere, nor was it confined to Siberia. It was to open up the one blockage which stood in the way of joint Allied intervention in Russia – the blockage in the mind of Woodrow Wilson.

Among the first to sniff out the possibilities here was that astute baronet Sir William Wiseman who, as head of the SIS station in Washington, acted as 'C's' liaison man with the State Department.

In a telegram sent back on 16 June,[15] he admits that all the arguments, including the military ones, so far put up to the President in favour of intervention were 'virtually exhausted'. Then he goes on: 'There remains only the Czecho-Slovak complication to use as a lever. Possibly an appeal to the President to extricate these unhappy people from their present grave position would be useful ... If they are to be saved at all intact as a force ... intervention must be undertaken at once. At all events, it seems worthy of consideration whether we should not make the most of this in dealing with the President.'

The most was duly made of the 'Czecho-Slovak complication' by America's allies, who found that, on this issue, they were pushing at a steadily opening door in the White House. The reason was simple enough. Already in the spring, when all Franco-British efforts to lure Austria-Hungary away from her German alliance had foundered, the president had agreed with Lansing that the Habsburg monarchy ought now to be dismantled, and its component peoples given their independence. The Czechs were at the top of Wilson's 'self-determination' list in this respect. In Masaryk they had always possessed the most respected and influential of all the émigré leaders in America, and now the exploits of his legion had turned them into comrades-at-arms. Protecting that legion was more than a fig leaf to cover a presidential somersault over intervention. It was a moral compulsion, and Wilson was a very high-minded man. But in the weeks before that somersault was completed, a great deal else was happening in the Baltic and in Moscow and it is to these events we must return. Lockhart, as usual, was in the thick of things.

During May and June he had been making what he hoped was steady progress towards the achievement of one Allied aim, the destruction or neutralization of the Russian fleets. This had been laid down by the Admiralty as a top priority and the naval attaché, Captain Cromie, had submitted various plans to London as to how the aim might be achieved as regards the powerful Baltic naval force at anchor in Kronstadt. Clearly, the best prospect was to persuade anti-Bolshevik officers on board to lay the demolition charges themselves, before the German army, which was threatening Petrograd, could march in and secure the vessels. Ideological arguments between the Russian destroyer flotilla, some of whose officers were prepared to blow the fleet up, and their more cautious comrades on board the heavier vessels had delayed matters. (Cromie had, in fact, concentrated on the four dreadnoughts as his prime targets.)

But the key to the solution lay in bribery rather than ideology and that meant millions of roubles being scraped together for Cromie to dole out among his contacts. A sum of 1.5 million (some £30,000–£35,000, depending on exchange rates) was authorized in a 'Very Urgent and Secret' telegram sent to Petrograd on 14 May and on the same day[16] Lockhart in Moscow was told to drop all his own money requests and concentrate on the emergency fund for Cromie. This, it was made clear, had to be met in full.[17]

Lockhart not only helped with raising the cash; he also served as the main link with Trotsky, now Minister of War, over the matter. The Bolsheviks had good reasons of their own for not wanting their fleet, or their old Tsarist capital, to fall into German hands and earlier in the year Lockhart had held several discussions with Trotsky on the matter. Now, the day after getting London's urgent fund-raising demand, he took Cromie himself along with him to discuss with the Soviet minister how the Baltic fleet could be destroyed. With the presence of the naval attaché at such a meeting, Lockhart was laying all his cards on the table. They were not, however, picked up.

'Trotsky,' he reported, 'stated that destruction should be carried out in case of necessity; that special men had been chosen for this task and a sum of money set aside for them and their families in the shape of special award.'[18]

As things turned out, there was never to be a joint action to destroy the Baltic fleet, nor was it disabled in 1918 by either Trotsky[19] or Cromie acting individually. As will be recounted later, its near destruction was only achieved by the British the following year, in an escapade which would have filled Cromie's heart with pride, had he but lived to witness it.

Lockhart also got caught up in the main military problem confronting the Alliance as a whole during these weeks: what to do about the Czechs. Quite apart from helping the legion to battle its way east to Vladivostok, the argument had to be resolved as to where they should go from there. The French insisted that they should all be sent to France to strengthen the Allies on the western front; this had earlier been agreed with the Allies and Clemenceau was adamant (in his best thunderous manner) that the arrangement should stand. The British, on the other hand, now thought that the legion might be better employed to go on fighting the Bolsheviks in Siberia, alongside the Japanese and any other Allied force which might be landed there. British estimates were putting the legion's strength at only 25–30,000 men – too few to be a major factor in France (which they could anyway not reach for three months) but strong and united enough to make a powerful contribution where they stood, in the Far East. As a somewhat fanciful compromise (probably only a delaying tactic) it was debated at one point whether half should be sent north to help protect Archangel, before being eventually shipped home. Here, it was pointed out, they might at least get the chance to fight Germans, which was all they cared about, rather than Bolsheviks, with whom they had tangled only out of necessity. This view was eventually to prevail.

Lockhart had had his first political contact with the Czech representative in Moscow only days after that tussle on the railway line began. Should the legion, asked the vice president of the Czech National Assembly, make for Archangel or Vladivostok? Lockhart told him to press on eastwards for the time being while he discussed the Archangel option further with London. The episode shows how far Lockhart had ranged from his brief of 'informal contacts with the Bolsheviks' and how far he was prepared to stick his neck out in the process. Throughout May and June he continued to be involved, successfully protesting with the French, for example, against a Bolshevik demand that the Czechs should be disarmed before travelling anywhere. All his telegrams to London about the Czechs had been coupled with further pleas for immediate Allied intervention.

'The German wall is now closing in on every side,' ran one such appeal. 'If Allies do not act immediately it is difficult to see how our intervention can be successful.' The climax came in a telegram of 6 June[20] when he not only wagged his finger at his London audience ('I have already warned you and I repeat again' etc.) but threatened his own resignation 'in the event of any further delay'.

This hectoring tone proved too much for the Whitehall mandarins, who anyway resented him as a political appointee and therefore an outsider. They now sharpened their quill pens and tried to stick them in the hide of this bumptious young Scot. Their message is interesting for what it reveals about the dilemmas facing the Alliance as a whole. 'You have at different times advised against Allied intervention in any form; against it by the Japanese alone; against it with Japanese assistance; against it at Vladivostok; in favour of it at Murmansk; in favour of it with an invitation; in favour of it without an invitation, since it was really desired by the Bolsheviks; in favour of it without an invitation, whether the Bolsheviks desired it or not.'

There was no point, the lecture continued, in complaining about indecision, since the problem was lack of agreement among the Allied governments: 'Britain, France and Italy have thought the dangers of intervention less than its advantages; America has thought the advantages less than the dangers.' Nothing could be done without overcoming America's rejection of active participation and all that could be done was to 'press our views on the Administration in Washington'.[21]

What the paper might have laid more stress on in explaining the Allied quandary was that, quite apart from the lack of agreement among themselves, there was a chaotic lack of any central authority inside Russia itself. That gap in the argument was eloquently filled by the Prime Minister, in a debate on Russia held at that same time in the House of Commons.

Mr Joseph King, the Liberal MP for Somerset, was constantly pestering his leader for more decisive action to help the Bolsheviks who, he declared, were the 'only government'.

At that, Lloyd George jumped up: 'That is exactly where he is wrong. What is the Government of the Ukraine? What is the Government in Georgia? What is the Government when you come to Baku? What is the Government in the northern parts of the Caucasus? What is the Government in any town and city of the Don? What is the Government, I will not say in Siberia, but in any city of Siberia? He will not find the same Government in any two villages there.'

The riposte had been quite extempore, delivered without those sheaves of pre-prepared texts which came, in later years, to deaden parliamentary 'debates'. But even had the Prime Minister been speaking from a brief, he could not have given a more telling survey. It will stand in good stead when the final frustrating stages of Allied action in Russia are described.

Back in Moscow, the Allies were about to learn another lesson from the diffuse struggles for power which the British Prime Minister had described. Again, it was a case of separate and probably unconnected acts of violence producing profound consequences. That it should be Boris Savinkov who would throw down the strongest political challenge to Lenin was not, in itelf, unexpected. It will be recalled that, at the end of May, 'C's' chief man in Russia, Commander Boyce, had identified the idealistic Socialist-Revolutionary leader as the only man who might conceivably bring the regime down.

Ten days before that, Lockhart had reported, in a 'Very Secret' telegram to London,[22] a long conversation he had had in Moscow with one of Savinkov's right-hand men. The emissary said that his leader hoped to stage a counter-revolution 'in which he himself will be Minister of Interior with some well-known General at its head'. But, to succeed, such a move ought to be coordinated with Allied intervention: what were the prospects?

Ten days later Lockhart (having received guarded consent from London to pursue the contact) had another session with Savinkov's 'confidant' who now felt able to go into much more detail. The French mission, he told Lockhart, was behind them and had given assurances that intervention had already been decided upon. Accordingly, Savinkov now proposed 'to murder all Bolshevik leaders on night of Allies' landing and to form a government which will be in reality a military dictatorship'. That, in fact, was what Savinkov and his supporters were aiming at when they struck their blow in the first week of July. The trouble was that their timing was wrong and their efforts were uncoordinated. The *coup* collapsed in a mixture of heroism and farce.

The most dramatic incident took place at 3 p.m. on 6 July when two left SRs[23] gained access to the German embassy, a splendid private house in Moscow's Denejni Pereulok, and killed the ambassador by emptying a pistol into him and then finishing him off with that traditional weapon of Russian assassinations, a bomb. The main aim of their movement had always been to resume the war against Germany (which was why they were so favoured by the Allies) and they hoped – vainly as it turned out – that such a gross provocation would somehow start the fighting up again.

Boris Savinkov was nowhere near Moscow at the time, but on that same day he raised the banner of revolt at his stronghold in Yaroslavl, a town some 150 miles to the northeast and roughly halfway towards Vologda. Savinkov's aim seems to have been to ring the Soviet capital with a series of similar insurrections. However, the fuses of rebellion failed to ignite elsewhere and his Yaroslavl uprising was finally quashed by the Bolsheviks after a fortnight of fierce fighting, with heavy artillery rushed up from Moscow playing the decisive role.

For forty-eight hours, the Soviet capital itself became the scene of some desperate skirmishing between the SR rebels (who had built up strong cadres of supporters inside Dzerzhinsky's secret police, including its combat detachment) and forces loyal to the Bolsheviks. At one point Dzerzhinsky himself was captured and Lenin was even contemplating evacuating the Kremlin. He was saved only by the Lettish mercenaries who had been hired to protect his regime in Moscow and other key centres.[24] General Vatsetis, their commander, had a mere 1,500 men at his disposal and was outnumbered by the rebels. But he and his well-disciplined troops knew how to fight and the rebels did not. By midday on 7 July it was all over and the arrests began.

Vatsetis had also sent some of his men to surround the Bolshoi Theatre, and with good reason. The Fifth Congress of the Soviets had opened there on 4 July, 470 of the 1,425 delegates being left SRs. At least one of their number knew exactly what was being plotted outside the building. This was Maria Spiridonova, a veteran pre-war revolutionary who knew neither fear nor pity. She also seems to have had no nerves. Having organized both the assassination and the armed uprising in the streets, she calmly took part in the dialectical debate inside the Opera as to the rights and wrongs of Lenin's policies. Lockhart, who sat in on the Congress proceedings throughout, has left the only full account of what happened next.[25] Parts of it matched the setting: opera buffa as well as high drama. Fittingly, ST 1 makes a brief and highly theatrical appearance.

The proceedings on the 5th had been stormy enough, with both Lenin and Trotsky defending the peace treaty and the left SRs calling them 'the lackeys of German imperialism' and yelling, prophetically, 'Away with the German butchers! Down with Mirbach!' It was expected that some resolution would be passed when the session resumed on the afternoon of the following day, Saturday, 6 July. But though the parterre filled up again with delegates, there was no Lenin or Trotsky on the platform and by 5 p.m. most of the other senior Bolsheviks had left. Count Mirbach's box was empty. Clearly, something was seriously wrong.

The first news from outside came from none other than Sydney Reilly who, at 6 p.m., burst into Lockhart's box. There had been a challenge of some sort to the Soviet authorities, he reported, and there was fighting in the streets of the capital. At this: 'Reilly and a French agent began to examine their pockets for compromising documents. Some they tore up into tiny pieces and shoved them down the lining of the sofa cushions. Others, doubtless more dangerous, they swallowed.'

As it happened, they need not have bothered. Nobody in the Western box was searched when Karl Radek, a senior member of the Foreign Office with whom they were on good terms, arrived an hour later to give a brief explanation to the diplomats: their German colleague had been murdered by the left SRs who had planned to storm the Opera House and capture the entire Bolshevik leadership assembled there. Instead, the rebels had themselves been trapped.

Though the assassination was duly described by an official Soviet communiqué the next day as the work of 'Russo-French-English Imperialists', no immediate sanctions were launched against Western missions. Nor did the German army march on Moscow to exact revenge. Nonetheless, the excitements of 6 July had left some lasting marks. The left SRs had been eliminated as the one serious political threat to Lenin. Savinkov himself fled the country to continue his dogged campaign against the regime from abroad – an exile from which he was very foolish to return. The Bolshevik leadership knew full well that the British, and even more the French, had been pouring millions of roubles into the coffers of certain anti-Soviet movements; this had now shown Lenin what that money could try to achieve. He took certain highly secret decisions accordingly.

Nor should we ignore the effect of 6 July on the 'master spy'. Reilly had been working underground for some two months and, though he had kept contact with his superiors (otherwise Lockhart would surely have expressed surprise at seeing him again), there is no record in his files of any written reports on this period given either to Commander Boyce or the consul.[26] But Reilly did not need to record what he had now seen for himself: the power of the Lettish 'Praetorian Guard', which alone had stood between Lenin and disaster on that day. There was a mighty lesson to be learned from that.

Though even more hectic months were to follow, three more major events still lay ahead in July. The first – and the most important one as regards Allied policy in Russia – was Wilson's final surrender to Anglo-French pressure to participate fully in joint intervention. This pressure had reached a new peak with the appeal drafted by the British and approved by the Supreme War Council in Paris on 2 July. It pulled out all the stops, some of them very squeaky ones. There were references to saving the 'Russian nation' and 'liberal Russia', both of which were known to be phantom phrases. There were warnings that the German army, by now checked in the west, would return eastwards with renewed savagery and violence to swallow Russia up as a vast German colony, another dubious proposition. There was also much play on rescuing those 'brave allies', the Czechs, now fighting desperately for survival in Siberia.

Though the Czechs were in reality doing very nicely on their own, this was the theme which, for the reasons given above, constantly recurred in the crucial aide-memoire which Wilson delivered on 17 July to all the Allied envoys in Washington. It was, in fact, a belated capitulation to the arguments they had been putting forward for months, but it was blandly presented as if Woodrow Wilson had worked it all out himself. While American military action would be limited in scale and restricted in particular, it was now declared 'admissible' and its main aim would be to 'help the Czecho-Slovaks consolidate their forces and get into successful cooperation with their Slavic kinsmen'. The President even specifically mentioned 'sentimental grounds' as being partly behind his decision. For America's allies, neither Wilson's Slavic susceptibilities, nor the modest military contribution he was starting off with, mattered for the moment. The principle of joint Allied support action had been established at last. It was to be applied, with varying degrees of enthusiasm and success, from now on.

Ironically, it was on that very day, 17 July 1918, that news of a second major event reached the West. This time, the Allied camp had no cause to rejoice but plenty of reason to examine its conscience. Tsar Nicholas, together with his wife and children, had been murdered by the Bolsheviks at Ekaterinburg, the Siberian town which had become their final place of confinement. The slaughter had taken place in the cellar of the House Epatiev, almost directly opposite the building where Thomas Preston,[27] formerly a mining prospector, had set up his office as honorary British consul. As usual, Lockhart was centre stage. Official confirmation of the 'executions' was given to him in Moscow on the evening of the 17th by the Assistant Commissar of Foreign Affairs, Leo Karachan, and Lockhart became the first person to pass it on to the West.

Almost until the day of his own murder, Count Mirbach had been pressing the regime in vain for assurances about the ex-Emperor and his family. That was more than Britain had done, despite the fact that Tsar Nicholas was a cousin (and a spitting image) of King George V. The King had in fact been more emphatic than the Foreign Office that the doomed imperial cousin should not be rescued and given political asylum. The government was nervous about the danger of hostile reaction in the liberal camp and left-wing demonstrations in the streets. The monarch was nervous lest this might even threaten his own crown. Who lagged behind whom in this has been hotly debated. The fact remains that in all the hundreds of messages passed between London and the various British missions in Russia during the first six months of 1918, only one has been traced which makes any anxious enquiries on behalf of the captive Romanovs. Even this draws back from taking any action on their behalf.

On 3 May Balfour had telegraphed to Lockhart:

> The King is greatly distressed by the reports which have reached him with regard to the treatment of the ex-imperial family at Tobolsk. I entertain grave misgivings whether any representations you will make would not do more harm than good to these unhappy victims. But it is impossible for us here to form any opinion worth having on this point, and I must leave it to your tact and discretion to do what is in your power to diminish the hardships of their confinement. If it were generally believed here that they were the victims of unnecessary cruelty the impression produced would be most painful.[28]

Even the hand-wringing being indulged in by Whitehall and Buckingham Palace was of the flabbiest order. But there is no doubt that when the news of the Ekaterinburg slaughter reached King George, it produced more than a painful impression. He was so haunted by remorse that, six months later, he despatched a British officer to the aid of the deposed Austrian Emperor Charles, another fellow monarch in distress and danger, albeit an ex-enemy one.[29]

The most important event of the month affecting the personal lives of Lockhart and his Western colleagues in Moscow was the departure of all the Allied missions from Vologda and the abrupt ending of that town's brief spell as a diplomatic centre. That existence, always a blend of the unreal and the surrealistic, ended in appropriate fashion. After mid-July pressure increased on the clutch of Allied ambassadors and chargés d'affaires cooped up there to fold their tents and move. But where to?

On 17 July, one Captain McGrath arrived as an emissary from General Poole, Allied commander-in-chief in the north, but behaving as though he were Allied viceroy. The general informed the diplomatic colony that he was expecting to be reinforced soon and would land in Archangel.[30] Their presence in Vologda might then hinder his subsequent military plans – presumably meaning a march on Moscow. There seems to have been nobody in the colony with the nous to realize that the general was simply going off his rocker. It was some 350 miles from Archangel to Vologda and another 300 from there to the Soviet capital. Had the Allies even been contemplating a campaign on such a Napoleonic scale, their envoys in Russia must have been informed and consulted. In that case, the venerable American ambassador in Vologda, David Francis, would have known full well that a veto would have come from his President. Nonetheless, the Vologda colony started twitching with anxiety and made provisional decisions to set out for Archangel and home.

But it was pressure applied simultaneously, and contrarily, from the Bolsheviks which decided the matter. Lenin wanted all these envoys back in Moscow (where they might come in very useful as hostages) and the Foreign Affairs liaison official Karl Radek was sent up to persuade them. Where he failed, an electrifying message from his chief, Georgi Chicherin, did the trick. The commissar warned the envoys that a great battle was looming, with Vologda in its path (unless he was thinking of an anti-Bolshevik thrust coming from the east, he was clearly suffering from the same delusions as General Poole). At all events, the envoys were said to be in mortal danger unless they returned to the protective arms of the Kremlin. The offer of such protection was worse than any distant din of battle. The diplomats boarded their special trains which were always on standby and, in the early morning of 25 July, steamed north to Archangel, without daring to tell Chicherin their destination. Vologda returned to the keeping of its many priests and monks.

It had been something of a scuttle and it ended on one of those notes of farce which always seem to echo in the wings of the Russian drama. As the evacuation party finally boarded their ships at Archangel on 28 July they were joined at the last minute by the members of a high-level British economic mission which had arrived on 22 July on a goodwill visit to Moscow and St Petersburg. Their party, which now scampered up the gangplanks, was headed by no less a dignitary than Sir William Clark, comptroller-general of the Department of Overseas Trade. Its activities, which in the circumstances were totally ludicrous, had presumably been launched without Mr Balfour's knowledge or approval. It was a classic Whitehall mix-up.

Whoever was to blame, Lockhart and his other consular colleagues were now left entirely alone and isolated in Moscow. He had not been told one word in advance about the Vologda evacuation, nor warned about the planned landings in Archangel.

As he grimly put it, the Allied consuls in Moscow had now taken over the role of hostages hitherto earmarked for the Allied envoys at Vologda. Despite Chicherin's assurances as to their safety, the consuls were understandably nervous. The events of August would show how right they were.

Part Two

The Allied Conspiracies

5

The Plot, As Presented
Down the Years

There had been a steady build-up of pressure during August before
the boiler exploded at the end of the month. The first serious
confrontation between the Bolsheviks and the Western powers was
triggered by General Poole's landing at Archangel which had indeed
marked the real beginning of Allied intervention.[1] As had been the
case with Western landings in Siberia, the numbers involved became
wildly inflated in the rumours which now swirled around Moscow.
Some versions put Poole's force at anything up to 100,000 men and
spoke of a joint drive on the Soviet capital with seven Japanese
divisions advancing from the east. Reports, equally unfounded, that
the Allies were carrying out mass executions of Soviet partisans
in the north inflamed Bolshevik tempers even more.

All these stories had not reached Moscow until 4 August, but
the regime lost no time in retaliating. Before dawn on the following
morning, about 200 British and French residents in the capital had
been rounded up by the Cheka and interned as hostages and both
their consulates-general raided by force of arms. (The Americans
were left, for the time being, untouched. It was not yet known that
fifty of their Marines had given symbolic support to the Anglo-
French battalions.)

The diplomatic immunity of the consular officials themselves
was eventually respected; what the Chekists were thought to be after
was any evidence which might enlighten them as to the real strength
and purpose of the Archangel landings and of any threat to Moscow.
Again, a touch of farce intrudes. The elderly consul-general, Oliver

Wardrop (who had been chatting to Lockhart when the raid began) later described how well his pre-arranged action plan for such an emergency had functioned: while two of his vice-consuls engaged the intruders in conversation in the offices, their chief retired to the bedroom – where the most confidential documents were kept – and, behind a locked door, made a holocaust of them in his large fire-place. By the time the Chekists, alerted by the columns of smoke which were pouring out, got into Wardrop's private apartment, they found the consul-general, half-dressed, in his sitting-room with the bedroom beyond so full of heavy acrid fumes that even a profes-sional fire-fighter might have hesitated to go in. Still, Wardrop was puzzled that the raiding party took only a perfunctory look at the piles of charred fragments which remained. One of them enlight-ened the old gentleman before leaving. It was a pity, the Chekist said, that all those files had been destroyed; he and his men had been given no authority to seize papers or property of any kind.

Wardrop's American colleague, de Witt Poole, in a report sent to Washington the next day, warned that 'there was no assurance that the American Consulate-General would not be violated at any moment'. Accordingly, he was asking his Swedish opposite number to take over American interests while he prepared to leave Russia immediately with his entire staff via Petrograd. In fact, as we shall see, Poole stayed on for some weeks, giving a very stout gesture of Allied solidarity. But his cypher codes, as well as his records, fol-lowed those of Wardrop up his consulate's best-burning chimney, in yet another bonfire of Allied papers. It is not surprising that American intelligence reports for the period should be almost non-existent. The ones on file had presumably been destroyed and there was no direct means of transmitting any more since the Americans had no separate secret service codes. This is a pity, for the heyday of rival intrigues was just about to begin with the emergence of the first fuzzy outlines of the 'Lockhart plot'.

We are dealing in this chapter with the published version of events – Communist and Western – down the years. It will be convenient to start with the Bolshevik side and how the Soviet press and radio described the dramatic developments at the end of August 1918. We can then work back exactly a fortnight from there, to the point at which the stage was actually set. It had been panic which had prompted those relatively modest police raids in the first week of August and it was panic which again triggered off police action in the last week of the month. This time, the emergency which threatened the regime was far greater, and so was its reaction. The threat came from the political weapon they feared most because they had used it to great effect themselves: assassination.

On the morning of Friday, 30 August, the head of the Petrograd Cheka, M.S. Uritsky, was gunned down and killed on the steps of his office by a young man wearing a leather jacket and an officer's cap who had turned up casually riding a bicycle. He was in fact a Russian military cadet called Kannegieser and his motive seems to have been repugnance at the mass shootings which Uritsky had been carrying out. He tried to get away through a nearby house where the English Club of Petrograd had once had its quarters and, though the club building was now empty and the young gunman had merely used it as an escape route, that was enough for the Soviet press to pin the blame for the murder on the British.

That same evening, something far worse took place. Lenin had been addressing a workers' meeting held at the large Michelson factory in the Moscow suburbs and, whilst he was leaving, a young Social Revolutionary fanatic – a Jewish girl called Dora Kaplan and a soulmate of the redoubtable Maria Spiridonova – approached him saying she wanted to talk about the food situation in the capital. When Lenin stopped to listen, she produced a revolver and fired two shots at him point blank. One went through the left upper lung, just missing the heart; the other entered his neck, close to the main artery. An inch or two either way with either bullet and Lenin would have perished and with him, in all probability, his regime. For a day or two, his condition was indeed critical but then his temperature steadily dropped and by 2 September he was out of danger. By then, the Soviet press was already pointing to 'agents of the English and French' as the sources of the attack.

The Cheka had struck, and struck hard while their leader was still fighting for his life. In the domestic field, a round-up was carried out of those who, in police jargon, would be called 'the usual suspects'. The Western press later reported[2] that among the 521 'counter-revolutionaries' seized in these raids were three grand dukes, one prince, two counts and four army generals. But it was in the diplomatic sphere that the heaviest impact came. At 3.30 in the morning of 31 August, only a few hours after the wounding of Lenin, Lockhart and his assistant, Captain Hicks, were pulled out of bed by Cheka gunmen and taken to the Lubyanka prison.[3] For Lockhart, this was to be the start of a muddling process of arrest, release and re-arrest. On this occasion he was asked three questions, each of which he refused to answer. The first was routine: 'Do you know the Kaplan woman?' The second was more tricky: 'Where is Reilly?' The third was the most awkward of all: 'Is that your writing?' Lockhart found himself looking at a pass he had signed earlier that month recommending the bearer to General Poole in Archangel.

Before tracing that signature back, we must look at the most serious incident of that same 31 August which took place at Petrograd. At about 4.45 in the afternoon, the British embassy building (which was now operational again, despite the absence of even a chargé d'affaires) was stormed by a squad of eight armed Chekists.[4] They were looking for British officials and not simply for documents. According to the only British eye-witness account[5] we have of the affair, the sworn affidavit given the following day by Nathalie Bucknall, the wife of a staff member, one of the Chekists told her that a death list of five embassy officials had been given them that morning. The only name she clearly recognized was that of Boyce, 'C's' station chief who had his office in the building. In fact, though Boyce was held overnight with the other male staff present in the room of the ambassador's secretary, no harm came to any of them.

It was another story with the naval attaché Captain Cromie, who, as the Cheka well knew from Trotsky, had his own network of informers and potential saboteurs to accomplish his mission of destroying the Russian fleet at anchor in the nearby harbour. The most heroic description of the tragedy was that of the gallant captain being shot down at the head of the embassy staircase, while firing away with a revolver in each hand at the ascending marauders. Both Allied and Soviet accounts[6] agree that he sold his life dearly. One of the Chekist raiders, named Ianson, was killed in the exchange of fire and another severely wounded.

Mrs Bucknall's account is somewhat less heroic. She saw Cromie running down the staircase with Chekist gunmen pursuing him. Apparently, he had fired his shots from an upper room and was now brought down mortally wounded on the last step of the staircase as he tried to escape.

The raiding party withdrew the next day, taking with them all the documents they could collect but releasing all their captives unharmed. The fact remained that the embassy of a major foreign power, with whom Bolshevik Russia was in diplomatic relations, had been stormed and the senior officer present murdered. The victim was treated with particular brutality, partly because the Bolsheviks recognized, among the medals he was wearing, a Tsarist decoration. This was the Cross of St George, which a Chekist either crushed under his foot or pinned mockingly on himself (the versions differ here).[7] At all events, this testimony that their opponent had been honoured by the Tsar was enough for them to refuse the dying man even Mrs Bucknall's drink of water, let alone medical attention or the services of the embassy chaplain, Mr Lombard. After a period of semi-consciousness, with his lips moving faintly, Cromie was dead within the hour.

On 2 and 3 September the Moscow press and wireless gave the Bolshevik version of events to the world. Among the froth of anti-imperialist jargon were many hard bits of information. The first of these official bulletins announced

> the liquidation of a conspiracy of Anglo-French diplomats, headed by the Chief of British Mission, Lockhart, the French Consul-General Grenard, French General Lavergne and others.

Object of conspiracy was to seize, by bribery of Soviet troops, the Soviet of People's Commissars and to proclaim a military dictatorship in Moscow . . .

There passed through the hands of one of Lockhart's agents – English Lieutenant Riley [*sic*] – more than one million two hundred thousand roubles for the purpose of corruption during the last week and a half alone . . .

Full details are published, with time and place of meetings between Lockhart or Riley with Soviet military commanders etc. and of exact sums of money handed over on each occasion. Capture of Soviet together with Lenin and Trotsky was fixed for about 10 September. Compromising documents with signatures of Lockhart and Riley are in the hands of the Extraordinary Commission . . . including a scheme drawn up by Riley for arrest of Soviet leaders and their despatch to Archangel, with the exception of Lenin and Trotsky, whom it would be more prudent to shoot immediately after arrest.

'Compromising correspondence' was said to have been found during the raid on the British embassy at Petrograd, when 'forty persons, mostly British, were arrested'. Cromie's death was reported with no comment, except for the allegation that it was he who had commenced the firing.[8]

There was, as yet, no mention in all this of the identity of the 'Soviet military commanders' approached by the plotters. The omission was partly rectified by another official announcement the next day headed 'Attempted bribery of the Letts'. This, as will be seen, came much nearer the bone.

Ten million roubles assigned for this purpose. Lockhart entered into personal contact with the commander of a large Lettish unit, trying in personal interviews to play on his national feelings. Should the plot succeed Lockhart promised in the name of the Allies immediate restoration of a free Latvia. Immediately the Lettish commander was approached by the English, he asked instructions from the [Soviet] Extraordinary

Commission and was told to accept the invitation. To his surprise, he was taken at once by the agent of the British Military Mission Shmegkhen [*sic*] to Lockhart's private flat, where he had his first interview with Lockhart himself on 14 August. All moneys received by the Lettish commander were immediately handed over to the Extraordinary Commission.

Though the emphasis in all this was heavily on documents seized from the British, a raid on various French premises was also reported, and this had produced the most startling piece of alleged evidence about the plot thus far paraded. It concerned the discovery of a letter addressed to the President of France, Raymond Poincaré, and written by René Marchand, the correspondent in Russia of the foremost Paris paper, *Le Figaro*. The writer alleged that he was present at a crucial meeting of Allied representatives which had been held at the American consulate on 25 August to discuss a joint venture strategy against the Bolsheviks. Poole's French colleague, Grenard, was present, though (unfortunately for the Soviets' picture to be painted a week later) not Lockhart himself. However, all three chief espionage agents were there: Reilly for the British, 'Colonel de Vertement' (still being wrongly labelled) for the French and Kalamatiano for the Americans.

The main purpose of the meeting, according to Marchand's disclosures, was to coordinate a mass sabotage campaign against the Soviet rail network and other key targets, especially around Petrograd, with the objective of creating famine and fomenting such discontent as would ultimately topple the regime. It was designed as a 'stay-behind' operation, to be launched by the three underground intelligence networks after the anticipated imminent departure of the diplomatic missions. Marchand's 'disclosures' stopped there; they gave no details about any impending *coup d'état* in the capital though we know from other sources that he had also passed on to the Cheka a full account of the 'Moscow plot' as discussed at the Allied meeting.[9]

There was no doubt, as was later established, that this Allied conclave had, in fact, taken place when and where stated, nor that

Marchand had attended it. The French journalist was also something of an authority on Russian affairs (he had published, before the war, a series of books on Tsarist diplomacy). Moreover, he was a trusted confidant of the French Consul-General, whom he had accompanied the year before on a tour of Southern Russia. It was at the invitation of Grenard, the senior diplomat involved, that Marchand had attended the meeting of 25 March, rather to the surprise of the other Allies present.[10] The mystery was how and why this incriminating letter had been left lying around and why, in view of the tremendous publicity given to it in the Soviet press at the time, Marchand was never to be called as a witness. In due course there would be a good explanation of all this but no hint of it emerged at the time.

The Marchand letter was one of many things which troubled the political masters of 'arch-conspirator' Lockhart at home, and it is to the reaction in London which we must now turn. The first official confirmation of the outrage at the Petrograd embassy seems to have reached the Foreign Office via Copenhagen just before 6 p.m. on 3 September. The Danish minister at Petrograd reported to his government who passed on the news of the forcing of the British embassy four days before, including an account of Cromie's death and the 'horrible manner' in which his corpse had been treated. The embassy archives, it was stated, had been sacked 'and everything was destroyed'. (The Foreign Office must have rather hoped that had, indeed, been the case.) The message added that the French Military Mission had also been forced, with several Frenchmen being arrested 'but that everything had already been recovered'.[11] (It was later to emerge that de Verthamon's secret service hideout, set up early in August in the Catholic Girls' High School of St Peter and Paul, and run by a Frenchwoman, Jeanne Morens, had also been raided. The agile sabotage expert made his escape over the rooftops and was never captured.)

A further sombre message from Copenhagen described how their minister in Petrograd had, on 2 September, found Cromie's 'half-decapitated body thrown into a cellar'. He had taken it to the

British Church where it was properly buried, though wrapped in a Danish flag as the British one was unavailable. Arrangements were being made for the remains to be placed in a zinc coffin and sent to England.

There were two reactions in London to this harrowing news, the day after the official confirmation had been received. Both were curiously muted. The first was at a War Cabinet meeting where the Petrograd outrage was among the items on the agenda. It should be recalled that the great British breakthrough at Amiens had taken place only three weeks before and minds were very much on what seemed, at long last, to be the turning point on the western front and, therefore, victory in the war. Despite this, the comment which the First Sea Lord, Admiral Wemyss, made on the murder of his naval attaché appears excessively muted. This was, he said, 'very grave news for the Admiralty as the death of Cromie had severed the last links of communication which the Admiralty had with Russia'.[12] Their Lordships seemed almost to be reproaching Cromie for laying down his life.

Lord Robert Cecil of the Foreign Office Russia Committee had been called in to attend, and it was left to him to say that 'some action was called for'. Perhaps they ought to imprison, or at least intern, the Soviet envoy in Britain, Mr Litvinov?

The action turned out to be a decidedly limp slap on the Bolshevik wrist. On 4 September Balfour sent a round-robin telegram to all Allied capitals on the crisis. It began: 'I fear we really have little hold at present over Bolshevik Government, but I feel we must do all we can to show that we are in earnest.' But the most he felt able to do sounded modest indeed. 'The only further course that occurs to me is to get neutral governments to express their reprobation of such acts as the murder of Captain Cromie and to declare that, in the event of the perpetration of further crimes of this nature the authors will be regarded as outlaws.'[13]

The five neutrals approached (Sweden, Norway, Denmark, Holland and Switzerland) promptly agreed to make the joint démarche, but found they had been pre-empted by, of all people, the representatives of the Central Powers in Petrograd. Already on 3 September, the envoys of Germany and Austria led an address to the Bolshevik authorities protesting 'in the name of humanity against these wanton murders of peaceful and innocent citizens'. To underline that they were not simply referring to the mass executions of the Russians arrested a few days before, they had telegraphed for authority to join with the neutrals in the protest over Cromie's murder.

Ironically, therefore, the language of the Entente powers was not so strong as that of their enemies, who, moreover, delivered their protest directly and not through neutrals. Further British action was confined to the despatch of a telegram to Petrograd (again via Copenhagen) conveying to all British officials and citizens 'the deep sympathy of H.M.G. in their difficult and hazardous situation and assuring them that we are doing, and will do, all in our power to secure their safety'.[14]

All that appeared to be in their power was to put Litvinov and the members of his Soviet mission under 'preventive arrest' until such time as British representatives in Russia were freed and allowed to leave the country via Finland. This was the beginning of a drawn-out process of bargaining between London and Moscow. But though, in the exchanges which followed, the accusations against Lockhart and Cromie were rejected as 'trumped-up', relatively little emphasis, and even less publicity, was devoted to this. The reason was clear. The British government was already well aware that all the charges were not trumped up and was probably nervous as to how much more the Russians could produce and back up. A small sample of things to come was given by their chargé d'affaires, Lindley, who was in Archangel when the outrage in Petrograd took place. When he received the news of Cromie's death on 6 September, he immediately sounded a cautionary note to London. The captain's activities in trying to secure the Baltic fleet, he pointed out, had been 'carried out for months in daily danger of his life and brought him ... into cooperation with Russians hostile to Bolshevik regime and therefore claimed as reactionaries.

His plans may very well have included destruction of certain bridges, as Bolsheviks declare.'[15]

What all three Western capitals urgently needed were first-hand reports from their diplomatic or intelligence officials on the crisis (cyphers had by now been largely destroyed, except in the northern ports). That meant, above all, from 'arch-conspirator' Lockhart. It is his version of the affair which is at the heart of the Western case, as it has been presented.

Lockhart's accounts down the years come in two principal instalments: his *Diaries*, kept during the crisis but not published in London until 1973,[16] and a fuller version given in his *Memoirs* which came out over forty years earlier. By then, the name of the mysterious officer who was the presumed agent provocateur of the Cheka had long since been produced; indeed, Colonel Eduard Berzin, the commander of a Latvian artillery regiment, was paraded as the star witness in the mass trial of the conspirators held in Moscow between 28 November and 3 December. (Lockhart, Reilly and de Verthamon were among those tried *in absentia*.) Many other details of what looked like an embarrassing fiasco for the Allies were also recited at the trial so that, when he put pen to paper for posterity, Lockhart had a lot to explain. Boldly, he described his account of the plot as 'the whole truth, so far as I know it'.

In summary, his story is that at lunchtime on 15 August (the real date was probably the day before) two 'Lettish gentlemen' appeared at his flat. One was 'a short sallow-faced youth called Smidchen' (clearly the 'Shmegkhen' of the Soviet story) and the other, the impressive figure of Colonel Berzin ('tall, powerfully built with clear-cut features and hard, steely eyes').[17] They produced a letter of recommendation to Lockhart from Captain Cromie in Petrograd which was instantly recognizable as genuine, not only from the handwriting but from the idiosyncratic spelling mistakes. When asked what they had come for, the men said that they could not go on fighting the Bolsheviks indefinitely and now desired to go north to prevent any conflict between the Lettish troops up there and General Poole's forces. Could they be given a laissez-passer?

This seemed a plausible proposition but before deciding Lockhart wanted first to talk it over with his French colleagues, Consul-General Grenard and General Lavergne, and also with Sydney Reilly. (ST 1 was at the time in the consulate – which was his semi-official refuge in Moscow – and, with Lockhart expected to depart for England shortly, was due to take over any operations planned from underground.) Here we reach the nub of the matter. The two Letts were duly given their passes to be used when needed and Reilly was then introduced to Berzin. The prospect of a working alliance with one of the Praetorian Guard commanders in Moscow, who now seemed to be genuinely turning against his Bolshevik employers, sent Reilly's imagination racing. Two days later, he returned to the consulate suggesting that, after it had been closed down (and when no official involvement could therefore be imputed), 'he might be able, with Lettish help, to stage a counter-revolution in Moscow'.

The next words of the *Memoirs* need remembering: 'This suggestion was categorically turned down by General Lavergne, Grenard and myself, and Reilly was warned specifically to have nothing to do with so dangerous and doubtful a move.'

At that, Reilly, whose reaction is not recorded, disappeared into hiding and Lockhart did not see him again until the two men met in London, Reilly having travelled by a much more dangerous and circuitous route than the consul.[18] Lockhart was to spend another, longer spell of nearly three weeks under arrest (this time in the relative luxury of a well-furnished apartment in the Kremlin) before being released at the end of September – in return for the release of Litvinov in London – and starting the journey home. While in the Kremlin, he read from the Moscow papers the unfolding story of the Bolshevik case against him, with repeated revivals of the René Marchand allegations. Interestingly, in neither the contemporary diary nor the *Memoirs* is there a flat and categoric rejection. Both use identical phrases: the Soviet accounts of an Allied conspiracy were 'fantastic'; their version of the Lockhart plot 'reads like a fairy-tale'. But Lockhart admitted some worry about Reilly: 'Unless he

had completely lost his head, the whole story was a tissue of invention.' The nearest thing to a denial, when it comes, is qualified.

Both *Diaries* and *Memoirs* suggest that Lockhart was equally
seized during those fraught September weeks by storms of romance
as well as of conspiracy. Earlier in the year, he had been swept up into
the most violent and all-consuming of his various extra-marital
affairs. The lady in question was Marie Zakrveskaia, the daughter of
a Russian senator, who had made a brilliant match in 1911 when she
married Count von Benckendorff, then the Tsarist ambassador in
London. He was murdered by the Bolsheviks after the revolution,
leaving the beautiful and talented Moura (as she was always called)
unattached. She eventually attached herself to Lockhart and, this
time, the affair could be flaunted openly without fear of diplomatic
repercussions. There was no British ambassador to issue rebukes;[19]
social constraints hardly existed as there was no such thing as society;
and the flames of an obsession such as this only grew fiercer in the
heat of the political furnace surrounding it.

Both *Memoirs* and *Diaries* for 1918 vibrate with Moura: the joy
which swept aside all his political worries when, on 28 July, she
rang from Petrograd to say she was safe and on her way to Moscow
to join him; the torment when they arrested her as the presumed
confidante as well as the known mistress of the 'arch-conspirator';
the relief when she was released and allowed to visit him in the
Kremlin, bringing him news and books; and the passion of the last
days they were able to spend together in freedom when he was on
his way to Finland. The Foreign Office had found it 'quite incred-
ible' that he should have requested a brief delay to his arranged
departure 'to wind up his affairs'. The affair Lockhart was winding
up was Moura.

Before taking a final dip into his *Diaries* (which were the last
of the British eye-witness accounts to appear) it is worth looking
at the other published versions. The theme of the 1918 conspiracies
is touched on by most of the early post-war writers on Soviet affairs
and most of them accepted the offical denial of any involvement
more or less at face value.[20] These commentators simply had

nothing else to go on. Then, in 1931, the ghost of Reilly's voice was heard in a book, published by his second bigamous wife, the Latin American beauty queen Pepita Bobadilla. It can only have been based on accounts which he had earlier given her and the caution always called for as to Reilly's veracity has to be doubled when his stories are passed through the magnifying glass of Pepita, who was out to make a splash and a tidy sum of money with the book. Nonetheless, for the first time from the British side, there came an admission of the Reilly–Berzin contacts in August 1918, hatching a plot whose aim was to unseat the Bolshevik regime.

This may well have prompted the guardians of the secret in Whitehall to sanction the publication of more reputable first-hand accounts. It can be no coincidence that Captain George Hill's intelligence reminiscences and the Lockhart *Memoirs* both appeared the following year, 1932. Hill's book[21] now gave officially sanctioned confirmation that a *coup d'état* had been planned in Moscow, but described it as a purely personal venture of Reilly's. Hill stated that he had never even met Berzin, let alone sat in on any discussions; he had, however, been fully informed about developments in case it might fall to him to carry the project out.

Hill also gave a vivid account as to how the Cheka stumbled on to the identity of many of the Allied agents involved in the plot. One of the girl couriers employed by Kalamatiano had apparently lost her head and broken down during a police raid on an Allied safe-house; a body search soon produced the incriminating evidence. Her chief was arrested that same afternoon. Hill helped Reilly's escape (of which more later) while he himself reverted to his cover as a technician in a Moscow film studio and carried on as best he could with organizing courier services and sabotage gangs, underground work which had now become doubly hazardous. Lockhart was totally exonerated in Hill's account. All the Bolshevik charges against him (and therefore by implication the British government) were 'quite false and from political motives'. This cleared the tracks for Lockhart's own *Memoirs* which, as we have seen, came out the same year and painted the same picture as regards involvement.

It was not surprising that when, thirty-four years later, Lockhart's son produced the first biography of Reilly[22] he should also place ST 1 at the centre of the plot, indeed, as its prime and only mover. Lockhart Senior figures only as a collector of roubles for good anti-Bolshevik causes. It is curious that the son nowhere cites any information given to him by his father. Critical information from other sources was not available, including the very secret report on the whole affair which his father had made on his return to London.

The author remembers being called on in London in the mid-1960s by Robin Bruce Lockhart to ask for any guidance as to where and how this material could be obtained. The answer at the time was regretfully negative. In fact, had he been able to wait another four years in preparing his Reilly biography, some enlightenment would have been found in a learned article in the *Journal of Modern History*. The writer accepted and expanded on fresh claims made by Soviet sources about the Cheka's manipulation of the whole conspiracy scenario; he also cited some of the admissions which Lockhart had himself made in 1918 about his personal involvement in the affair.[23]

The pointers to the truth were inadvertently presented for all to see when Lockhart's *Diaries* were published in 1973, fifty-five years after they were written. Yet only fragments of the 1918 material were reproduced, even after this lapse of more than half a century. The editor of the *Diaries* tells us that Lockhart was a compulsive chronicler, keeping three regular accounts of his doings. These ranged from a brief log of his appointments to the fullest of the three daily records now being printed – but printed in a severely censored form, in which no item of a politically sensitive nature has survived. The most drastic example of this censorship concerns the last three weeks of August 1918; they are left totally blank. Yet these were the very weeks when, as Lockhart's *Memoirs* recorded, he was caught up in the Berzin–Reilly affair, which had massive military and diplomatic ramifications – whether or not a *coup* took place in the Soviet capital.

The entries before the gap are on a daily basis, ending with a note on 7 August about the publication of the murdered Tsar's diaries; they resume on 31 August with his arrest following the attempted assassination. They then continue, also in regular sequence (with only two one-day omissions), right down to his departure for England on 2 October. The entries covering his confinement in the Kremlin pull no punches as regards the Bolsheviks; the constant references to Moura make it clear that he was not the man to keep quiet out of deference for the feelings of his wife and family. Moreover, the compulsive diarist, and his editor, would have been expected to provide some explanation for this large and critical gap. The assumption must be that the entries between 8 and 30 August contained material which was politically rather than personally embarrassing, and remained so down the decades to follow. We can leave it there for the moment, and turn briefly to tracing how the Lockhart affair came to be presented by the Soviet side over the years.

Here a preliminary note of caution needs to be sounded. All too often, these Soviet versions have been quoted and more or less accepted at face value in Western literature, as though they constituted a reliable chronicle of record. This ignores the fact that the Soviet regime was, from the start, founded on the two dark pillars of lies and violence. The lies embraced the techniques of manipulative propaganda, which shifted with changing political requirements.

The first presentation of the Soviet case after the arrests was the statement for the prosecution at the 'open trial' (later known under the name 'show trial') of the defendants which was staged before the Supreme Revolutionary Tribunal in Moscow between 28 November and 2 December 1918. According to a French intelligence report which was passed later to their British colleagues,[24] the twenty-four accused were divided into six separate groups.

By themselves at the head come the two diplomats, Lockhart and the French Consul-General Grenard, who are accused in general terms of 'organising counter-revolutionary activities in order to create famine and to overthrow and destroy the government of workers and peasants ... and restore the capitalist bourgeois regime'. This was referred to as 'The envoys' plot' (in view of the status of the two accused) and was largely based on the text of the Marchand letter. There was never any doubt that, simply by encouraging and financing anti-Bolshevik movements (with the approval of their governments), the two men had functioned as 'counter-revolutionaries'. There was no case, therefore, to answer as regards the broader conspiracy.

The other five groups were all associated with the 'Lockhart plot' itself – i.e. the detailed execution of the broader plan. The first of these again contained only two names, the intelligence agents Reilly and Kalamatiano. (Strangely, the misspelt de Verthamon is omitted from this group, though his name does appear when the sentences were announced.) Reilly's attempts to bribe Lettish groups and 'prepare them for revolt' are mentioned.

The second of the 'Lockhart plot' groups includes the names of Kalamatiano's principal Russian collaborators, Colonel Friede and Major-General Zagriajsky, accused of directing the spy network and collecting more recruits. The third lists six of these helpers, ranging from a customs officer and a prison guard to the manager of the military vehicle depot in the capital.

Then come the female couriers who were trapped: 'the former actress Otten; the former teacher at the French school for young girls, Friede,[25] and its director Morens'. Finally comes a mixed batch of Russians and Czechs said to have provided safe-houses for the network. When sentences were passed, two were condemned to death; eight were given prison sentences of five years' hard labour and the rest pardoned. The two condemned men were Colonel Friede (who was executed on 14 December) and Kalamatiano who, as will be described below, survived a gruelling spell in the Lubyanka jail. The court also passed death sentences *in absentia* on Lockhart, Grenard, Reily (*sic*) and Vertamon (*sic*), noting that 'they had all fled'. They would all be shot if ever found on Soviet soil.

The case for the prosecution in 1918 cannot be accused of serious falsification or even exaggeration. The various groups were listed correctly as regards their functions and the charges against each group came to be broadly substantiated. If there was anything remarkable about the proceedings, it was the relative leniency of the sentences (compared with later Communist show trials and purges). Indeed, the official journal *Izvestia* commented on this, suggesting it showed 'how secure the regime feels itself to be'.

Subsequent Soviet treatment of the 'Lockhart plot' was intermittent and somewhat haphazard; but the trend was gradually to flesh out the bare bones of the trial accusations.[26] The first such expanded account appeared in 1920, written by the veteran Latvian revolutionary, M. Latsis. Exiled to Siberia in 1916, he had escaped in time to join Lenin's Bolshevik revolution and, in 1918, became one of Dzerzhinsky's closest colleagues, serving on the Cheka's ruling Collegium. For the most part, Latsis followed the official account of the plot as given at the trial two years before but added a few more details. Thus he described how, after Lockhart had told Reilly to arrange matters with Berzin, four meetings took place between the two conspirators in the second half of August, the dates being 17, 22, 28 and 29. Reilly's alleged plans for his two principal captives, Lenin and Trotsky, are also gone into for the first time. The original idea had been to take the pair under close guard to Archangel but then Reilly had changed his mind and decided to shoot them.

Four years later, another Latvian Bolshevik, who also became a principal lieutenant of Dzerzhinsky's, added further details in his memoirs. This was the extraordinary figure of I.K. Peters, who had a revolutionary record longer than his arm. He had been lucky to avoid a criminal one as well, lucky, indeed, to escape the British hangman's noose. Peters had spent the last years of his foreign exile (1909–17) in London, where he worked as a tailor's presser. Under surveillance as an anarchist, he was arrested in connection with the notorious Houndsditch shootings, carried out by fellow Latvians on 16 December 1910, when three London policemen had been murdered. He stood trial at the Old Bailey the following May but managed to get off by pleading the most beguiling of alibis: he had, he said, spent that evening at his lodgings, mending his mouse-trap.[27] Peters had then married an English girl, May Freeman, whom he left behind when he returned after the revolution. He kept a soft spot for England (and especially, perhaps, for the magnanimity of British justice) and got on very well personally with Lockhart when their paths crossed in such a strange fashion in 1918. It was Peters who had questioned him gravely but politely after his initial arrest on 1 September; Peters who released him and was then obliged to re-arrest him a few days later; Peters who brought him books during his second confinement in the Kremlin; Peters who organized the release of Moura; Peters who later brought her to the Kremlin to rejoin her lover, at least for a visit; Peters who announced his freedom, and even tried to persuade him as a friend to stay on in Russia because 'capitalism is finished'.

But in his memoirs six years later, Peters did nothing to spare the Englishman's reputation. For the first time, details were given to suggest that Britain's Russian expert had been thoroughly duped. It was only in August, according to Peters, that he and his Cheka boss Dzerzhinsky had decided to 'investigate' Lockhart and for this purpose he, Peters, had contacted a Latvian officer, 'Comrade Berzin'. (The colonel, he confusingly added, had already been approached by one of Lockhart's agents.) The meetings of 14 and 15 August, with the involvement of Grenard and Reilly, are related almost exactly as Lockhart later described them in his *Memoirs*, but for the first time the American Consul-General de Witt Poole is also brought into the Soviet account. Without giving the date (25 August) Peters tells how the Cheka had learned of that Allied conclave held in Poole's office at which the underground 'stay behind' operations had been discussed, including the 'planned coup' in Moscow. (The source of all this had, of course, been Marchand, though the Frenchman is not cited.) Peters concludes by saying that the attempt on Lenin's life had forced the Cheka to hurry things up and 'act prematurely'.

Nothing more of interest was produced from the Soviet side for the next forty years. Then, in 1962, one K.A. Peterson, political commissar of the Latvian Rifle Division, took matters a step further by claiming that the 'Lockhart plot' had been penetrated by the Cheka from the beginning, again giving early August as the start of the operation. This version has Peters as the controller, suggesting that Berzin be persuaded to act the role of agent provocateur. (The Cheka did not use this phrase, which, to them, reeked too much of Tsarist practices.) Reilly's plans for Lenin are now given as to 'remove,' instead of to murder, the Bolshevik leader.

Finally, in 1964, a Colonel V. Kravchenko published two interviews with the mysterious 'Schmidkhen' who had flitted in and out of the story from the start, as a presumed double agent. He was now revealed as one Ian Buikis (yet another Latvian). As early as May 1918, Dzerzhinsky had sent him to Petrograd with a fellow countryman to make the initial contact with Captain Cromie which, in turn, led to the meetings with him, Reilly and the French. According to this version, the Allied conspirators had been out-conspired. Their famous plot was now presented as being entirely of Bolshevik hatching.[28]

All the Soviet accounts contain a degree of confusion and contradiction; yet on the whole, they do not appear to have been manipulated. Manipulation has clearly been at work, however, in the various versions of the 'Lockhart plot' as given in that ever-changing bible of Bolshevik history the *Great Soviet Encyclopaedia*. In Volume 37 of the first edition (1938) the Latsis version is summarized but with the omission of Trotsky as an intended victim. (Banished from the Soviet Union, he was soon to be murdered in Mexico and had long since become a political non-person.)

Volume 25 of the second edition (1954) gives a startlingly different version of events. This edition, produced at the height of the Cold War, is made to serve as Soviet propaganda ammunition in that conflict. American involvement in the 1918 drama, hitherto almost sidelined, is now presented as crucial. The French are virtually omitted as villains and the conspiracy becomes Anglo-American, with vastly inflated proportions. De Witt Poole and Lockhart are said to have organized between them everything from the Savinkov revolt of July 1918 to the attempted murder of Lenin at the end of August. Finally, in 1957, comes an official version which turns full circle by restoring the French and British as the arch-conspirators.[29]

The contradictions, variations, omissions or partial admissions in all the versions, official and personal, Soviet or Western, leave key questions unanswered on both sides. The Russians have never made clear, for example, who was really responsible for the alleged infiltration of Berzin and the other agents provocateurs; who controlled the operation; and when it was launched. Nor has the mystery of the famous Marchand letter ever been cleared up: was it a chance discovery or a Cheka plot?

On the Western side, the true extent of Lockhart's own knowledge of, and involvement in, the conspiracy which bears his name is still left unclear by all the versions given above. That leads straight to the bigger question: how much did his government know, and has there perhaps been a massive cover-up extending down the century on this? Then there is the hazy picture of Allied involvement. Were the French in it up to their necks, and how much did the Americans know?

Finally, however far-fetched they may appear in the end, there were the suspicions (harboured above all by the Americans at the time) that 'C's' ST 1 was not so much a British master-spy as a two-faced double agent and that it was none other than Reilly who, from first to last, was behind any Cheka frame-up that took place.

We can now look at these questions in the light of much unpublished – indeed hitherto unknown – evidence and testimony which has come to light. At least some of the question marks which have surrounded this eighty-year-old mystery can be removed.

6

The Plot: What Really Happened

The most common label attached down the years to the Allies' anti-Bolshevik conspiracy of 1918 has been 'the Lockhart plot', the name of the alleged arch-conspirator himself. Other versions, however, including that given by Lockhart's son, present it as 'the Reilly plot', on the grounds that ST 1, flouting categoric orders to have nothing to do with any Moscow *coup d'état*, went ahead defiantly on his own with a one-man mission to topple the Bolshevik regime. Finally, as more indications filtered down through Soviet sources that the Cheka had penetrated the operation, it was even referred to as 'the Dzerzhinsky plot'. But according to a formidable body of testimony which came into the author's hand almost by accident while this work was still under preparation, none of these labels really fits. The great Allied conspiracy seems to call for a very different and far more prestigious label.

The unpublished – and indeed hitherto unknown – memoirs[1] left behind by the top Soviet defector, General Alexander Orlov, after his death in America contain among many other things a detailed description of this 1918 Moscow drama. It was put together by Orlov to satisfy his own curiosity while he was serving at the Lubyanka headquarters in the early 1920s and had the opportunity both to see material on the episode and to question those of his colleagues who had been principally involved in the affair. The picture which emerges is of Lenin not merely launching the massive deception campaign in person, months ahead of the dénouement, but of intervening to exploit new twists to the affair as and when they cropped up. General Orlov's account begins: 'Early in the summer of 1918 Lenin came to the conclusion that the British and French were definitely plotting the overthrow of the Soviet government. He suggested to Dzerzhinsky that it would be a good thing if the Cheka could catch the foreign plotters red-handed and expose them to the world.'

When Dzerzhinsky and his aides got down to discussing how their leader's plan could be carried out, they seized straight away on the same instrument which they knew the Western Allies were almost bound to go for themselves: the Lettish troops.

'Among the informers of the Cheka there was a former Tsarist ensign by the code-name of Smidchen, of Lettish origin, who had made the acquaintance of the British naval attaché in Petrograd, Captain Cromie. Smidchen had reported that, on two occasions, Captain Cromie had tried to obtain through him secret information about the Red Army.'[2]

This gave the Cheka their obvious opening and so 'Smidchen was instructed to tell Captain Cromie that he had a friend, Colonel Eduard Berzin of the Lettish Artillery Brigade who, though in the service of the Soviets, hated the Russian Bolsheviks and could be made to work for the "Allies".'

The date given for this was 7 August. A week later, 'Cromie asked Smidchen to bring Colonel Berzin to the private apartment of the British envoy Bruce Lockhart, in Khlebny Lane in Moscow.' The account of this first meeting between the three men follows in broad outline that given by Lockhart in his *Memoirs* and by 'Smidchen' himself, under his real name, in 1964. But Orlov makes some significant additions to the story in describing what happened next. Thus, on the next day, 15 August, when both the French Consul-General Grenard and 'the important British intelligence officer' (Reilly) joined in the talks, it was the Frenchman who made the running with the first mention of a possible *coup d'état* in Moscow: 'The French Consul brought up the question of overthrowing the Soviet government and tied it in with the fate of Latvia.'

Orlov's account (which could only have come, directly or indirectly, from the two Latvian agents) is also interesting on the subject of money: 'When Berzin was asked how much money he thought he would need for indoctrinating and influencing the men and officers of the Lettish Brigade, he feigned disinterestedness and casually dropped the figure of four million roubles. The diplomats immediately agreed and said he would get two million in a couple of days and the rest a little later.'

The meeting ended with Lockhart supplying the evidence of complicity against himself which the Cheka wanted. The handwritten laissez-passers he gave to Berzin read: 'Please admit bearer, who has an important communication for General Poole, through the English lines.'

Orlov's narrative continues with the meeting in a Moscow café two days later at which the British agent 'turned over to Berzin 900,000 roubles as the first instalment of their agreement'. Then follows an interesting passage which, for the first time, indicates that it was again the French who were putting daring ideas into Reilly's head (not that ST 1 needed much encouragement).

> The British agent outlined to Berzin the plan for overthrowing the Soviet government which, he said, had been suggested by a French general.[3] According to the plan, two Lettish regiments would have to be transferred to the city of Vologda, where they would go over to the side of the Allies and open the front for the Anglo-French troops advancing from Archangel. *The Lettish troops remaining in Moscow would then assassinate Lenin and the members of his government.*[4]

Orlov next describes how it was that the Cheka stumbled by accident on the address of one of Reilly's Russian mistresses who was, in fact, a key member of the courier chain. Reilly had failed to turn up on time at the house of another of his lady friends to keep a rendezvous with Berzin. While waiting, the Lettish colonel noticed a sealed envelope which, the maid told him, had just arrived and was lying on the table. Berzin recognized from the handwriting that the letter was from Reilly. As it was not marked for him, the colonel did not open it. But what looked extremely useful was the return address which Reilly had put on the envelope: Sheremetiev Lane #3, Apartment 85, Moscow. Berzin jotted the address down and left, to hand the information on to the Cheka.

This gave them a vital breakthrough when, a week later, they launched their raids on suspected Russian targets. Apartment 85 turned out to be the home of Elizabeta Otten, an actress at the Moscow Art Theatre. The rest was plain sailing.

> She admitted that she had served as liaison between Sydney Reilly and his spies and that her apartment had been used as a meeting place for the conspirators.
>
> The Cheka set up an ambush in her apartment and arrested everyone who ventured in. One of those detained was Maria Friede who walked into the trap with a large batch of secret documents in her possession. She had got them from her brother, Colonel Friede of the General Staff of the Red Army. The next to be seized was Colonel Friede himself. He admitted that he regularly supplied Sydney Reilly with data regarding the strength and movements of Red Army units. Among other things, Friede confessed that he had furnished the American intelligence agent Kalamatiano with a false identification certificate in the name of Sergei Serpukhovsky and that with this document Kalamatiano had left for the Eastern front to pick up espionage data.[5]

Invaluable though Elizabeta Otten's address proved to be, the disclosure was of far less significance compared with another twist to the tale which also took place in the last days of August 1918, a twist which brought Lenin himself back into action. Orlov's next revelation solves the long-standing mystery of the Marchand letter.

'At about the same time, the Moscow correspondent of the French newspaper, *Figaro*, called up the head of the Cheka, Felix Dzerzhinsky, and asked for an appointment. He said he had something important to convey but was shy [sic] to come to the Vecheka building. Dzerzhinsky immediately despatched an aide to fetch Marchand and bring him to his private apartment outside the Kremlin.' Once there, Marchand related how

> on 25 August he had witnessed a highly secret conference in the American Consulate-General, in which a few British and French diplomats and officers of the military missions had taken part. The French Consul-General presided. The American Consulate was chosen for the meeting because it was thought to be a safer place, due to the more considerate attitude shown by the Soviet government towards the Americans. Marchand said he had been invited to the conference by Consul Grenard who by some misconception considered him to be a confidential agent of the French government.

The first part of Marchand's report to Dzerzhinsky follows closely on the disclosures soon to be broadcast in the Soviet press, i.e. plans for an Allied 'stay-behind' operation to be conducted by the three heads of espionage operations, de Verthamon for the French, Kalamatiano for the Americans and Reilly ('aided by Captain Hill[6] of British Intelligence') for the British.

But the details which followed in Marchand's story, as recounted by Orlov, were never published by the Bolsheviks, then or later. The Frenchman described to Dzerzhinsky aspects of the sabotage operation which was to be mounted in connection with the Lettish mutiny. It bears the hallmark of General Lavergne's advice and influence:

> After that, two sabotage agents made a report about the steps they had taken to cut off Petrograd from food supplies. One of them said that everything was made ready to blow up the bridge which spanned the River Volkhov near Avanka. The other reported that he was only waiting for a specific order to blow up the Cherepovetz Bridge, which connected Petrograd with the Eastern provinces from where the city's food supply came. According to the plot, the blowing up of the bridges was

supposed to be timed with the mutiny of the two Lettish regiments in Vologda, in order to prevent troops of the Petrograd garrison from reaching the attacking mutineers.

Then Marchand described Sydney Reilly's 'active part in the conference'. As neither his political master, Lockhart, nor his intelligence chief, Boyce, had appeared at this meeting, the stage was left clear for ST 1, and he made the most of it. He began by informing his fellow conspirators that he had personally promised the Lettish commanders involved that they would get high posts in the government of an independent Latvia which he would guarantee on the Allies' behalf.

Reilly then described exactly how he proposed to execute the Moscow *coup d'état*:

> Reilly told the small audience that, in three days, on 28 August, a session of the All-Russian Congress of Soviets was to take place at the Bolshoi Theatre, with the whole Russian leadership in attendance. At this conference, he and his band of daring conspirators, armed with pistols and hand grenades, would be concealed in the theatre behind the curtains. Then, at a signal given by Reilly, the Lettish soldiers would close all exits and cover the audience with their rifles, while Reilly, at the head of his band, would leap on to the stage and seize Lenin, Trotsky and the other leaders. All of them would be shot on the spot![7]

Though Dzerzhinsky already knew about the plot from the reports given him by Colonel Berzin, here was a new element, a foreign witness, a Frenchman, who had sat in at the heart of the conspiracy and could testify to official Allied involvement. There was only one man who could decide how this hugely important development should be handled. The police chief informed Lenin and asked for guidance. The plot had, after all, been his leader's idea in the first place.

What was extraordinary was how, in Orlov's account, Lenin found time, amidst all the massive problems which confronted him, to steer this pet concept of his to fruition. He began by asking whether the French correspondent would agree to his story being published in the Soviet press. When the question was put to Marchand, he demurred, saying that that 'would mean the ruination of his journalistic career and he would be ostracised by all the Western countries'. To report it to his own government would, on the other hand, 'be all right'. Lenin immediately came up with the appropriate formula.

> 'Ask him,' he said to Dzerzhinsky, 'to describe what he had been a witness to in a letter to President Poincaré, and tell Marchand that the Cheka will search his apartment and find the copy of his letter to the French president.'
> To this, Marchand agreed, for he knew Poincaré personally. He wrote a lengthy letter *which was edited by Dzerzhinsky,*[8] and settled down to wait for the 'search'. He didn't have long to wait.

Two things shifted the scene further during the next forty-eight hours. First, the Bolshoi Theatre Congress was postponed for nine days, until 6 September; Reilly declared himself unperturbed by the postponement which, he felt, would only give him more time to perfect his plans. But he, and everyone else involved in plot and counter-plot, reckoned without the second and crucial happening – the assassination on 30 August of the head of the Petrograd Cheka, Uritsky.

At this point, Orlov's account provides another remarkable revelation. It was Uritsky's murder which, by itself, sparked off the Cheka's raids and mass arrests and it was Lenin, still unharmed on that Friday afternoon, who gave the order to strike back: 'He ordered Dzerzhinsky to Petrograd and instructed him to swoop down on British and French embassies and consulates simultaneously in Moscow and Petrograd.'

Only a few hours later, on the same evening, came the near-fatal attack on Lenin himself. But this was not before he had personally sprung the trap which he had both devised and baited.

The 'Lockhart plot' should really be called the 'Lenin plot', with Lockhart and Reilly as the chief dupes in the Allied camp.

As for the degree of involvement between the Allies, Orlov's account makes it clear that the French (and especially General Lavergne) were in the forefront of the *coup d'état* plan.[9] This, as Reilly had grasped, was the natural, even inescapable complement to an operation designed to bribe the entire Lettish brigade into changing sides. The events of the abortive domestic *coup* had shown as recently as 5 July that only the Praetorian Guard of the Letts stood between security and disaster for Lenin and his regime. These were the men who not only protected the party Congress meetings and the Kremlin itself, but also the Russian gold in the National Bank, key centres of communication and even those roving armoured trains with which the Bolsheviks sought to restore order. It was the Letts who largely staffed the prisons and the Letts who usually pulled the trigger when executions were carried out. If their regiments in the field could be persuaded to desert en bloc to the Allied camp, their comrades in Moscow would have the capital, with its unreliable Soviet garrison, at their mercy. The smallest defection there would have meant chaos and a vacuum of power, at a time when anti-Bolshevik armies were already beginning to mass on three fronts. The only problem with the plan was that it was a figment of the Allies' imagination. Its only real existence was as a deception ploy in the mind of Lenin, with Marchand as his principal volunteer stooge. So much for the unanswered questions on the Soviet accounts of the affair as given down the years.

If we now turn to the gaps and contradictions in the Western versions, Orlov's contributions play only a minor supporting role. For the irony is that Lockhart, the central figure in the conspiracy and its main chronicler, can be shown to have exposed himself to the charge of distortion and downright deception, once his rueful secret reports to his Foreign Office masters over the fiasco are compared with the bravado of his published works. These reports need considerable unearthing and collecting, dispersed as they are among the fifty volumes of documents headed 'War, Russia 1918'.

Some of the evidence has clearly either been lost or left deliberately incomplete (a feature which also applies to the much scantier American official records on the affair).

The first sign of the British government's queasiness over the 'Lockhart plot' emerged on 20 September 1918. This was three weeks after all the thunderous allegations had appeared, unanswered, in the Soviet press and when the central figure, a fortnight into his spell of confinement in the Kremlin, was 'unavailable for comment', to use the official phrase. The British Legation in Stockholm (which was by now established as the main clearing house for reports about events in the Soviet Union) had reported on 19 September two disturbing items of news. Their American colleagues had received confirmation from one of their men in Petrograd saying that the Bolsheviks 'have got hold of all Cromie's and Lockhart's documents which they intend publishing'. At the same time, Arthur Ransome,[10] the left-wing correspondent of the *Manchester Guardian*, had received an ominous letter in Stockholm from Karl Radek, who often functioned as Dzerzhinsky's spokesman. The gist of his message was that 'the Bolsheviks had enough evidence against Lockhart to shoot him'.

This obviously came as no great surprise to London. The significant thing is the Foreign Office minute on the Stockholm telegram: 'Presumably the cyphers have been taken with the rest. I am afraid they will have got a good deal of compromising material.'[11]

That was all that could be said for the moment, while Lockhart was still incommunicado. But even before Lockhart and his colleagues were able to tell their own story, London had received another advance warning of trouble ahead, again from an American source.

On 7 September, a party of 125 Americans and 75 Italians who had been allowed out of Russia arrived in Stockholm. To ensure their safe and smooth passage out, the American consul-general in Moscow, de Witt Poole (who had remained at his post until the whole Allied evacuation programme had been arranged), had sent one of his junior diplomats, Norman Armour, to lead the group. The British minister in Stockholm, Mr Clive, was naturally all agog for any first-hand news about the startling allegations just levelled against the Allies in the Soviet press.

Armour told him that he had seen Captain Cromie only two days before the attack on the embassy and that the secret documents seized during that raid were probably 'Cromie's lists of Russians to be recruited etc.'. Then came a vital piece of information which the British envoy immediately sent on to London:

'Armour . . . told me that when he was in Moscow three weeks ago Lockhart had told him he had opportunity to buy off Lettish troops *and that the scheme was known to and approved by French and American Consuls.*'[12] (This passage in the telegram was specially marked 'Secret'.)

Armour, the report continued, did not think that Cromie had had anything to do with 'Lockhart's schemes in Moscow regarding Lettish regiments'. He could only suppose that these schemes had collapsed because the 'Letts commander had given the show away'.[13]

Three weeks back from 7 September would have been 14–15 August, the very days when Lockhart, Grenard, Lavergne and Reilly were debating how to undermine the Bolshevik regime. They also marked the exact time when Lockhart's private diaries, in the form in which they were eventually published, were brought to an abrupt if only temporary halt. The position of the British government in all this is examined below. All that needs observing here is that their head of mission in Moscow would hardly have left them uninformed about launching the most daring anti-Bolshevik venture of the year if he had already told his Allied colleagues about the plan and secured their approval. As we have seen, Lockhart was always meticulous about securing Whitehall's advance approval for any activities directed against the regime, such as his contacts (eventually forbidden) with emissaries from Savinkov. What London needed to know from Lockhart now was not whether a conspiracy had existed, but how much incriminating evidence about it had fallen into Bolshevik hands. The urgency was all the greater after 24 September, when the full text of Marchand's famous letter had been published in the Soviet press, containing what purported to be the full details about the Allied plot.

For this, the Foreign Office could only await Lockhart's own arrival in Stockholm. Messages from Finland reported that he had left Moscow at 10 a.m. on 6 October, reaching the Finnish border that evening. The next day Lockhart at last re-emerged on the wires himself with a telegram from the Finnish town of Haparanda signalling the safe arrival of his Allied party. All he gave was the detailed make-up of the liberated group, all of whom were from Moscow: Consul-General Wardrop with his staff of 11; Lockhart's own mission with a total of 21 members; and the French official party, also numbering 21, including Consul-General Grenard and General Lavergne. Both men, and Lockhart himself, would, in a month's time, be sentenced to death *in absentia* on charges of plotting the regime's overthrow.

Lockhart got down to the tricky business of tackling those charges on his arrival in the Swedish capital three days later. This first report of his on what had patently turned out to be a British-led fiasco was both sketchy and defensive. What he had to say on the subject was 'too long to telegraph', he began. He continued: 'I may state, however, that charges were mainly invented or greatly exaggerated . . . and that in view of Captain Cromie's murder which was certainly not foreseen nor intended by Bolshevik government, conspiracy was then exaggerated still more to justify that murder.'

The message, for obvious reasons, contained no denial that a plot as such had taken place. On the crucial point of proof, Lockhart was by no means reassuring: 'as far as Moscow is concerned Bolsheviks have little documentary evidence and practically nothing against the British. They have however a considerable amount of verbal evidence and it is possible that in Petrograd certain material may have been found.'[14]

His telegram goes on to give a rambling preliminary account of how he foresaw the future of Allied policy towards Russia. He underlines the current supremacy of Bolshevism and the (hardly surprising) recent increase in the leadership's strength and self-confidence.

Then comes yet another appeal for immediate Allied action to topple the regime, phrased in those apocalyptic terms which always sent shudders down Whitehall's spine: 'If our intervention is to be successful it must be on a really large scale and must entail occupation and administration of the country for some time to come.'

This much-needed blow, in his opinion, could now no longer be struck from the north, and the southern front seemed the best alternative: 'An Allied force landed in south through Black Sea might be able to march rapidly on Moscow.'

As we shall see, the Allied powers were soon to be considering such options. However, for the time being, the British government seemed less concerned with Lockhart's views on grand strategy than on his disquieting remarks on what might have been found in their Petrograd embassy. An urgent enquiry was sent via The Hague to the Dutch minister in Petrograd, M. Oudendyke, who was in charge of British interests there. His partly reassuring reply was relayed back to London on 22 October. 'Most documents of Embassy are intact. Forty boxes of provisions, a quantity of wine, some diamonds and money have been stolen.'[15] Such conventional looting would not have caused as much concern as the fact that at least some of the embassy papers were missing.

By now Lockhart himself was back in London, where he had arrived on 19 October. He was soon left under no illusions that he had permanently blackened his diplomatic copy-book, which already, to the eyes of mandarins such as Lords Hardinge and Cecil, had quite a few unseemly blotches on it. Neither wished even to see him, branding him in their clubland talk as an 'intriguer' and 'a hysterical schoolboy'.[16] On the other hand, King George, with whom he had a forty-minute audience, and Foreign Secretary Balfour were both kindly and indulgent.

Lockhart could only preserve his reputation and thus improve his dwindling career prospects by producing reports on his mission which would either gloss over the conspiracy fiasco or present it in as unembarrassing a light as possible. Reports there would have to be for, despite the almost overwhelming official preoccupation with the imminent collapse of Germany, there were MPs who continued to press in Parliament for the truth about the 'Lockhart plot'. The Liberal member, Mr King, his obsessive interest in Soviet affairs sharpened now by his suspicions about the government's involvement, led the enquiries. On 29 October he tabled a question to ask the Foreign Secretary 'whether he has now received and considered the Report of Mr Lockhart on his experiences in Russia ... and whether any charge was made against him to justify his imprisonment'. It fell to Lord Robert Cecil to draft the reply that no elucidation could be given as no report had yet been received. This was purely a holding operation, for Lockhart was already busy with the drafting of two quite separate memoranda.

The first, though marked 'Secret', was given a fairly wide official distribution as a so-called Foreign Office print and was passed on, with important omissions, to the American embassy. It was copiously minuted upon by the Foreign Office and Lockhart was shown these comments by one of his few supporters in that building, Rex (later Sir Reginald) Leeper. Thus, Lord Cecil had found the paper 'very interesting' but feared its conclusion was 'impracticable'. The same line was struck by Balfour: 'A most able paper – whatever I thought of its conclusions.'[17] The conclusions referred to followed a long survey covering the regime's prospects, the various anti-Bolshevik movements, and the general military and economic situation. They fell into the almost tediously familiar trio of options for Allied policy: cut losses and pull out altogether; confine activity to supporting anti-Bolshevik forces with arms and money; or (Lockhart's preferred choice) 'intervene immediately on a proper scale'.

This was all familiar, almost routine stuff and the only reference to the midsummer mayhem which had seen all Allied consulates and embassies raided or threatened and one naval attaché killed came in the introduction. Here, Lockhart expressed to Mr Balfour his 'deep regret that, owing to circumstances over which I had no control, I was unable to leave Russia without falling into the hands of the Bolsheviks', adding further apologies for the 'trouble and inconvenience this caused to His Majesty's Government'. The fact that there was not one word in the eleven-page printed document which followed as to how and why Lockhart had 'fallen into Bolshevik hands' and what their reasons had been for seizing him and his Allied colleagues led to suspicions then, and down the subsequent decades, that this was not the only report submitted to Balfour and that Lockhart must have spelt out the embarrassing truth in another, more private paper.[18] Today, those suspicions can be shown to have been justified.

On 5 November 1918, two days before the submission of that anodyne memorandum on Russia which became a Foreign Office print, Lockhart submitted a private personal report to Balfour 'dealing with the alleged Allied conspiracy against the Soviet government'. It is marked 'Very Secret', also 'Secret and Confidential' – not surprisingly, since paragraph after paragraph of the seventeen-page document shows the word 'alleged' to be a complete misnomer. Though Lockhart almost falls over backwards to minimize his own part in the plot which would forever bear his name, here is the admission that an Allied conspiracy there certainly was, with Lockhart standing in the middle of it. Moreover, though the word 'dupe' is avoided, there is an oblique confession that he and his colleagues had been bamboozled by the Soviet regime which was their intended victim.

His account of events up to the appearance on the scene of Colonel Berzin is revealing only for what he says about communications. He confirms that his cyphers had already been destroyed before the first round of Cheka raids on 5 August but that other safe lines remained open, for example, the secret service link with General Poole up at Archangel. (This is important, for other Whitehall records show that messages from Lockhart were being sent up to 17 August, i.e. after the critical mid-August meetings.) His record of those meetings follows broadly along the lines of the Soviet 'allegations', as based on Berzin's own reports to the Cheka, but there are fresh details about the money payments. Of the 'three to four million roubles' which Berzin had asked for to buy off the Lettish regiments, a 'first instalment of 700,000 roubles was given to Reilly for Berzin' some eight days after the August 14–15 conclave. For the first time the involvement of the Americans is mentioned. They produced 200,000 of this sum, the remainder coming from the French. Lockhart later advanced another 700,000 himself, making 1,400,000 in all (the exact figure given in Soviet versions).

There is no mention of General Lavergne's plan for toppling the Soviet leadership by using one of the three Lettish regiments to seize them in the capital, so the entire responsibility for what is coyly described as 'an operation in Moscow' is placed on Reilly's shoulders. There follows a marked difference in the language now quoted as having been used to Reilly compared with the words which Lockhart in his *Memoirs* claims to have used. In the latter version, Reilly's proposal for a counter-revolution in Moscow backed by some of the Lettish troops (the Lavergne plan) was 'categorically turned down' by Lockhart, his French colleague Grenard, and by the general himself (!). Moreover, 'Reilly was warned specifically to have nothing to do with so dangerous and doubtful a move.'[19]

The memorandum to Balfour, which might be regarded as a *mea minima culpa* confessional, strikes a very different tone. Here Lockhart reports that he told Reilly only that 'he saw no point in a movement in Moscow as we were too far away'; and later, when Reilly raised the idea again with the French present, that 'we all demurred and pointed out that there was nothing to be gained by this'. Dissuasion certainly, but not a veto. In other words, Reilly seems merely to have been left in no doubt that, whatever he got up to in Moscow, the responsibility would rest entirely on his shoulders and his activities would be officially disowned if things went wrong. Not for the last time in his colourful career, Reilly played the role of the West's volunteer fall-guy. At least this time he was able to flee the peril.

This is precisely the picture given by Reilly's principal British collaborator Captain George Hill in the lengthy report which that much-underestimated officer was eventually able to make to his Director of Military Intelligence in London on 26 November 1918.

Like Reilly, he faced up to the plain truth from which Lockhart had backed away: 'The proposed turning of the Lettish troops to our cause on the fronts could not be achieved without seriously affecting the Moscow and Petrograd centres. The simultaneous change on the fronts and at Moscow and Petrograd would have destroyed the Soviet government ... In the event of failure and our being found in any plot, Lt. Reilly and myself should have simply been private individuals and responsible to no one ... The whole brunt would have been borne by us.' Elsewhere in his report, Hill makes it clear that the plot had been discussed with and actually backed (though in nervous fashion) by the British SIS chief of the Moscow station in person. Hill writes (on page 22 of his report): 'About midday on the 31st August he [Reilly] got into touch with Lt. Boyce and they had a conference together. Lt. Reilly explained to him the whole of the Lettish plan and Lt. Boyce said he considered the whole thing was extremely risky *but agreed that it was worth trying* [author's italics] and that the failure of the plan would drop entirely on Reilly's neck.' This arrangement was surely far too tailor-made for Lockhart's convenience for him to have been unaware of it. Indeed, Hill adds the damaging sentence: 'Telegrams from Mr Lockhart and ourselves were despatched to General Poole, informing him of what had been done, and what we proposed to do.'

The way in which the 'Very Secret' report to Balfour was handled itself smacks of official equivocation. It was filed quite separately from the main chronological series of his telegrams and reports on the Moscow crisis and appears as an isolated release on the subject eleven volumes later down the line[20] in the Foreign Office series 'War, Russia 1918'. There it sits, wedged incongruously between a claim from a Mr Percy Calvert about 'compensation for losses sustained' and an anti-Bolshevik proclamation to the Peoples of the Northern Region, both irrelevant to the theme of Lockhart's 5 November report. Moreover, unlike that circularized print of his, dated only two days later, this private memorandum has no Minute Sheet attached, no mandarin or departmental comments and not even a distribution list. It was clearly intended to slumber on unnoticed as an only copy for as long as possible; which is precisely what happened. It has lain on the files for some forty-five years.

The saga of Xenophon Dmitrivich Kalamatiano, the chief field agent of American intelligence, is best recounted later on, for it stretches well beyond 1918. But one mention of his Moscow network is relevant in conclusion here – for what was left out rather than for what was said. After leaving Russia, Kalamatiano's political control officer, the former US Consul-General de Witt Poole, sent his own reports to Washington on that crucial meeting on 25 August in his Moscow office.[21] Before going into the Allied 'stay-behind' strategy discussed at the conclave and the disquieting presence of René Marchand (all by now familiar material) Poole tells Washington: 'I judged unwisely in permitting Mr Kalamatiano to come too closely into contact with these agents [an obvious reference to Reilly and de Verthamon], a mistake which I regret very profoundly.'

However, reasons for such a deep professional apology, though they must logically have been given, did not survive: that part of the page which precedes the apology is missing from the despatch as handed to the American National Archives for preservation. As other indications will also suggest, the attempt to smother the truth about the 'Allied Conspiracies' does have a transatlantic dimension.

The irony is that any such efforts are now seen to be almost irrelevant. If anything needed obscuring for the historical record, it was not so much what the Allies were planning against the Bolsheviks in the midsummer of 1918, as how thoroughly the Bolshevik leader and his minions had duped them into concocting their plots.

7

New Options: the Rethink

The Great War ended with a steady rush that knocked the breath out of the victors as well as the vanquished. It was not until 25 September 1918 that the curtain rose on the final act when Bulgaria, the weakest and wobbliest of Germany's fighting partners, sued on the Balkan battlefield for a separate armistice with the Allies. 'This has smashed the bottom out of the barrel' was the graphic comment of the Austrian Foreign Minister, Count Burian, when the news reached Vienna.

His own monarchy was the next to go. On 27 October, barely a month after 'Foxy Ferdinand', the Bulgarian king, had deserted the Central Powers' alliance, Charles, the mild and well-meaning young man who was destined to become the last of the Habsburg rulers, also sued for a separate peace over Berlin's head. The move came too late to shore up the social and political landscape that was crumbling away around the dynasty.

In the space of the next fourteen days, the multi-national empire which had held the Central European patchwork together for seven and a half centuries came to an end. It had first been crushed by a humiliating defeat on the Italian front and then ripped apart along its racial seams as, one after the other, its peoples ignored their sovereign's offer of autonomy within the empire and elected instead for independence outside it. The Czechs, whose legion was fighting for dear life during these same weeks in far-off Siberia, were among the first in the queue at home for instant and painless nationhood.

Even the collapse of the German military juggernaut, which had lumbered on for so long with the Central Powers' alliance on its back, came about more swiftly and completely than anyone had predicted. At the beginning of September 1918, Foch and the other Western commanders were only just beginning to believe that the conflict might conceivably be over that year, instead of dragging on, according to the rosiest of existing estimates, until the spring or even summer of 1919. As it was, Germany's chief warlord, General Erich Ludendorff, was forced to throw in the towel before the end of October 1918, leaving the Armistice he had been doggedly opposing to be signed less than a fortnight later. Compared with the seemingly interminable slaughter of the past four years, the end seemed to have come before anyone could blink.

It had certainly come before anyone in the Western camp had fully worked out the consequences for a Europe whose face had suddenly been transformed for ever, with the Habsburg and Hohenzollern empires now joining the realm of the Romanovs in oblivion. The Allies had known what they wanted for Germany: the public clamour to 'hang the Kaiser', though too extreme to follow, echoed the official view that a chastened and weakened post-war Germany would be safer in the hands of a republican president than in those of Kaiser Wilhelm, or indeed any of his arrogant Hohenzollern brood. The German generals had already sorted out that question for them by packing their emperor off by train to exile in Holland, like an unwanted piece of excess baggage, the very day before the Armistice was signed.

It is now known from the French intelligence files recently returned from Moscow, that Lenin had been fishing in those stormy autumnal waters closing over the head of the German empire. According to a secret service message sent to Paris from Zurich on 9 October 1918,[1] Prince Andronikoff, a 'grand seigneur' of the old regime who had come to terms with the new, had just spent three days at the German Supreme Headquarters at Spa, where he had held discussions with the Kaiser and with the two men who held what power was left in his government, the Generals Ludendorff and Hindenburg. What Lenin's emissary was trying to find out was whether there was any chance of re-enacting Brest-Litovsk by concluding another separate Bolshevik peace with the now crumbling German colossus. But the move – never a likely starter anyway – had come too late. The victors had other plans for Germany.

The Allied leaders – with Woodrow Wilson very much to the fore on this issue – had also come round to agreeing on the desired fate for the Habsburg monarchy: dismemberment. Again, the work had been accomplished for them just before the fighting ended. Yet there was no consensus as to how the violent heirs to the Romanovs should be treated, if only because the credentials of the Bolshevik regime were still in dispute and its prospects for survival were cloudier than ever. Clear for all to see was that huge hole which had opened up in such joint policies on the problem as the Allies had managed to cobble together during 1918. The basis for all their uneasy agreements had been the military imperative to secure the western front by keeping the German army extended in the east. Now, with the surrender of Germany, that imperative had vanished. What could be put in its place to justify further Allied involvement in Russia? Ought the Bolsheviks to be opposed not, as hitherto, because they often appeared to be passive instruments of German power but, quite simply, because they were Bolsheviks? And, bearing in mind the recent embarrassing fiasco of the 'Lockhart plot' (whose true dimensions the Allies had not begun to guess), what form and what scope should future involvement assume?

The secret service, which was now at the sharpest end of the business, had been among the first to ask for guidance – indeed, on occasions, to clamour for it. That is the only description one can apply to the appeal which 'C' received from his Stockholm station just ten days after the Armistice had been signed.[2] It began: 'It is absolutely necessary to lay down principle as to whether Russian officers in Finland and Russia should be encouraged to join forces like the PSKOV Army,[3] lately under direct instructions from BERLIN but an anti-Bolshevik safeguard to ESTHONIA, or be withdrawn . . . and sent to some British-run force.'

The station chief reported that, after consulting with the French and British military attachés in Stockholm, he had in fact sent secret word to the officers concerned that they should remain at their posts with the Pskov army 'until other arrangements are made'. Otherwise, he pointed out to London, Estonia would have nothing to defend it from the Bolsheviks. But this had been his own decision, taken without London's authority. 'I urgently need instructions on general principles of action [sic] of Russian officers in Finland and Baltic provinces. At present I do not know what to do.'

The answer he got back was not entirely encouraging.

Yes, the Russian officers in Estonia should remain at their posts 'if they can assist in organization of anti-Bolshevik Esthonian forces for whom we are sending arms'. But, the reply stressed, 'Russian officers must use their discretion as to where they can most usefully serve, and you must not commit us by endeavouring to influence.' This sounded like an echo of that ambivalent guidance which Whitehall sent to Lockhart during his six-month reign in Moscow: intervene but do not interfere. However, this message to Stockholm did contain one unqualified statement: 'The only enemy now to be considered are the Bolsheviks.'[4]

Once again the British Foreign Secretary, Arthur Balfour, was among the first to put pen to paper in an attempt to square this circle of dealing with the Bolsheviks as enemies while not declaring them as such. (It was because they were not formally an enemy regime, he was to point out in a later paper, that they could not legally be submitted to an enemy blockade.) This earlier memorandum,[5] circulated to the King and the War Cabinet when the German collapse was imminent, is notable for the moral tone which Balfour interjects into all his realism. While accepting as obvious that the original strategic motive for opposing the Lenin regime has vanished, he goes on to stress that any large-scale Allied military intervention in the post-war situation would be ruled out for political as well as strategic reasons: 'This country would certainly refuse to see its forces, after more than four years of strenuous fighting, dissipated over the huge expanse of Russia in order to carry out political reforms.'

The old mantra is repeated that 'it is for the Russians to choose their own form of government'; but then follows a key passage of semi-contradiction. The Allies should, in effect, continue to try to determine that choice for them:

> But it does not follow that we can disinterest ourselves wholly from Russian affairs. Recent events have created obligations which last beyond the occasions which gave them birth. The Czech-Slovaks are our allies and we must do what we can to help them. In the south-east corner of Russia in Europe; in Siberia; in Trans-Caucasia and Trans-Caspia; in the territories adjacent to the White Sea and the Arctic Ocean, new anti-Bolshevik administrations have grown up under the shelter of Allied forces. *We are responsible for their existence and must endeavour to support them.*[6]

A ringing declaration indeed of Allied duty; but a much flatter note emerges as to how that moral obligation was to be discharged: 'How far we can do this, and how such a policy will ultimately develop, we cannot yet say.'

Only American help, Balfour indicated, would be powerful enough to produce any real results, though there was one region where Britain could intervene effectively on her own. That was in the Baltic provinces, where protection could be given to 'the nascent nationalities by the help of our fleet'. In this one respect, at least, Balfour's ideas were to be realized with gusto.

The War Office weighed in with their own assessment, a paper by the Chief of the Imperial General Staff, General Sir Henry Wilson, which examined the military options in post-war Russia front by front.[7] His memorandum is interesting in that it fore-shadows, by nearly half a century, the doctrine of 'containment' evolved by the United States to meet the threat of Communism which was to arise, more menacing than ever, in the aftermath of the Second World War. In 1918, the general professed himself sceptical whether 'the cult of Bolshevism' would even survive 'the re-establishment of normal conditions in the rest of the world'.

But, if it did, one response for the West would be 'to create a ring of states all around Bolshevik Russia, the object being to prevent Bolshevism from spreading'.

Yet there were immense practical snags. This policy would involve garrisoning the protective cordon, a task which was beyond the Allies' strength unless the Americans were prepared to provide troops, which appeared 'unlikely'. Even the Czech Legion in Siberia, he pointed out, would hardly be willing to fight on now that the Armistice had been signed. As for the British Army, this had enlisted on a 'Duration of War' basis. That term could not be held to cover 'a desultory campaign of indefinite duration in Eastern Europe and Asia against an enemy with whom the British public has no particular quarrel'.

Attempts had been made during that autumn to persuade neutral Sweden to hold part of the protective ring. The West had enquired in Stockholm whether a Swedish force might be sent to fill the gap in the northern sector and 'act as big brother to a free Baltic bloc'. But that country, which had emerged prosperous and unscathed in a war-scarred continent, was not prepared now to lift a finger to help its vulnerable little neighbours. The Swedish government expressed nervousness about 'the danger of armed conflict with the Bolsheviks', adding that, in any case, their army had been 'laid low by Spanish flu'.[8] This unedifying response had caused little surprise in the Allied camp.[9]

The final War Office recommendation, therefore, was for a speedy withdrawal of troops, at least from European Russia, and the continuation of operations through assistance to anti-Bolshevik movements which were based there: 'We should take immediate advantage of the opening of the Baltic to provide our friends with warlike stores and of the opening of the Black Sea to occupy such ports on its eastern shores as may be necessary to extending a hand to those elements in the Caucasus which tend to make a stable Russian government.'

In plain English, this talk of helping 'friends' in the Baltic and 'extending a hand' from the Black Sea meant fighting the war after the war by proxy: from the north because that was the only direction from which Petrograd could immediately be threatened and from the south because that was the most practical route by which Moscow itself might eventually be taken. The Bolshevik capital could hardly be captured from the east after both the Americans and the Japanese had refused to allow their forces in Siberia to advance any further into the Russian heartland beyond Lake Baikal.

As for the Czechs, still the most effective single force fighting the Bolsheviks, they were in dire straits on the ground while all these lofty memoranda on Allied strategy were floating about in the air. One of the few surviving secret service messages about the Siberian situation in the autumn of 1918 paints a grim picture: 'The Czechs are falling to pieces. Morale and discipline are going owing to heavy losses and the growing belief that the Allies will not come.'[10] Other messages spoke of a joint force of 20,000 Czechs and 40,000 Russians falling back from the Volga front towards Ufa before a combined attack from 200,000 German and Bolshevik troops.

Only a decisive blow struck against the regime from the north or south could, it seemed, shore up the anti-Bolshevik campaign in the east. But special intelligence assessments needed to be delivered first. Was General Yudenich, the unimpressive commander of the relatively small North-Western Army, capable of delivering any such blow? And what sort of a figure was General Anton Ivanovich Denikin who had just taken over command[11] of the much larger 'Volunteer Army' formed in the south?

To try to answer that second question, 'C' was to send out a well-tried team to the Black Sea at the turn of the year. Meanwhile, he had some unfinished business of his own to deal with in and around Petrograd, which he had just managed to penetrate again, only weeks after the September rout. Much of the previously closed intelligence material on both these missions is now available.

Part Three

The War After the War

8

The Baltic: White Sea Heroics

Osea Island was an isolated speck of land set in the marshes and mudflats of Essex's Blackwater River, whose wide tidal flow shielded it from intruders. It made a drab-looking launch pad for what was to become the most scintillating adventure the secret service had so far known in its ten-year existence. Moreover, in that winter of 1918–19, these gloomy surroundings were more than matched by the mood of depression among the young Royal Navy officers gathered there for training. Even the extra food rations and the presence of a unit of their female colleagues, the Wrens, to cook and serve the meals failed to lift their spirits. It looked as though the days of their precious 'Skimmers' were numbered, and therefore their own usefulness.

The Skimmers, or CMBs as they were officially called, had been the Admiralty's pet project during the final months of the war: light motor-boats with hydroplane hulls, a top speed of over forty knots and a draught of less than three feet of water. This made them both the fastest and most manoeuvrable of any naval craft afloat. They also carried their own sting: one torpedo mounted on the 40-foot long version and two on the larger 55-foot model. Though the first of these vessels had not been delivered until early in 1918, they rapidly justified the enthusiasm of their designers in raids against German bases on the North Sea coast, notably in support of the daring attack to block the Zeebrugge channel on the night of 22 April. The Admiralty and their eager young volunteers on Osea began to dream of attacking German battleships at anchor in harbours hitherto made invulnerable by mine-screens. Then, in the autumn, came the rapid military collapse of Germany and her Central Powers partners, culminating in surrender and the Armistice of 11 November. It seemed that Osea was just another tiny cog in the giant Allied military machine which was now due for mothballing or dismantlement. Odd jobs were still coming, such as some post-Armistice patrols in the Caspian Sea; but hopes of any major operation seemed buried.

All was to be changed by a visit which an unfamiliar Royal Navy captain paid to the island in January 1919. The visitor declared neither his identity nor the purpose of his call and it was assumed by all concerned on Osea that this was simply another routine Admiralty inspection. But the latest caller was no ordinary naval captain. It was Mansfield Cumming, 'C' in person, and he was there on secret service business of the highest priority. How high and how secret was made clear a fortnight later in Whitehall when Cumming received the young officer from Osea who had been selected for his use, the then unknown Lieutenant Augustus Agar.[1]

'C' described to the bemused volunteer the almost total breakdown that had occurred in communications with Bolshevik Russia after the closure during the previous summer of Allied embassies and consulates. He then came to the point. There was 'a certain Englishman' (no details given) who had got back into Russia (no date or place mentioned) to start collecting intelligence again for London. His reports, the only source of reliable first-hand information, were already proving of such vital importance to the government that a special operation had to be mounted to keep his courier service open via Finland and, when the need arose, to bring him out to safety. Would Agar like to lead a team of two CMBs out to the Baltic to take on the job, and was he ready to become a civilian and transfer immediately to the secret service for the purpose?

Agar did not take long to accept; nor, on returning to Osea Island, did he have any difficulty in filling his team of three fellow officers and two mechanics (one for each 40-footer). This handful of

Sir George Buchanan, British envoy to the Tsarist regime and the epitome of old style diplomacy.

Robert Bruce Lockhart, Britain's 'unofficial' envoy to Lenin's Bolshevik regime. He found himself at the epicentre of all the 1918 upheavals.

The 'Ace of Spies', here depicted in 1919 in an unpublished cartoon portrait by one of his SIS colleagues. Reilly was then at the height of his professional prestige and is shown wearing the Military Cross medal awarded for his exploits in Russia. Two years later, all contacts with the Service were severed.

Reilly in real life.

Xenophon Dmitrivich Kalamatiano, the very resourceful head of
American Secret Service operations against the Bolsheviks.

Paul Dukes, the special agent 'C' smuggled back into Petrograd in 1918 after the collapse of the Western networks. He performed brilliantly and became the only SIS operative ever to be knighted to services in the field.

The 'Lubyanka', the dreaded police headquarter building in Moscow where the Western 'plotters' Kalamatiano and, later, Reilly, were captured and incarcerated in turn.

Felix Dzerzhinsky
(1877–1926). First head of
the Bolshevik political police
and Lenin's implacable
instrument of terror.

Boris Savinkov, the 'great
revolutionary', an idealistic
Communist who came to
oppose Bolshevism for its
tyranny. Stalin feared
Savinkov above all émigré
opponents and eventually
lured him back to his doom.

General Alexander Orlov, the most senior Soviet intelligence officer ever to defect (1938) to the West. His secret reminiscences have been drawn on for the first time in this book.

young naval officers, who had already commanded small craft on special missions, stood a world apart in temperament from those millions of infantrymen now only too anxious to escape from the memories of mud, poison gas, shell-shock and barbed wire which had haunted their nightmare of trench warfare. The Osea volunteers were individuals operating in a clean and stimulating environment of their own, one which whetted the appetite for more adventure. Like many a fighter pilot at the close of the Second World War, with neither fame nor challenge awaiting them in civilian life, they were half-sorry that the fun was over. By the time Agar was back in 'C's' office forty-eight hours later, as instructed, he could name his three officer colleagues. All were under twenty-one and, like their leader, were neither married nor engaged (a point 'C' had insisted upon).

Agar was now inducted into some of the mysteries of the secret service they had joined. Petrograd was named as the target. Finland and the Baltic states would serve as the intelligence contact points and bases for his mission which would be controlled, like all 'C's' operations in the area, from Stockholm.[2] Sydney Reilly, it will be recalled, had been given the code name ST 1. From now on Agar would be known as ST 34; the mysterious Englishman in Petrograd – still unnamed – had already been designated ST 25. Agar later wrote: 'Speculation about this man became an obsession. Who was he? What was he like? How came he to be there at all? Was he still alive? Would I be in time to get to him?'

The mystery man was in fact the then obscure Paul Dukes, whose approach to the secret service world had been as eccentric as his departure was to prove only three years later. While still a young boy, Dukes had decamped from England to St Petersburg (as it was then called) to study music at the city's prestigious Conservatoire. He was helped by the fact that the English composer Albert Coates was then conducting at the Marinsky Theatre opera and after Dukes had graduated from his four-year course he was invited to become the conductor's assistant. But the outbreak of war changed the path of the young musician's career, as it was to transform the lives of millions of others. Because of his excellent knowledge of the language, he was offered a job, early in 1916, on the newly established Anglo-Russian Commission and, for the next two years, he alternated between liaison duties in London and fact-finding trips in Russia. His intelligence credentials had still not been formalized. It was not until June 1918 that Dukes was whisked back to London from the YMCA Headquarters in the Volga port of Samara,[3] put on 'C's' payroll, and given his Petrograd mission.

Elaborate preparations had been made for this. Dukes was later to be described as 'a master of disguise'. It would be more accurate to call him adept at wearing disguises which had been carefully crafted for him. When, in November 1918, he finally arrived in Petrograd (via Archangel and Helsinki) he had four different identities to choose from, each complete with photograph and the appropriate Soviet stamps, seals and signatures. They had been prepared for him by 'C's' forgery section which, though as young as the service, had benefited from intensive practice during the four-year war with Germany.[4] None of these sets of false papers was to let him down, including the first and the boldest. This certified that he was 'Joseph Afirenko', a Ukrainian office clerk working for no less than the Petrograd Commissar of the Cheka.

Dukes would more than justify the almost instinctive faith placed in him by Cumming and all the trouble taken to camouflage him. The only one of his many reports to London which he was allowed to reproduce (also in doctored form) has sections on strikes and the Communist party but deals mainly with the food situation in Petrograd, the disease and mortality rates, the sanitation problem, the financial chaos and the general atmosphere of desolation in the former capital.[5] In terms of new intelligence disclosure, it is roughly on a par with that general survey[6] with which Lockhart and the Foreign Office had attempted to cloak what had really gone on in Moscow in the turbulent summer of 1918. Moreover, this one published report of Dukes's (the reference number significantly omitted) did not reach London until May 1919, having allegedly been smuggled out via Stockholm concealed in the boot of a Russian officer.

But, as we have seen, 'C' had already been galvanized into action four months before, in mid-January 1919, and the Agar operation had been set in motion with great secrecy and urgency early the following month. The reason for this speedy launch was a stream of reports which Dukes had been smuggling out via Finland within weeks of settling in as 'Comrade Afirenko'. In subject matter, details, authority and highest-level sourcing these were a spymaster's dream and quite probably superior to anything that had landed on 'C's' desk throughout the four years of war against Germany. Dukes had not merely established a network of informers, civilian and military, throughout the city and its great port.[7] He had penetrated the top Bolshevik Councils of Petrograd to such an extent that he was able to transmit to London translations of the highly secret minutes of their meetings in full. A selection from these remarkable CX dispatches is published below for the first time.

Naval power was the key to control of the whole Baltic region. Command of the White Sea would determine not only the fate of Petrograd itself but the outcome of the battle against the Bolsheviks being fought by the Allies and the North-Western Army of 'Whites'. It would also decide the destiny of the three former Russian provinces of Latvia, Lithuania and Estonia. Though, under the terms of the Brest-Litovsk Treaty, the Bolsheviks had tacitly admitted their right to become independent states, Lenin was determined, as *Izvestia* had put it, that 'The Baltic must become a Soviet Sea.' The man whose job it was to stop this happening at the time of Agar's mission was Rear-Admiral Sir Walter Cowan.

The career of this extraordinary officer had taken off back in 1898 in the upper reaches of the Nile, when his shallow-draught little gunboat, the *Sultan*, had helped Kitchener's army to rout the Khalifa's dervishes at Omdurman and retake the besieged Khartoum. His active service life was not to end until 1944 when, aged nearly seventy-five, he was supporting Tito's Yugoslav partisans in the Adriatic. But the high point of that long career was this year of 1919–20, spent in conducting the Baltic struggle against the Bolsheviks,[8] and the key to it, apart from his own seamanship, was intelligence. The force he was sent out with consisted of two light cruisers and ten destroyers. His largest vessel, in which he flew his flag, was the *Caledonia*, displacing 4,120 tons and armed with five 6-inch guns.[9]

Estimates had varied about the strength of the former Tsarist fleet, now in Bolshevik hands, which faced him behind the barrages and minefields of Petrograd's Kronstadt harbour. But it was known that this included three vessels more powerful than anything he possessed. There was one heavy cruiser, the *Oleg*, which displaced 6,650 tons and had twelve 6-inch guns. The *Oleg* was herself overshadowed by two Russian battleships at anchor there: the *Andrei Pervozvanni*, a ten-year-old pre-dreadnought vessel of 17,680 tons and equipped, among other weapons, with four 12-inch guns; and, above all, the four year-old *Petropavlovsk*, a giant dreadnought of 23,370 tons whose armament included twelve 12-inch guns. These ships, if properly handled, could blow anything that Cowan possessed out of the water. Among other things, he needed to know – and to know accurately – what their state of readiness was; what the ever-shifting command structure looked like; what the state of fighting morale was in a fleet split between ex-Tsarist officers and Bolshevik revolutionaries; what orders they were under from the Soviet leadership; and, if possible, what they were expecting him to do. To all of these questions, including even the last, Dukes was providing the answers in his smuggled messages, passed by 'C's' stations in Helsinki and Stockholm back to his Whitehall Court office and transmitted by him to Naval Intelligence.

Thus, the first of Dukes's 1919 despatches contained, among a wealth of military and naval intelligence, the following account of a meeting summoned by the Petrograd Bolsheviks on 17 January to discuss the key problem of the fleet's morale.[10] It must have brought comfort to their lordships at the Admiralty: 'All admirals, divisional commanders and ship commanders of the first grade were summoned to a special meeting at the Military Revolutionary Soviet to discuss the fighting value of the fleet. Irrespective of the proof furnished that the fleet could be re-established and even utilised at the present moment, a resolution was carried that the fleet was of no fighting value.' Dukes's informer then eavesdropped on (and perhaps took part in?) the lively discussion which followed the resolution. His account contained the following two gems:

> After the meeting, Commissar Penkaitis,[11] in conversation with some officers, enquired into their relations with each other; between them and the sailors; and between the sailors and the commanders. He asked why the fellowship which had existed before the revolution did not exist now.
>
> One of the officers present answered that, on the one side [sic] a mass of spies prevent better relations and on the other, the officers are considered class enemies. On asking what measures are taken, should the commander's orders not be carried out, he was told that generally no steps are taken; sometimes a report is sent in but no attention is ever paid to it.
>
> Pinkaitis[11] [sic] then said that it would be possible to enforce obedience by force of arms, *referring to the Red Army where, in cases of disobedience, every tenth man is shot.*[12] The officers replied, 'Give us the authority'.

The second revealing item was an account, given in the same Dukes message, of a Commission of Enquiry into the case of a certain Lieutenant Raskolnikov, commander of the Russian destroyer *Avtroil* which, with its sister ship *Spartak*, had been damaged and captured in an engagement with the British fleet in the Gulf of Finland three weeks before, on 26 December. F.F. Raskolnikov was not just the destroyer's commander. He was also the political head of the Soviet Admiralty and therefore, in effect, the Bolsheviks' First Sea Lord. It was he who had led this major sortie of the Kronstadt fleet with the object of blasting the Estonian capital of Reval (later Tallinn) into submission. The cruiser *Oleg* had joined a force of destroyers for the operation, with the dreadnought *Andrei Pervozvanni* lurking menacingly in the rear. The sortie had proved a fiasco and a highly embarrassed Raskolnikov did his best to avoid being taken prisoner on his captured ship. (He was finally found hiding under twelve bags of potatoes.)

Now the Commission of Enquiry wanted to know what had gone wrong. Dukes was again able to pass on the actual minutes:

> One witness, on being questioned regarding the officers and men said: 'The officers behaved as befits officers but the crew [improper word follows].'
>
> *Judge*: 'Why do you use such coarse language?'
>
> *Witness*: 'How can I help it when the crew hid themselves on the decks from their own guns?'

Even more revealing was an exchange when the presiding judge, thinking of the future, questioned a sailor from the submarine *Pantera* which had also taken part in the attack:

> Judge: 'Will you attack the British?'
> Sailor: 'If the commander orders it, we will.'
> Judge: 'But will you fire on them?'
> Sailor: 'Yes.'
> Judge: 'Will you hit them?'
> Sailor: 'No.'

Whatever satisfaction these reports were to produce in London, they infuriated Trotsky who, in March 1918, had been appointed Commissar for Military and Naval Affairs by Lenin to rescue the Bolshevik regime from its many enemies and challengers.[13] It was to prove an inspired choice, for what this intellectual Bolshevik lacked in military experience he more than made up for in sober pragmatism, coupled with a frenetic energy in reacting to crisis. This he displayed now as he set to work in Petrograd to sort out the confusion and to galvanize the demoralized fleet into action. Dukes sent two reports on his forty-eight-hour emergency visit. The first[14] shows that Trotsky, true to his controversial policy of preferring ex-Tsarist officers to revolutionary numbskulls for key positions, had shaken up the naval command structure in Kronstadt from top to bottom. The new Chief of Staff he installed, for example, was a senior captain called Dombrovsky who had only just been released from a Soviet prison.

In the same message, Dukes also passed on the following secret order issued by Trotsky which showed Admiral Cowan that there was no cause for British complacency: 'Within three months, the flower of the Baltic Fleet must be ready for action, namely *Petropavlovsk, Poltava, Andrei Pervozvanni,* the cruisers *Oleg* and *Svetlana* (being built) and the *Rurik* (questionable).' A separate report from the 'Chief Engineer Mechanic' showed that the fleet had enough coal reserves (two million *poods,* or some 321,100 tons) to undertake the spring operations Trotsky was demanding.

The next message from Dukes arrived in London almost simultaneously.[15] It represented an even greater *coup* for, by now, ST 25 had got an informant who had attended two emergency meetings in Kronstadt of the Revolutionary Military Soviet presided over by Trotsky himself. One session was again devoted to the shake-up needed in the naval command structure, and Dukes's message passed on more details of the changes. There was also a direct quote from Trotsky who told the meeting bluntly that he 'preferred to have to deal with specialists, even if not reliable from a political point of view, rather than with stupid commissars'.

At the other meetings, the fighting value of the fleet was once more examined, though this time with the War Minister himself in the chair. One revealing passage in the minutes shows Trotsky losing his temper in true revolutionary fashion while at the same time conserving good old bourgeois manners. A speaker had described how officers in the fleet were being systematically humiliated by Bolshevik committees of sailors who were forcing them 'to clean the water-closets, sweep the cabins and be sent ashore to buy provisions'. At this, 'Trotsky, perturbed by the facts brought before his eyes, thumped his fist on the table, smashing an inkstand, and declared in an excited voice "I dare not call this sort of thing by its right name, as there is a lady present."'[16]

In a further long despatch,[17] Dukes turned from what the Bolsheviks were hoping to achieve against their enemies to their fears over what that enemy might be planning to do against them, and the counter-measures they were taking accordingly. These were listed in details in a 'Report sent to the Revolutionary Soviet of the Northern Front' of which Dukes had somehow obtained the full text.

The report, which had been translated, worked on the assumption that 'in the spring, when the seas are rid of ice, the enemy will undertake the landing of troops in the districts [sic] of the Finnish and Riga Gulfs.' Ten key places were listed as 'the most favourable' sites because of their sloping sandy shores. Eight were in the Finnish Gulf, with the approaches to Kronstadt at the head of the list. The 'anti-landing' measures ordered covered everything from the installation of 3-inch gun batteries to the provision at each site of observation derricks, repair shops, motor boats, rowing boats and searchlights. Exact numbers of each were laid down, together with the cost. But it was the mines which mattered most:

> Minefields are the principal mainstay of the anti-landing stations. Well-placed mines undoubtedly present insuperable obstacles for small ships, motor boats etc. In order to hinder the movement of such craft, taking into consideration their small draught, the mines must be laid at a depth of 2½–3 feet from the surface. Each minefield must consist of 4 rows of mines. The mines must be laid at a distance of 175–200 feet from each other; the distance between the rows must be about 700 feet ... Such mines must be laid in each harbour in such a manner that the enemy cannot outflank them, i.e. laid right up to the shore ... The guns, 2 batteries at each station, are to be set up so that the whole area of the minefields is covered by their fire.'

Finally came the numbers of the new mines to be laid. Of the 8,500 ordered for all ten sites, 1,000 were allotted to the Kronstadt defences.

When this intelligence reached 'C', both he and Agar would have seized on one vital point – the depths at which those thousand new mines were to be laid. The Skimmers, with their draught of two feet and nine inches, might just about roar over them, even if the paint could be scratched from their hulls in the process. It was a matter of millimetres rather than inches. The Osea operation was still desperately risky, but it had now been shown to be technically just possible. The sunken breakwater at Kronstadt was known to be three feet below the surface, while the harbour's old minefields lay three feet deeper still. Even with the new mines, the courier service could be launched; perhaps much more as well.

By the time Dukes's reports reached London, Agar had his broad plan of action ready. Somewhere on the Gulf of Finland would be their obvious operating base, so it was to Helsinki that his party sailed in two groups. The two CMBs were shipped out separately on a small coaster from the West India docks. No attempt was made to conceal them. On the contrary, they went as deck cargo, painted gleaming white, to fit the agreed pretence that they were the latest creation in pleasure boats with Agar and his men as their keen commercial salesmen. The whole team wore, of course, civilian clothes, bought ready made at Moss Brothers. It might have stayed that way had 'C' not been troubled by a pang of conscience when bidding Agar farewell. He had been obliged to give the ex-lieutenant the standard warning issued to any intelligence agents operating without official cover: if caught the wrong side of the line, it would be their own funeral, perhaps literally. Then the naval officer in Captain Cumming had second thoughts. He had to give Agar and his team 'some sort of chance'. Each of them could therefore keep one set of uniform concealed on board, for use only in dire emergency.

A second concession, which fully matched the first, came when Agar, once he had reached the Gulf of Finland, called in his civilian clothes on the admiral commanding the British Baltic Fleet to reveal his mission. (To all other naval personnel he had met en route, Agar had passed himself off as a Foreign Office messenger.) But the commander of the fleet had to know the truth, and Agar was fortunate in the man he found sitting in the cabin of his flagship, the light cruiser *Cleopatra*. Rear-Admiral Cowan had an attitude towards active service which was in keeping with his adventurous career. His guiding motto was always to choose the boldest choice on offer, because this had the best chance of success. The plan which his young caller outlined fitted this motto perfectly. Agar was proposing to base his two 'pleasure launches' in the one-time Tsarist Yachting Club of Terrioki, a village close to the Finnish–Russian border and only some twenty-five miles by sea from Petrograd. From Terrioki, during the long white nights of the Baltic midsummer, he would make the run into Petrograd flying, if need be, the special pennant used by all Bolshevik Fleet commissars. (The invaluable Dukes had provided the description, from which copies could be made.) On each trip the Skimmers would have on board one of the Russian couriers whose job it was to take and deliver messages, with a small rowing-boat in tow, nicknamed 'the pram', for them to go ashore in and later regain the CMBs. The Skimmers also needed a pilot who could thread their course through the maze of breakwaters and known minefields. All this was arranged by Agar's industrious new colleagues, ST 30 and 31 of 'C's' station staff at Helsinki.

It is not quite clear how the question of the torpedoes arose. Agar's tiny craft were still unarmed when his talk with Cowan began. By the time he left, the admiral had given instructions for two torpedoes to be issued (one for each 40-footer) with two spares. One version has the admiral deciding on this move himself. Agar's account gives it as his request, made on the strict understanding that the weapons would be fired in defence only and that he and his men would don their emergency naval uniforms for the occasion. The issue is irrelevant, given that there was such a meeting of minds between the old sea-dog and the young lieutenant turned secret agent. There could also have been already an unspoken understanding about future possibilities.

By June Agar and his team were all set to operate from Terrioki, having squared the local Finnish commandant and even secured his support in return for a promise of intelligence material. As we have seen, that month marked a high point in Bolshevik nervousness over their future, with even the ice-cold, iron-strong Lenin showing signs of frayed nerves. Petrograd itself (where, rumour had it, yachts or submarines were standing by to take the regime's leaders to safety) was in a state of panic with the White Army of General Yudenich pressing in from the west. This was made plain in a brief report which Dukes had smuggled out of the city on 14 June.[18]

Dukes described the violence of the repressive measures taken by the city's newly appointed Director of Defence, Iakov Peters (one of Dzerzhinsky's chief trouble-shooters) as 'exceeding everything previously known'. The wives and children of suspect officers were being taken hostage and shot out of hand if the suspicion seemed justified. A new rule was being enforced under which nobody could hold a position of authority under the regime unless his near relations were on Soviet-Russian soil and thus within the Cheka's grasp. Occupation by the Allies and Yudenich's White Army was thought to be imminent. Dukes had already (!) made contact with the head of the Bolshevik Counter-Intelligence unit which had been set up for Petrograd on the assumption it would fall to the enemy. This would have represented normal practice. A more mystifying item in this Dukes report ran: 'Bolsheviks printing English and French money for use after occupation' A showdown of sorts was clearly in the offing but the drama which unfolded in June took a different turn for both sides from what anyone had expected.

On the 13th, the garrison of Krasnaya Gorka, the main fortress on the southern shore of Kronstadt bay, hauled down the red banner and, together with its smaller sister fort, ran up the white flag in its place. This was a signal of defiance, not surrender. The garrisons, which had long been suspected of anti-Bolshevik sympathies,[19] had taken their courage in their hands after hearing reports of White Russian attacks on Petrograd and had mutinied in sympathy. In fact, the attacks had been sharply repulsed. The Soviet commanders, realizing that the right flank of the entire Petrograd front, as well as the Kronstadt harbour itself, fell under the fire of the rebel fortresses, ordered every warship under their control to bombard Krasnaya Gorka into submission. Watching through binoculars from a church top in his Terrioki lair, Agar saw with mounting despair how the main fort was being blasted to pieces by curtains of shells rained down on it by the heavy warships across the bay. He had slipped past these silent giants already in his first midnight courier runs with pilots and prams. Now the giants were aroused, and were pulverizing an anti-Bolshevik strongpoint.

The fighting man in Agar got the better of the spy in his civilian suit. There was no time to contact Admiral Cowan. Instead, on the morning of 16 June, he despatched one of his new colleagues, ST 31, to the nearest British cypher station (the consulate at Vyborg) with a message to London asking for permission to abandon his sailing orders and use his two CMBs for an attack on the bombarding ships. The reply from Whitehall reached him late that same evening: 'Boats to be used for intelligence purposes only stop. Take no action unless specially directed by SNO Baltic.'

The second sentence gave Agar his opening, provided he had the confidence and the courage to take it. The Senior Naval Officer was, of course, Cowan and, as every hour counted (the bombardment had started again that afternoon), Agar decided to take the admiral's backing for granted.[20] He had been priming and preparing the torpedoes all day as if indifferent to what Whitehall would say. If Krasnaya Gorka was to be saved, he had to attack that very night. Out came the uniforms, to be donned in the open sea, and he even took small white ensigns to be flown during the action. It was a faint echo of the Nelson touch, though when the hero of Trafalgar risked his judgement he had his fame as an admiral behind him. In the obscure Finnish port of Terrioki a century later, it was an equally obscure ex-lieutenant who was taking the entire responsibility on his young shoulders. If things went wrong, little mercy could be expected, either from the Admiralty or from 'C' himself. In the event, after initial setbacks, things were to go spectacularly right.

The first attempt, made by both craft soon after midnight, had to be abandoned when Agar's companion boat, CMB 7, struck an obstacle on the approach run and smashed its propeller shaft. (It was probably a loose floating mine, in which case both the vessel and its crew were lucky not to have been blown to smithereens.)

There was nothing to be done but to tow the damaged boat back to Terrioki, and think again. Indeed, some hard thinking needed to be done. A new propeller shaft would take weeks to secure and install. That left Agar's boat as the only craft available, not only to communicate with Dukes but also to bring him out in safety, an operation that had been provisionally fixed by 'C' for mid-July. Could Agar risk jeopardizing all that by attacking alone? He decided that he must try, this time risking even more in the event of disaster.

He left Terrioki at 10.30 p.m. on the night of 17 June but a disappointment awaited him when he slipped past the Tolbukhin Lighthouse which marked the approach to Kronstadt. Both the Soviet battleships had withdrawn to their island harbour, seemingly safe behind its screen of forts and breakwaters. Agar's prime targets had vanished, but an adequate substitute loomed up in the half-light: the three funnels of the heavy cruiser *Oleg* which was still at anchor in the harbour roads, guarded by a screen of six destroyers and patrol boats.

There was a distinctly awkward fifteen minutes when the firing charge of his one torpedo went off accidentally as he was nearing the screen of destroyers, and had to be replaced at dead slow speed in a heaving sea. Then he opened throttle and the Skimmer raced at full speed between the startled patrol boats and roared at forty knots towards the cruiser. He fired almost at the stroke of midnight when less than half a mile off her port beam. The torpedo struck home close to her foremost funnel, throwing up billowing smoke and a high column of water.

At this, pandemonium broke out among the Soviet defences. Fire rained down on the tiny CMB both from the destroyers and from the harbour forts, some shells landing within a few yards of her. But as Agar safely ran the gauntlet out to the open sea he had the delight of seeing the *Oleg* slowly sinking by the head, smoke belching from her funnels as she tried in vain to get under way. One and a half hours later, CMB 4 was back in Terrioki, with no physical damage to either vessel or crew. But there had been damage of another sort. Sub-Lieutenant Hampsheir, the man who had been responsible for replacing the torpedo charge, was a nervous wreck and had to be sent back to Helsinki, on doctor's advice, to recover. Agar himself seemed quite composed as he submitted his formal report to Cowan.

The CMBs went back to their courier duties and the Krasnaya Gorka mutineers were eventually blasted into submission after the White Army in the north-west failed to march on Petrograd. Things seemed to have reverted to the situation at the beginning of June. In fact, the sinking of the *Oleg* had changed everything.

After seeing what the torpedoes of the Skimmers could achieve against heavy armour plating, Admiral A.P. Zelonoy was less inclined to allow his dreadnoughts to venture out again into the Finnish Gulf. Yet, even in harbour, they remained the battering ram of a powerful fleet in being. Somehow, they had to be put out of action, as the Admiralty had insistently demanded more than a year ago when the ill-fated Captain Cromie launched his sabotage attempts. Agar's feat pointed the way: destroy them at their moorings. After air raids on the dockyard had proved ineffectual (the heaviest bombs carried by the nine British planes involved weighed only 112 lbs), Cowan decided on a massive assault by his CMBs. Seven more of them (mostly the 55-footers with two torpedoes) were towed out by destroyers from Osea Island to Biorko Sound, where Cowan had his headquarters. Technically, the whole party were still, like Agar, under 'C's' orders. But the attack which this deadly little flotilla launched on Kronstadt harbour on the night of 18/19 August 1919 was a naval operation, planned and executed in naval style, with air support but no intelligence tasks in the programme.

Cowan had given them three priority targets to destroy or disable: the two battleships *Petropavlovsk* and *Andrei Pervozvanni*, and the submarine supply ship *Pamiat Azova*. Agar, in his smaller 40-footer, led this swarm of hornets into the inner harbour soon after midnight, to be met by a hail of fire from every shore and ship battery and machine-gun post in the basin. By the time the frantic action was broken off, all targets had been dealt with: both battleships had been put out of action and the supply ship sunk at her moorings. This time, there had been a physical price to pay. Three of the CMBs had been sunk, mainly by destroyer shells, with the loss of eight officers and men killed,[21] and another nine had been taken prisoner. Yet compared with the achievement, the losses were negligible. As a jubilant Cowan put it later, 'After this, nothing larger than an enemy destroyer ventured out.' Allied naval mastery in the Baltic was assured.

Agar himself, who seemed destined both to court disaster and to escape it, had been untouched in all the mayhem of the raid. But he had a narrow shave three weeks later when making one last attempt to bring out ST 25 (two earlier trips in August had failed when the rendezvous went wrong). His CMB was caught in the cross-beams of two searchlights from the harbour forts and, while trying to weave away into darkness, it crashed at full speed into a rocky breakwater on the northern shore of Kronstadt island. He and his two crewmates were dazed but unhurt. The boat, however, was a near-wreck, without rudder or propeller and taking in water through the thin shell. The twinkling lights of their haven on the Finnish coast could just be seen. But they lay fifteen miles away with two fortresses in between and dawn was due in four hours. Somehow they made it, refloating their leaking craft, baling with a bucket and empty petrol cans as the breeze and swell started them drifting in the right direction. Using spare petrol cans as an improvised rudder (sea boots replacing them as balers) and a strip of deck canvas tied to two boat-hooks for a sail, they grounded on the shoals of Terrioki exactly twelve hours after setting out. (Two Russian fishermen, whom they came upon in the blessed cover of a morning mist, had been persuaded by their machine gun to lend them a proper sail.)

All thoughts of yet another rescue mission for ST 25 had to be abandoned; as things turned out, it proved unnecessary. Dukes, who had received an urgent summons from 'C' to return to London at any cost, had managed, in the first week of September, to make his way overland to the British Mission at Riga, travelling with the papers of a dead Bolshevik. Three weeks later, Agar was himself back in London (travelling in safety and style from Stockholm) to receive from King George the VC he had been awarded for the *Oleg* exploit. And so it was in Whitehall and not off the Tolbukhin Lighthouse in Petrograd bay that the two men saw each other for the first time. 'C' had carefully stage-managed their encounter by arranging for them to appear almost simultaneously in the passage outside his office. Their greeting was a model of British taciturnity.

'Are you Dukes?' Agar asked, on a hunch, as the lean, sharp-eyed stranger joined him.

'Yes.'

'Well, I suppose you know I am Agar.'

At that, the naval hero and the master spy (an epithet Dukes deserved just as much as Reilly) shook hands and entered 'C's' office together.

At Buckingham Palace a few days later, Agar found King George eager to hear, down to the very last detail, the story of the sinking of the *Oleg*. Then, at a private audience, he pinned on the VC, adding the DSO (to Agar's astonishment) as an extra award for his part in leading the Kronstadt raid. They talked about the remark-able Paul Dukes. He also deserved the VC, the monarch observed; but, being a civilian, was precluded from receiving it. Some other recognition would, however, be found. That 'some other' was the KBE which Dukes received on 1 January 1920: the first and only time in the history of the secret service that one of its members was to be knighted for services in the field. Thus both men stood side by side on the pinnacles of professional recognition though, as we shall see, their later careers were to differ sharply.

The citation for Agar's VC referred to his 'conspicuous gallantry, coolness and skill in penetrating a destroyer screen, remaining in close proximity to the enemy for twenty minutes while his tor-pedo was repaired and then successfully completing an exceptionally difficult operation in far from ideal weather conditions, finally escaping, notwithstanding heavy fire from enemy warships and forts'.

Following the precept that the British secret service did not officially exist, there was no hint in all this of the fact that Agar was in fact a civilian, one of 'C's' agents who had been despatched to the Baltic on a purely intelligence mission. But the protocol observed at Buckingham Palace established the true parentage of the affair. Agar was presented to his monarch not by the First Sea Lord, Admiral of the Fleet Lord Wemyss, but by Captain Sir Mansfield Cumming. Apparently, 'C's' only regret over the great occasion was that, on this rare opportunity to be received by the King, he could scarcely get a word in edgeways.

9

Black Sea Hopes:
Secret Service in the South

Sydney Reilly's reappearance as a secret agent on the Bolshevik stage was a great deal more dignified than his debut. When, at 4.30 p.m. on 12 December 1918, he left London bound for the Black Sea on his second mission for 'C', he was not preceded by unflattering messages about a 'Jewish-Jap type ... carrying sixteen diamonds value £640.7.2'. Moreover, his new alias was as a government official, a great advancement over the 'diamond buyer' of April. The chief had personally drafted and initialled his movement orders:[1] 'Please arrange for Mr Reilly and Captain George Hill to leave London not later than Thursday afternoon for Paris and Marseilles to arrive on Saturday in time to catch the SS Isonzo ... They are to travel as civilians and assistants to Mr Bagge, Commercial Secretary in South Russia.'

That the task in hand had little to do with commerce was made clear in a letter of introduction from 'C' which Reilly carried for Mr John Picton Bagge: 'With regard to their work, I understand that political information is urgently needed from the whole of South Russia – Ukraine, Don, Kuban and Astrakhan ... Especially full reports from Kiev and Ekaterinodar.' Secure communication with London was clearly going to be a complicated affair, as it had been from Moscow and Petrograd in the spring:

Mr Reilly brings a code with him, one copy for his own use, one for Captain Hill and one which he will give you. As we arranged, however, it will be more convenient if you will forward these special reports in your own cypher, the prefix 'Following for Campbell' will ensure their reaching the right quarter. Should you wish, for any reason, to make use of my own code in telegraphing to England, the prefix should be 'Following for Campbell, following for C'.

We should be glad of course if you will add any comments of your own to their reports when you forward them.[2]

As well as his key reports to London and a good deal of background material, Reilly's meticulously kept diaries for the whole of his two-month-long mission have survived in his service file. They show him reaching the Black Sea at Sevastopol only twelve days after leaving London. The entries for his outward journey are peppered with complaints ('13 Dec. arrived Paris, frightfully full. Dined at Larue'; '14 Dec. Horrible night. Arr. Mars. 11 am'; '17 Dec. Arr. Malta noon. Lots of silly formalities . . .'; '19 Dec. En route to Constant. *Rowan* dirtiest ship ever.') But he arrived on Christmas Eve at Sevastopol in style and in good spirits aboard a British warship and the next day collected a useful Christmas offering which had been pre-arranged in Whitehall. This took the form of a letter signed by the British Commander-in-Chief Mediterranean, Vice Admiral Calthorpe, and was addressed 'To all British Naval Officers'. It read: 'Mr. S.C. Reilly, the bearer of this document, is a member of the staff of the Commercial Secretary to Russia appointed by the Foreign Office. I request that all British Naval Officers will afford him any assistance he may require.'[3]

Never before – and, for that matter, never afterwards – was Reilly furnished with such prestigious credentials. It is perhaps worth noting at this point that, if the advice of the Americans had been adopted, Reilly might never have been issued with an official travel document of any sort again.

A 'Personal and Most Secret' telegram sent to London in the aftermath of the Moscow plot fiasco had conveyed a warning from de Witt Poole, the former American consul-general there, that Reilly had been in touch with Soviet agents provocateurs and might quite possibly be a traitor himself.

'There is a strong suspicion,' the message read, 'that an agent named Riley [*sic*] ... has either compromised Lockhart ... or has even betrayed him ... United States Consul-General suggests that, in view of the serious danger involved, Allied authorities in Northern Russia and elsewhere should be warned that, if Riley appears in Allied districts, he should not be trusted, at any rate until he has completely cleared himself ... United States Consul-General has informed his government.'[4]

The only grounds quoted for these suspicions were somewhat flimsy: that Reilly and his chief Russian contact had escaped arrest, in contrast to Kalamatiano, who had been seized in Moscow in broad daylight. But, as described in Chapter Fourteen, this had happened because the American decided to run the gauntlet of Cheka police surrounding his embassy and had been grabbed in the act of trying to scale the walls. Reilly, on the other hand, gave all Allied missions a wide berth once the Bolshevik round-ups began and had melted away to safety along an escape route of Hill's safe-houses interspersed with his own chain of love-nests.

It was not until early November that Reilly got back to London (via Petrograd, Riga and Stockholm) to give his own assurances. The perils of that journey gave advance proof, in themselves, that he had been running for his life. But Whitehall had already joined ranks on his behalf. Lockhart, who returned home a fortnight earlier, was emphatic that, loose cannon though Reilly undoubtedly was, he would never have turned his fire against England. The Foreign Office was typically less emphatic, but at least went so far as to say that they had always found his information 'quite satisfactory'. More vigorous support came from the War Office, whose Director of Military Intelligence deemed Reilly to have been both a valuable and trust-worthy operator. Cumming, who was already recommending his special agent for the Military Cross (anything more would have made him too conspicuous), would have been capable of ignoring depart-mental verdicts, even had they all gone against his man. His faith in Reilly's basic political allegiance was rock-hard and, as we shall see, it was to be borne out by everything that lay ahead in the coming years.

Nonetheless, this general Whitehall backing made it easier to despatch Reilly to Russia again, barely a month after his escape, and this time on a mission whose political requirements were laid down for him in advance. 'C' had acted entirely off his own bat in launching the parallel intelligence operation which took such a spectacular turn in the north. But this Reilly–Hill inspection tour in southern Russia was in response to specific pleas from the British War Cabinet, echoed in the Allied Supreme Council, for first-hand information on which Western policy after the Armistice could be based.

Allied involvement with anti-Bolshevik movements in southern Russia had, of course, long preceded the Armistice. Only weeks after the October Revolution, contact had been established with the Cossack general, A.M. Kaledin, the 'Ataman' or leader of the Cossack communities in the Don which had declared their independence from Moscow. His panache stirred enthusiasm in the Allied camp, and on 3 December 1917 Lloyd George impulsively pledged unlimited British financial aid to the general. This action flew in the face of very negative intelligence estimates about the general's merits and indeed the usefulness of the volatile, squabbling camp of the Cossacks as a whole. The mistrust of the experts was to prove fully justified.[5]

The so-called Volunteer Army, the other main anti-Bolshevik fighting force in the south, had seemed from the start to be a much more promising affair. Its founder, General Michael Vassilevich Alexeyev, was no parochial Cossack firebrand but a former Chief of Staff to the Tsar who had been hired, sacked and rehired by Kerensky to run the demoralized post-Tsarist Russian Army. When Lenin took over power, he became a marked man in Petrograd and headed south, to raise an anti-Bolshevik army alongside the Cossacks in its wide and relatively secure spaces. He was joined there by other Tsarist generals who knew their days were numbered if they lingered too long within the grasp of the new regime. These included another former Russian Army Commander-in-Chief, Lavr Kornilov, who had once led an abortive *coup d'état* to unseat

Kerensky, and Denikin, who had supported him. The Volunteer Army was thus launched with a trio of considerable military experience at its head, a trio, moreover, who worked well together until the death of his two fellow commanders[6] left Denikin in the autumn of 1918 in sole charge.

By the time Reilly and Hill appeared on the scene three months later, the White Volunteer Army was volunteer only in name. From June to August it had marched steadily south from the Don to drive the Bolsheviks out of the entire Kuban region, thus providing it with a manpower reservoir for conscription. It had now swollen tenfold from the puny force of some 3,000 with which Alexeyev had started out into an army of more than 30,000, buoyed up by high morale and the battle honours of the victorious midsummer campaign behind it.

Thus Reilly was to arrive at a Black Sea littoral which seemed to provide a fairly stable White Russian platform on which to operate. Before following his whirlwind activities there, it is worth describing just how unstable that platform had been over the previous six months. An unpublished first-hand account of the confusion is given in reports which one Mr Jerram, the acting British vice-consul in Novorossisk, managed to pass back to London via Tiflis. Copies of these telegrams are in Reilly's personal CX file, suggesting that he was given them to read as background. They form a miniature picture of the general mayhem which was confronting Allied officialdom throughout Bolshevik Russia.

In June 1918, when the narrative begins, the port was in the hands of Bolsheviks and the great issue was the fate of the Russian Black Fleet at anchor there. Would it scuttle itself in the harbour to avoid seizure by the Germans, as Trotsky was promising the Allies, or would it sail away unscathed? The answer was a bit of both, but rather more in the way of destruction than escape. On 17 June, the dreadnought *Volja*, accompanied by a cruiser and seven torpedo boats, weighed anchor and left the outer roads, heading for Sevastopol. But the next day every warship left in the inner bay was sunk by its crew, taking its full complement of guns and ammunition with it to the bottom. The scuttled vessels included two dreadnoughts and six destroyers which would have been a sizeable prize for the Germans to capture.

However, that had still left some thirty transport and cargo steamers in the port, including British, French, Italian and Belgian vessels. The next step was to arrange for their destruction before the German fleet, which was steaming at full speed for the port, could arrive. The Novorossisk narrative shows it to have been a desperate Allied race against time. On 20 June, a special French mission from Moscow under a Commander Saboureau arrived to take a hand in things. The commander lost no time, with money talking loud. That same day, he 'obtained permission from the ruling Bolsheviks to sink the steamers under the condition that the crews were paid three months wages in advance'.

The money was produced and, within twenty-four hours, all the Allied vessels, except one British steamer which still had to discharge her cargo of coal, had been blown up and sunk. She was still unloading her coal (wanted by the Bolsheviks) when the German-Turkish fleet loomed up on the horizon. It was headed by that formidable battle-cruiser *Goeben*, which had won world fame in 1914 by helping to browbeat Turkey into the war on Germany's side. It could win no more laurels now in a Black Sea which was anyway fast becoming a very different ocean from that which the *Goeben* had dominated for the past four years.

Indeed, her admiral was to be denied even one modest extra leaf to his crown, when he just failed to seize the only Allied vessel left afloat in the harbour, the British coal-carrier *Trevorian*. The steamer was still hastily unloading the last 500 tons of her cargo when the *Goeben* neared the harbour and the Bolsheviks reluctantly agreed to do without their coal and let the carrier go to the bottom. The vice-consul's narrative continues:

Before however I could get the wrecking crew together and move the steamer away from the pier the Germans were already so near that it was absolutely impossible to take her outside the breakwaters and I therefore gave orders to take her over to the north side of the bay. A charge of dynamite was placed in her engine room and five minutes after I had left her with the wrecking crew she blew up and sank. Although the vessel sank in comparatively shallow water she was utterly useless to the enemy owing to the heavy damage done by the explosion.

Soon after the *Goeben* anchored in the bay, the German admiral paid his adversary the compliment of sending an officer ashore with a conciliatory message. Though well aware that the British vice-consul had led the wrecking operation, neither he nor the British colony would be molested in any way 'provided he would undertake not to agitate in any way against them'. Jerram had no choice but to agree and undertook to obtain similar assurances from his French and Italian colleagues. For the next two months they remained virtual prisoners on their word of honour while the Germans were 'on more or less good terms' with the Bolshevik authorities in the town.

Then, at four o'clock on the afternoon of 26 August, the first Cossacks of General Krasnov's command appeared on the heights of Novorossisk and the port's fortunes abruptly changed again.[7] How abruptly is described in the vice-consul's report:

> By about nine o'clock that evening the town was in occupation of the Cossacks, whose losses in the fight were two dead and eight wounded, whilst the Bolsheviks were completely smashed up, losing many killed and wounded ... All the members of the Soviet have been captured and are now in prison, awaiting their trial by court martial. The Cossacks were out of hand, wishing to pay off old scores and, in consequence, many of the Bolsheviks were shot on the spot ... The new Governor has declared martial law ... and is now engaged in restoring things as they were before the revolution.

Some German forces, however, remained in the town, while the one or two gun boats or armed trawlers which they kept in the port assured them the continued mastery of the sea. For the next three months, a somewhat Kafkaesque situation reigned in Novorossisk. The Germans were secretly funnelling arms and ammunition to any Bolshevik bands in the region while managing to remain on polite talking terms with the administration set up by the Volunteer Army in the town (the Cossacks having ridden off elsewhere). Its governor meanwhile was busily engaged in bringing the past back to life in every way he could devise. He even ordered engineers of the Vladikavkas railway company to raise the SS *Trevorian*, sunk by Jerram in the bay. This worthy man duly protested that the engineers were tampering with British property. But they went ahead regardless and, having succeeded, they renamed her, with great ceremony and Tsarist flag-hoisting, *General Korniloff*, after the great Cossack commander who, twelve months before, had launched his pathetic mayfly revolt to try to restore the monarchy.

After the Armistice and the surrender of German forces, it was all change again. The German-Turkish fleet melted away and on 23 November Jerram was able to report the arrival of an impressive Allied naval squadron at Novorossisk: the British cruiser *Liverpool*, the French cruiser *Ernest Renan* and two destroyers. The vice-consul's first action was to get the squadron's Royal Navy commander, Captain Napier Tomlin, to have the resuscitated but still battered *Trevorian* handed back to him under her proper name. Order and sanity, it seemed, had descended on the port. This impression was strengthened when, two days later, the Royal Navy destroyer *Northesk* arrived, bearing the members of separate British and French Military Missions to General Denikin's headquarters at Ekaterinodar.

At the head of the British mission was Major-General Frederick C. Poole, who had been withdrawn from his command in Archangel in September because of his abrasive colonial-style behaviour which had outraged both his Russian partners and all his Allied colleagues – the Americans in particular. This second chance he was afforded only two months later gave less scope for dictatorial antics. His brief from the War Office was quite specific: to report on the nature and quantities of supplies Denikin should be provided with, assuming that the Volunteer Army qualified for large-scale military aid. Reilly's task was to assess those qualifications, and he lost no time about it.

He was finishing his first despatch a week to the day after landing in Sevastopol. It was based, his diary shows, on four days of talks in the Crimea – technically the responsibility of the French – followed by three more with White Russian leaders in Novorossisk and Ekaterinodar. His main informants were Baron Noelken, Chief of Staff of the Volunteer Army in the Crimea; Admiral Kanin, the Crimean Minister of Marine; the Army's Political Officer for the area, Kirpichnikov; General Shulgin, the delegate from the Southern White Army fighting around Voronesh; the ill-fated Governor of Novorossisk, General Kutyepov;[8] an assortment of Allied civilian and military officials, including 'some of our best-informed agents who are accidentally here'; and finally General Lukomsky, Denikin's so-called Minister of War. Reilly called this Despatch No. 1 his 'preliminary impressions', but they are no less emphatic for that:

> Notwithstanding shortcomings enumerated below Volunteer Army represents only concrete dependable force and living symbol Russian unity. It has now passed its heroic period and reached critical point when must either become determining factor for rallying all constructive elements or slowly but surely disintegrate. This will entirely depend upon promptitude and extent of Allied support. Although total strength estimated at 150,000, field force only 60,000.[9]

Among the 'shortcomings' Reilly went on to list were the Volunteer Army's lack of supplies in almost everything (ranging from ammunition to warm clothing and boots for the soldiers) and the friction between Denikin and the Cossack General Krasnov over the supreme command and field operators. The latter, he noted, was refusing to allow his men to fight outside their own territories.

Apart from 'immediate if at first moderate assistance in equipment and armament' the Allies could also intervene, Reilly argued, by declaring their moral support for the Volunteer Army and thus help to solve the command problem. (This course had, in fact, already been decided in principle a fortnight before, when General Poole had persuaded Krasnov to put his Cossack forces under Denikin's command.)

Reilly ended by painting the glowing prospect of a 'Novorussia' or 'New Russia' arising under the wings of the Volunteer Army. This would extend northwards and eastwards from the Crimea and the Black Sea littoral to embrace the Kharkov provinces, the Donetz Basin with its coal and iron and the oilfields of Maikop – the whole vast area to be a *place d'armes* for the decisive advance against Bolshevism'. This was heady stuff indeed, though, as we shall see, there were those in London prepared to take more than a sniff at it.

The crucial question, however, was how far England or France, who shared Allied operational responsibility in the region between them,[10] were prepared to back the creation of any sort of 'Novorussia' with their own manpower. Reluctantly, and, as things turned out, ill-advisedly, the French had concluded that they would have to commit troops to secure their western zone of southern Russia. There were no established anti-Bolshevik movements fighting here and a dangerous vacuum arose when, after the Armistice, the German troops started to pull out. It seemed that the only way to stop the Red Army filling that vacuum by marching down from the north was immediately to mount a French occupation force. Its advance guard of 1,800 French and Moroccan troops duly landed at Odessa a month after the Armistice had been signed and the garrison eventually swelled to over 60,000 men, with Czech, Polish and Senegalese forces joining the French units.

Such a motley band possessed neither coherence nor morale, and its fate was dismal. The wobbly swathe of occupation which it marked out originally extended up to fifty miles inland, only to be steadily dented and then pushed right back to the coast by nothing more formidable than bands of Cossack and Anarchist partisans.

After less than four months, the French government threw in the towel and, on 6 April, Odessa itself was evacuated.[11]

This humiliation of their closest ally and joint operator in southern Russia was, of course, not even envisaged by the British at the turn of the year. But the question had already arisen as to whether they should follow the French example by landing men on their own eastern sector, despite the fact that in this region they enjoyed the luxury of powerful and confident White Russian forces to fight the anti-Bolshevik battle for them. Poole, who was replaced by an even more senior officer (Lieutenant-General Briggs) in January, recommended in his final report that, in addition to tanks and aircraft, British troops should be deployed with the Volunteer Army, though on a fairly modest scale: one infantry and one artillery brigade had been his suggestion. Such was the state of play when, on 10 January 1919, Reilly, accompanied by Captain Hill, held face-to-face discussions with Denikin. The meeting, one of the keys to Reilly's mission, was described to 'C' and the Foreign Office in a message sent the following day.[12]

It begins with a shrewd assessment of the White Russian leader:

General Denikin is a man of about fifty, of fine presence, the dark Russian type with regular features, he has a dignified and very cultured manner and could be classed as belonging rather to the higher Staff officer type than to the fighting man. He gives one the impression of being broad-minded, high-thinking, determined and well-balanced – but the impression of great power of intellect, or of those characteristics which mark a ruler of men, is lacking.

The general should have been in buoyant mood for the meeting. A week before, he had launched his troops into a very promising offensive against the Bolsheviks in the North Caucasus. (Before the month was out it was to end, to the consternation of Trotsky, in the annihilation of the Soviet Eleventh Army, with the capture of 50,000 prisoners, 150 pieces of artillery and 350 machine guns.) Moreover, the very day before his discussion with 'C's' envoys, he had been able to issue an official Order promulgating his status as Commander-in-Chief of 'all land and sea forces acting in the south of Russia' – thus confirming the deal with the Cossacks brokered by the departing Poole. Yet Reilly found Denikin very sober on both counts.

On the Cossacks, he was even pessimistic. The agreement with Krasnov had been very difficult to achieve, and it was going to be harder still to carry it out in practice. 'Nowadays, discipline has deteriorated and everybody wants to command.' As for the general outlook, Denikin gave a remarkably down-to-earth verdict which Reilly passed on to London in full. It is worth reproducing parts of it here:

> People think that in order to pacify Russia, all one has to do is to take Moscow. To hear again the sound of the Kremlin bells would, of course, be very pleasant, but we cannot save Russia through Moscow. Russia must be reconquered as a whole, and to do this we have to carry out a very wide sweeping movement from the South – moving right across Russia. We cannot do this alone. We must have the assistance of the Allies. Equipment and armament alone are not sufficient. We must have Allied troops which will move behind us, holding the territories which we will reconquer, by garrisoning the towns, policing the country and protecting our line of communications. Only then shall we be able to mobilise fresh troops ... and move forward without anxiety.
>
> ... We will do all the fighting, but you must stand by and protect us from being struck in the back.

Denikin was invoking that eternal apparition of Russia's vastness which confronted any campaigner on her soil. It had defeated Napoleon a century before and was to frustrate Hitler a generation later. The problem was just as formidable now and its scale was spelt out to Reilly and Hill in another talk they had at Ekaterinodar later that day. General Dragomirov, Denikin's Political Assistant, told them that no fewer than fifteen Allied divisions would be needed to secure the rear of the Volunteer Army on its forward march. This was a tall order, too tall, it seemed, even for the exuberant Reilly to sponsor. Indeed, this is in some ways a new Reilly. Nowhere in any of his long despatches from southern Russia does he advocate the sort of massive intervention which he and Lockhart had been demanding from Moscow during the summer. In other ways, however, the old Reilly continues to pop out from the records of this two-month tour, the Reilly of dubious personal repute.

There is a faint sign of it on the money front, in a letter written from Ekaterinodar on the same day as his long political despatch. The proper rate of exchange, he maintained, was £1=42 roubles, whereas he had changed sterling in Novorossisk at 26 roubles. Could the State bank there be contacted, he asked the vice-consul, 'to see whether a better rate could still be squeezed out of them'. He seems to have ended up with more roubles in his wallet, though at 33 rather than 42 to the pound. However, this was a perpetual problem and a perpetual grumble with all the Allies.

Much more incongruous is the way in which Reilly's marital and amorous affairs suddenly obtrude into the archives. Thus on 10 January 1919 an urgent appeal for news about her estranged husband had arrived in Whitehall from Reilly's first (and only legal) wife, Margaret. It is a sad letter from a discarded though still seemingly devoted woman. It was penned to 'The Air Board' on 4 January from Brussels where, she said, she had been 'surprised by the war whilst my husband was in St. Petersburg where he had an important business'. She had not seen or heard from him ever since though she had now learned through the British Legation in Brussels that he 'had been working against the Bolsheviks in Russia and, being compromised, had escaped into Finland'. Then followed the appeal: 'Will you not have pity for me, gentlemen, and let me know as soon as possible what has become of my dear husband? If you can communicate with him, please let him know that in health I am well but that I desire ardently to hear from him. My financial situation is also rather strained . . .' And she enclosed a photo of the man who had shooed her out of Russia and out of his life in order to 'marry' Nadine Massino.[13]

The letter must have been passed to the Intelligence Service and so on to Reilly in southern Russia, for his response some weeks later was sent back to London in secret cypher: 'Please pay Mrs. Reilly for [sic] my account £100. Please inform her I shall [make?] further provision after I return.'[14] There is no trace in his official file of any 'further provision' for Margaret, nor indeed any indication whether he ever saw her again. As we shall see, however, other women in Reilly's life were to plague Whitehall right down to the outbreak of the Second World War.

Back in the winter of 1919, neither Margaret (in Brussels) nor Nadine (in New York) would have taken kindly to the frequent references in his diary to another Russian lady whom he was pursuing at the time. In between details of his official appointments come frequent references to his letters to 'Kissenka', sometimes abbreviated to 'Kis' or simply 'K'. On 29 January he notes that 'Kissenka Letter No. 7' was on its way to her, courtesy of the British warship *Temeraire*. Six days later comes the entry 'Cabled F.O. for Kissenka' – this despite the fact that, as he well knew, communication channels to London were difficult and heavily overburdened.

The richness of his behaviour – and this is vintage Reilly – is that he nonetheless found space in the same diary to criticize the morals of the head of the British Military Mission. One of the many outrages laid at General Poole's door in Archangel was that he had openly installed his Russian mistress in the large mansion he had requisitioned for his sole use. Similar behaviour in Ekaterinodar was provoking Reilly's righteous indignation three months on. Thus, on 14 January: 'Gen. still fooling about with Mme. P. and Tundukoff. Bad impression. Never saw such ugly women . . . Everyone disgusted Gen. P.'s carryings on with Mme. P.' One wonders whether Reilly would have been quite so censorious had 'Mme. P.' been a beauty.

Odessa, from where he had been virtually shamed into cabling that £100 to his abandoned wife, was, of course, his birthplace. But, for Reilly, the past was not merely a foreign country; it was a country which no longer existed on the map. The British officer and special agent, now on his second important mission for 'C', lived on another planet from the bastard Jewish Sigmund Georgievich Rosenblum who had been born in this great Russian port in 1874, and fled it abruptly sixteen years later. Thus, though his diary for the journey contains many personal notes and comments, there is not a word about revisited childhood haunts in Odessa, let alone trying to look up surviving friends or relatives there. His closest colleague, George Hill, who was still with him, observed only one outward trace of contact, when Reilly suddenly turned pale on passing a particular house in the town. The 'master-spy', however, said nothing, then or later, about his birthplace. As far as we know, he was never to see it again.

By the time of that final visit to Odessa, Reilly and Hill had finished their official tour. Apart from the study of Denikin and his Volunteer Army, it had included assessments of two other possible centres for anti-Bolshevik operations in southern Russia. The first was the Ukraine where, for centuries, the spirit of separatism had sprouted alongside the wheat. It had burst out again after the Bolsheviks' seizure of power: an independent Ukrainian People's Republic was proclaimed by the so-called 'Rada' or nationalist council in Kiev, only to be overthrown early in 1918 when Bolshevik troops marched in to restore a Soviet regime. This despite lavish Western financial aid for the separatist cause, supplied along any available channel. On 11 February 1918, for example, a British contribution of fifteen million roubles was handed over to nationalist leaders at Kiev's Grand Hotel; the paymaster, who had raised the money locally on London's behalf, was a certain Mr Perervoins of the Premier Oil and Pipe Line.

Lenin's peace negotiations with the Central Powers swung the door open again for secession. The Ukrainian delegates at Brest-Litovsk had little trouble in signing their own separate treaty with the enemy, though German control of their province – through puppets stiffened with military decrees – continued until the Armistice. Only then could an independence of sorts be established;

it was still only a chaotic semblance of statehood. A new Directorate was proclaimed as successor to the Rada but its leaders were the same ineffective and quarrelsome figures of old. The President was Vladimir Vinnichenko, an intellectual Marxist who was all for cooperation with the Bolsheviks. Such power as the Directorate possessed rested with an ex-journalist named Simon Petlyura, a firebrand and dreamer who, as Minister of War, had raised a peasant army more than 100,000 strong within weeks of the German surrender on the promise of land grants. Petlyura, seeing himself as the mini-Napoleon of the steppes, resolved to set up his own Ukrainian dictatorship, whatever the Bolsheviks or anyone else thought about it. What the Allies wanted to know was whether anything could be gained by supporting this quixotic figure. Reilly's verdict was speedy and emphatic:

> Petlyura, Vinnichenko and Co. are not Bolsheviks but their tactics lead fatally to Bolshevism. Peasants will leave them either as soon as they get their land, or when imminence Allied intervention makes prospect land-grabbing remote. Then Petlyura will be left only with town proletariat and transition to Bolshevism becomes unavoidable. Notwithstanding Petlyura's orders to the contrary, in Odessa Bolshevik Soviets had been instantly organised, in Kharkov they are actually ruling. Petlyura now in vicious circle. Either he will be squashed by Allied intervention and then he must invoke Bolshevik help, or he will be swamped and ousted by Bolsheviks, whose mottoes he only adopts for tactical considerations.[15]

The Cossacks weighed much more heavily in the anti-Bolshevik balance, above all on the military scale. In contrast to Petlyura's horde of unskilled peasant soldiers, these famous horsemen, born to the saddle, formed the largest and fiercest cavalry force in existence. But though they had occupied their homeland, the Don, for some 500 years, they were a race rather than a nation, and certainly not a state. They had their 'Great Kroug', or Parliament, which chose their Ataman, or leader. At the time of the Reilly–Hill tour, this was General Peter Krasnov, a relatively obscure ex-Tsarist officer who had been playing the German card and had eventually been re-elected in August 1918 as the German Army's nominee.[16] This military dependence weakened Krasnov's control; his political foothold became even wobblier as scores of Cossack commanders throughout the territory created their own fiefdoms. Was he, therefore, worth continued Allied support?

Reilly spent nearly a week in the Don in mid-January 1919 trying to find out. It was an exhaustive enquiry. Over five days, he reported that he had seen not only Krasnov himself but also his principal ministers, members of the Kroug, the archbishop, leaders of the regional Cadet and Monarchist political parties, Cossack officers and 'the most prominent merchants, bankers, manufacturers, newspaper editors, railway directors, foreign Consuls etc.'. His verdict was discouraging in the extreme.

Krasnov, in his view, was the tool not merely of the Germans but of a Camarilla of his own advisers who were 'universally detested as reactionaries and intriguers of the worst type'. Anarchy and corruption ruled the Don between them:

> Rostov, the largest town, with a population of 300,000 is administered by a half-crazy autocrat by the name of Grekoff who is seconded by a certain Illaieff, the former chief of a band of robbers and continuing, in a barely disguised form, to follow this lucrative occupation. Bribery and abuse of power abound everywhere. The law courts, which contain some of the worst judges of the old regime, have entirely lost the confidence of the people. The police in the towns and the militia in the 'Stanitzas' [Cossack villages] are a law unto themselves.[17]

While accepting that Krasnov had performed 'a truly Herculean task' in raising, training and equipping an army of 60,000 men, Reilly had grave doubts about the 'intrinsic stability' of this force. In any case, the Cossacks would probably need heavy bribes to induce them to fight outside their territories. A great deal depended on whether Krasnov's recent pledge to put himself under Denikin's command would be honoured in practice. The omens were not good. When Reilly complimented Krasnov on his 'wise and unselfish attitude' over the question, the Cossack general had immediately flared up, criticizing the Volunteer Army for thinking only 'of grasping the maximum amount of power'.

Reilly's thoughts on Allied assistance echoed those of Denikin: the need was not simply for arms and equipment but 'for troops to assist in holding reconquered territories and to protect lines of communication'. There was already widespread disappointment over the laggardly pace of Allied action: 'The Russians,' Reilly noted, 'have become used to the rapidity and decisiveness of the Germans and they cannot understand our deliberate methods which are interpreted as weakness.'[18] But the trump cards remained in the Allies' hands and they should play them by making it clear to Krasnov that in southern Russia they would stand by the Volunteer Army 'not only militarily and economically but also politically'. If need be, the general, who had virtually been appointed by the now-defeated Germans, could be replaced by the now-victorious Allies.

All in all, Reilly's reports give the impression of being balanced yet decisive, and authoritative though not dogmatic. His brief from 'C' had been closely followed and well discharged, with no theatrical touches and no flourishes of self-importance. He is, in fact, hardly recognizable from the firebrand who had operated solo at the centre of all that midsummer mayhem in Moscow. Whether he achieved more as sober analyst than as special agent on the rampage is hard to assess. In his time (unlike today) there was no mechanism by which all intelligence input could be coordinated and presented regularly to the policy-makers for consideration. But London was the one Western capital where, at the beginning of 1919, all these field assessments from southern Russia might well have had a direct political impact.

On 14 January, Winston Churchill had become Minister of War, an appointment which automatically inflamed the itch he always felt for grand strategic designs. Post-armistice war weariness and reluctance to fight the Russians' battle for them was common to all the victorious Allies. Yet there was no uniformity among them as to how swiftly or completely their swords should be sheathed. President Wilson was all for the scabbards. He had always lagged behind in joining Allied intervention plans in the first place and had then hobbled these ventures by imposing strict limits on America's contribution and deployment. Now, at the Paris Peace Conference, he was reiterating his position that the Allies should clear out of Russia as soon as they could scrabble up the gangplanks and leave the people there to determine their own fate.

The French felt more caught up in the Russian imbroglio, for historical as well as economic reasons. But, as with the Americans, their history also inclined them to look more tolerantly towards the Bolsheviks as the rough-hewn but hopefully well-intentioned apostles of revolution and republicanism in post-war Europe. Lenin's slogans had the vague appeal of the 'Marseillaise' about them, as disaffected French sailors in both the Baltic and the Black Sea flotillas had demonstrated. Nor could that French military fiasco at Odessa be easily put aside; even a table-thumper like Clemenceau would be tempted to murmur: 'Never again!'[19]

Churchill was the odd man out, not only among his own government colleagues but among the Allied Council as a whole. Even before taking over the War Office (he had previously served as Minister of Munitions in Lloyd George's wartime Cabinet) he had been arguing for large-scale joint military intervention by all five principal Allied powers to bring down the Soviet regime; and if, as seemed likely, Wilson would not allow the Americans to take part, then the other four – the British Empire, France, Japan and Italy – should simply go ahead by themselves. Within his own government, the Prime Minister was Churchill's most powerful and most persuasive opponent. Lloyd George argued that the difficulties – political even more than military – of launching such a massive operation in peacetime were too formidable and also that the expectations of anti-Bolshevik support on the ground were far too optimistic. In his view, Denikin, for example, controlled 'only a little backyard on the Black Sea'. The most he was prepared to accept was that, in such areas as were not in Bolshevik hands, the Allies should supply practicable amounts of financial and material support but on no account provide troops. This was the state of the debate when Churchill took over the War Office.

The new minister would have had, on his desk, both General Poole's final report from Odessa in early January and, soon afterwards, Reilly's account of his meeting with Denikin on 11 January – copies of which 'C' had sent to the service departments in Whitehall. It is surely no coincidence that the language used in both these assessments finds an echo in the keynote speech on the post-war Russian problem which Churchill delivered at the Mansion House a month later, on 19 February 1919.

While repeating the mantra that 'Russia ... must be saved by the Russians', Churchill made it clear that the Allies should take a powerful hand in that salvation process by aiding the forces which were engaged in fighting 'the foul baboonery of Bolshevism'. This aid, he said, could be given by 'arms, munitions, and technical services raised on a voluntary basis'. The final words of the proposal opened the door even for the despatch of troops, though not on the scale for which the White Army commanders were hoping. The Churchill formula was the nearest thing to a positive but pragmatic policy for Allied post-war involvement that had so far been enunciated. The problem was whether it was not too pragmatic to succeed.

General Sir Henry Wilson put the matter bluntly in the memorandum he had penned only forty-eight hours after the Armistice.[20] In the middle of all his assessments about the merits of giving Allied aid to anti-Soviet Russian forces comes the sentence: 'If the Bolsheviks are the better men, we cannot indefinitely continue to protect the others.' After a series of wild fluctuations in the fortunes of Whites and Reds, the year 1919 was to prove which of them indeed had 'the better men'.

10

Peace Flutters

Before the clash of arms reached its turning-point, some unlikely-looking doves of peace flapped unsteadily above the battlefield. The first was released, quite unexpectedly, by Lloyd George, when the New Year had barely dawned. On 2 January 1919, he floated the idea of a peace conference in Paris between the Allied powers and 'all the various groups contending on Russian territory'. Its purpose would be to reconcile their differences and so lead to a general settlement. As a precondition, hostilities were to be suspended by all the 'parties and peoples in the States and territories concerned'.

This phrase was so all-embracing by implication as to be almost meaningless. Included, alongside the Soviet regime in Moscow, was the whole of that heaving and amorphous swathe of opponents which surrounded it. This comprised not only the commanders of the three White Russian armies which were preparing to assault the Bolshevik citadel from the north, south and east, but also the Ukraine, the Baltic provinces and that plethora of anti-Soviet 'governments' – some provincial, some regional, some purporting to be national, mostly venal and mostly quarrelling with each other – which had sprung up under the protection of those armies.

If the size and make-up of such a motley band of delegates made it unlikely that they would reach agreement wherever they assembled, Clemenceau made sure that, whatever happened, they would not be coming to Paris to join in with the general peace conference. On the day, 11 January, that Lloyd George arrived in the French capital to attend the opening of that mammoth assembly, his Russia plan was leaked to the French press, only to be opposed by the French Foreign Minister, Stephan Pichon. The minister did not, of course, give the real reason for his rejection – Clemenceau's phobia, already noted, about the peril which the Bolshevik bacillus presented for the health of the French nation, a threat which might deepen if Bolshevik propagandists descended on Paris to spread the contamination. Instead, he argued, with some plausibility, that there already were enough Russians of various political affiliations present in the French capital to fill up a conference table.

The men he was thinking of (without enumerating them) did indeed add up to a formidable collection. The most prestigious was Prince Georgi Lvov who in 1917 had briefly taken over the reins of government from the deposed Tsar. Lvov had sailed to Paris from North America with a group of other monarchist expatriates to hold a watchdog brief for his cause at the Peace Conference and had asked whether he might visit London on the way. In agreeing, the Foreign Office paid him this waspish tribute: 'Prince Lvov is a sincere and honest patriot, absolutely disinterested, and we cannot refuse to see him. He will be as admirable in conversation and nearly as feeble in execution as his compatriots.'[1]

Lvov was the president of the so-called 'Russian Political Conference' which had its seat in Paris, where it had been cobbled together by Vassily Maklakov, Kerensky's one-time envoy in the French capital. This body was indeed 'feeble in execution', not only because it was without any formal credentials but because of its disparate make-up. Thus it included not only Sergei Sazonov, who had served both the Tsar[2] and Kerensky as Foreign Minister, but also the veteran Socialist Nikolai Chaikovsky, head of the 'Provisional Government of Northern Russia' up at Archangel before he departed in disgust at the dictatorial antics of Major-General Poole. A particularly incongruous member (in such law-abiding company) was Boris Savinkov, the dedicated revolutionary who had tried to topple Lenin's regime during the previous summer. He was now in exile in Paris as propagandist and fund-raiser for the anti-Bolshevik cause in general, whereas Sazonov claimed to be acting jointly for the White Army commanders both in Siberia and in southern Russia.

This 'Russian Political Conference' had only one long-term element of symbolic significance: it established Paris in the Bolsheviks' eyes as the centre of all later attempts to overthrow them. As we shall see, the French capital did indeed serve as the staging-post for separate bids by Savinkov and Reilly to topple the Soviet government and later on as the scene of Stalin's most outrageous terrorist exploits. But in January 1919, the émigré group could be dismissed as a political factor, representing, as Lloyd George put it, 'every opinion except the prevalent opinion in Russia'. The Bolsheviks themselves, he insisted, would have to be involved in any talks about a Russian settlement. The only alternatives, he told the Allied Council on 16 January, were to crush them by military force ('pure madness') or to erect a besieging circle around Soviet Russia which would bring starvation to millions ('a cordon of death').

After some heated exchanges between the British and French leaders, Clemenceau's intransigence over any dealings with the Bolsheviks was eventually softened. This was due partly to Lloyd George's assurances that there was no intention of giving them formal recognition as a government and partly to his dropping the idea of using Paris as the venue (Clemenceau's 'bloody capital' and no place to hold a peace conference anyway). It was President Wilson who drafted the eccentric compromise formula. The American President, just as anxious to make contact with the Bolshevik leaders[3] as Clemenceau was to avoid them, suggested Prinkipo, the largest of a group of Turkish islands in the Sea of Marmara, as the new venue.

No greater contrast with the French capital could have been imagined. The Princes Islands, to give them their Western name, were by 1919 a summer resort, which meant that there would at least be an abundance of out-of-season hotel space available, and no problems over objections from the defeated Turks. (The Czechs had previously vetoed Salonika and Lemnos as possible conference sites.) The Bolsheviks might well have seen the Princes Islands in a different context. The Byzantine emperors had long used Prinkipo as a place of banishment and Lenin's emissaries would have found themselves in something of a prison camp atmosphere now. To sail in Allied vessels straight from the Black Sea to the Sea of Marmara, and back by the same means along the same route, would have left the Soviet delegation tightly enclosed on the journey and with little chance, once they were landed in such a remote location, of generating the world publicity they desired. The bizarre way in which the project was launched was in keeping with its other oddities.

For the first time since the invention of radio an international conference was convened entirely by Morse signals despatched over the short airwaves on 23 January to the parties concerned. This had been a deliberate ploy by the Allies to avoid any direct diplomatic contact with a Soviet regime which they were still refusing to recognize. In view of this, the broadcast's preamble was grotesque. The Allies, it affirmed, 'recognise the revolution without reservation and will in no way and in no circumstances aid or give countenance to any attempt at counter-revolution'. The threadbare formula of intervention without interference was being trotted out again, and the equivocation did not go unanswered in the reply broadcast from Moscow on 4 February. This noted acerbically that 'the capacity for resistance of the enemies which Soviet Russia has to fight depends entirely on the aid which they receive from the Allies'. However, precisely because these powers represented the 'only real adversaries' of the regime, it was prepared to enter immediately into negotiations with them, 'on Princes Island or in any other place'.

The tone of part of the Soviet message irritated the Allied leaders because it harped on the financial and economic concessions which Moscow proposed to make, thus suggesting that the conference was little better than a bazaar-style bargain. But the remarkable thing was the acceptance in itself, for it was not just the Allies whom the Bolsheviks would be dealing with at Prinkipo. The invitation had gone out, as Moscow conceded, to 'all *de facto* governments in Russia'. This meant that, if all the recipients had

accepted, and if the Allies had then been able to broker a settlement between them, the Bolsheviks stood to sign away control, not
merely of Finland and the emerging Baltic states in the north, but
of Siberia and all the Urals in the east; of the bulk of the Ukraine;
of Poland and the Don; of Transcaucasia and the Black Sea littoral
in the south. Lenin himself had voiced fears on this score, in
telegrams to Trotsky.

This was all speculation; the reality was very different. Soviet
spokesmen in the Ukraine and the three provisional Baltic administrations followed Moscow in accepting the invitation. But it was
flatly rejected by every element in the anti-Soviet camp: by the White
Russian leaders in the east, south and north (each a form of 'de facto
government') and by the Russian Political Conference speaking on
their behalf on the spot in Paris. For all these groups, the mere idea
of sitting down with the Bolsheviks to talk peace at a conference
table was heresy; their mission was to crush them on the battlefield
and so restore Great Russia to its rightful place in history. So far
from trying to talk the protestors round, Clemenceau, who had
disliked the conference project from the start, gave them quiet
encouragement from the sidelines. This was decisive in torpedoing
Wilson's Prinkipo plan, which duly sank below the waters of the Sea
of Marmara without so much as a bubble breaking the surface. The
President's invitation had called on all willing participants to turn
up for talks by 15 February 1919. Not a soul had appeared by the
deadline and so on 16 February, the Princes Islands reverted to their
role as an off-shore Turkish holiday camp.

Churchill was naturally delighted by the collapse of the Prinkipo
project and, by an appropriate coincidence, on the very day its term
expired, he was in Paris[4] arguing for its antithesis – 'joint military
action by Associated Powers [i.e. the Allies] acting in conjunction
with the independent border states and pro-Ally governments in
Russia'. With President Wilson also temporarily back home (to
attend the Congressional elections) the anti-Bolshevik 'hawks' in
the Allied Council were enjoying a moment of glory.[5] It was brief,
for their ideas proved too much for even the second echelon of

Allied leaders to accept (Clemenceau was also absent, recovering from an assassin's bullet wound). Moreover, even while the martial clamour was sounding, another peace dove had appeared in the Paris skies. This one was young, all-American, snow-white in his idealism and ready to fly solo to Moscow.

William Christian Bullitt (one of his ancestors had been Fletcher Christian of *Mutiny on the Bounty* fame) was the golden boy among that vast assemblage of so-called 'Argonauts' who, in December 1918, had set sail as President Wilson's advisers for the Paris peace conference. He came from a wealthy and well-connected Philadelphia family; was intelligent and good-looking; and, at twenty-eight, had already made a name for himself as a wartime State Department analyst. His job in Paris was to prepare daily intelligence briefings about conference affairs for the leaders of the American delegation and this brought him into regular contact with the most important of them all – Colonel Edward House, Wilson's special adviser and alter ego who often spoke for the President at Allied Council meetings. It was House's sponsorship which had got Bullitt on to the American team in the first place and it was the colonel who now helped to launch his young protégé on the most important journey of his life.

The idea of sending a fact-finding mission to Moscow to assess the strength of Lenin's regime and its true stand towards the Allied camp had been floated by Bullitt as a junior official in Washington in February 1918. It now resurfaced in Paris twelve months later as a serious proposition to replace the fiasco of the Prinkipo approach. Bullitt had been assiduously lobbying to take on the job (not just, as he coyly put it, 'as a general bootblack') and on 18 Febuary, three days after the collapse of Prinkipo, he got his heart's desire. A formal letter was sent to him by Secretary of State Lansing authorizing him 'to proceed to Russia for the purpose of studying conditions, political and economic therein [*sic*] for the benefit of the American commissioners' plenipotentiary to negotiate peace'.[6] The very wording of the assignment showed that Lansing's previous complaint to Masaryk, that he had 'no idea what was really going on in Russia', still held good. Indeed, with most of the Western diplomatic missions and all their secret service appendages cleared out of the Soviet capital six months before, and only the lone Paul Dukes still operating in Petrograd, the Western picture of Lenin's regime had become hazier than ever. An authoritative, on-the-spot assessment was badly needed. But by 22 February, when Bullitt left Paris for Britain, where he took ship for Russia, the young Philadelphian had become more than a special intelligence scout: he was halfway towards being a peace-broker all on his own.

Bullitt had held several informal talks on the Russian problem earlier in the year with Philip Kerr, Lloyd George's private secretary, to whom he had now been authorized to reveal his mission. (It was an early example of the Anglo-American 'special relationship', particularly regarding cooperation on intelligence matters; at this stage, the secret was kept from all the other Allies, including the French.) In return, Kerr was asked to sound out his government on Britain's ideas for a Russian settlement; the outcome was an eight-point set of conditions passed to Bullitt the day before he left Paris.

As far as officialdom was concerned, the mission started off in a fog just as it was eventually to evaporate in a fog. Thus, on the American side, President Wilson is known to have been informed of the plan only just before leaving for America on 14 February. The fact that he did not forbid it was taken as his endorsement, though no explicit blessing is recorded. The involvement of Britain's leaders is even less well defined. Both Lloyd George and Balfour obviously knew of the mission but whether either of them took a personal hand in drafting Bullitt's brief is much less clear. At all events, Philip Kerr must have known what the Prime Minister's general ideas on the subject were when he sent his young American friend a set of proposals to present in Moscow, proposals which he coyly claimed had 'no official significance and merely represent suggestions of my own opinion'.

Most of the points dealt with routine matters such as the normalization of Russian port and railway controls, the free entry and movement of Allied nationals, and the restoration of trade relations.

The crux was whether Lenin was prepared to endorse his acknowl-edgement of the anti-Soviet forces fighting against him on Russian soil. The requirement was spelt out in Condition Two: 'All *de facto* governments to remain in full control of the territories which they at present occupy.' This formula hardened the language used in the Prinkipo preliminaries. It turned Lenin's tacit acceptance of his opponents' existence into a formal pledge to recognize their claims.

To Bullitt's delight (and perhaps also astonishment) Lenin was to raise no objection. The young American envoy had been accorded what, in later political parlance, was to be called 'VIP treatment' from the moment his ship docked at Petrograd. In Moscow, where he arrived on 10 March, he was given palatial quarters, fully heated and staffed, and fed with the best food to be found in a stricken capital where proper tea had become nearly as much of a delicacy as caviare.[7] After three days of almost continuous talks with the Soviet Commissar for Foreign Affairs Georgi Chicherin and his deputy Maxim Litvinov (back from his stint in London), there followed a long conference with Lenin himself. The outcome was a seven-point reply, handed to Bullitt on 14 March.

The only condition in the Anglo-American proposals not to be met was the call for the cessation of hostilities on all fronts – suggesting that the Soviets, who were doing rather well at the time on the battlefield, felt they could improve their position even more. The other Western requirements were agreed to, with changes only in phraseology, and the crucial clause that all de facto governments on Russian soil should be confirmed in control of the territories they occupied was accepted more or less as it had been put forward. That would have meant giving up, at least for the time being, some two-thirds of the old Russian empire, in return for an end to Allied intervention and the prospect of recognition for a rump Soviet state.

A year later, when the whole issue had been decided by deeds, not words, Lenin was to explain away this sweeping concession by arguing that even a peace treaty with the Bolsheviks on these favourable terms would have been rejected by public protest in the capitalist West. That was a bold assumption. Yet it was partly borne out by what happened when young Bullitt, flushed with success and singing loud hymns of praise for the Soviet leadership, returned to Paris on 25 March, clutching what he imagined to be an historic treaty of peace.

Several factors would combine to toss Bullitt's precious document on to the scrap heap; but the most immediate, at least for Lloyd George, was a ferocious attack launched straight away by Lord Northcliffe's *Daily Mail* on any peace deal with the Bolsheviks. The editorial[8] excoriated anyone in the Allied camp who would 'directly or indirectly, accredit an evil thing known as Bolshevism'. Then, descending a few steps down that ladder which leads to gutter-press journalism, it suggested that the whole operation was an attempt by Jewish influences in Moscow to bribe the West into recognizing the Soviet regime with 'prospects of lucrative commercial enterprise in Russia'. Lloyd George brandished a copy of the paper's Paris edition at a meeting of his advisers. 'As long as the British press is doing this kind of thing,' he exploded, 'how can you expect me to be sensible about Russia?' Sensible or not about Russia, Lloyd George was to become outrageously devious over Bullitt's mission, to the point where, a month later, he disclaimed to a sceptical House of Commons any knowledge of what it had really all been about.

So, in this respect, Lenin's hunch had proved correct. But anti-Bolshevik feeling in the Western camp was not the only pressure which thrust the Bullitt mission into oblivion, like Prinkipo before it. For the Allied leaders, the Russian problem had itself been sidelined by the urgent need to get into place the keystone of the whole Paris conference, the peace treaty with Germany. Clemenceau and Foch had throughout been demanding severe, even savage, terms in order to banish (as they fondly hoped, for all time) the giant shadow of German might from along their borders. Lloyd George, whose country's frontier with Germany was the North Sea, not the Rhine, could afford to be less extreme: he was opposing any settlement whose harshness might drive a defeated and humiliated Germany into the clutches of Bolshevism. The confrontation, which

was reaching its climax the same week that Bullitt arrived back in
Paris, had to be resolved above everything else. President Wilson,
as determined as ever to end American involvement in Russia
as soon as was decently possible, was not the man to steer his
colleague's mind back to the Soviet problem. Parallel with this shift
in political priorities came a sudden change of fortunes on the
Russian battlefields. In March, the anti-Soviet forces on the eastern
front had launched a massive offensive which seemed to be
sweeping the Red Army from its path. So much so that the Allied
leaders began to ask themselves whether the man they really ought
to be sounding out over the shape of things to come was not Lenin
in Moscow but the leader of that offensive in Siberia. His name,
Alexander Kolchak, was already being spoken of as that of the
saviour of the Great Russian fatherland.

Part Four

Battle Tides – Surge and Ebb

11

The Siberian Tragedy

The man to whom both the White Russians and the Allies now looked to win the land battle against the Bolsheviks was, paradoxically, a naval man born and bred, whose whole life thus far had been the ocean. His father had served as a naval artillery expert in the Crimean War and two of his uncles were also naval officers. The fifteen-year-old Aleksander Vasilevich Kolchak was enrolled, almost automatically, in the Russian Naval Academy in 1889 and when he passed out six years later it was to embark on a triple career as Arctic explorer, naval planner and battle commander. He achieved distinction in all three fields, and especially on active service.

Kolchak had begun the Great War as flag captain in the Baltic before (to his own genuine surprise) being promoted rear-admiral in July 1916 and transferred south to command the Black Sea fleet. Here he promptly achieved the not-inconsiderable feat of putting to flight the German cruiser *Breslau* which, together with her sister ship the *Goeben*, had been terrorizing the Tsar's southern ocean. In 1917, after the first Russian revolution had broken out, he showed that he had as much integrity as valour. When the naval Soviet which had formed in his fleet called for the immediate disarming of all its officers, he assembled the crew of his flagship and announced that he had no intention of following such a needless and insulting order. He then unsheathed his sword, tossed it overboard, and went ashore to send a telegram to Kerensky resigning his commission and command. Not many Tsarist officers nailed their colours to the anti-Bolshevik mast with such dash and dignity. The Kolchak legend had begun among his countrymen.[1]

What the self-retired admiral did next helped to establish that legend among the Allies. Within a month of disowning the revolution he was in America where – such was his professional reputation – he had been invited to advise on the use of naval mines. On the way to Washington he had talks in London with Admiral Jellicoe, the First Sea Lord, who was duly impressed by his visitor. Kolchak made an even greater impression on the British government when it read a telegram sent by their ambassador in Tokyo, Sir Conyingham Greene, on 8 November of that year. Kolchak had been in the Japanese capital en route for Russia when the news came through that his homeland was now in the hands of Lenin. Within twenty-four hours, Kolchak had presented himself to Greene with an extraordinary offer: in order to fight the Bolsheviks he was prepared to join the British Army even as a common soldier. (His senior rank, he pointed out, would have made it awkward for him to be absorbed into the Royal Navy.) For a man of his talents, the offer was as ludicrous as it was magnanimous. The envoy must have been a blinkered bureaucrat to accept it and arrange without demur for his posting to the Mesopotamian front. Wiser British and White Russian councils prevailed. The ex-admiral was halted en route at Singapore and told that he would be of far greater use if he returned home to raise an anti-Bolshevik army in Siberia.

His wanderings were still not over. He had an uncomfortable stay in Manchuria, where he was dismayed at the duplicity of the local Japanese commanders at Harbin, and the Cossack forces under Grigori Semenov which they controlled. After a fruitless trip back to Tokyo to try to persuade the Japanese General Staff to stop sitting on their hands in Siberia and give active help in the field, Kolchak set out in disgust to join up with the Volunteer Army in southern Russia, more than 3,000 miles distant. He finally came to rest, halfway on his journey, at Omsk, where the White Russian government of Western Siberia had just established its capital as the most impressive of all the anti-Red regional administrations. There he stayed, at first accepting the post of Minister of War with the task of turning some 200,000 raw recruits into an army.[2]

It was by now mid-October of 1918. Kolchak was not to remain Minister of War for long. Four days before his arrival, the so-called 'All Russian Provisional Government', fleeing from Ufa in the Urals before the advancing Bolsheviks, had also turned up at Omsk, to seek not merely refuge but recognition and a share of power. Nothing illustrated better the tangled and unpredictable complications of the White Russian scene. A stand-off immediately developed between the newcomers, headed by a liberal-minded five-man Directorate and the sitting tenants of western Siberia who were right-wing Tsarists to a man. Though they all initially agreed to merge, there were constant brawls and verbal battles between the two sides, with the occasional assassination enlivening the wrangle for power. In a happy phrase, General Vassily Boldryev, the Directorate's Commander-in-Chief, described the scene as 'Mexico amid snow and ice' (winter had already begun to set in at Omsk).

The hopeless situation certainly had a Mexican-style ending. On the night of 17 November two of the left-wing Socialist Revolutionary members of the Directorate were kidnapped and arrested by Tsarist officers; a third resigned in protest; the fourth (General Boldryev) had gone off to visit the front, so that only a timorous fifth, one Vologodsky, remained. Somebody else had to be put in charge to end the chaos. On the morning of 18 November, Kolchak (who had in fact been sponsoring the cause of the absent general) was informed that the choice had fallen on him. From now on, all political and military power in Siberia was to be vested in his person; in addition, he was henceforth to be styled 'Supreme Ruler' of all Russia.[3] Never did a less ambitious and self-seeking man become, overnight, a dictator.

Tongues started wagging immediately, among both the Allied and White Russian camps, as to what part the British had played in all this, and the mystery has never been completely solved. Attention centred on the role of Major-General Sir Alfred Knox

(Lockhart's bitterest critic the previous year when the two men were serving in Petrograd). Knox had arrived in Vladivostok on 5 September 1918 to take up his new post as head of the British Military Mission in Siberia, and though not the senior Allied officer on the scene[4] he was certainly the most active. He spent some ten days in Omsk during the second half of October and both he and the two British officers accompanying him made no secret of their support for Kolchak, with whom they had several discussions. That there was advance on-the-spot British lobbying for the admiral (as he was now again being called) is undeniable.

That the British actually engineered the *coup d'état* which put Kolchak in power a month later is more questionable. Knox had long been back in Vladivostok when these events took place. The central role, even if a relatively passive one, was played by another British officer – an unusual man with a strange mission in an extraordinary setting. Lieutenant-Colonel John Ward was still a serving Trade Unionist Member of Parliament when he arrived at Omsk, also in mid-October, in command of the 25th Battalion of the Middlesex Regiment. This was one of the two British Army units (the other being the 19th Hampshires) which had been despatched to Siberia with the vaguely non-political tasks of garrison and escort duties. Like the Hampshires, the Middlesex was a low-grade military unit made up mostly of elderly, unfit soldiers who had somehow passed their Hong Kong medicals. (It had indeed been dubbed 'the Hernia Battalion'.)

But however many of its members were suffering from ruptured stomachs, there was nothing wrong with their machine guns. It was these weapons which the colonel had mounted all around the building in which, on the morning of 18 November, the crucial decision on leadership was being thrashed out. The symbolism of their conference being held under the protection of British arms could not have been lost on those inside the building, especially as it was known that Colonel Ward was another enthusiastic convert to the Kolchak cause. (He had assigned special guard details to protect the admiral on his travels.)[5] Thus it seems fair to claim that, even without overt interference, influential British nods and winks had been given in Kolchak's direction at the critical moment. The fact that the *coup d'état* caught the Foreign Office on the wrong foot at the time (it had been on the point of sending a telegram of recognition to the Directorate on the day of its dissolution) is significant only in that it absolves the British government from any formal involvement. The nods and winks had been dispensed locally. It was yet another example of knee-jerk Allied reaction to another shift in the endlessly unpredictable scenario of Russian politics.

Kolchak's assumption of supreme overall power in the White Russian cause was accepted in the Allied camp, though with differing degrees of enthusiasm. The Japanese had cold-shouldered him in Tokyo as a potential rival. In Washington, President Wilson needed to overcome doubts about his Tsarist loyalties and his unsavoury Cossack partners. Even in the Anglo-French camp, there were large cracks underneath the surface façade of joint support. General Maurice Janin had arrived in Vladivostok at the time of the Kolchak *coup*, invested with no fewer than three posts. First, he displaced Otani as the Allied Commander-in-Chief; second, he took charge of the French Military Mission; and, third, he assumed personal control of all Czech forces in Siberia (having already served in overall command of their legion). It was this last responsibility which caused the problems. For Janin (and his master in Paris, Clemenceau, who had never forgiven the British for trying to reroute the Legion via the far northern front on their way home) the Czechs were the key to triumph over the Bolsheviks. White Russian forces hardly figured in French plans for Siberia, whereas these were central to British thinking. Indeed, Janin seems to have regarded Kolchak almost as Knox's puppet.

As will be seen, this was to stir up trouble and controversy in the year ahead. But, personalities apart, there was broad agreement that if the Bolsheviks were ever to be replaced by a liberal/democratic regime, the transition would first have to pass through a phase of military dictatorship as the only framework by which order could immediately be imposed on chaos. Now, it seemed, the hour had produced the man. In the words of General Knox, his most powerful champion: 'Everything now seemed to depend on Kolchak.'[6] It was a mammoth load to set on any one man's shoulders.

That this middle-aged admiral – unassuming amidst a horde of pompous opportunists and unstained by the sea of corruption around him – failed to lead the White Russian cause to triumph was, in retrospect, hardly surprising. The sailor now had to embark on a land battle whose scale and complexities would have daunted even a second Napoleon. In addition, he had to cope with problems which the first Napoleon never faced: dissension in his councils and high-level intrigues behind his back.

The key to his success had always turned on the scale and the manner in which the Allies were prepared to support him. By the spring of 1919 the troops they had despatched to serve under the 'Supreme Ruler' were beginning to look respectable enough on paper. At the time of the first Kolchak offensive, the Japanese had supplied much the biggest contingent (28,000, to rise eventually to 75,000). They were followed by 7,500 Americans; 12,000 Poles; 4,000 each of Canadians, Serbs and Poles; 2,000 Italians; 1,600 British, with a group of 760 French bringing up the rear. Together with the 55,000 Czechs and his own White Russian soldiers, this gave Kolchak a polyglot force of some 200,000 men to face the roughly equal Red Army troops along the 900-mile fighting front.

On Kolchak's side, however, the numbers were illusory. As far as the actual campaign went, both the Americans and the Japanese were his allies in name only. The former, on President Wilson's orders, stuck like glue to his face-saving formula that they had come to Siberia only 'to help the Czechs'. Before the winter fighting of 1918–19 started, General William Graves, the commander of the American contingent, had been told that his forces should not be established at Omsk 'or any other point in the Far Interior'. Moreover, Washington would not undertake to send even its supplies anywhere west of the Urals to sustain the Czechs. In the American view, these should anyway be retired east of the mountains

– a proposition which, once it was followed, put paid to any serious White Russian threat to either Petrograd or Moscow.

From the first, the Japanese were playing a game of their own. Their large parade of troops seemed to have been designed as a shield to protect the Far East from the spread of Bolshevism and as a screen for economic penetration and, perhaps, eventual colonization. Like the Americans, the Japanese refused to contemplate any movement west of the Urals. Even in the east, they remained a presence only, leaving the fighting to their mercenaries, Cossack Atamans like Semenov and Kalmikov, brigands whose looting and atrocities further besmirched the anti-Red cause. Surrogates like these drew Japan into the extreme right-wing camp, in contrast to the Americans who, to begin with, played the White Russian field as far to the left as was respectable.

Those ideological differences among the Allies were as nothing compared with tensions and squabbles which racked Kolchak's camp. The admiral-turned-land-forces-supremo (a few river gunboats were the nearest thing in his command to a navy) had proved a poor judge of men. More damaging still, he proved equally bad at calling them to order. Thus when his Chief of Staff, the impetuous 36-year-old General Lebedev who had Moscow already in his sights, started quarrelling with the cautiously bureaucratic Minister of War General Stepanov, the best Kolchak could think of was to hold almost daily conferences of mediation. It never seems to have occurred to him to sack one of them, or else knock their heads together. The admiral lacked one vital requisite for any dictator: to be a good butcher.

When the first reports of the political imbroglio at Omsk had reached London, the Foreign Office commented: 'Nothing will apparently prevent these Russians intriguing against one another in such a way as to destroy all chance of stable and orderly Govt.'

'They are hopeless,' added another official. Mr Balfour, by simply initialling the paper, did not dissent.[7]

Out in Siberia, the British Training School which General Knox had set up on Russian Island near Vladivostok was soon experiencing similar problems.[8] Here the sheer indolence and self-indulgence of the recruits was the main complaint of their instructors. One of these wrote of the attitude of their typical Russian trainee: 'Tomorrow is better than today and the day after tomorrow is better than either. He does not appear to be able to exist without his womenfolk and feasting and holiday-making, as important in war as in peace.' The aggrieved British officer added that, in addition to the recruits downing tools for the holidays themselves (four of which had fallen in one week), they had needed 'half the previous day to prepare and the whole of the day after to recover'.[9]

Despite all this, the attempt was made on both the political and military fronts to prop Kolchak up for as long as he showed any prospect of becoming the hoped-for saviour of all-Russia. This hope was, of course, wrapped from the start in a desperate optimism which amounted almost to delusion. Though the title of the 'Supreme Ruler' came to be recognized both by General Denikin in the south and by General Yudenich in the north, his forces never managed to link up with either. All the while, central Russia remained in the grip of Lenin's Bolsheviks and even Kolchak's hinterland all the way back to Vladivostok was insecure. His fiefdom as dictator was confined to western Siberia and the Urals; even here the writ of power ran in a wobbly fashion.

All this was reflected in the equivocal political backing which, after lengthy debate, the Allies finally extended to Kolchak in mid-June 1919. Largely to appease President Wilson's qualms over the Supreme Ruler's democratic credentials, Kolchak had first been asked to subscribe to a list of high-minded preconditions ranging from a pledge to hold free elections in any territory he controlled, to a promise to join the League of Nations. After the admiral had given his broad consent, the Allies confirmed an earlier provisional offer 'to assist the Government of Admiral Kolchak and his associates with munitions, supplies, food and the help of such as may volunteer for his service, to establish themselves as the Government of all Russia'. The vital word 'recognition' was missing. In a philosophical sense, this helped the Allies to act out the convenient fantasy that they could 'intervene without interfering' in Russia's domestic concerns. But the omission hinged on something much more down to earth. By the time that telegram from the 'Allied and Associated Powers' in Paris was despatched to Omsk, the admiral was already looking like a lost cause.

There is no purpose in describing here the extraordinary gyrations of fortune which swirled around the Siberian battlefields in the spring and summer of 1919. No new light can be thrown from secret intelligence archives on this confused campaign because the Deuxième Bureau, the only one of the three Western intelligence services operating in Siberia, supplied no military surveys. As for the guidance provided at the time from other sources (Allied military missions, consular posts, Red Cross officials, commercial representatives and so on) this had only one common factor: it was nearly always wrong.

Thus the Allies had been agreeably surprised to the point of astonishment by the initial success of Kolchak's spring offensive. On 14 March 1920, his troops, streaming forward from the Ural Mountains, had retaken from the Bolsheviks Ufa, the former base of White Russian government in Siberia, which lay to the north-west of its new capital at Omsk. A month later, Kolchak was threatening another one-time White capital, Samara, the key to central Siberia and less than 500 miles from Moscow itself. Kolchak's northern forces, which had retaken Perm at Christmas, destroying the third Bolshevik Army in the process, were moving further up the railway line leading to Vologda and, ultimately, Petrograd. (The Army's commander was the 28-year-old former Czech officer Rudolf Gayda, who had once led the legion.) Combined with the surging advance of Denikin's Volunteer Army in the south (which also had Moscow in its long-distance sights) it all looked too good to be true; and it was.

At the end of April the Red Army, strengthened by fresh troops drawn from the Ukraine and Turkestan, counter-attacked, smashing the left wing of Kolchak's forces. Though Gayda continued for a while to press forward on the northern Siberian front, it was soon all over for the admiral's forces in the south, and a general retreat, sometimes descending into a disorderly rout, set in remorselessly on all sectors. On 4 June the Red Army retook Ufa; on 1 July Perm; on 14 July Ekaterinburg; on 23 July Chelyabinsk;[10] and on 23 July Kurgan. By 12 August, Kolchak had been driven back across the Ural River near Orenburg; three days later, he had retreated behind the River Tobol; and by the end of the month Soviet troops had entered Tobolsk.

By September, mixed signals were coming from the Allied camp. Ships laden with rifles, millions of rounds of ammunition and other war material were still being landed for Kolchak at Vladivostok; on the other hand the Middlesex Regiment, one of the two British Army units 'protecting' the Supreme Ruler, sailed for home from that same port on 6 September. The other battalion, the Hampshires, remained for a while and Knox was still there with his Military Mission, though doubtless feeling that its days were numbered. There was a brief glimmer of hope in the middle of September when, after more reverses, Kolchak's forces counter-attacked and drove the Red Army back almost a hundred miles in the Tobolsk sector. But that was like the last convulsion of a dying animal.

Throughout October, the Bolshevik troops were able to resume their steady march eastwards. By the end of the month (when the Hampshires were also embarking for home) they had taken the key town of Petropavlovsk, only 170 miles from Kolchak's capital. A fortnight later, on 15 November, they entered Omsk in triumph. In the battles before the city, whole regiments of Kolchak's forces were captured, together with several divisional headquarters. Some of the latter had been riven by mutiny, with soldiers shooting their officers before surrendering in their name. In Omsk itself, the Reds took some 40,000 prisoners, including nine generals and a thousand other officers. Kolchak and the remnants of his government had already retired eastwards along the railway line. They left behind them 2,000 machine guns, 30,000 spare sets of uniform and four million rounds of ammunition, together with vast stockpiles of artillery shells and high explosives. These on-the-spot estimates, which were later roughly confirmed, had been supplied by a Mr Emerson of the American Railway Commission which was still working on the Siberian line – a graphic illustration of the distinctly unofficial intelligence on which the West often had to rely.

It is worth noting that the Red Army's eventual victory in Siberia was not due to any significant superiority in numbers or equipment. Nor was it the product of any grand master-plan being systematically implemented by the commanders in the field. In such a vast terrain, one successful flanking raid could open the way to a great sweep forward, so that tactics often shaped strategy. In any case, the determining factor was not ability or capacity to fight so much as morale once battle was joined. When the crunch came, the Bolshevik forces, held together by savage discipline as well as by a broadly shared revolutionary creed, maintained a unity denied to Kolchak's army, split as it had always been by squabbles in the field and political dissension in the rear.

Whatever the causes, that army was now in tatters, and so was the regime which had raised and commanded it. The question loomed: what was to become of the Supreme Ruler himself? His fate turned into a sombre tale, not without taints of betrayal, the most blatant of which came from an unexpected quarter.

In July, Kolchak had quarrelled with General Gayda, dismissed him as C-in-C and expelled him from Omsk. It was a dubious decision militarily, for Gayda had proved by far the most successful of the Siberian field commanders. But the young man, who departed eastwards in style in his own armoured train manned by his own Czech guards, proved equally effective as a political intriguer; and the victim for the plots which he now spun in Vladivostok was the admiral, on whom he had sworn revenge.

His tool was the Social Revolutionary Party, tolerated by the White Russians and their Allied protectors because the declared aim of its leaders was the defeat of its Bolshevik rivals. Gayda helped to raise SR command cells in key towns along the Siberian railway line, one of which was to prove deadly for the admiral. On 17 November, Gayda even tried to launch an uprising in Vladivostok itself but was thwarted by Kolchak's local commander, General Rosanov, who secured Japanese support. The young firebrand was captured and eventually shipped out of the port; but though he had departed the scene, his vengeance, as things turned out, was assured.

Nor was Gayda the only Siberian commander who was intriguing behind the admiral's back. The French secret intelligence files which can now be drawn on for the first time show that Kolchak's unsavoury Cossack partner, the Ataman Grigori Semenov, was developing political ambitions which encompassed an even wider field than Russia. In the autumn and early winter of 1919, the Deuxième Bureau's base at Vladivostok was closely monitoring the movements of a number of individuals setting out on special missions for the 'Atman de Campagne des Troupes Cosaques d'Extrême Orient' as Semenov was described. Some, like one Pierre Mikhailovich Tcherkess, a lieutenant of Signals, had been earmarked for special liaison missions to the White Russian commanders Denikin and Yudenich, to set up links with Cossack forces fighting in the south and north.[11]

By December, when it was clear that Kolchak's days in power were numbered, Semenov launched a bid to replace him on the world stage. French intelligence identified a group of people who had requested, and in some cases received, passports and visas to visit Europe, and even Canada, as political envoys of the Cossack leader.[12] These included Erich Freiberg, a Baltic colonel who had commanded one of Semenov's armoured trains; Vladimir Stepanov, now posing as a 'quick change artist' but who had earlier served as Freiberg's second in command; and one Michel Iogolevich, a Jewish medical doctor now posing as a purchaser of agricultural machinery. He had served at the front in 1916 and had latterly been living in New York. The same file contains a long survey of Semenov's campaign, warning against its dangers, especially arising from the Cossacks' strong pro-German sympathies. The paper is signed by General Lavergne (famous for his part in the Moscow events of 1918). Curiously enough for a file which is otherwise precisely sourced, there is no indication of where or when his signature was appended.

The fullest official account of Kolchak's final weeks was given by one Captain Stillings of the West Riding Regiment, an officer of Knox's mission attached to Kolchak and at the admiral's side throughout the final phase of the tragedy.[13] The end of the year found the Allied High Commissioners meeting at Irkutsk on the western shore of Lake Baikal to assess the situation. Kolchak, his army disintegrating at every stage of his flight, telegraphed them from Nijne Udinsk, 300 miles westwards up the line, to say that he had decided to transfer 'supreme power for the whole of Russia' (the great illusion was still being floated aloft in words) to General Denikin, his more successful opposite number in the south.[14] To sign and give effect to the act of transfer, he needed clearance for his train to continue eastwards, but henceforth under formal Allied protection. That message was received on 4 January 1920. The High Commissioners, who had already agreed to provide such protection if needed, sent the necessary orders to the Czech commander at Nijne Udinsk the following day and then returned to Vladivostok, imagining that the admiral's person was now secure, even if his army had been blown to pieces. They reckoned without the fluctuating military and political pressures of the day, the scruples of the admiral and, above all, the equivocation of General Janin, the Allied Commander-in-Chief in Siberia, who had agreed with their orders and was now supposed to execute them on the ground.

Kolchak had muddled the issue by telegraphing that, as only one wagon seemed to be available for his transport, he could not abandon his large retinue by simply steaming off and leaving them to their fate. He would therefore, if need be, stay behind with them and face whatever came. Janin, who had long disliked Kolchak as the nominee of the British, found his moral scruples too much to fathom, let alone stomach, in this frantic situation. He accordingly wired back telling the admiral that he was now on his own: no further responsibility could be accepted for his safety. The general was either unable or unwilling to seek the consent of the High Commissioners to this abandonment of their pledge.[15] Worse was to come.

Had Janin really washed his hands of everything to do with Kolchak, that might have given the beleaguered admiral a better chance of survival. As it was, his was the hand which, deliberately or not, struck Kolchak down. The Supreme Ruler's train arrived at Irkutsk on 15 January still bearing the trappings of status. The 'government' at Nijne Udinsk had carried out their orders and draped it in Allied flags; but real protection there now was none. When Janin, who was some miles away at the time, was asked what should be done with the admiral, he replied that Kolchak should be handed over to the so-called 'Political Centre' which was in control of Irkutsk. The centre was, in fact, a front party of the Social Revolutionary, Gayda's chosen instrument, and they promptly removed him, flags or not, to the district prison. When, a week later, the SRs handed over power to the increasingly dominant Military Committee of the local Bolsheviks, Kolchak's fate was sealed. At 2 a.m. on 6 February, the committee, alarmed that White Russian force might be threatening the town in order to liberate Kolchak, ordered his execution. Three hours later, without even the semblance of a trial, he was shot. They gave him even less in the way of a funeral. That same morning a hole was smashed in the ice of the river Ushakovka, which flowed through the town, and Kolchak's body was pushed through it – a riposte no doubt to the way in which a batch of thirty-one SR prisoners had been finally disposed of by the Cossacks the year before.

Captain Stillings's report, on which the above narrative has been mainly based, was circulated in the the War Office before being passed on to the Cabinet. A staff colonel with an indecipherable signature entered the first comment on the Minute Sheet: 'This version exonerates Janin.' His superior, the Director of Military Operations (a major-general with an equally unreadable surname), had a different view. He commented acidly: 'I cannot imagine any British officer behaving like Janin.'[16] Winston Churchill, the War Minister who circulated the paper, did so without comment. The Foreign Office made it plain that it would take no action in the matter.

General Denikin later accused Janin directly of Kolchak's betrayal.[17] Janin himself (ignoring the wise French maxim '*Qui s'ex-*

cuse, s'accuse') issued a somewhat hysterical defence of his actions, claiming, among other things, that he had been no more able to save Kolchak at Irkutsk than anyone could have rescued the Tsar at Ekaterinburg. Whatever the truth, the end of Kolchak, on whom all hopes had been based, automatically meant the end of Allied involvement. On 19 February, less than a fortnight after his execution, Lord Curzon, who had succeeded Balfour as Foreign Secretary, told the French government that 'in view of the present situation in Siberia, we propose to abolish the post of High Commissioner'.[18] Ten days later, the French followed suit.

On 12 March when the British office in Vladivostok was formally wound up, the Foreign Office engaged in a little banter at the expense of the failed venture which their department had once supported. 'So ends a not very creditable enterprise,' minuted Lord Hardinge. His fellow ex-viceroy replaced the 'not very' with 'highly dis-'.[19] There was not a word of regret over the admiral's end nor of tribute to what he had struggled to achieve on their behalf. The ice was closed over Kolchak's cause just as firmly as it had closed over his body.

12

Petrograd and the Baltic Tangle

No leader who could hold even a Russian candle to Kolchak emerged in the north. Moreover, compared with the breathtaking sweeps of the Siberian campaign, there were only pigmy-like movements across this dreariest of landscapes – much of it swampy forests of pine and birch. It was sweltering in the brief summer when the sun never set, making sleep a problem, and piercing cold in the Arctic night of winter, when barely two hours of milky daylight broke into the gloom.

As we have seen, the initial Allied landings in Murmansk and Archangel during the summer of 1918 had been designed to protect the vast stores of war supplies[1] stockpiled in both ports and prevent them from falling into German hands. By the beginning of 1919, a mixed force of over 18,000 men was garrisoned at Archangel, with 6,220 British, 5,100 Americans and 1,680 French as the main Allied contingents. At Murmansk, a separate command, there were some 16,000, mostly British and Russian, with only 700 French and no Americans at all.[2] But by now Germany was out of the war and, though the Allies were still to find themselves entangled with German troops in the nearby Baltic provinces, the case for defending the ports seemed over. The British had always been the prime movers in these operations, largely owing to the key role which their navy played throughout in northern waters. Fittingly, it was the War Cabinet in London which, on 4 March 1919, took the lead over evacuation: British forces would be withdrawn in the early summer of that year.

Then, three weeks later, came one of those quirky little happenings which were always shaking up the Russian kaleidoscope. A volunteer reconnaissance detachment of ten British and five French soldiers, led by a British officer, had set out from Archangel on a risky trip through Bolshevik territory to probe the extent of Kolchak's great spring offensive, which was then sweeping in from the east. Towards the end of the month, this tiny Anglo-French party had covered 400 miles all the way to the western foothills of the Urals, and there, on the Pechora River, they met up with some of the admiral's advance guards. Could this be the signal for reviving that old master-plan of linking up the White Russian armies of the north and east in order to strike the decisive blow against the Bolshevik regime? Not surprisingly, the man who made the most of the signal was Winston Churchill, three months into his new post as War Minister. For him, the rendezvous on the Pechora brought visions of the Allies handing over to a secure anti-Bolshevik government in the north, while both Petrograd and Moscow fell under the direct sights of the combined White Russian armies. For the Allies, this would spell an evacuation not only in honour but in triumph.

As we have seen, the stemming of Kolchak's offensive by one vicious counter-attack on his left flank, followed by the general retreat of his forces, eventually put paid to all such grand designs. In any case, General Janin, who, as Allied Commander-in-Chief, had done so much to frustrate British policy in Siberia, vetoed Churchill's most ambitious plan[3] the moment he heard of it in early July. This would have meant that the axis of repatriation for his beloved Czechs would have switched away from Vladivostok and the Siberian railway up to the British-dominated Arctic. Clemenceau had opposed any such idea in 1918 and the French were even less inclined to support it a year later.

By now, however, Churchill had contrived to have British reinforcements despatched to Archangel despite the doubts of his colleagues and in the teeth of a public opinion climate dead set against the notion of risking even one more soldier (or one more penny) in the anti-Bolshevik cause. The pretext was that the existing garrisons there were now so weakened and demoralized that they faced annihilation by the Red Army before they could eventually board their transports for home. Churchill sold the idea to his Cabinet by claiming that the extra troops were needed 'to secure the health, comfort and nourishment' of the garrison forces. It was sold to the nation by raising the British reinforcements (two brigades each of 4,000 men) entirely from volunteers, all apparently eager to rescue their comrades from Bolshevik clutches in the frozen north. To demonstrate how evil those clutches were, a stream of atrocity stories had been fed to the British press.[4] Whether or not it was these stories which had shocked President Wilson into a response, a modest contribution was finally secured from the Americans. It looked appropriately non-combatant: two companies of engineers, one for maintenance and one for operations, to work on the Murmansk railway.

It was, of course, true that the Allied garrisons in the Arctic ports were of poor quality and dubious morale. The British units were largely made up of Category 'B' men, matching those in the 'Hernia Battalion' of Siberia; the Americans were fit but totally untrained; while the French soldiers, like their comrades afloat, had had whatever fighting spirit was left in them sapped almost to extinction by revolutionary propaganda. Mutinies had taken place, mostly in Russian battalions serving under Allied command but some in mixed or even all-British units.

On the other hand, the relief army was, by itself, two brigades strong, each of 4,000 men. Moreover, it had showed itself capable of grit and determination in action against the Bolshevik forces, once the redoubtable Major-General Edmond Ironside had been installed as its commander.[5] Indeed, the final assault he masterminded on Bolshevik positions as a preparatory screening operation for the evacuation ended with one of the most stinging tactical defeats which the Red Army had ever suffered at Allied hands in the field. He launched his attack with 3,000 British and 1,000 Russians on 10 August 1919, his target the Bolshevik forces astride the Drina River, roughly halfway to Kotlas. The enemy was outflanked and routed, losing some 6,000 men – killed, wounded or taken prisoner. The losses of the Allied brigades were fewer than 150 with no prisoners taken. For a while, there was even talk of their marching right down to Kotlas, to effect a major link-up with Kolchak's men.

Ironside could never have taken Petrograd with his miniature army, however reinforced and led. But it could have given useful backing to a major White Russian assault on the old capital which, the left-wing press in England argued, had been its real aim.[6] Indeed, the thought can never have been far from Churchill's mind, which accepted the inevitability of Allied evacuation only when the collapse of Kolchak's army had become irreversible.[7] But why, even without the support of an Allied intervention force in the field, was Petrograd never taken? We have seen, in a previous chapter, how the Bolshevik-held city had seemed on the point of surrender in the summer of 1919, when Paul Dukes was still operating there and Lieutenant Agar, officially only 'C's' contact man, was busy in a sideline activity of crippling the Red Fleet at Kronstadt with his Skimmers. Part of the reason lay then in the ruthlessness and ferocity, as witnessed by both agents, with which the local Soviets, inspired by Trotsky, were bludgeoning both the garrison and the civil population into resistance. Any Red Army officer even suspected of failing in his duty knew that his wife and children would be shot out of hand. Whenever resistance flickered up inside the city confines, it was crushed without mercy, as the mutineers at the Krasnaya Gorka had learned when their fortress was reduced to rubble by the pounding of Red naval guns.

There was nothing on the White Russian side to match this iron will and the clamps of discipline it imposed on soldiers and civilians alike. Almost the contrary. The commander of the North-Western Army investing Petrograd was the elderly General Nikolai Nikolayevich Yudenich. He had been appointed by Kolchak in April 1919 and supplied with gold from the hoard seized by the Czechs (some of which seems to have stuck to his hands). He was to show, in this supreme test, little of the fiery reputation won when fighting the Turks in the Caucasus; and once General Mannerheim, who had driven the Bolsheviks out of Finland, declined to join in a further offensive eastwards,[8] Yudenich was on his own as regards ground troops.

These, admittedly, were not very impressive. A French secret service report has survived which dates from the time of the build-up to the final battle for Petrograd. It paints a sorry picture of the state the besieging forces were in:[9] 'The army until very recently has been deprived of essentials. The men have not drawn any pay for the past three months. Three-quarters of them are bare-footed and clad any old how [à la diable]. There is an almost total lack of arms and ammunition which prevents operational developments.' However, the report adds, this last problem had been alleviated by the arrival, on 12 August, of two British military transport vessels at the Estonian port of Reval. Among the supplies they unloaded for Yudenich were 'four small tanks, thirty howitzers, ammunition and 10,000 sets of uniform'.

The deliveries noted by the French were only part of the total British aid rushed out to the Baltic for the planned assault on Petrograd in the early autumn. When Yudenich launched his final offensive, on 12 October 1919, his North-Western Army of some 17,000 men (now mostly wearing boots and proper uniforms) went into action with 57 heavy guns, around 700 light artillery and machine guns and two armoured trains, the real battleships of Russian land fighting. This was modest compared with the extravagant requests the general had been putting forward. One of his shopping lists, passed to London via Paris in the spring, for example, had demanded no fewer than 50,000 rifles with 3,000 rounds per rifle, 30,000 machine guns and 200 field guns. Then, almost as an afterthought, he tacked on: 'Required, 100 tanks.'[10]

That preposterous addendum is quite in keeping with the impressions of the man which his contemporaries have passed down. The picture which emerges is a cardboard caricature of the Tsarist generalissimo, all show and no substance. A British newspaper correspondent was impressed most of all by his magnificent moustaches and his seemingly limitless capacity to absorb alcohol, 'a head which defies the utmost efforts of the unbridled hospitality of his hand', as the journalist elegantly phrased it.[11] Lord Curzon regarded him politically as a dangerous loose cannon, reactionary to the point of dreaming how to re-annexe all the neighbouring Baltic provinces into a new Greater Russia of the Romanovs. Most damning was the professional verdict passed on Yudenich by the great soldier whose help he had sought in vain. Mannerheim found him 'physically slack and entirely lacking in those inspiring qualities which a political and military leader of his standing should possess'.

It was this lack of leadership which sapped the determination of the North-Western Army in action. Indeed, there was a lack of any top-line presence at all at the front. Yudenich had left the field command to General Rodzianko, a cavalry officer and renowned international sportsman with whom, in true Russian fashion, he had been squabbling almost down to the day the attack was launched. Once battle was joined, Yudenich remained, in great comfort, at his base headquarters in Narva nearly fifty miles behind the line.

At first, things went well; not surprisingly, as the raw Seventh Red Army defending Petrograd was initially no stronger and far less well-equipped than its attackers.[12] These were also enjoying some highly unusual combat support from their principal backers. The supplies finally delivered to Yudenich had included six Mark V tanks with a detachment of fifty officers and men from the Tank Corps, commanded by one Lieutenant-Colonel Hope-Carson. Officially they were all instructors, sent out to teach the North-Western Army how to use the machines. But, as with Lieutenant Agar and his torpedo boats, the temptation to get into battle proved too much. Carson's tanks were in action almost from the day they were unloaded, at first around Narva and finally on the outskirts of Petrograd itself. The shock of seeing these strange contraptions coming at them head on did even more damage to Seventh Army morale than their six-pounder guns, and they were scurried around by Rodzianko from point to point until the machines started to break down and their crews were exhausted.

Nor was this the only combat help which the British extended to their protégés. The guns of Cowan's Baltic Fleet covered the landing of Yudenich's forces near the ruins of the Krasnaya Gorka coastal fortress, now again in Bolshevik hands, while the hotch-potch squadron of British Camels and sea-planes which had been in action during Agar's exploits now launched another series of bombing raids, losing four pilots killed in the process. Casualties like these highlighted the tricky problem of explaining to a restive public opinion at home why British servicemen were still risking their lives in obscure Russian causes long after the German war had ended. The answer hit upon was to present them all as volunteers. Like all the best lies, the outer shell enclosed a kernel of truth; but it amounted to another exercise in deception. The Allies had started off with the suspect formula that, though they were intervening in the Russian power struggle, they were not interfering with it. Now that the interference was palpable, it was excused as being only voluntary, and therefore bearing no official status.

Had Petrograd fallen that would, of course, have been excuse enough. But Petrograd did not fall. The White Russian story as it unfolded on other fronts was re-enacted here. Rodzianko made sweeping advances, capturing Yamberg after a ten-mile advance on the first day. In the next four days his forces covered another sixty miles to take the town of Gachina. After Bolshevik troops had again panicked at the mere sight of British tanks, Rodzianko set up his headquarters in the Tsarist palaces of Tsarskoe Selo, in the suburbs of the old capital. By 20 October, he was on the Pulkovo hills, with the city whose centre was now only ten miles way spread out beneath, seemingly inviting capture.[13] Then his fortunes suddenly changed.

It was White Russian sloppiness and Bolshevik dynamism which combined, first to hold, then to repulse and finally to tear into pieces the North-Western Army. The sloppiness was in failing, during the advance, to cut important railway lines into the city, along which reinforcements from the garrison could be fed. It was the dynamism of Leon Trotsky which made sure that those reinforcements were raised off the streets and then hurled into battle. Lenin's ubiquitous War Minister had gone to Petrograd during the previous winter to sort out the troubles in the Soviet Fleet. Now, on 16 October 1919, he was back again, this time to galvanize the Seventh Red Army into action, and save the city in the process. Unlike Yudenich, who still languished in the rear, Trotsky led from the front, on horseback, turning retreating troops round and driving them again into the attack. When inspired or terrorized like this, Bolshevik troops could fight with a frenzy which the stolid valour of the White Russians could never match.

As with Kolchak's armies in the east, so now in the north retreat turned into rout. By mid-November, the North-Western Army troops had been driven back 150 miles, past Yamberg, and hard against the Estonian border. An epidemic of typhus struck them even harder than the Bolsheviks on the retreat, killing some 11,000 men. At the end of the month, the army of Yudenich on which so many hopes had been pinned and (thanks largely to Churchill) so much British treasure spent[14] had ceased to exist as a fighting force. The survivors were allowed to cross the frontier but only after being disarmed. Their commander lingered on for a while in the Estonian capital, Reval, where, thanks to Kolchak's gold, he and his staff were able to live in style at the city's Golden Eye Hotel. Eventually Yudenich managed to board ship for France, where he settled as yet another piece of human flotsam on the ebb-shore of Tsarism. Petrograd, renamed Leningrad, was not to be threatened again until the autumn of 1941 when Hitler's tank commanders looked down from those same Pulkovo heights on a Soviet city that would again defy its besiegers.

The tussle between the Allies and the Bolsheviks on Russian soil is what we have been concerned with, particularly where any fresh light could be thrown on that scene from the parallel conflict between the rival secret services. In the north, the key to the battle, once Allied intervention forces had been withdrawn from Archangel and Murmansk, was the White Russian attempt to take Petrograd, whose failure helped to secure Bolshevik control over the country as a whole. But close to Petrograd, on what, officially, was now no longer Russian soil, lesser battles had raged as the old Baltic provinces of Tsarist Russia fought to win their statehood which the Lenin regime had promised them. It is a tangled tale, best summarized separately from the Petrograd campaign, if only because hardly anything in the story is straightforward. The tangle begins with the very nature of the three emerging states: Estonia, Latvia and Lithuania, to take them north to south down the Baltic Sea.

Though part of the Tsarist Empire since the days of Peter the Great, the bulk of their populations was not even Slavonic, let alone Russian in character. Riga, the Latvian capital, had, for example, been founded by the fighting Bishop Albert of Bremen as far back as 1201 and the Order of the Knights of the Sword which he created a year later set a German stamp on these Baltic lands which the two centuries of Tsarist rule had never effaced. Commerce was in the hands of the merchants of the Hanseatic towns, who came in the wake of the German soldiers. The countryside was dominated by the estates of the so-called Baltic Barons, most of them distant descendants of those medieval Knights of the Sword and as tough, closed and hidebound a feudal class as could be found anywhere in Europe.

Not surprisingly, they were hated by the population at large, and especially by the peasantry, on whose backs they rode. The barons were both the symbols and the instruments of reaction. In Tsarist times, they had joined with gusto in suppressing any stirrings of liberal or nationalist feeling. The Russian revolution presented them with the more serious threat of Bolshevik regimes set up locally in the Baltic capitals. But by now they had an all-powerful ally on hand who was very much to their taste – the German imperial army. In the spring of 1918, this had struck north from East Prussia, overrunning the provinces which, for the next six months, were ruled as a German colony. The Balts, as the barons and their Latvian henchmen were called, were enchanted to see a German military governor shooting nationalist leaders and decreeing that German should be the sole language of instruction in Baltic schools. To their delight and surprise, an even more inspiring saviour arrived on the scene some ten weeks after the German surrender.

On 1 February 1919, a quintessential Prussian officer, Major-General Count Rüdiger von der Goltz, blue-eyed and square-jawed, disembarked at the Latvian port of Libau to take command of the local German garrison and the VI Reserve Corps. It was the victorious Allies who had sanctioned, indeed ordered, the continual presence of these troops and von der Goltz had himself been appointed on an Allied mandate. There were compelling reasons for this topsy-turvy situation. The Bolsheviks were by now strongly entrenched in the Baltic lands (the Libau area was, for example, almost the only part of Latvia not in their hands at the time) and the only forces capable of taking them on were the Germans.

The nascent Baltic states were still struggling to raise small armies of their own, while the various freebooter White Russian bands which roamed these lands were incapable of agreeing with one another, let alone tackling the common foe. The problem had been foreseen when Article XII was written into the peace terms. This stated that German forces still anywhere outside their national frontiers at the time of the general laying down of arms should return home when the Allies 'shall think the moment suitable, having regard to the internal situation of these territories'.

What neither the peace-makers in Paris – nor anybody else – had foreseen was that Rüdiger von der Goltz would prove an even worse headache for them than the Bolsheviks he had been sent to deal with. It was a classic case of the cure proving worse than the ailment, for the count had already resolved on landing to redraw the post-war map of Europe. His dream was to create a new Teutonic superstate in the east which would recompense his defeated countrymen for the imperial realm they had just lost in the west. Its ruling race would be the indigenous Germans, reinforced by thousands of new colonizers from the homeland; its subject people the Slavs, incorporating not merely those of the Baltic provinces but as many Russians as could be absorbed further north. For him, this was not foreign conquest but the restoration of a racial patrimony. Riga had, after all, been founded by Germans as far back as 1201. Now, after more than seven centuries of vicissitudes, a new Bishop Albert had landed on those Baltic shores, a man who seemed well equipped for the task in both mind and mettle.[15] His crusade is the key to much of what happened in the muddled conflict of 1919. Part of the muddle was that, though the Allies were fighting the Red Army, through direct involvement as well as through their surrogates, they were not formally at war with Soviet Russia (a paradox which teased Balfour's intellect when contemplating the 'legality' of imposing a blockade). There was just as much built-in confusion over the Germans. The forces of General Goltz were de facto partners in the struggle to expel the Bolsheviks from the Baltic provinces, yet they remained the troops of the defeated enemy. Allied support would have to be tailored accordingly.

The British were throughout the leaders among the Allied powers in all these northern Russian campaigns, their naval power dominating their involvement. It was only natural, therefore, that the first formula for squaring the German army circle in the Baltic should have come from the Admiralty in London. At the end of 1918, a light cruiser squadron based in Copenhagen was being readied for active service in the Baltic. What instructions should be given to its commander, Rear-Admiral Sinclair, especially regarding operations in Estonia, which was under Bolshevik threat? The Admiralty, together with the Foreign Office, produced the following formula:

> As regards naval support to the Estonians, it was agreed that in the event of their fighting with the Bolshevik forces, Admiral Sinclair should be at liberty to support them by his guns from the sea but that under no circumstances should we put ourselves in the position of metaphorically [sic] fighting shoulder to shoulder with German troops who might be acting

> in concord with the Estonians and we should not concern
> ourselves with any German military activities . . . in a district
> removed from the coast.

To make matters slightly less metaphorical and rather more muddling, the admiral was, however, authorized 'to send a party of, say, Marines, ashore on the recognised sort of mission that has hitherto been carried out in coastal warfare by the navy'.[16] In the event the marines were to stay on board, though British naval guns fired more than once to support the energetic Goltz.

The general eventually succeeded in raising a regular army of more than 30,000 men, whose core was his so-called 'Iron Division'. Far less regular, and much more disturbing, was the so-called 'Army of Western Russia' which he had raised partly from demobilized German soldiers in the homeland. These were to be the first volunteers for his Teutonic Empire dream, having been lured to the Baltic on the express promise of land and long-term settlers' rights. This had helped to swell their numbers to around 12,000 men, who clearly spelt trouble if the pledge were to be carried out – and even more so if it were broken. To make the prospect more unsettling, Goltz had selected for their commander one of the loosest cannons to be seen anywhere on the heaving Russian deck: Colonel Prince Paul Bermondt-Avalov, a military freebooter from Georgia devoted to the German cause. A British intelligence intercept from Berlin showed that even the White Russians were involved in the affair: Russian émigrés were trying to work out a deal with the Weimar Republic under which the new Germany would be given massive economic and financial aid to fight the Bolsheviks in return for a charter of colonization in the Baltic. Other intercepts spoke of Bermondt-Avalov snapping up more recruits from Russian prisoners of war handed over to the Germans.

The secret service was, of course, continuously involved, alongside regular military intelligence channels, in answering two vital questions: what was Goltz really up to and what resources did he have at his command? Not surprisingly, the French were the most concerned, dreading as they did anything which might herald a resurgence of German power anywhere on the continent. The activities of Bermondt-Avalov were a prime secret intelligence target, as shown by two long reports of the Deuxième Bureau which were presented in the spring of 1919.[17]

One puts the total of Germans serving with Bermondt-Avalov as 'several thousand' as opposed to the officially admitted figure of 600. Several senior German army officers were said to be among his recruits, including one major from the General Staff. They were serving alongside an estimated 4,000 Russian officers and men recruited by Bermondt-Avalov. The other report, among much technical detail, offers two opposing perspectives from which the Bermondt-Avalov menace could be viewed – and concludes with engaging frankness that it simply cannot decide between them (leaving this to higher Deuxième Bureau authorities, who possessed a wider range of reports).

The fairly harmless view of Bermondt-Avalov's forces ran as follows: 'They are supposed to be engaged in fighting the Bolsheviks. But according to our agents who have succeeded in gaining the confidence of some of them, they are very little inclined to go on fighting a war. They are well paid and could easily turn into pillagers in the Baltic lands.'

The alternative scenario was much more alarming. Other informants had told French agents that the secret purpose of Bermondt-Avalov's 'Army of Western Russia' (which, as British intelligence had confirmed, maintained its recruiting base in Berlin) was not so much to fight the Bolsheviks in the Baltic as to suppress their Communist comrades, the Spartakists, in the German capital. 'This would amount to a monarchist plot. The money to finance some of these detachments would be provided by one of the Krupp syndicates.'[18]

Substantiated or not, the very existence of reports like this only heightened concern at the highest Western level to get rid of Goltz and his unsavoury White Russian *condottieri* as soon as was practicable, if not before. Clemenceau was understandably the most insistent when the subject was debated at the Allied Supreme

Council in Paris.[19] The mere mention of the dreaded Krupp armament concern having a finger in the politics of post-war Germany
was enough to make 'The Tiger' bare his claws. The problem was:
how could the Prussian general and his satraps be removed from
the scene once their immediate usefulness was over?

The Allies were not helped by the problems of direct communication which they had created for themselves. The so-called
chains of command they had set up functioned more as a festoon
of loose ribbons when it came to passing effective orders up to the
Baltic. The British had despatched to the area (apart from Sinclair
and his naval squadron) two missions with different remits
reporting primarily to different masters. Their Military Mission
(described in an ambivalent phrase as 'possessing an inter-allied
character') arrived in Latvia in the early summer, headed by a very
senior officer, Lieutenant-General Sir Herbert Gough, a jovial
Anglo-Irish cavalryman with a controversial war record.[20] His task
was to quell the Bolsheviks, thus helping the three provinces
towards statehood, and above all to get rid of Goltz. He reported
in the first instance to the War Office and to the British delegation at the Paris peace conference. Then there was Colonel Stephen
Tallents, a former Irish Guards officer who had been wounded and
invalided out of the army in 1916 to take up a series of posts in
Whitehall, concerned mainly with food supplies. He now arrived
in Latvia at about the same time as Gough, as the head of a diplomatic and economic mission. His remit partly overlapped that of
the general but his master was the Foreign Office, to whom his
reports were sent. Neither of the two departments in London shared
all their information with the other; nor did either repeat everything to their political chiefs in Paris.[21]

These worthies faced enough complications of their own in
imposing their will on the Baltic muddle. As there was as yet no
formal recognition of the post-war republic declared in Germany,
the Allies had to work at first through the German Armistice
Commission in Paris and then through the German Peace
Delegation at Versailles. Only after May 1919 could their own Baltic

missions[22] be brought into play alongside the German authorities in Berlin, fully recognized or not. By now Count Rüdiger von der Goltz was well established as the main Allied headache.

Following repeated Allied complaints that the Prussian commander was resorting to every excuse to delay the withdrawal of his forces, Goltz had been summoned back to Berlin in the spring for talks. But Allied hopes that this would bring a swift end to his mission were dashed when the general returned to the Baltic more arrogant than ever.[23] At the same time, he became more effective than ever in discharging his anti-Bolshevik task. On 25 May, his troops took the Latvian capital Riga by storm, driving out the Red Army garrison which had carried out a reign of terror in the city since the beginning of the year. (A White Russian terror of reprisals promptly followed.)

The capture of Riga marked the high point of Goltz's prowess and prestige. There is a revealing account[24] of a conference he attended with Gough in Latvia on 19 July in which the two generals discuss the current position on terms of absolute equality, as though they were Allied officers having a businesslike talk, as opposed to one being the spokesman of the victors imposing their will on the local representative of the vanquished. The Germans turned up with a 'delegation' which even outnumbered the strong five-man British team. Goltz also made it clear from the start that he was not going to be out-gunned. He had, he said, received no instructions from Berlin about German withdrawal, which he intended to carry out based purely on 'military considerations'. They would require a total of 214 trains to effect the withdrawal (evacuation by road was not an option given 'the inflamed state of Lettish opinion'). If the lines were cleared and proper rolling stock provided, the operation might be completed in thirty-seven days. Otherwise it would take twice that time. The British side seem to have accepted both the demands and the time-tables without comment, though their verdict, as passed to London, was that Goltz was merely obstructing the withdrawal 'in the hope that some excuse for their further intervention in the country might arise'.[25]

Goltz did not attempt to deny that he had recently received fresh troop reinforcements; these, he said, were purely for 'railway protection'.

Even the future of the Landeswehr, a 2,000-strong local force of Balts, was used as another pretext for delay. Gough had insisted that all the Germans fighting in it should be dismissed for repatriation and a fresh commander appointed.[26] The process would take some time, Goltz replied, and would further delay his evacuation. It was only now that Gough asked the question which ought to have set the mood of the meeting from the start: did or did not General Goltz recognize the Peace Treaty signed on 28 June by Germany at Versailles which imposed on him the obligation to withdraw?[27] The response as rendered by the translator was a plain affirmative. What the Prussian actually mumbled was that he 'had nothing against it' ('*Er hätte nichts dagegen*').

As things turned out, the Germans managed to prolong the withdrawal of their Baltic forces long after Goltz's 'maximum' time-table of seventy-four days. After sustained top-level Allied pressure on Berlin,[28] he was finally dismissed as Commanding General on 3 October 1919, and departed, still spitting defiance. In an interview given to the military journal *Die Trommel* six days later, for example, he attacked the 'shameless ultimatum of the Entente', derided the Berlin government for bowing to it, and declared that German soldiers and German settlers would stay on to continue the struggle against Bolshevism whatever the authorities at home might do or say.[29] The evacuation by rail of the bulk of the 'Iron Division' was not, in fact, completed until early December. Even then, other elements of the army were making for the Lithuanian port of Memel with the intention (so Allied intelligence supposed) of keeping a strike force in being to overthrow their own government in Berlin.

In the end, it was the steadily expanding armies of the new provincial governments which, with Allied and White Russian help, drove the last German units from the Baltic. Lenin had also given up any hope of hanging on to the provinces, whose independent statehood was recognized when Russia signed three separate peace treaties with them during 1920.[30] The Baltic governments, together with Finland, had started their negotiations with Moscow in the early autumn, a move which had a direct impact on the impending White Russian offensive against Petrograd. Yudenich had been counting on the support of Estonian troops (the pick of the Baltic forces) for his attack and a joint action plan had indeed been drawn up under British supervision.

The peace talks certainly put an end to that. Yet it remains dubious whether a few thousand more Estonians would have swung the battle in favour of the attacking force. Had they been led into action by a commander who was the White Russian equivalent of General Count Rüdiger von der Goltz, however, it could easily have been a very different story. As it was, the year 1920 saw the end both of the Bolshevik and of the German military menace to the Baltic states. The latter was to return with a vengeance in 1940, when Hitler's Wehrmacht snuffed out their twenty years of freedom.

13

Denikin: 'One Last Packet'

We left southern Russia at the beginning of 1919 after both General Poole, reporting to the War Office, and the Reilly–Hill mission, reporting to 'C', had sung the praises of General Denikin's Volunteer Army and pressed the need for further Allied military supplies. At the same time, they passed on the general's sober warning that even mountains of such aid would not be enough if he were expected to wrest the whole of European Russia, including Moscow, from the Bolshevik grasp. Allied soldiers would also be needed in large numbers, not to do the fighting, which his men would carry out, but to garrison towns in the vast hinterland of their advance, and guard the immensely long lines of communication.

The general had by then already notched up some successes in his mid-winter campaign; the spring offensive which followed brought more spectacular gains. During three weeks' action in May, his forces routed four Red Armies along the entire southern front from the Caspian to the Sea of Azov, capturing 22,000 prisoners, 150 guns, 350 machine guns, four armoured trains and 'an immense quantity of other booty'.[1] This was at the time when Goltz was at his most rampant up in the Baltic and when the ill-fated Admiral Kolchak was running into trouble in Siberia. Denikin, already Churchill's favourite, now seemed to be displacing the admiral as the White Russian to bet on. June 1919 was the month when British bets of all sorts were laid.

To begin with, some useful British military units arrived, including No. 47 Squadron of the RAF. This had been moved up from the Balkans, after the Allied victory there, to give direct air support to the Volunteer Army. The squadron, composed largely of Sopwith Camels, bombed Bolshevik targets for Denikin steadily throughout the summer, though its personnel, like the tank crews who also went into action, were officially only 'instructors'. Their most significant contribution was probably to the capture of the key Volga town of Tsaritsyn (famous in military annals as the Stalingrad of the Second World War). In the last days of June, as Denikin's army, helped by the British tanks, closed in on the town, the RAF squadron blasted away at 'enemy' wharves, railway yards, troop convoys and cavalry units all around the great Volga bend.[2] The squadron also developed a deadly system of dive-bombing in support of the Tsaritsyn action. They flew on ahead directly over the heads of the Bolshevik troops, scattering them so that they could be dealt with by the sabres of the White Russian cavalry who galloped close behind the planes.

This was just the sort of highly selective support for which both Poole and Reilly had argued. Churchill also followed their advice (though he scarcely needed the encouragement) over the despatch of a most impressive Military Mission to Denikin's headquarters. This eventually totalled no fewer than 356 British officers and over 1,000 other ranks, under the command of Major-General Herbert Holman, Poole's more forceful successor. Special service units and hordes of staff officers did not exhaust the encouragement Holman brought out. He also carried with him to Ekaterinodar the insignia of the Order of the Bath, which King George had been persuaded to bestow on Denikin. It can only have been Churchill who engineered this unique gesture of moral support. The Foreign Office knew nothing of it, and were furious. Their pursed-lip departmental comment on the matter noted that it was 'highly irregular' for such awards to be bestowed on non-British nationals without their previous blessing. The general, however, was enchanted by the decoration. Its ribbon was to bind him tightly to England.

Denikin's steady steamroller progress seemed almost too good to be true, especially when compared with the problems which

White Russian forces were facing on other fronts. Another expert survey was called for to judge just how far the steamroller could travel: was this indeed the military machine with the best prospects of crushing Bolshevism in its path? This brought 'C' into play again, for the need was for a political intelligence verdict to go with the military assessments of Holman's mission. And so Captain George Hill also turned up in Ekaterinburg at the beginning of June. Hill's was a solo mission (Reilly, though still employed by SIS, did not return with him) and it was set up in an unusual way. Possibly in order to overcome the appalling communication problems which had dogged the winter tour, Hill reported entirely through Foreign Office channels. Though copies of all his despatches were sent both to 'C' and to the War Office, the originals bear the extraordinary inscription 'Captain George Hill, 4th Manchester Regiment to Earl Curzon'.[3]

The good captain eventually developed a rush of blood to the head at the exalted company he was keeping but his reports remained throughout models of well-researched fieldwork.[4] They covered assessments of all three Territorial governments in southern Russia (the Kuban, the Don and the Terek); a brave attempt to analyse the anarchy and chaos which still convulsed the Ukraine; economic and political surveys and, above all, a judgement about the future of the Volunteer Army itself, by now under the nominal command of the Supreme Ruler in Siberia.[5] Hill's reports radiate confidence on Denikin's prospects; indeed the final victory of the combined White Russian forces is almost taken for granted. One sample of his optimism: 'Denikin may yet get to Moscow first but there is no doubt that he and Kolchak will eventually join up and form the most important factor in Russia.'

Hill had managed to get some of his couriers deep into Bolshevik territory and the stories they brought back sounded equally encouraging for the White Russian cause. Thus the food situation was reported as 'desperate', matching the mood of the regime. Lenin was said to be fearing not only the loss of Petrograd but of Moscow itself and preparations were therefore under way to evacuate the capital to the Ukraine. Though Kolchak was feared the most, the main concern of the regime in the short term was Denikin, whose advance on the Donetz basin would bring the loss of coal supplies and thus cripple the whole Bolshevik transport system.

In one 'Very Secret and Confidential' enclosure to Lord Curzon, Hill gave it as probable that the Bolsheviks would simply abandon their formal hold on power, scatter and go underground to continue their 'war against civilisation' from abroad. He adds: 'For over a year the Bolsheviks have been putting by for a "rainy day" and they now possess large stocks of platinum, some gold (gold is too bulky for them), diamonds and various other special stones, obtained by the nationalisation of jewellers' stores, confiscation from the bourgeoisie and plunder of the churches. In addition, they have managed to obtain a certain amount of valuta and in some countries they have bought landed property.'[6] This may have made startling reading, but later testimony was to show that the idea of a Bolshevik 'scuttle' in the summer of 1919 was not fanciful.[7]

In the meantime, everything that Hill sent back to London resounded as loud music in the ears of Winston Churchill, the interventionist par excellence. He was never in a majority in his own War Cabinet (and even less so, thanks to American diffidence in the Allied Supreme Council); yet Churchill's personality, the strength of his convictions and the eloquence with which he presented them ensured that he often carried the day-to-day arguments though not the ultimate decisions. It must be added that, throughout the summer, Denikin went on presenting the arguments for him, by force of arms instead of force of oratory. On 25 June, Kharkov fell to the Volunteer Army, and Tsaritsyn a week later. Denikin was already launching his 'final advance' on Moscow when, on 25 July, Churchill successfully presented the War Office plan to concentrate all future British military aid on the general, at the expense of Admiral Kolchak, who was reeling backwards in Siberia. Denikin was by now regarded almost as one of the family by the service departments in Whitehall. The Air Council, for example, had successfully proposed the appointment of a Russian air attaché in London to reflect the scale of what were coyly described as 'aeronautical relations' with the general.[8]

However, adopting Denikin as the new all-Russian saviour brought some deliberate political problems in its wake. Denikin had often been tarred, by liberal-minded observers in the West, with the label of a 'reactionary'. As far as the general was personally concerned, the accusation was mainly based on his declared plans for agricultural reform, which were the opposite of Kolchak's aims. Hill had spelt out the contrast in his report of 22 June 1919 to Lord Curzon: 'Denikin's policy stands for ... the restitution of landowners' property: all seized land to be handed back to the owners pending the final solution of the question, i.e. in every district a standard acreage will have to be taken and adhered to – any surplus being handed over to those not possessing land.' Kolchak's policy, on the other hand, seemed to be: 'Peasants to hold all that they now possess, including the land seized by them, pending the decision of the National Assembly.'

The danger of a political confrontation between the two White Russian leaders over the land issue grew ever more remote as it became increasingly unlikely that they would meet up in the first place. A bigger blot on Denikin's reputation were the pogroms launched against the Jewish colonies in towns taken by his troops. These reached horrendous proportions especially in the Ukraine, which the Volunteer Army occupied in September 1919. The persecutions were neither ordered by Denikin nor were they approved by him. But, like the excesses of some of his Cossack units, there was little he could do to prevent them. Anti-Semitism had been endemic in Tsarist Russia and the fact that so many of Lenin's henchmen, especially in the secret police, were Jewish had caused the virus to flare up again. In any case, the Jews usually had the valuables and were the natural targets for local looting.

The problem could be contained in and around headquarters and at other towns where Allied liaison units were stationed. The same, though only after immense pressure by General Holman, applied to some extent as regards lawlessness and corruption. Hill reported the clampdown on absentees and looters[9] which had taken effect in Ekaterinodar by the end of June. 'A special committee has been formed to control the towns and the railways and enforce order and discipline. Offenders are punished the first time, and treated as deserters under martial law if caught again . . . All restaurants now close at 11 pm . . . Places of amusement – unless they subscribe 50 per cent of their net proceeds to the army – are generally closed.'

From London, the War Minister took a personal hand in remonstrations with his White Russian protégé. Throughout the early autumn, he fairly bombarded the general with telegrams urging him to curb the pogroms and put his unruly house politically in order. At one point, Churchill even ruminated whether he might go out to southern Russia himself to help Denikin fashion a suitable new constitution for his country. These were the weeks when the sceptics in the Allied camp were also beginning to think that the Volunteer Army might be blazing the trail into a post-Bolshevik era. Even Lloyd George had to concede that Denikin now controlled much more than 'a backyard on the Black Sea', as he had contemptuously dismissed the general's position a year before. Through he still put the odds of the Volunteer Army's reaching Moscow at 'hardly an even chance', the wager could no longer be ignored. He had been forced to admit that Denikin now occupied an area of 20 million people, from which an army of 2½ million could be raised. And so, on 19 August 1919, the day that Denikin took both Kherson and Nikolaiev (while, in Siberia, Kolchak was fleeing back across the Tobol River) Churchill started to put together Britain's 'one last packet' of military aid for the battle in the south.

This had been agreed in principle by a somewhat dubious Cabinet the week before. Lloyd George made it clear that he still did not see Denikin as the future master of Russia. On the contrary, the packet was being offered to provide him with a bargaining counter to use in reaching some sort of power-sharing arrangement with Lenin. For the British Prime Minister, the best chance of a satisfactory peace in Russia now lay 'in the firm (but not too firm) consolidation of Denikin's position'. The final packet would carry the general up to the point where he was more than self-sufficient in coal, oil and food and he should negotiate with Lenin accordingly: 'If both sides were fairly strong Lenin would say "Denikin is powerful enough to prevent me getting any coal"; and Denikin, on his part, would say "Lenin is too powerful to give me any chance of reaching Moscow".'[10]

The idea that the apostle and executor of the great proletarian revolution would ever sit down with the White Russian leader, the declared champion of the landowners,[11] and amicably proceed to share power with him was a flight of Celtic fantasy on Lloyd George's part. It is doubtful whether he even believed in it himself. What the formula did provide was a face-saving device to accommodate both the fiery enthusiasm of his War Minister and the scepticism of most of his government colleagues. It was obvious that the struggle between the White Russians and the Bolsheviks would have to be resolved, not around a conference table, but on the battlefield.

For two more heady months, it looked as though this armed struggle would go Denikin's way. On 23 August, Denikin retook Odessa, scene of the French expeditionary fiasco. On 2 September, he entered the Ukrainian capital of Kiev and on 20 September, Kursk, the scene in the Second World War of the greatest tank battle in history. The first weeks of October brought still more sweeping gains. Voronezh fell to the Volunteer Army on 6 October, followed by Orel on 13 October. He was now only some 200 miles south of Moscow and pushed closer still when he took Navosil two days later. By now, mid-October 1919, Denikin's 'backyard' covered an area of 600,000 square miles free from Bolshevik rule, with some 50 million inhabitants spread across eighteen separate provinces. It was the sheer vastness and complexity of his military realm which, in the end, defeated Denikin – as he had, indeed, forecast both to General Poole and to Sydney Reilly when the great march north was being launched. Expansion without outside reinforcements for garrison work had made him weaker, not stronger. The over-stretched lines of communication gave the Volunteer Army spindly legs of paper. The moment the head was knocked back, the whole body would collapse.

That lethal blow was delivered by the Red Army at Orel, after Denikin had been in the town a bare week. By now the Red Army enjoyed a general superiority along the front of some 5:3 in manpower with a twofold superiority in artillery and machine guns. But, as with the savage flank attack, mounted by reserves, which had sent Kolchak reeling in the spring, so too, here at Orel it was a sudden encircling movement by Red Army reinforcements which stopped Denikin in his tracks. The Bolsheviks had mobilized a special assault force of Ukrainian cavalry and Latvian infantry (the Praetorian Guard yet again!) and sent it south of the town across Denikin's unguarded lines of communication to attack from the rear. His garrison of elite troops was driven out of the city only after bitter fighting which had seen a new star appear in the Red Army's ranks: General Simon Budyenny, who in the space of eighteen months had established himself as the finest cavalry commander anywhere on the battlefield.[12]

By now Denikin had been further weakened by troubles far behind the front line. His Cossacks, though professing allegiance, had often turned out to be allies in name only, as Reilly had predicted. Indeed, the Kuban Cossacks, after months of surly non-cooperation, came out in the autumn in an open revolt, which had to be suppressed by brute force. Another rebellion flared up at Dagestan, a mainly Moslem province on the Caspian Sea some 1,200 miles away to the south-east, just as the battle for Orel was at its height; some 15,000 men of the Volunteer Army had to be detached to deal with it. These again were typical of the problems endemic in a huge and thinly manned occupation zone, many of whose provinces were ethnic tangles which defied any attempt to sort them out. (Dagestan, for example, numbered thirty different nationalities, scattered among its mountain valleys. They were united only in their historic defiance of any outside rule, as the Tsars had found to their cost.)

But whatever the determining factors were, either at the face of battle or far behind it, the loss of Orel had marked the turning of the battle tide in the south. With it came the end of any threat to Moscow, the death of the White Russian cause in general and the consequent collapse of the Allied bid to fight an anti-Bolshevik war by proxy. The Volunteer Army made some determined stands, and even launched sporadic counter-attacks, as it retreated. But the ebb-tide dragged it inexorably back to the shores of the Black Sea from where it had surged north with such confidence in the spring. Kursk fell to the Red Army on 19 November, Kharkov on 11 December and Kiev on 16 December. On 31 December the Donetz basin was again in Bolshevik hands and with it those vital coalmines which Lloyd George had wanted to put up as a bargaining counter.

Lenin had no need to bargain now. Kolchak had fought his last battle in Siberia and was heading for imprisonment and execution; there was not one Allied soldier left in the Arctic ports; Petrograd was also safe, with the North-Western Army of General Yudenich in shreds, together with his reputation. The liquidation of the Volunteer Army in the south was the only task which stood between the Bolsheviks and total victory in 1920. It took longer than anyone – the Allies, the Red Army or even the White Russians themselves – expected because it was to be stretched over two quite separate phases.

The phase under Denikin's command lasted until the end of March. There was one last show of defiance on 20 February when his Volunteer Army, with uncertain Cossack support, took back Rostov from the Reds. But success here was even more fleeting than it had been at Orel the previous October: within three days, the Soviet Army had re-occupied this key city of the Don. Denikin's forces had delivered their final kick and they then crumpled. The headquarters town of Ekaterinodar fell on 15 March and everyone – soldiers, officials, camp followers, merchants and refugees alike – streamed into the port of Novorossisk, where Denikin and some 5,000 of his men were evacuated across the Black Sea to the temporary safety of the Crimea. It was from there that Denikin issued his last order of the day, appointing General Baron Wrangel, who had displayed great dash and determination in the field, to replace him as Commander-in-Chief of the Southern Armies.[13]

By now the British, always his only effective supporters, were preparing to abandon his cause for good and all. They had been wobbling for some weeks, despite all Churchill's efforts to drive the intervention policy forward. Indeed, a despairing telegram sent by General Holman on 16 February 1920 revealed that even the aid grudgingly promised by Lloyd George six months before had still not been fully delivered. 'Denikin needs the final packet and thanks you most sincerely for your promise to complete it,' the head of the Military Mission told his War Minister.[14]

At the end of March, Denikin was formally requested to hoist the flag of surrender in a telegram from the Cabinet inviting him 'to give up the struggle'. The latest of a series of emissaries, Brigadier-General Terence Keyes, installed as chief political officer of the British Military Mission, was instructed 'to urge on him that Russian interests would best be served by making peace at once' and that, furthermore, Britain would offer to act as intermediary with the Soviet government, 'with whom we would endeavour to arrange an amnesty and terms of capitulation'. Then in what may have been a twinge of Whitehall's uneasy conscience, it was suggested that 'General Denikin and his chief supporters should be offered the hospitality of this country'.[15]

This was to be the form in which Britain's final packet of aid was at last completed. A British destroyer took Denikin and his wife from Sevastopol to Constantinople, where they were transferred in style first to a hospital ship and then to the dreadnought *Marlborough*. They arrived at Southampton on 18 April 1920.[16] If the packet had not brought victory for the general, it had at least ensured his safety.

Though the struggle was ended for him, it was far from over for the Volunteer Army. Wrangel was immediately offered by London a similar deal to the one which Denikin had reluctantly accepted: surrender to the Bolsheviks, in return for British mediation to secure an amnesty and the offer of 'refuge outside Russia'. The new

Commander-in-Chief, aged only forty, was made of far sterner stuff than Denikin. Ignoring London completely, he set about rebuilding the demoralized rabble of an army evacuated from Novorossisk into the toughest White Russian force ever to be thrown against the Bolsheviks. It was a phenomenal feat of reorganization, achieved within the space of two months by draconian disciplinary measures and the driving force of his own personality. By the summer, Wrangel's revitalized and expanded army of some 25,000 men was ready for battle. The question was, where?

The answer was provided by Poland's armed struggle to secure the independence it had proclaimed after the Armistice but still needed to impose on the Lenin regime. At the end of April, the Polish army, led by Marshal Pilsudski, drove into the Soviet Ukraine, capturing its capital, Kiev, on 6 May. That was the signal for Wrangel to break out of the Crimea, whose exits at the Perekop Isthmuses had been held by the Thirteenth Red Army. He then launched simultaneous offensives to the north, to come to the aid of the Poles, and to the east, to spur the Don Cossacks into a new anti-Soviet revolt. In the process, he further divided those vacillating patrons of White Russian resistance, Britain and France.

The two powers had established parallel Military Missions with his forces in the Crimea but they now moved in opposite directions. The British government, furious with Wrangel for ignoring their advice, used the launching of his June offensives as the welcome pretext for breaking off all relations with this troublesome swashbuckler. His actions, the Cabinet decided, 'must be taken as a final release for us from our responsibilities to all forces under his command'. The British mission was ordered to distance itself from all his operations, to wind up their own work without delay and prepare to be evacuated from the Crimea as soon as shipping was available to collect them.[17] It was left to Churchill as War Minister to despatch that telegram, and he evidently did so with a heavy heart, protesting in particular at the decision not to afford Wrangel the assistance during any eventual evacuation given to Denikin, who had played London's game.

The French, on the other hand, did all they could to egg Wrangel on, particularly in his attempt to aid the Polish struggle, which had long been the apple of Clemenceau's eye. Indeed, in August, when Wrangel was bleeding his army to death in an attempt to stem a Polish retreat, he was officially 'recognized' by France, with promises of military aid (which never materialized). It was only after Lenin, faced with a massive new offensive by the Poles, decided in October to cut his losses and open peace talks with them that Wrangel's cause was lost. The Don venture in the east had already foundered on the predictable lethargy and double-dealing of the Cossacks; now, Wrangel found himself faced by an overwhelming Red Army force gathering to his north, as whole divisions were transferred from the Polish battlefield to deal with him once and for all. He went down all guns blazing, fighting his way in the first fortnight of November back into the Crimea and then down to the coast against an enemy four times his strength.[18] This was the last battle to be fought by the White Russians, effectively bringing to an end the four-year-old Civil War.

One of the reasons why Lloyd George had determined to be so unyielding over Wrangel, arch-enemy of the Bolsheviks, was that negotiations were now well under way in London to reach an Anglo-Soviet trade pact. Trade had always been the opening in the door which barred a settlement between the Allies and Lenin's Russia. The gap existed by mutual agreement. The West had always kept their foot there because of the political as well as the economic openings in prospect. For the same reason Lenin never slammed the door completely shut. It will be recalled that at the height of the misnamed 'Lockhart plot' crisis in the summer of 1918, a British trade and economic mission had been despatched to Russia and accepted by the Bolsheviks (its members finally scampering to safety up the gangplank of the vessel taking the released Lockhart himself back to England). February 1920 in southern Russia produced an equally ironic reminder of the significance of the commercial weapon. The final proof that Britain was preparing to abandon the White Russian cause came when a British economic mission, originally destined for Denikin, was directed to Moscow instead. It was another nudge at that partly opened door which was gradually to swing on its hinges to allow full Western recognition of the Soviet regime. The question remains: why had all the anti-Bolshevik armies failed, allowing the merchants and the bankers to take over instead?

It is worth pointing out that the final outcome was not a foregone conclusion; indeed, there was a time when, as he later admitted, Lenin himself feared that those armies would win the day. 'C's' emissary, George Hill, had reported at the end of June 1919 that by then the Soviet leader had grown so pessimistic about the Red Army's prospects on the battlefield that he was contemplating abandoning, for the time being, the struggle on Russian soil and decamping with his principal lieutenants to continue the fight underground from abroad. The British agent was closer to the truth than even he had realized. The papers of General Orlov, which illuminate so many of the dark corners of these early years, also shed new light on this episode.

In 1928, when, as *Rezident* in Berlin, Orlov was heading the Soviet intelligence network in the Weimar Republic, the chairman of the Soviet State Bank, Scheinmann, turned up – ostensibly for a medical check-up, but in reality to defect to the West. The Soviet ambassador to Germany at the time was Nikolai Krestinsky, who had known Scheinmann well from their work together during the Civil War. He described how, during the summer of 1919, Lenin had told the party's Central Committee that, as 'only a miracle can save us', extraordinary measures would have to be taken in the face of an impending defeat.

One such measure he had decided upon was to smuggle five million dollars in notes out of the country into Sweden to finance any Bolshevik campaign mounted from abroad. Scheinmann, a trusted Bolshevik, was selected as the carrier, largely because he had uncles who were bankers in Stockholm. Krestinsky, at the time one of Lenin's personal aides, told Orlov that he personally handed over the stash of foreign currency to Scheinmann who duly took it to

Sweden and deposited it in the bank of his relatives. The messenger returned to Moscow but not a cent of the money came back despite later attempts to reclaim it.[19]

The evidence is clear, therefore, that in the midsummer of 1919 Lenin was despairing of victory. Yet, less than six months later, that victory was in his grasp as, one by one, the White Russian armies advancing from north, south and east fell to pieces. The suddenness and completeness of this transformation in fortunes must have been hard for the leaders themselves, on either side of the battle lines, to comprehend. Yet the factors which led to the failure of the attacking forces stand out even in a brief look back at the campaigns: the over-extended and vulnerable lines of communication, especially in the vast areas of the south and east; the squabbles and intrigues over policy and strategy on all three fronts; uncertain command in the east and disastrous command in the north; the absence of any coherent master-plan to enable a link-up between even two out of the three White Russian armies.

The contrast on the Bolsheviks' side was always stark and, in the end, decisive. They fought throughout with shorter internal lines of supply and reinforcement, a key advantage in any campaign. Moreover, in the days of crisis, such as in the October 1919 battle for Petrograd, the Red Army could be fired up into a frenzy of energy through a combination of savage discipline and ideological ardour. Trotsky showed what this could achieve for the Bolsheviks in the suburbs of the old Tsarist capital. Wrangel demonstrated a year later in the Crimea what this might have achieved for the White Russians. As it was, the Bolsheviks had shown themselves to be, in the end, 'the better men'.

The role played by the Western Allies was also hobbled by disputes over policy (with the Americans dragging their feet from start to finish, and the French and British often pursuing different aims). It is true that, on the whole, Western military aid came too little and too late to be effective. It is also feasible that had it been possible (in political as well as logistical terms) to launch a major Allied offensive with three or four regular divisions, then certainly

Petrograd and perhaps also Moscow could have been occupied in the summer and autumn of 1919. Churchill with his 'damned maps', as his colleagues called them, had a special fondness for grand attacks on the enemy from the south – the Dardanelles in the Great War, now through Denikin in the intervention campaign and, later, against 'the soft underbelly of the Axis' in the war to come. But Russia in 1919 was a special hazard, for even military success would not have solved the problem. What then? That was the question which was all too rarely put, and never answered.

One of the few Western leaders to pose it starkly was the Chief of the Imperial General Staff, Sir Henry Wilson. In a memorandum to the Cabinet on 1 December 1919 (by which time he had been promoted to field-marshal) Wilson warned of the remorseless way in which commitments would steadily increase, seemingly with no check and no end, once a military operation were launched in a distant arena like the Russian battleground. Though he did not live to see it, the process by which, in the 1960s, America was sucked ever deeper into the military morass of Vietnam was to be the classic vindication of Wilson's warning.

Moreover, even if the Allies had succeeded in occupying key Soviet-held cities, how would they have fed, let alone administered them? When the battle for Petrograd was looming, an alarm note was sounded on this score by one Vorobiev, the president of the city's Corn Exchange. In a memorandum which landed up in Whitehall, he estimated that to feed the city's 700,000 inhabitants, for two months only, 24,000 tons of flour would be needed (6,000 per fortnight). The cost of shipping this out from London via Helsinki he put at £603,600, including freight charges and insurance. In addition, 'supplies of tinned meat and soups, fish, salt, sugar, tea, etc' would be required.

Not surprisingly, M. Vorobiev's memorandum[20] was marked 'No Action'. It had probably been read with a shudder and dismissed. By now the bill, for Britain alone, in trying to keep the proxy fight going, amounted to the formidable sum of £94 million in the money of the age. £15 million of this had gone to Yudenich and the north Russian campaigns; almost as much again had been spent on aid for Kolchak in his Siberian venture; while the lion's share, some £26 million, had gone to Churchill's special protégé, General Denikin in the south.

These huge sums had largely been dispensed after the Armistice when, in Britain as in other Allied countries, the need for further sacrifices of either blood or treasure in an obscure cause was being severely questioned. A nation which had already tightened its own belt down to the last notch of rationing would hardly have accepted the despatch of tens of thousands of tons of food a month to keep the teeming millions of Russia alive. Nor could all the Allied powers in concert (and they were now less in agreement than ever as to how the Bolshevik problem should be tackled) have easily provided the military forces needed to garrison such a vast area of occupation even after its conquest, nor the legions of civilian officials to help with any post-Bolshevik administration.

That rapidly forgotten memorandum from the president of the Petrograd Corn Exchange had revealed the hidden irony of the whole intervention saga. For the Allies, it was almost certainly a blessing in disguise that they had lost their 'war after the war'.

14

Transitions

The process by which the West came to terms at the official level with their defeat in Russia, and thus with the reality of Lenin's power, is mostly familiar terrain and can be skipped through accordingly. The unlocked door of trade began to swing on its hinges early in 1920 when the army of General Denikin, the most successful standard-bearer of the anti-Bolshevik crusade, was being driven back to the shores of the Black Sea. On 16 January, more than two months before their warships started evacuating the remnants of his troops, the Allies announced, through the Supreme Council in Paris, the first step towards a formal commercial accommodation with the victors.

Some face-saving niceties were preserved. The reason for this new policy was described as 'remedying the unhappy situation of the population of the interior of Russia, which is now deprived of all manufactured products from outside Russia'. Moreover, the trading partner selected was not the Bolshevik government as such but the 'Tsentrosoyuz', the Moscow headquarters of Russia's powerful agricultural cooperatives, which had been allowed to preserve a nominal measure of independence for its 25 million members vis-à-vis the regime.[1] Lloyd George had had a tough last-minute struggle with his own Cabinet to get the policy adopted. Some, like Lord Curzon, opposed it as being tantamount to recognition of a still-hostile government. But the ground had rather been cut from under his feet by the steady progress being made between London and Moscow over an exchange of prisoners of war, both military and civilian. The Anglo-Soviet agreement on this was finally signed, after nine months of negotiations, on 12 February 1920. It removed the smell of cordite from the air and enabled both sides to breathe more normally.

The proposition that the West had to reopen trade with Russia in order to save the people of that country from dire distress was equally devious. Indeed, so far as food supplies were concerned, it was the other way round. The Allies desperately needed Russian grain to avoid starvation in Poland and in the vanquished countries of Germany, Austria and Hungary; this was where the real distress loomed, and it threatened to provide fertile ground for Bolshevik agitation. What the Soviet Union, for its part, needed above all were locomotives and other railway material to bring the mangled communications network back into operation – a military as well as an economic imperative. Hovering above all these concerns were the political factors. Lenin, now safely in power, wanted to end the diplomatic isolation of his regime; the Allies, having accepted that he was probably there to stay, also wanted to end that isolation if only to stop Germany creeping in again through the Russian back door.

But if Curzon had lost the early arguments over restoring commercial ties with Russia so soon, there was no disputing his conclusions. The Anglo-Soviet Trade Treaty, signed on 16 March 1921, marked the de facto recognition of the Bolshevik regime. Full *de jure* recognition followed steadily, as night follows day, with Britain leading the way on 2 February 1924. Though the White House had been so effusive in greeting the arrival to power of Bolshevism, Washington proved the last Allied capital fully to accept it. Not until 1933 did the White House appoint an ambassador-plenipotentiary to Moscow. He was none other than William C. Bullitt, who as a 28-year-old diplomat had been despatched on that extraordinary one-man peace mission to Lenin in the spring of 1919. This time, he was to have even less luck in building any magic bridges of East–West fellowship.[2]

The story of the rival intelligence services during this transition period is far less familiar than the record of inter-governmental relations, of which it emerges as the mirror image. Like their governments, the Western secret services sought to remove, wherever practicable, the embarrassment of their failed challenge of 1918 and the Bolsheviks occasionally obliged. The best example is the case of Kalamatiano. The State Department's master-spy (it is idle to call him anything else) was not in Moscow when the Chekist raids on Western missions and their intelligence outposts took place. He had left the capital only a few hours before they were launched, on a special mission to Siberia agreed with Poole. The American consul shared the general Allied conviction that the regime could be toppled militarily only if the various anti-Bolshevik forces operating in the east, north and south of the country could somehow join hands. Samara, a key city in central Siberia where the great railway crossed the Volga, could serve as this strategic link and was already the seat of an imposing regional government. It was when Kalamatiano reached there after a week's arduous travel that he first heard of the mayhem in Moscow and Petrograd; even then, he had no idea how serious things were until he got back to the capital on 18 September.[3]

Kalamatiano described his arrest in a long memorandum he was able to deliver to Washington later on, and corroborative details have been supplied by both American and Soviet sources.[4] He realized the game was up as soon as he got back to the capital and learned from those of his contacts who were still on the run about the evacuation of Western diplomats, the disappearance of their key agents and the imprisonment of Lockhart. The arrest which troubled him most was that of Colonel Friede of the Red Army Moscow Communications Centre.[5] Among other vital services to the network, Friede had supplied him with a genuine Russian passport made out in the name of Sergei Nikolayevich Serpukhovsky, under which he was now travelling. The colonel had presumably been made to tell all. The alias was not merely useless; it was damning.

Before leaving for Finland a few hours before, Poole had placed the American consulate-general under the protection of Norway, and its flag now flew over the building. Even the Cheka would surely not dare to raid those premises, and Kalamatiano's hopes were raised when he cautiously reconnoitred the area by daylight. There were Red Guard sentries posted around the building but all seemed peaceful enough and he could even see some of the Allied refugees who had already made it to this safe haven playing football in the gardens, as though their cares were over. All that was needed to join them was a fifty-yard dash through the adjoining grounds of the British church and then a clamber over the high perimeter fence around the consulate itself. He decided to wait until after dusk to make his attempt. Rain set in which made the ground slippery but, as he had hoped, the sentries outside the main gate started huddling over a wood fire to keep warm. He waited until the comrades still on patrol were on the other side of the perimeter and then rushed towards the fence – elegantly dressed in a dark coat and hat with grey spats over his well-polished shoes and clutching his precious walking stick in his left hand. That ornate cane proved his downfall in more senses than one. By refusing to abandon it, he was left with only his right arm to seize the top of the fence and lever himself over it. It was not enough. As his grip began to slacken on the wet top rail he felt a pair of arms grab him by the waist from below and heard the owner of the pair of arms yelling out for help. It was the janitor who had his hut by the gate which Kalamatiano had overlooked.

The second doleful consequence of hanging on to that cane came later that night when the top Cheka official, I.K. Peters (whom we have met already interrogating Lockhart), came to join in questioning the false 'Serpukhovsky'. The Cheka had already raided Kalamatiano's apartment and found nothing; a body search of the prisoner, who was refusing to talk, had been equally fruitless. The Chekists seemed at a dead end when eyes started to focus on that heavy walking stick, which the American was refusing to put down, even when moving across the room. The reason why was revealed when they took it from him for examination. It turned out to be hollow and the space inside was stuffed with bundles of roubles, cyphered messages and, most damaging of all, receipts for money from more than thirty coded informants. Kalamatiano had proved the case against him without uttering a word.

So much for the bizarre way in which the top American agent in Moscow fell into Chekist hands. His fate in the Butyrka prison was equally striking. It was notable, in the first instance, for the pressure which Washington started to apply on his behalf almost from the first reports of his arrest. Thus, already on 11 October 1918, the State Department was urging the Norwegian government to do all in its power to secure the release of Kalamatiano, coyly described as 'a former employee of the Moscow Consulate'.[6] The inadequacy of this description was promptly demonstrated by the prisoner himself. Only a fortnight after his incarceration he managed to smuggle out of the notorious Butyrka jail a long report to his spymasters describing not only the circumstances of his arrest and current prison conditions but also his prospects of escaping the death penalty. Finally came details of how many of his espionage agents were still safe; how Poole (who received this in Archangel four months later) was to get in touch with them, supply them with money and generally keep his fractured network of Russian agents in some sort of operation:

> On September 1st, No. 5,[7] his sister, mother, other sister and brother were arrested when his sister carried a report to Riley's [sic] place where she was arrested and the report taken ... All others, i.e. 24, 10, 11, 8 were caught by the watch on No. 5's house. No. 12 was arrested after I was through a receipt found on me. No. 7 was arrested because of the blackmailing letter he had written and which I had kept in my old home ... No. 28, 2 and 4 are safe. You could communication with the former. The Ukraine organisation is safe and you could get in touch with it through No. 2 at Charkov [sic]. We have there No. 2, 3, 16, 17, 18, 21, 23 and two couriers.[8]

Given his isolation and plight, he was remarkably calm in evaluating his own prospects for survival, almost as though this were just another intelligence assessment. He felt that at the trial, which he knew was impending, he and No. 5 and No. 15 were the most likely to be given a death sentence. He continued:

> Believe at present our fate depends either on international situation or possibly we could be exchanged. If you ever consider this please take our men into account. They could be useful in Archangel or Siberia – can only speak most highly of their conduct . . .
>
> Still many chances [sic] that we may be taken out and executed some day. Believe this depends on fight now going on between terrorists (Vecheka) and moderates (Chicherin-Petrovsky).

He went on to detail the line he was taking under interrogation and which he intended to continue with at the trial, namely that he had been collecting only the commercial and economic information he needed for his business work and that he had nothing to do with any alleged Allied plotting for a *coup d'état*. He gave an account of his arrest and even included a brief survey of conditions in European Russia.

He ended: 'Present letter very hard to send – hope to manage however as anxious you know exactly how arrested, what my testimony [will be] and that you can get in touch both with 26 here and 23 in Charkov.'[9]

The phrase 'hard to send' was a considerable understatement for a prison cell intelligence operation which had been conducted almost as thoroughly as though he had been sitting, still undetected and at liberty, in his own Moscow house. It was a masterly exercise which finds few, if any, equivalents in the contemporary annals of Allied espionage. He managed to follow it with another smuggled message giving conditions in the prison, the categories of prisoners held, the number of executions, and the tensions in the Moscow leadership in the face of White Russian military advances on the capital. Again the mood is one of calm evaluation.

His spirits deteriorated rapidly when he was returned to the jail two months later after being duly sentenced to death and put in the row of cells reserved for condemned prisoners. It was probably during these early weeks of his incarceration that he was taken out two or three times into the courtyard for what turned out to be only his mock execution – all part of the increased psychological pressure to get him to tell more. He stuck to his story but at a cost. Norwegian consular officials were now his only link with the outside world as well as for representations to his Moscow jailers. The Norwegians managed, via the Russian Red Cross, to make his food supplies more than tolerable. Three times a week they sent in a parcel containing a pound of meat, a pound of potatoes, some bread, tea, sugar and cigarettes. There were also three weekly deliveries of very British fare (roast beef, mutton chops and veal cutlets for example) prepared especially for him at the former British consulate. Moreover his cigarette ration was eventually increased to the heavy smoker's allowance of fifty per day. But despite these creature comforts, his health continued to fail badly as the months went by in 1919 with seemingly no prospect of his release – so much so that his Norwegian consular visitors feared at one point that he might even be going mad.

In fact things began to swing, slowly and silently, in his favour and it is here that the fate of Western spies reflects the transition in relations between the Soviet Union and the Western camp as a whole. America was, from the start, a special case in Soviet eyes. Its President, though representing capitalism at its most rampant, was also a declared anti-imperialist and it was evident that he had been dragging his heels before joining the Allied armed intervention campaign. What would impress Lenin far more than Woodrow Wilson's nebulous philosophy was the stark fact of his power. At the Paris Peace Conference he stood head and shoulders above the other Allied statesmen – not, even remotely, because of any superior intellect or personality, but because he led the country with the strongest economic and military forces in the post-war world. This was not a leader to be needlessly provoked. On the other hand, Kalamatiano was not a trifle to be disposed of thoughtlessly or surrendered cheaply. Lenin realized from the start that the

American was no use to him as just another bullet-ridden body sagging against the wall of a prison courtyard. As a live hostage he could command a price, though even Lenin could not have imagined at first how high that price would go.

The fact that Kalamatiano's death sentence at the 'Lockhart trial' had been immediately suspended (as opposed to that passed on his chief agent Colonel Friede, which was promptly carried out) sent a signal to the White House. That signal became much stronger when the State Department first learned (through a telegram dated 21 February 1919 from its Stockholm legation) that the sentence was being formally commuted to one of imprisonment. But nearly thirty months of tortuous haggling[10] were to follow between Washington and Moscow before the prison doors were finally opened.

For more than two years the negotiations, conducted mainly through neutral intermediaries, centred on some form of prisoner exchange. The opening bid on this from Moscow (in February 1919) was turned down because it did not include, along with Kalamatiano and others, the American consul in Tashkent, Roger Tredwell, who had been arrested, for no valid reason, by the Bolsheviks of Turkestan on 20 October 1918. It was not until April 1919 that the diplomat was freed and American efforts could be concentrated on the plight of their special agent (still referred to in all exchanges either as 'a former consular employee' or simply 'a United States citizen'). But by then the various White Armies, with massive Allied support, had begun their advance on Moscow and it was the turn of the Bolsheviks to give the cold shoulder.

Thus in July 1919, in a telegram to an unofficial go-between in Stockholm, the Bolshevik government announced flatly that, as Kalamatiano had 'committed the highest crime against the Soviet state, was properly tried according to Russian revolutionary law and is still considered dangerous to Soviet Russia', he could not be set free unpunished. This was, of course, the time of maximum threat to the regime from the White Russian armies, and the telegram pointedly went on to reproach the United States for 'having officially associated itself with Kolchak and Denikin'.

Clearly Kalamatiano, together with other Western hostages, would have to stay behind bars as long as the regime was still fighting its unresolved 'war after the war'. Even Dr Fridtjof Nansen, the famous Arctic explorer who had been negotiating directly with the Soviets as a representative of the International Red Cross, failed to make a breakthrough in this chilly political climate.

After the White Russian threat had been eliminated and the Western Allies had started their trade talks, which amounted to peace talks, with a seemingly secure Bolshevik regime, Lenin still dragged his heels over releasing his prize hostages. Throughout 1920, dogged American efforts on Kalamatiano's behalf suggesting a variety of live body exchanges, even on an Allied basis, got nowhere. Lenin hung on in the hope of striking a better and still better bargain. Ironically, in the end, it was he who had to come almost cap in hand to Washington. The gradual change in the air seems somehow to have penetrated the prisoner's cell. On 19 November 1921, after a long period of silence, he managed to smuggle out another letter to the outside world – this time addressed personally to Professor Harper, the Harvard academic who had discreetly recruited him for intelligence work six years before. Even more remarkable than the addressee was the chirpiness of the message:

Moscow – Butyrki Prison, 19/11/1921.

My dear Harper,

Just a few words to tell you, and whichever of my friends you run across, that I am still very much alive – although skinny . . .

Yesterday celebrated my 30th month of imprisonment in various institutions – Byke [sic], two different camps, 8 months of Kremlin and the Butyrki solitaries – a liberal education in itself.

However, as whatever happens outside finally is concentrated here I consider I have been given a box seat to watch the revolution and am not complaining of [sic] such an [un] usual opportunity.

... Several of your acquaintances have been here at various times. I trust sometime to tell you more about them all. At the present, names on paper are odious things ...

If I pull out alive, and I have every hope of doing so now – although at one time chances seemed to be rather on the undertaker's side – I hope we will have a chance of talking things over.

With best wishes
Yours very truly
K.B Kal—[11]

And, in a PS he even mentions Huntingdon, once his Petrograd case officer, by name.

There was no longer any danger of Kalamatiano going mad with despair; his message sounds more like a letter sent from a spartan but fascinating convalescent home. What may well have been feeding his confidence was the evidence, coming in steadily with new inmates from the Moscow just outside the prison walls, of the regime's growing economic plight, a plight which it could not resolve unaided. On 20 June, *Pravda* came out with the grim truth. As a result of drought and crop failure, the paper admitted that famine was raging in the country and over 25 million Russians were facing starvation. At a stroke, the bargaining positions were reversed. Instead of the Allied powers relying on Russian wheat to feed a famished central Euope, the Bolshevik regime now had to secure Western food aid to keep its own people alive. And famine, as Lenin well knew, also spelt foment. For Kalamatiano and his fellow detainees, it spelt freedom.

On 27 July, five weeks after the *Pravda* article had appeared, the new American Secretary of State, Charles Evans Hughes, warned the Soviet Foreign Minister, Maxim Gorky, in writing: 'It is manifestly impossible for the American authorities to countenance measures of relief for the distress in Russia while our citizens are detained.' Herbert Hoover, the future president who was then directing the American Relief Administration, sent a similar message to Moscow.

The climb-down in Moscow was almost instantaneous. Three days later, on 30 July, the Bolsheviks agreed to release their American prisoners in return for ARA emergency help. The change in Kalamatiano's fortunes had exactly mirrored the sudden tilt in the East–West balance.

After some face-saving bureaucratic delays by the Bolsheviks, the secret agent and five other American prisoners crossed the border into Estonia and freedom on 10 August 1921. Kalamatiano looked the neatest and most composed of the bedraggled batch, who were instantly taken over by the local American Red Cross for a hot bath and delousing. They then went shopping.

In early September, the State Department's faithful servant and sorely tried hero got back to base, to find no effusive plaudits awaiting. Instead, the department received him with what could only be described as a welcome at arm's length. They had done their level best to bring him home but, once he was back, they seemed equally determined to bury him. After a sixty-day leave of absence, he was not only obliged to resign as a government employee but was also dissuaded from producing any account of his achievements and sufferings. His old spymasters, Professor Harper and de Witt Poole, both assured him that 'the mood of the country' was not propitious for any such publication at the time. What they meant, of course, was the mood of official Washington, which, as we have seen, had sought all along to throw a blanket over American involvement in Allied secret service operations.

The last years of his life, which were few and rather dismal, can be described when, at the end of this account, we summarize the fate of all the leading players in the great confrontation, Bolshevik as well as Western. Suffice it to note here that Kalamatiano's career ended, as it had begun, under a shroud of furtiveness, a shroud first cast over Washington by a president's allergy to the word 'secret' in any context.

The career of Sydney Reilly in the early post-war years also reflected, though in a very different way, the change taking place in all relations between the Bolsheviks and the Western world. For him, the transition began much more comfortably than was the case with his old Moscow partner, though it was to end more savagely. In between came ups and downs which were extraordinary mainly because Reilly himself was such an extraordinary character.

Reilly's uncertain honeymoon period with the secret service continued for about two years after his return in February 1919 from the productive reconnaissance mission to General Denikin in southern Russia. Among the papers in his file later on that year is a request sent by Major Morton of the SIS to Colonel Menzies at the War Office to have his name put forward for an honorary commission as a major in the army, to replace his temporary commission as a lowly lieutenant in the air force. The minute continues: 'He is now engaged on important work for the Foreign Office which necessitates his conferring with soldiers and civilians of high rank and he finds his temporary low rank a great hindrance. I am certain the Foreign Office would back this up.'[12]

This received a double-handed brush-off. Menzies replied that, as Reilly was on air force strength, he could hardly intervene nor did he wish to: 'In any case, the W.O. are adamant in their refusal to give even honorary promotions as, in the event of the officer becoming a casualty "Finance" are responsible.' The hand of the Treasury was never to leave Reilly's shoulders.

This is perhaps the moment to record that, on a mission to the Paris Peace Conference eleven months later, the irrepressible secret agent seems to have taken matters into his own hands as regards his service garb. On 3 September 1920 the Admiralty sent the SIS a brusque Information Required note concerning 'Sidney [sic] Reilly, Address Paris': 'This man is reported from a reliable source to be wearing naval uniform in Paris and his conduct is not satisfactory. Is he still employed by "C"?'

Reilly's chief (now knighted under his new name of Mansfield Cumming) sent a rasping reply back to the War Office, in defence of his protegé: 'Sydney Reilly is employed by me and is engaged at present on a highly important and confidential mission. Will you cause further enquiries to be made as to the precise respect in which this ex-officer's conduct is not satisfactory?' And Cumming went on to express the opinion (probably not held too fervently) that it was 'at least possible' that Reilly had been behaving himself after all. This is one of the scarce messages to survive bearing the chief's famous green ink initial of 'C'.[13]

That was firm top-level support indeed and other papers show that Reilly had been in need of it. On 4 January 1920 'Production' (probably the same helpful Major Morton) sent him a New Year greeting care of the British Legation in Prague with a very personal message about his future. This was jolly but not totally reassuring. It read: '*You* are quite safe, or ought to be now, after the numerous efforts that have been made by various swells to apply the boot. I expect when you get pushed away you will not go alone, as all our nefarious past will by that time have come to light, in which case I think we had better club together, buy an island in the West Indies and start a republic of our own. You may be President if you will give me the job of Chancellor of the Exchequer.'[14]

The letter told Reilly clearly if flippantly that the knives were out for him; with some powerful fingers around the handles. However, he was still kept busily employed throughout that year and he redoubled his own efforts to be of value to the service whose recognition he craved. In March, for example, there was a flurry of activity concerning a secret mission to Berlin which Reilly was arranging for a certain M. Bazarov. Its purpose, not spelt out despite voluminous correspondence on the subject, seems to have been to establish what likelihood there was of a pact between the Bolsheviks and the Weimar Republic in Germany, now that the latter had put down the Communist uprising.

'Berlin is today the navel of the world and the German–Russian Monarchist plot more interesting than ever,' an excited Reilly wrote from Paris (where he was comfortably installed in the Hotel Lotti) on 14 March. Bazarov duly went, furnished with £300 of SIS money, but there is no trace of what came out of it all.

The autumn of the year shows Reilly at full stretch on the department's behalf, both as an informant and as an emissary. In

September he compiled a large intelligence report on Bolshevik clandestine operations, which, as the archives show, everybody in Whitehall involved in Russian affairs wanted to get their hands on. This was not surprising. Its six sets of papers included a list (clearly extracted from some Soviet card index) of Bolshevik 'missionaries' with linguistic knowledge being sent abroad on propaganda work; an index of Red spies, with their portraits; a map showing the location of resident Soviet agents in Europe; and finally a copy of a circular from Moscow giving them their instructions.[15] This was intelligence material of the highest order.

The following month, Reilly set out on a European mission of his own, evidently with 'C's' backing, since telegrams announcing his forthcoming arrival were sent to Warsaw, Reval, Riga and Berlin. In Warsaw, he teamed up with an old colleague, Paul Dukes of Petrograd fame, and a telegram at the end of the month shows that 'ST 1 and ST 25' had left for Pinsk, then the headquarters of Boris Savinkov's anti-Bolshevik forces. Reilly was now emerging as Savinkov's main political lobbyist in the West. A few weeks later, we find him writing personal letters to London with a profile of the undaunted revolutionary, whom Reilly was about to escort on a visit to Britain. He suggests some of the people he would like Savinkov to meet: 'Winston Ch., Leeper, the P.M.'s secretary, Sir Edw. Grigg'.[16] Thus, after a shaky start, 1920 ends on a positive note all round for Sydney Reilly and the SIS. Yet the following year, official relations were severed for good.

There is something of a mystery about this parting of the ways. We know from later SIS papers (which will be quoted in due course) that 1921 was the year when all official links with Reilly were cut. But there is no reference to this in his personal file. Indeed, there is no entry about him at all during the whole of that year, the only such completely blank space in his post-war record. The explanation may be that this was the time when the 'Ace of Spies' asked to be taken on the permanent strength of the service as a full-time career member, only to be rejected. The approach is believed to have been made orally to 'C', who then had the awkward task of explaining why it was turned down. There were a variety of reasons for Cumming's decision, not all of which he would have passed on to his protégé and none of which would have been put down on paper.

Among the factors he could readily have mentioned was lack of money: the department's peacetime budget had been slashed[17] savagely so that the need was to reduce staff levels rather than to expand. He could also have made the obvious point that his wartime 'contract agent' was anyway, in the jargon of the service, completely 'blown'. Reilly's identity was known to every diplomat and official of the Soviet regime, let alone to everyone in its political police. His photograph was in all their files and the face was unmistakable and virtually undisguisable. Here we get on to reasons which were probably not spelt out. Reilly's features, to quote that telegram of 'C's' which began this narrative, were of the 'Jewish-Jap type, brown eyes very protruding'. He was a Jew who looked almost like the caricature of a Jew and both the SIS and the Foreign Office mandarins who oversaw its activities were, at the time, strongly anti-Semitic.[18]

Then came his personal record and character which in peacetime were just as unacceptable to the same elitist circles as his face. He was not only a womanizer but a bigamist; not merely a fortune-hunter but an unscrupulous and probably crooked businessman. Scandal and sensationalism had always swirled around his head and it seemed likely that they always would. This was the opposite of the quietly spoken London clubman who, when living in the country-side, would sit on the parish council and support the village cricket team as though he were just another inconspicuous civil servant. Finally, and here we again come to the linkage between politics and intelligence, Reilly, the flamboyant anti-Bolshevik buccaneer, was the last man needed for a secret service whose government was now steadily moving towards de facto recognition of the Lenin regime. Reilly's ties with Boris Savinkov, the sworn and very active enemy of the Soviet government, represented a major potential embarrassment. The 'Ace of Spies' would henceforth have to continue his crusade from outside the corridors of Whitehall. This he now proceeded to do, and with redoubled vigour. Unfortunately for his standing with the Foreign Office, it was the controversial Savinkov to whom he moved ever closer, at first acting as his standard-bearer and then as his principal financier.

The problem is perfectly expressed in the first entries in Reilly's file for 1922, when his story in the Whitehall records is resumed. In January the head of 'C's' station in Vienna writes a personal note to 'B.M.'[19] in London requesting guidance: 'Will you kindly wire me whether Sydney Reilly, who occasionally blows into this office and says he is part of our London show, is really your representative and should be talked to in all confidence . . . We have nothing definite and I have the strongest intuitive mistrust of him, which I only hope is unfounded . . . I expect him here at any moment.'[20]

A telegram, followed by a letter, put the Vienna station chief in the picture. The former advised: 'Give Reilly no more information than is absolutely necessary . . . Reilly is not a member of our office and does not serve "C" in that he is not receiving any pay from us. He worked at one time during the war for "C"s' organisation and is now undoubtedly of a certain use to us. We do not altogether know what to make of him.'[21] The follow-up letter[22] added: 'There is no doubt that Reilly is a political intriguer of no mean class and it is therefore infinitely better for us to keep in with him, whereby he tells us a great deal of what he is doing, than to quarrel with him when we should hear nothing of his activities . . . He is at the moment Boris Savinkov's right-hand man. In fact, some people might almost say he is Boris Savinkov.[23] As such he is of undoubted importance.' But the warning was added that in no way should he be given any help in promoting Savinkov's cause, for example, by providing travelling facilities: 'The last thing in the world we should wish is to become embroiled in any way with Savinkov, although of course we are not averse to hearing all about the gentleman and his plans.'

The messages vouched for Reilly as being 'not anti-British and never had been'. Moreover, he was 'a genuine hater of the Bolsheviks'

– albeit 'an astute commercial man, out for himself'. This last description fitted what the rejected spy did next. He plunged back into business to raise money for himself and for his anti-Bolshevik crusade. Business for Reilly meant a return to America, and it was for New York that he set sail in July 1923. His old department, who were keeping a close watch on his movements, saw to it that he did not do them any damage on the other side of the Atlantic as well as in Europe.

'S.G. Reilly,' they informed their New York station, 'worked for us during and after the war in Russia, and knows a certain amount about our organisation as it was then constituted ... but in case he rolls up, this is just to warn you that he now has nothing to do with us.'[24]

This, then, was the background to the final phase of the Reilly–Savinkov saga. SIS were happy to exploit them for any information about Russia while denying them any assistance. Both men faced the threat now being mounted against them without any Western shield of protection.

Part Five

The Scam

15

Spinning the Web

It became known, both within Russia and to the world outside, as 'the Trust'; an ironic title indeed, for the operation it described was, quite simply, the greatest scam of the century.

The Bolshevik system had rested from the start on lies and terror, the same twin pillars which were to support all the Communist dictatorships to follow it. Moreover, the Cheka had already ventured out at least once into the murky waters of deception. This was in 1920, when 'Mayak' or 'The Beacon' had been launched to sow mutual suspicion between White Russian movements in exile by spreading rumour and confusion among them. Yet, by virtue of its scope, sustained brilliance of execution and time-scale, the Trust stood in a category apart. Its remit was audaciously ambitious: to deceive the regime's enemies, both in the homeland and within the émigré movements scattered throughout Europe, that there existed inside Russia an anti-Bolshevik underground so resolute and broadly based that it needed only the appearance on the scene of an anti-Marxist Messiah to sweep the devilry of Leninism off the map.

This meant that the western Allies, who had only just abandoned their 'war after the war' against Lenin, now had to be persuaded of the lie as well. And they were persuaded (albeit with some qualms of doubt) mainly through the device of feeding their secret services with a stream of useful and sometimes unadulterated Soviet intelligence. This purported to come from Trust supporters who had infiltrated even the top echelons of the Cheka and its successors, the GPU and the OGPU.[1] Other secret members of the Trust – so the fable went – were ensconced in every branch of the Bolshevik hierarchy and every department of government: party members, going right up to the Central Committee and the Politburo; officials in the ministries, and even some of the ministers themselves; officers in the army, including some generals; the intellectuals; the professional classes; the church leaders and a vast supporting staff of key workers in the factories and communications.

Later in the century, when the Cold War revitalized the intelligence conflict between East and West (a rare example of frost actually encouraging growth) the vivid phrase 'wilderness of mirrors' was coined to describe the maze of deception which had been constructed between the two sides. The Trust can be seen as the beginning of that wilderness and it was strewn with barriers much more solid than plain sheets of glass. But, if one stays with that picture, it must be added that some of these Soviet mirrors were convex and some concave so that the image was always distorted. Some were one-way looking glasses; other panes were frosted so that only a shadow could be glimpsed. This gigantic multi-faceted illusion was mounted not simply for a few weeks or months, but fashioned to be kept in place for years. One gross blunder at home or abroad would have shaken the operation and could even have smashed it. As it was, several smaller slip-ups – inconsistencies and even contradictions in the various stories being presented to the dupes – had to be hastily corrected and explained away. Yet it somehow survived until, after five years of continuous mass deception, the Trust had served the regime's purpose.

That purpose had been laid down, clearly if not explicitly, by Lenin himself in his speech to the Ninth Congress of the Soviets in Moscow on 23 December 1921. As we have seen, that year had brought the defeat of White Russian forces on all three battlefronts and the hasty transition of their pragmatic Allied backers into trading partners of the Bolshevik regime. But though the civil war had been won, the victory still rested on shaky foundations which now had to be shored up. The heart of this consolidation was Lenin's New Economic Policy or NEP, designed to raise the wretched living standards of the Russian people which had under-lain so much of the recent turmoil. There were two dangers threatening the reform programme which could only be pushed through with the impetus of private enterprise. The first was ideo-logical contamination from this emergency partnership. That could be dealt with by propaganda and, if necessary, by intensified repres-sion. But everything depended on the regime being left in peace by its enemies to put its ravaged house in order.

That was the threat which led to Lenin's impassioned appeal for 'vigilance'. The same watchword was to echo down the years in Moscow, to serve as the cover for many a policy purge or party intrigue. But when first uttered, the call was genuine enough. Millions in this newly established Bolshevik realm were still sus-picious, disorientated, and resentful that hardship and poverty persisted so long after the old order had been swept away. They formed the mass of sullen passive resisters, like a heavy subsoil which the Soviet plough needed to turn to its use. And, sprinkled among that mass, came the thousands of active resisters – liberals, bourgeois professionals and civil servants, monarchists, old fashioned 'Great Russian' patriots, unrepentant survivors of the vanquished White armies as well as the stranded followers of Boris Savinkov's 'Socialist Revolutionaries'. They were the domestic crop which the Cheka needed to reap, and the Trust did the harvesting for them. Hundreds of these anti-Bolshevik activists stepped forward to serve in the new movement and each, the moment he or she joined, went down in the secret police books, to be talked along for the time being and disposed of later on. Many, as we shall see, were 'turned' by torture, blackmail, sophistry or bribery to do the Trust's work for it.

The Cheka lost no time in following the leader's call. Lenin had identified their two main targets for them: the Western powers, who had to be lulled into inactivity while the NEP experiment was being put through; and the White Russian émigré movements, who needed to be neutralized and prevented, at all costs, from joining hands with the resistance at home. Signs of such a dangerous coalescence were detectable in the months right after Lenin's speech. In Moscow, for example, there had sprung up a fledgling resistance organization called the Monarchist Association of Central Russia or MOR[2] which was reported to be already in touch with White Russian groups in Petrograd and even further afield. It was the interception of one of these contacts which opened the door for the Cheka. The Trust was launched, as it was to be wound up, through a betrayal.

There is, for once, general agreement among the principal sources[3] as to how this came about. In November 1921, one A.A. Yakushev, a senior official in the Soviet Ministry of Waterways and a genuine member of the MOR underground, stopped off in Tallinn, the Estonian capital, at the beginning of a foreign tour for his department. There he met up with a friend, a former White Guardist officer, Yuri Artomonov, whose wife Yakushev may well have been pursuing. But the Waterways official, known to be a great ladies man, had more on his mind than dalliance. Without revealing the name or any other details about MOR, he described how anti-Bolshevik feeling in Russia had now crystallized around an organization which had penetrated the party and state apparatus in Moscow to such a degree that the regime itself was under threat.

His Tsarist friend was so electrified by the good news that he promptly passed it on, by letter, to one of the many émigré outposts, the so-called Monarchist Council in Berlin. The fateful message was somehow intercepted by the Cheka, who had their fingers everywhere and Yakushev was duly seized on his return to Moscow and thrown into the Lubyanka. Dzerzhinsky then played with his hapless victim like a cat with a mouse throughout the winter, though no physical torture was applied. Finally, in the spring of 1922, Yakushev, who had been in daily fear for his life, succumbed to an appeal to his 'patriotism' and agreed to work unconditionally for the Cheka.

It is at this point that MOR melts away out of the picture, at least for customers abroad, and the Trust (operating under the cover of the 'Moscow Municipal Credit Association') takes its place. The émigré centres which were the Cheka's targets would be issued with the plausible-sounding instructions that all secret communications between themselves and their Moscow contacts should henceforth be couched in a business language code appropriate to such a state association. The whole operation was placed by Dzerzhinsky (who at first seemed rather dubious about its prospects) under the control of one of his closest aides, A.K. Artuzov, then the head of the Counter-Intelligence Department. Artuzov had a classic party pedigree in everything except his birth. His father, one Fraucci, had been, of all people, an Italian-Swiss cheese-maker who had settled in Russia in the late nineteenth century. The boy's record soon put the image of foreign bourgeois Emmenthal far behind him. He was among the first to join the Bolsheviks in 1917 and had served on the Archangel front the year after and with the Cheka in Poland during the Russo-Polish war. Most of the Trust's stratagems abroad were devised by him, and all the threads, genuine or bogus, led back to him.

One of the first émigré centres which Yakushev contacted proved also the most difficult to fool. The Yugoslav capital Belgrade had become the 'Little Russia' of the emigration, a city whose solid Slav character, complete with reassuring Orthodox churches, had been relatively undiluted by cosmopolitanism. Moreover, it was here that General Baron Wrangel, the formidable hero of the last Crimean offensive, had set up his headquarters. Wrangel was eventually to become persuaded of the Trust's credentials. But the first meeting Yakushev had with three of his emissaries was sticky going. General Klimovich, the Baron's Chief of Intelligence, was dubious. Nikolai Chebyshev, who served as Wrangel's political adviser, declared outright afterwards that the smooth-talking 'Foreign Minister' of the Trust was nothing more than a Cheka stooge. It was time to aim at a softer but more prestigious target, the Grand Duke Nikolai Nikolayevich, uncle of the murdered Tsar and a one-time commander-in-chief of his armies. The elderly Grand Duke had established himself in Paris which had emerged, soon after the revolution, as the political centre of the whole White

Russian diaspora. If he could be won over, the Trust's credentials would be impeccable.

It was a crucial move, so crucial that Dzerzhinsky took part with Artuzov's team in the planning. Obviously, Yakushev would be inadequate for the assignment on his own; the Grand Duke was not likely to be impressed by a former official of the Waterways Ministry. But there was an ideal reinforcement at hand in the person of a General Potapov whom, in the old days, the Grand Duke had occasionally received at court in St Petersburg. Superfluous to add that this former Tsarist stalwart was now firmly in the hands of the Cheka. The team still had to be coached and provided with expert counselling on the spot in case any awkwardness arose. Thus, yet another figure is pushed forward on the chess board, the OGPU agent known by his *nom de guerre* of Federov.

Orlov, in his 'March of Time' manuscript, accords Federov a key role in Trust operations from now on.[4] He describes the man as being at this time in his early thirties, short and on the portly side. He always spoke slowly and with great deliberation. His favourite tactic when trying to win someone over was to present both the pros and cons of the proposition – seemingly in an objective fashion, though with a hidden balance tipped the way he wanted it to fall. This ambivalent approach was for ordinary mortals whose minds were not made up. For the Grand Duke there could be only one method: an outright pledge to restore the monarchy with undiluted powers and an outright promise that the Trust could and would achieve this.

General Potapov and Yakushev were admitted to the grandducal presence in Paris on 24 August 1923, with Federov, the watchdog and counsellor, nowhere in sight. The talks lasted three hours, during which the bogus monarchists dropped more than one hint that when it came to selecting the new Tsar, the Grand Duke's name would be high on the list. The MOR, still working under that name inside Russia, would leave the underground when the time was ripe and emerge publicly as the country's official Monarchist Party. Its ruling body would in turn choose the Romanov to be placed on the throne. The scenario sounded plausible and, to the

Grand Duke, very promising. Artuzov's emissaries departed with his blessing and a promise to consult them over any major decisions in the future. The OGPU, as the Cheka had been restyled, now had more than a foot in the door; they were right across the threshold and would be privy to any plans their opponents made.[5]

It remained only to fool, or at least lull into inactivity, the Western powers, so that no more Kolchaks or Denikins would advance across Bolshevik soil. The channels used for this part of the deception programme were their secret services. These had had their budgets slashed (especially in England) after the abandonment of armed intervention in Russia and were now all too willing to conduct their intelligence work by proxy, if the opportunity arose, just as they had fought their 'war after the war' by proxy. Artuzov and his fellow-schemers provided that opportunity. We are now able to watch this process of penetration through the eyes of one of its principal targets, Harry Carr, who ran the British secret service station in Helsinki during the 1920s.[6]

Carr describes how the first reports about a powerful anti-Bolshevik underground organization known as the the Trust reached him at the beginning of 1922. It soon became clear that secret couriers between the Trust in Moscow and centres of White Russian activity abroad were criss-crossing several of the frontiers between the Soviet Union and the West. What made Carr sit up and take greater notice was when he learned that the military intelligence departments of Estonia, Poland and Finland 'had become involved and were facilitating this secret traffic and activity'.[7] This prompted Carr to detail one of his own agents, a certain Nikolai Bunakov, to find out what the Trust was really up to and 'to try and exploit it for providing intelligence for the USSR'. The Moscow plotters could not have asked for more: the hand of British intelligence was actually being stretched out towards them. However, Carr was too astute an operator to accept at face value the offerings which soon started to come his way.

He became concerned, for example, when his requests for sensitive military information consistently produced poor responses. He recalled:

Some military information was forthcoming but political questions and questions on internal conditions in the Soviet Union were answered more readily. Though the reasons for this, as gathered by us from the Trust's replies, seemed plausible enough, their hesitation to provide information on military matters nevertheless caused me to regard them with some misgivings.[8] The theme song running through their explanations was that the Trust was first and foremost a secret underground anti-Bolshevik organisation, aiming to overthrow the Bolshevik regime when they considered the moment ripe and that it was undesirable for them to undertake any intelligence operations of a kind that might jeopardise their primary political objectives. This seemed a sensible policy to follow but the possibility that such explanations were nothing but an excuse could obviously not be entirely discounted.[9]

Carr went on to stress that, at some point, somebody would have to be called on to solve the riddle. The attempt to provide that precious answer was eventually made, and it was to cause a storm of controversy to blow up and down the corridors of Whitehall. But for the time being, the mystery remained unsolved and the Trust had gained at least a beady-eyed recognition by the Western powers. It was all that Moscow needed. Even acceptance with reservations was enough to keep the Western governments passive and their intelligence networks hungry for more tidbits. By 1923, the steely web of deceit had been fully spun and was holding all around its vast perimeter. It was now strong enough for Dzerzhinsky to start luring the first of its major victims into the meshes.

16

The Entrapment of Savinkov

Boris Savinkov had been marking himself out for years as the prime target for Bolshevik vengeance. In his secret history of the era,[1] Orlov notes that when Savinkov came to Moscow in the autumn of 1917, he promptly made his first conspiratorial contacts with the French ambassador M. Noulens (described as 'the main plotter behind the anti-Bolshevik coups') and with the mission's principal military adviser, General Lavergne. By the spring of 1918, French and British funds were flowing briskly into the coffers of Savinkov's 'Union for the Defence of Fatherland and Freedom'. One of the main channels was via a certain Vilenkin, who was the official Russian lawyer of the British Consulate. By midsummer, Savinkov's Union was already organized into six separate staff sections and most of the Anglo-French money was going to the front line departments: the armed detachments, commanded by General Rychkov, and a group of units specially trained in street fighting by the former commander of a Lettish brigade, General Gepper.

According to Orlov's account, the Union, which already had its armed branches formed in Kazan, Yaroslavl, Rybinsk, Muram and Kaluga, originally intended to launch the uprising, based on a French plan, in June 1918. But this first plot was 'blown' through a romance which had blossomed in Moscow's Iberian hospital between a young cadet and one of the nurses. He had fallen in love with the girl and wanted to protect her from the violence which, he warned her, would soon break out in the capital. He told her that many other 'patients' in the hospital were, like himself, healthy members of Savinkov's movement in hiding for the great day and she should leave Moscow at once for her own safety. The nurse foolishly gossiped about this alarming news and the Cheka duly swooped on the hospital, persuading some of the 'patients' to talk. As a result, several of the key passwords to networks outside the capital were revealed. It was then that Savinkov decided to strike in the Upper Volga, in the Yaroslavl putsch of July 1918 which has already been described.

The failure of that putsch and the defeat of the White Russian armies he supported two years later, had only driven him abroad in search of yet another banner under which to fight the tyranny he perceived in the Kremlin. He found it in Poland in the winter of 1920, when the Russo-Polish war was at its height. In December of that year, this fanatical apostle of human freedom founded the last of his many organizations designed to bring the Bolsheviks down. He called it 'The People's Union for the Defence of the Country and of Liberty' and one of his visitors at the time[2] recorded that he had the same supreme power over that movement as Marshal Pilsudski possessed for the whole of Poland.

But Savinkov in Poland was much more than a political opponent. He also controlled from Warsaw a powerful guerrilla band which was fighting against the Red Army in neighbouring Byelorussia. Its commander was an ex-Tsarist officer, Colonel Sergei Pavlovsky, who was to remain fiercely loyal to Savinkov almost to the bitter end. Dzerzhinsky feared – with reason as it turned out – that this guerrilla force might one day expand into a serious military threat and he set up a special operation (codenamed in the service 'Syndicat 1') to neutralize it. Orlov's unpublished papers give a vivid description of its launch in the thick of the Byelorussian forests.[3]

The guerrillas, with the help of the local peasants, had been having a series of successes in hit-and-run raids on Soviet camps and in derailing military freight trains. The Red Army repeatedly sent out punitive detachments, known as the Chon, to liquidate the guerrillas; they could never even find them, let alone engage them. Then, one day, a detail of Red Army soldiers, armed with

Agar's 'skimmers' anchored at the Finnish port of Terrioki, whose yacht club he used as his clandestine base.

Terrioki, 2.50 a.m., 17 June 1919; the crew of CMB 4 back safely after sinking the 'Oleg'. Agar, quite relaxed with pyjamas and slippers under his uniform. His No. 2, Hampshire (left), was shattered by the adventure and was promptly repatriated with a nervous breakdown.

The armoured Red Fleet cruiser, 'Oleg', whose twelve-inch guns out-matched anything in 'the allied' navies of the Baltic.

The wreck of the 'Oleg' after Lieutenant Agar, while serving with SIS as a naval courier had torpedoed it in Kronstadt harbour in June 1919.

Red Army prisoners held on board ship by their captors, the anti-Bolshevik Czech Legion. For months during the Civil War, the Legion controlled the length of the great Siberian Railway.

American soldiers of the allied intervention force in camp at Vladivostok during 1914. President Wilson forbade them to operate anywhere west of the Ural Mountains.

A parade of British troops in Vladivostok in 1918. Some military units took part in operations directly supporting Kolchak's westward push towards Moscow.

The ill-fated Admiral Kolchak (seated) with Major-General Knox (standing) and the staff of the powerful British Military Mission supporting the White Russian leader. Soon after being proclaimed 'Supreme leader of Russia' Kolchak was betrayed, captured and executed by the Bolsheviks.

Officers of Admiral Kolchak's White Russian forces in Siberia pose before the severed heads of their Red Army captives. Some of the Admirals' allies – especially the Cossacks were notorious for their brutality.

Peasant Soldiers of Kolchak's army. Though he received many millions of pounds in arms and uniforms from the West his forces never quite lost this rag-bag quality.

An all-female fighting detachment in the Bolshevik army – resources denied to their White Russian and Western allies in the great Civil War.

A Red Army armoured train occupies Samara, a key rail junction in the Siberian Campaign. These trains functioned like mobile battleships in the vast terrain.

General Denikin (in uniform) Commander-in-Chief of the White Russian Army of the South, in which the Western powers invested heavily, but in vain.

rifles, turned up at a village in the midst of guerrilla territory. Their commander, a young man calling himself simply 'Grisha', was himself a Byelorussian, speaking in the vernacular of the people. He told the peasants that he had been sent out to collect grain levy from them for the Soviet coffers, but instead had decided with his men to desert and make his way to Poland.

The story was a pack of lies. Grisha was an emissary of Dzerzhinsky's Syndicat 1. His real name was George Syroezhkin and he was both an ardent Bolshevik and the youngest battalion commander in the Sixteenth Red Army engaged against the Poles. His mission as a 'deserter' was to infiltrate Savinkov's guerrillas with the object of luring them into a pre-arranged trap where the Chon could finally dispose of them. Such was the initial assignment given him by the Osoby Otdel, the intelligence department of the field army. But, as Orlov relates, Grisha soon went ahead in such spectacular style with his infiltration that Moscow was compelled to think again.

He first captivated the local guerrillas (who had turned up in peasant dress at a village festival in order to take a good look at these Red Army men) by winning all the wrestling and weight-lifting contests that were staged. He had great personal charm as well as the strength of a bull and joined in the drinking, singing and dancing (for two weddings were being celebrated) as though he had been born in the village. The local guerrillas not only accepted him as one of their own; the young 'deserter' was soon their second-in-command. He promptly established his credentials by leading a daring raid on the treasurer's office in the Soviet-held city of Minsk and escaping with large sums of cash.

Grisha made an equally good impression on Pavlovsky himself when he was taken to a conference of guerrilla chiefs summoned by the field commander. The colonel was looking for especially brave and resourceful men among his forces whom he could use as couriers to maintain regular contact with Savinkov in Warsaw. Grisha seemed to fit the bill perfectly and was one of three candidates to be offered the assignment. He accepted with alacrity, realizing what an intelligence gift was being placed in his lap. His Red Army controllers, with whom he could keep in contact through a pre-arranged channel, were equally delighted. A message was passed back to Grisha telling him to drop the original military plan and concentrate everything on the liaison mission with Poland. Even better things were to come.

The border crossings, Orlov explained, were organized either by the Polish Intelligence Service, who had bought up farmsteads in the no-man's-land, or by smugglers who were paid for their services. It was when he was making his third trip over the fron-tier that the group ran into a Red Army patrol. Fire was exchanged before the patrol was driven off and Grisha, hit in the groin and the right wrist, was one of the two men wounded. On earlier trips, Grisha had been interrogated with disconcerting thoroughness by the Polish Army Defensiva, or Counter-Intelligence, who had checked and rechecked his past and the circumstances of his defec-tion. Now, even these shrewdly suspicious minds were set at rest. Surely the Red Army would not have fired on their own agent, simply to establish his credentials once and for all? The question mark is just worth leaving in place.

Whatever the truth behind the skirmish, it brought Grisha finally into close contact with Savinkov, who invited the wounded youth to stay at the headquarters of the People's Union, the Hotel Brul in Warsaw, while he was convalescing. There was something about the zest for life and sheer brute strength of the unsophisti-cated Grisha which appealed to the slightly built, middle-aged nihilist, whose own vitality was already being drained by disen-chantment. Almost like a child showing off a prize toy, he would introduce his young friend to officers on the Polish General Staff, inviting them to 'just feel his biceps'. The prize soon bestowed on Grisha was the secret agent's pot of gold. He was installed in a large Warsaw apartment which was to serve as the delivery point and rest-house for the couriers being sent back and forth to all under-ground commanders in the heart of Russia. Moreover, Savinkov put Grisha in charge of the entire operation. Grisha could hardly believe his luck. Nor, when they were passed the news, could his intelligence chiefs. This was on a different plane from the courier duties he had fulfilled for the guerrilla bands in Byelorussia. From now on, all the instructions sent to Savinkov's underground in the Soviet Union, as well as all details of the network and every item of intelligence they reported back, would pass through the hands of a Bolshevik agent in Warsaw and thence, via the head-quarters of the Sixteenth Red Army,[4] to the Kremlin.

Artuzov's delight at this windfall was tempered by alarm at the size and strength of the underground network it revealed. As Orlov puts it in his memoirs:

> In less than one year Savinkov succeeded in creating a vast and active anti-Soviet organisation which covered the territory of Western Russia from Petrograd in the north to Odessa in the south with all the cities of Central Russia in between. The underground headquarters ... was located in Gomel. This centre guided the work of the Regional Committees which, in turn, directed the activities of the local networks. All were busy recruiting followers and anti-Soviet cells in government estab-lishments, in the Red Army and in the villages.
>
> The principal aim of the organisation was to create inside Russia a fighting force capable of overthrowing the Soviet regime. At the same time Savinkov had in readiness two army corps of 15,000 men each which he had recruited from the armies of Petlyura (former leader in the Ukraine) and other forces interned in Poland.
>
> According to an agreement reached by Savinkov with the Polish General Staff *and approved by the head of the French Military Mission, General Niessel,*[5] the two corps were to be transferred to the Soviet frontier on Savinkov's demand.

The great uprising, combined with this military threat from the south, was planned to erupt in early autumn of 1921, after the har-vest had been gathered in. Lenin forestalled it when, in March of that year, he cut his losses in Poland, and signed the Russo-Polish peace treaty. This left Pilsudski in triumph in Warsaw, but Savinkov in despair. Poland had been the last staging post from which, sustained by the armed forces of the host country, he could have mounted a serious challenge to Soviet Russia from across a common border. Moreover, he was now driven into real exile. As soon as the peace treaty came into force, the Soviet government began to demand his expulsion from Poland and the cessation of all support for his movement. For some months Pilsudski resisted the pressure but he had to give way in the end. Savinkov moved first to Prague and then to Paris – another distant émigré leader, as opposed to a formidable military challenger on the borders.

Yet his underground movement inside Russia remained, as did his own unique prestige. The OGPU struck at the former in July 1921, when raids were made on his networks in a number of cities (their details all on record thanks to Grisha in Warsaw) and several hundred of his supporters arrested. The round-ups, conducted in a blaze of publicity, gave the Soviets the diplomatic ammunition they needed to persuade the Poles to abandon their nihilist protégé. Yet Dzerzhinsky, with characteristic cunning, was careful only to maim the organization, not to kill it off altogether. Orlov suggests that the OGPU feared the prospect of Savinkov starting again from scratch if ever he knew that his existing movement had been wiped out – in which case they would face the task of another fresh intelligence battle against him. With this in mind, only one member of the courier chain to and from Warsaw was arrested. This gave some reassurance to Savinkov and left his precious Grisha in the clear.

But somehow the nimbus of Savinkov's prestige had to be blown away, and that could only be achieved through humiliation on a grand scale. And so, in 1923, the plot codenamed 'Syndicat 2'[6] was launched by Dzerzhinsky. Its forerunner had been aimed merely at defeating Savinkov on a regional guerrilla battlefield. This successor plan was designed to destroy him in public, before the eyes of the Russian people and the outside world. It was a formidable task, and Bolshevik deception tactics rose to new heights of make-believe to achieve it.

As Savinkov could no longer count on his armed intervention force, based in Poland, everything depended on convincing him that an anti-Bolshevik underground inside Russia would be strong enough to topple the regime unaided – provided that he, the great messiah of human liberty, returned in person to lead it. But there was a snag. The Trust, functioning as the foreign arm of a so-called monarchist conspiracy, would hardly be acceptable to an uncompromising idealist like Savinkov, who hated the Romanovs as heartily as the Leninists. So a new bogus front was invented by the OGPU task team,[7] the so-called Liberal Democratic organization, a label which would surely appeal. Artuzov, under a different name, posed as its president and the persuasive Federov (this time changing back to his real name of Mukhin) was to function as its smooth-talking salesman. Various despatches (all of them optimistic) were sent by the bogus LD to Savinkov, who was now established in Paris, coupled with exhortations for him to return and storm to victory over the regime.

However, there was a second snag. The only man whom Savinkov trusted implicitly was his faithful Colonel Pavlovsky, who had returned to what was left of the real underground in Russia, and who was in secret communication with him. The extraordinary story of how the OGPU surmounted this complication is described only in the unpublished Orlov memoirs.[8]

To begin with, through the control they still had over the courier services, they started tampering with the colonel's reports to his chief and Savinkov's replies from Paris. This was not difficult as the two men used an unsophisticated method of writing in block capitals, in invisible ink but uncoded. Bogus messages were now interspersed among the genuine ones. Some gave a suitably exaggerated impression of the underground's strength. One such report presented what had in fact been an ordinary criminal raid on the cashier's office at Moscow's Kazan railway station (*Izvestia* clipping duly enclosed) as the work of the rebels. Other bogus messages informed him that the paramilitary contingent of the movement was steadily growing in strength with the help of arms provided by sympathizers in government arsenals. All this was leading to a resuscitation of Savinkov's old Union for the Defence of Fatherland and Freedom which he had more or less left for dead after the smashing of the July 1918 revolts.[9]

Savinkov, who sensed that his time might be running out, was sufficiently encouraged early in 1924 to ask the real Pavlovsky outright whether the movement did, or did not, have the strength to seize power. The bogus Pavlovsky (i.e. Artuzov) sent back a complete 'order of battle' of the organization (which now allegedly included disaffected units of the Red Army) and a plan of action. This was reminiscent of the scheme Sydney Reilly had announced at that fateful gathering in the American consulate-general six years before: a lightning *coup d'état* in Moscow with the assassination of the top Bolshevik leaders. The only drawback, the false Pavlovsky warned, was sharp disagreement within the movement about the political programme to follow: how much autonomy should be accorded to the Ukraine and should agricultural reform still follow the old Social Revolutionary line? 'Only your presence and personal appeal could make them close ranks,' the letter ended. It was the sort of language any would-be liberator yearned to hear.

Savinkov might have been lured back there and then until, one day in April 1924, the following alarming message arrived from the real Pavlovsky: 'I am discontinuing writing to you. Don't believe the letters that come from me. Don't write to me. Wait until I find another way of establishing communication. Don't trust the couriers. Trust nobody until I succeed, with God's help, in straightening out the situation.'

The colonel had given this message to a courier in whom he placed particular trust, but it also ended up in Artuzov's hands. The OGPU now faced a tricky situation. One Moscow–Paris strand in the web of deceit was clearly broken; whatever they did, Pavlovsky would be sending no more genuine messages in the foreseeable future. But his position as the underground leader had to be assured in Savinkov's mind, as did the courier service itself. They therefore decided to pass the warning on as it stood and to seize

Pavlovsky (whose whereabouts, of course, they had known all the time) before he could make any more damaging disclosures. The colonel's part in the plot now had to be changed. He was to be pushed centre stage to play the key role in persuading his leader to return.

Grisha (at Savinkov's request) had gone to Paris, where he repeated the siren-song about the revolution waiting to explode. But the great conspirator was still unconvinced, even after the pleas of this young Russian whom he believed to be his friend and comrade. So he decided to send a really expert investigator to Moscow to see Pavlovsky and get to the bottom of the truth. That man, recommended for the task by the Chief of the Polish General Staff, was a retired head of the Warsaw secret police whom Savinkov knew personally from his time in that city. And so, in all probability, did Pavlovsky, as the OGPU realized when they heard who was coming. There was therefore no point in dressing somebody up to act like the colonel. The colonel would have to appear himself, with suitable safeguards.

This result seems, in Orlov's account, to have been achieved by psychological pressure rather than violence. Artuzov first had Pavlovsky brought before him to be told that his organization was merely a bubble that had now burst. The colonel was shown the OGPU's photostats of all the messages exchanged with Paris and the details of the complete structure of Savinkov's organization – the list of activists with their addresses, the locations of the arms caches and the illegal printing presses. Many of these accomplices were now being seized, and if Pavlovsky wanted them to be treated leniently and save his own life in the process, he would have to perform as directed when Savinkov's Polish emissary arrived. This pressure was kept up for a fortnight and, in the end, a shattered Pavlovsky agreed. And so we come to Artuzov's pièce de résistance, a hospital bed scene worthy of any Hollywood scenario.

Artuzov had planned it with the greatest care and not only, as Orlov points out, because of the importance of Savinkov himself. By now, Stalin was in charge at the Kremlin,[10] and the OGPU were already feeling his heavy hand on their backs. The new master of Russia seemed to be taking a greater personal interest in revenge for its own sake than his predecessor had ever done. He started meddling with the OGPU's latest plot for Savinkov, observing sarcastically that if they were left to do it by themselves 'I can see that it will end in a flop'. As was probably the intention, that made Artuzov doubly determined to make it a success. He certainly spared nothing in the way of ingenuity.

The man he sent to meet Savinkov's emissary at the rendezvous on the Russian–Polish border was Puzitsky, from his special action group. This former major in the Tsarist Army, who was also a Russianized Pole, had the ideal credentials, needless to say under another name, to act as 'guide' on the carefully planned tour of inspection. The Warsaw police chief was immediately informed that the meeting with Pavlovsky would not take place at Kharkov, as had been suggested, but in far-away Tiflis, where the colonel had been obliged to go to resolve a bitter dispute between the radical and moderate branches of the underground, which had now spread to the Georgian group. The journey by train to Tiflis took more than two days, which gave the schemers several opportunities to produce bogus evidence of the strength of Savinkov's support.

Then, when the train was only an hour or two from its destination, a message was delivered that, 'in true Georgian style', the arguing in the Tiflis convention had become so violent and abusive that shots had been fired and that, in the mêlée, Pavlovsky had himself been unintentionally wounded in the right shoulder. However, the messenger went on, the colonel was still looking forward to the meeting, though it would now have to take place where he was being treated, in the city hospital. A whole floor of this building had been taken over by the OGPU, and fitted with their own 'staff' of doctors, nurses and janitors. Artuzov had realized from the start that even the promise of limited cooperation dragged out of Pavlovsky was too shaky to risk any in-depth talk with his visitor. They had therefore – wisely as it turned out – staged a pantomime which would limit the vital exchanges to a sentence or two. The pantomime was later described with professional relish by several of the 'Syndicat 2' group to Orlov, who duly recorded it in his memoirs.[11]

When the retired Warsaw police chief and his guide presented themselves at the hospital, they were taken to a room where Pavlovsky, the only occupant, was lying in bed, his body heavily bandaged. The 'shoulder wound' had seemingly just been treated by the doctor and the nurse, who was still holding a tray bearing a bloodstained dressing. The visitors were warned that they could stay only ten minutes at the most, for the colonel, already weakened from loss of blood, was developing a fever. They were then left alone with the patient.

The policeman promptly put the first question on behalf of 'the Commander' (Savinkov's pseudonym): 'Was the time ripe for the uprising and were the paramilitary forces available in Moscow and elsewhere strong enough to guarantee its success?'

There was a long silence (agonizing for Puzitsky). Finally the answer that came from the bed was 'Yes', but the patient wanted to postpone any detailed discussion until he was out of the hospital.

The second question was even more important for Savinkov: did Pavlovsky consider that the presence of the Commander was indispensable for the success of the operation? Again, the response was 'Yes', but the patient now added, with even more emphasis: 'I cannot give my final answers to your questions until I am out of this place.' It was just as well for the OGPU that they had timed the next act of their pantomime to begin at that very moment. The doors of the room burst open and a bed-trolley was wheeled in, bearing another patient who, to judge by the strong smell of ether, had come straight from the operating theatre. The visitors, reasonably enough in such a scenario, were asked to leave and to resume their conversation at another time. But when the Polish emissary and his guide returned the next day, the third act of the pantomime was played.

They were met by Pavlovsky's 'physician' who came out to tell them that their sick friend had now developed such a high fever that he could not be allowed any visitors for 'at least five days'. The guide suggested that, in this case, the best course would be to go up to Moscow where something of the Savinkov movement in the capital itself could be inspected. The Polish emissary accordingly spent his last few days in Moscow, where various special events were staged for his benefit. One such conjuring trick was to produce a briefcase containing 80,000 of the new Chervony roubles, an issue of hard currency pegged to the value of gold. They were the result, the visitor was told, of another successful bank raid by one of the underground's 'battle groups'. In fact, of course, the notes had come straight out of the OGPU's safe, to which they promptly returned.

The Pole appeared favourably impressed by all this, and reported as much to Savinkov on his return to Paris. But the arch-conspirator was still troubled in mind – above all by those distinctly bizarre happenings at the Tiflis city hospital. He cast around for worldly-wise advisers who could be trusted with his secrets. They turned out to be an extraordinary mixture. One was Benito Mussolini, the new Duce of Italy, in whose social reform policies a rather desperate Savinkov thought he could glimpse those pennants of human liberty which he had spent his life chasing. The great man opined, not very helpfully, that the affair might be genuine but could also be false and advised his strange admirer to wait for more facts. One of the confidants, Vladimir Burtsev, an expert since Tsarist times on plots, believed the story from Moscow was genuine and urged Savinkov to 'go with God's blessing'. On the other hand, Sydney Reilly, with whom, as we have seen, Savinkov had kept in the closest contact, declared emphatically that the whole thing was a trap, and urged him not to fall into it. (An ironic verdict, in view of what lay ahead.)

In the end, it seems to have been a woman who nudged Savinkov literally over the brink by crossing the Russian border. The Commander, despite his ascetic appearance, had cut a romantic dash in his early days and was reputed to have bedded many a willing young handmaiden of his liberal revolution. But now, in his late forties and seemingly stuck in the morass of emigration, he was vulnerable to a man's change of life – in every sense. The woman with whom he fell passionately in love was none other than the wife of his own secretary, Baron Derental. Lioubov was a flighty creature with a long thin nose set in the middle of a pertly pretty face. She was a born adventuress, interested only in conquering men and making money. Boris Savinkov was to satisfy both requirements.

Savinkov's infatuation with the baroness (whose husband seemed content to play the *mari complaisant*) soon came to the ears of the OGPU. Their *Rezident* in Paris, on instructions from Artuzov in Moscow, persuaded her to become one of their special informants. Realizing how special she was, she demanded three times the standard rate of payment, and got it. Eventually Artuzov, who was being berated by Stalin in front of his colleagues for the lack of progress, decided to stake everything on Madame Derental as his last hope of success. In money, the stake amounted to the considerable sum of 5,000 dollars[12] which she demanded as her reward for luring Savinkov back into Russia. Moreover, she insisted on the sum being paid into her Paris bank account in advance. The OGPU gritted their teeth and paid up.

She soon fulfilled her part of the bargain, urging her lover to stop dithering and take his rightful place in Russian history. He had sent many others across the border and they had not flinched. The time had come for him to follow and, as proof of her love, she would go at his side. This was more persuasive than all the carefully crafted appeals, one of them in Pavlovksy's own handwriting, purporting to come from his Moscow supporters. On 10 August 1924, Savinkov left Paris for Warsaw accompanied by Madame Derental, her *mari complaisant*, and the two bogus 'messengers' who had brought Pavlovsky's last letter. He was travelling on a passport in the name of Stepanov, provided by the Italian intelligence service, which had standing instructions from Mussolini to render the Commander all the help they could. Five days later, on a dark and rainy night ideal for such operations, Savinkov, now accompanied by only the two Derentals, crawled into a forest through which ran the Polish–Byelorussian frontier. When they emerged at daybreak, drenched to the skin, and crossed on to the Soviet side, there, waiting for them as promised, was the welcoming party – two men in Red Army uniform standing by a horse-drawn cart. Savinkov was delighted and reassured to find that one of the two men was Grisha, in whom he still believed implicitly.

The final scene in this saga of deception and betrayal – as described by Orlov from first-hand accounts given him by all the OGPU actors involved – has a touch of farce in it, alongside the drama. Grisha produced a blanket for the shivering Lioubov and military raincoats for the two men – Savinkov's bearing a colonel's badge of rank. They then drove some fifteen miles to a forester's log cabin in the middle of a clearing. Inside they were introduced to three men, using false names, who were in fact their chief captors: the red-headed Puzitsky, who had led the Tiflis hospital charade; a thin young man who looked like a German village pastor but was in fact Pilar, the OGPU chief of Byelorussia; and the plump, well-groomed Artuzov himself, who could not resist coming in person to witness the moment of his triumph.

That moment came after a jolly interval (for each side was very happy in its way) during which the ubiquitous samovar started to hum and Madame Derental began setting the table and preparing an omelette from the eggs on display. Then, at a signal from Artuzov, Grisha politely relieved the visitors of any weapons they carried (the baroness producing with a giggle a small pearl-handled Browning pistol from her underwear). Grisha then frisked a puzzled Savinkov and pronounced what was in effect a death sentence on the prize victim: 'Boris Viktorovich, believe me, this is the saddest day of my life, but I must declare you under arrest. I came to like you very much but revolutionary duty comes first.'

Savinkov was probably too dumbfounded to hear Pilar adding his solemn warning against any attempt at escape, telling him that the cabin 'is surrounded by my men'.

Finally Madame Derental broke the ensuing heavy silence with a chirpy call to table: 'Gentlemen, please take your seats. The omelette is getting cold.'

Captors and captives then sat down together to a communal breakfast, passing around salt and sugar but without looking each other in the eyes or exchanging another word.

17

Inside the Web

As soon as that bizarre breakfast was over, two large motor-cars took everyone to Minsk, where Pilar ordered his personal railway car to be attached to the night express for Moscow. In the capital, the stage was already being set for a political show trial which would eclipse even that of the Lockhart conspirators.

Dzerzhinsky had given as much thought to the manipulation of his prize prisoner as he had to the entrapment. The use of physical torture would have been an affront to captors and captive alike. Behind their battle of wits had lain a battle of ideals. The only way the Bolsheviks could truly win that second battle was to convince Savinkov that, whatever he might have thought of them in the early days, by now they were here to stay, and that the Russian people had accepted the situation. Psychological pressure, flattery, bribery by inducements and promises – all these would be needed; but the time for trickery, which had won the first battle, was over. The 'great conspirator' had to be persuaded that there was simply no point in conspiring any more.

This approach became evident from the start. Savinkov was taken from the train to the 'Butyrka', the inner prison of the OGPU, where Kalamatiano had been held and normally a place of dread. But the accommodation which had been prepared for Savinkov looked more like the comfortable den of a writer, with rugs on the floor, mahogany furniture, including a handsome desk with paper and pencils, an armchair and sofa and shelves filled with the latest books and magazines. His food was served from the same kitchen which supplied the meals for Dzerzhinsky and his top officials. Orlov makes it clear that, in providing these comforts, the OGPU were deliberately presenting themselves as hosts rather than jailers. His account continues: 'Dzerzhinsky decided to treat him with all the decorum due to his previous rank and position. He did not threaten Savinkov with persecution ... He simply told him that his crushing defeat and the fantasy that there was an army waiting for him to be led against the Kremlin proved that he had been living in a world of dreams and had been utterly misinformed about the true state of affairs in Soviet Russia.'[1]

This reality he was now invited to see with his own eyes. Grisha, whom Savinkov could not bring himself to dislike, let alone hate, was brought back into play, this time as his guide. Tailed by a posse of plain-clothes police, the two toured the capital together, visiting new and reconstructed factories, rebuilt roads and railways, schools and universities, hospitals, nurseries and even a Red Army camp outside Moscow. The streets were peaceful and the people, if not radiant with joy, no longer looked sullen with resentment. This was clearly not a city smouldering with revolution and awaiting only the arrival of a liberator to lead them once more into action. They had anyway seen enough of action over the last decade, a factor which the eternal revolutionary had failed to weigh. The experience was more numbing for Savinkov than any of his defeats in battle. Was there now, he began to ponder, perhaps no battlefield on which to fight?

His captor homed in on that growing doubt. Orlov's narrative continues: 'Dzerzhinsky told Savinkov that he had always admired his magnificent courage and that he now expected him to display that courage once more and tell the world the real truth about Soviet Russia ... Some squealing [sic] journalists might, of course, write that Savinkov had got cold feet, that he was praising Soviet Russia to save his skin, but such slander could only discourage a weak man or a petty politician, but not someone of his calibre.'

After the flattery came the bribe:

Dzerzhinky reminded Savinkov that Soviet justice was based, not on revenge, but on the concept of protecting society from socially dangerous criminals. Should the court find that Savinkov is no longer dangerous to Soviet society, he will be sentenced to a limited term of imprisonment which could soon afterwards be set aside by the Central Executive Committee. After that he would be given the possibility of serving the Russian people in a field where his talents might be most useful.

On the personal level, Dzerzhinsky accepted Savinkov's word that Baron Derental had never played any political role as his secretary and had never been an enemy of Soviet Russia; the police chief would, therefore, consider setting him free. Dzerzhinsky must have found it hard to keep a straight face when his captive put in an even more impassioned plea for Madame Derental: the lady, Savinkov declared, was 'completely innocent and had joined in the border crossing out of personal devotion to him and to her husband'. This appeal provided the perfect cover for freeing the greedy little OGPU agent, who had provided the final bait in the trap but who had been seized with the others for appearance purposes. Dzerzhinsky accordingly ordered her immediate release, thus earning the gratitude of the infatuated Savinkov while preserving the secret of his deception.

Such was the background to Savinkov's two-day trial, which started in Moscow on 27 August 1924, less than a fortnight after that breakfast in a Byelorussian forester's hut. Orlov does not go into any detail about the proceedings which he clearly did not attend. However, no contribution from him is needed: an eye-witness account was given in the *New York Times* by Walter Duranty, one of only three foreign correspondents admitted to the courtroom for the final day. In his autobiography,[2] Duranty gives only a summarized version of the key event – the defendant's speech before the three-man Military Tribunal. A fuller account of what Duranty reported from Moscow[3] shows that Savinkov's peroration came from the heart of this disenchanted idealist and not from the propaganda machine of the OGPU.

Duranty's description of the prisoner might, at first sight, have suggested a man whose will had been broken by his captors: 'A small figure, quite bald, about forty-five, who walked with rather weak and faltering steps . . . His face suggested the pictures of the young Napoleon, but was white and drawn, with deep shadows under the eyes.' However, Duranty went on to note that Savinkov appeared 'quite unafraid', an impression which was borne out by the words which followed. They were a proud restatement of his life's work and philosophy. His voice was low, almost monotonous, but that was the way he always spoke.

He began: 'I am not afraid to die. I know your sentence already but I do not care. I am Savinkov, who always played on death's doorstep, Revolutionary and Friend of Revolutionaries . . .' Then came a calm but unabashed demolition of the Bolsheviks' record, once they had taken over the reins of revolution:

> I turned against you for four reasons. First, my life's dream had been the Constituent Assembly. You smashed it. Second, I believed the Brest-Litovsk treaty was a shameful betrayal of my country . . . Third, I believed that Bolshevism could not endure, that it was too extreme and that it would be replaced by the other extreme of monarchism so that the only alternative was the middle course . . . Fourth, and most important reason, I believed that you did not represent the Russian masses . . . I thought they were against you and so I, who had given my life to their service, set myself also against you.

This was strong stuff indeed for the picked audience of some 250 members of the Bolshevik elite to hear.[4] It became much more palatable when the prisoner went on to describe his growing doubts over some points: the treaty of Brest-Litovsk, for example, which he had to admit gave the Lenin regime the breathing space it needed. In the event, there was no denying that the regime had proven its 'durability through years of stress and hardship'. As for the genuine feelings of the masses, these could never be properly judged from abroad and were what he had come back to gauge for himself, of his own free will, 'without bombs or revolvers, without plots or supporters'.

That last rhetorical flourish was, to put it mildly, somewhat at odds with the fact that he had returned with the fixed objective of leading a revolution against the regime by imagined hordes of devotees. But it was his realization that these simply did not exist which led up logically to the key passage which closed his speech: 'Now ... surrounded by your soldiers of whom I have no fear, I say that I unconditionally recognise your right to govern Russia. I do not ask your mercy. I ask only to let your revolutionary conscience judge a man who has never sought anything for himself and who has devoted his whole life to the cause of the Russian people.' At that he sat down, asked for a cigarette and calmly began to smoke.

He had thus provided the evidence which Dzerzhinsky had asked for, to demonstrate that Boris Savinkov was 'no longer dangerous to Soviet society'. But this did not sound like an OGPU stage performance pre-rehearsed by his captors. His words have the ring of the real Savinkov, with the egotism humbled and the dreams turned into ashes. This is certainly the picture painted by Alexander Orlov who, though never involved personally in the entrapment of Savinkov or the machinations of the Trust, took an immense interest in a case which was the talk of Moscow, official even more than non-official. He relates how all his colleagues in the intelligence community who had dealt with the affair were adamant that, to their relief, Savinkov had been sincere in his change of mind.[5] This was an immense and rare boon for any show trial.

The sentence passed on the prisoner certainly suggested that Dzerzhinsky had been successful with his pledges under what the legal world was later to call 'plea bargaining'. When the court was reconvened long after midnight, Savinkov was pronounced guilty on four separate charges which included, accurately enough, incitement to partisan warfare and counter-revolution. The mandatory death sentence was imposed, but there immediately followed a recommendation for mercy and the penalty was commuted to a term of ten years' imprisonment. Savinkov returned to his comfortable quarters in the Butyrka inner jail. The old privileges were all restored, with some precious additions. According to Orlov, he was now allowed special visits, both from his family and from his devious mistress, Madame Derental, who occasionally stayed overnight. It was Bruce Lockhart and Moura Budberg in the Kremlin all over again. This time, however, there was to be no happy ending for the prisoner.

The decision as to whether 'Soviet society' (i.e. the Bolshevik regime) would really be safe if the great revolutionary were released among them was one for the Politburo to take, and they spent long months debating it. Savinkov was not helped by the wildly fluctuating outbursts about his case made in London by the one man who had warned him against returning, his old friend and greatest champion, Sydney Reilly. The 'Ace of Spies', never one to shirk the limelight, now went right over the top, and even managed to do so in opposite directions.

Reilly leaped into print for the first time a week after the news of Savinkov's arrest, trial and sentencing had been published in rapid succession in the Soviet press. Rejecting the suggestion already circulating that Savinkov had joined forces with the Bolsheviks (which, some pundits were claiming, had been his whole purpose in returning), Reilly began by assuming that the show trial had been held behind closed doors, 'with no correspondents of non-Communist, European or American papers present'. This, as we have seen, was totally untrue, and it remains a mystery how Reilly had failed to pick up the widely quoted press reports from Moscow of Duranty and others. But he then went further by claiming that the man in the dock had not been the 'great revolutionary' at all. Savinkov, he suggested, had been killed while attempting to cross the Russian border[6] and an OGPU agent, made up to look like him, had acted his role before the judges.[7] It was an improbable flight of fancy and Winston Churchill, to whom Reilly sent a copy of his effusions, replied with a gently worded letter of rebuke. Reilly's version, the great man pointed out, was not borne out by the facts as reported in the *Morning Post*.

Moreover, if it were true that the Bolsheviks had indeed commuted the death sentence, this seemed to be 'the first decent and sensible thing I have ever heard about them'.

Within a week, Reilly turned a complete somersault in his judgements of Bolshevik trickery. *Izvestia* began publishing what was claimed to be the verbatim text of Savinkov's final statement to the court. This added up to little more than an expanded and suitably highlighted version of what Duranty had already reported, the overall gist of which had been that – partly out of a desire to go on living and working but partly also out of sober conviction – Boris Savinkov had accepted the reality of Bolshevik power. To Reilly, these trial reports seem to have come completely out of the blue; yet instead of questioning them as more OGPU stage-management, he accepted them without demur, exactly as they were presented. From there, he jumped to conclusions more savage than anything the court had levelled against the prisoner. Savinkov, he declared in another letter to the press, 'has not only betrayed his friends, his organisation and his cause, but he has also deliberately and completely gone over to his former enemies'. And, like a pope proclaiming excommunication of a heretic, Reilly pompously declared that Savinkov's name was 'erased for ever from the scroll of honour of the anti-Communist movement'.

Winston Churchill, who had been so impressed by Savinkov when Reilly had brought the two men together in England, again spoke out for him and tried to bring perspective into all the speculation. Savinkov, he replied to Reilly's latest missive, should not be judged too harshly, especially on incomplete evidence. For his part, Churchill added, he would wait until the end of the story before changing his own views about the man.[8]

That end was not far away. Savinkov had been a hyperactive man all his life, whether in armed struggle or political intrigue. Comfortable though his conditions were, he fretted at being shut out of the Russian stage which had always been the centre of his existence. Time and time again, he demanded to know when the regime was going to honour its implicit promise to cut his prison term and allow him in some way 'to serve the Russian people', once he had recognized the regime's right to rule. Dzerzhinsky, who had offered that inducement, is said to have twice attempted, in the winter and spring of 1925, to have it honoured. He even suggested that Savinkov should be allowed to write and publish his memoirs. But the Politburo, under Stalin's dominance, turned all such ideas down. All Dzerzhinsky could tell his captive was that he would 'have to wait a little longer'.

Savinkov's frustration turned to torment and on 7 May 1925 he wrote what was to be his final cry of despair. In a letter to the police chief later published in the Soviet press,[9] he repeated the position he had consistently taken up with the OGPU before his trial: 'Either execute me or give me the possibility to work . . . I cannot endure the neutral position of being neither for nor against you, of merely sitting in jail as one of its inmates . . . I appeal to you, Citizen Dzerzhinsky. If you believe me, set me free and give me something to do. I don't mind if it is a subordinate kind of job. I might be well qualified for it. For I too was once a revolutionary and fought for the Revolution.'

According to Orlov's account, Dzerzhinsky again raised the matter in the Politburo and was again refused. The decision was presumably passed on to Savinkov. That could well explain why five days later, on 12 May 1925, the OGPU's most famous prisoner fell to his death from a fourth-storey window of his jail.

Over the years, several versions of his end were produced, both of murder and of suicide. According to one account, he departed this life not through a window but down a lift shaft of the Lubyanka, into which he was hurled by his jailers. One suicide account has him evading his guard after a stupefying vodka session they had had together and throwing himself from the unlocked window of the room. Another has him jumping out after returning, ill and depressed, from his last escorted car-ride in the countryside.

Suicide was the verdict which the regime stuck to at the time – not surprisingly since the Trust operation was still in full swing and any suggestion of foul play would have knocked a hole in that great deception game. It can plausibly be argued that Savinkov was more useful to the regime as live bait to lure back its other opponents from abroad than as a murdered martyr. Orlov is non-committal over the verdict but, as usual, adds some details to the story. He quotes an Order of the Day issued together with the announcement of Savinkov's death which reprimanded several OGPU officers because of their negligence over the affair. To prevent any repetitions of such suicides the prison commandant was instructed to fit steel netting to all the windows of the building.

This could easily be read as being simply the final twist in that long trail of OGPU trickery which marked out the Savinkov saga. On the other hand, it is even easier to imagine that, by May 1925, after ten months of prevarication over his fate, Savinkov was himself in a suicidal mood. On balance, therefore, it seems plausible that he took his own life, though the possibility that Stalin – rather than Dzerzhinsky – took that life for him can certainly not be ruled out. It is not unfitting that controversy should also swirl over Savinkov's death after raging over his whole life.

The most prestigious tribute ever paid to that life was that of Winston Churchill, who installed the revolutionary in his pantheon of *Great Contemporaries*.[10] Here, Savinkov (sandwiched between Hindenburg and Asquith) and in the broader company of Foch, Bernard Shaw, Trotsky and Clemenceau, is celebrated as one of the twenty-one most influential men of the age. The heart of the eulogy is this passage: 'Without religion as the Churches teach it; without morals as men prescribe them; without wife or child or kith and kin; without friend; without fear; hunter and hunted; implacable, unconquerable, alone. Yet he had found his consolation. His being was organised upon a theme. His life was devoted to a cause. That cause was the freedom of the Russian people . . . He was that extraordinary product – a Terrorist for moderate aims.'

Boris Savinkov was all of this (or almost all; in fact he had a wife and son as well as other blood relatives). But his uniqueness can be summed up in briefer fashion. He was the only Russian who would have assassinated both Lenin and the Tsar with equal gusto.

Part Six

End Game

18

Trumping the 'Ace of Spies'

Boris Savinkov's removal from the scene had disposed of the one Russian émigré whom the Kremlin feared above all others. But the OGPU knew that Stalin would not allow them to rest until Sydney Reilly had also been lured back into their maze. They were aware that the former British agent had latterly emerged as the driving force behind Savinkov's anti-Bolshevik machinations; moreover, he had stood under sentence of death ever since December 1918, for his leading role in the Lockhart affair. Vengeance and cold calculation both demanded that he should no longer be left at large.

The enticement would have to be the same – the chance to return to Russia and march at the head of that invincible anti-revolutionary movement so persuasively depicted by the Trust. Yet unbeknown to them, Artuzov and his fellow puppet-masters had a well-meaning helper in the Allied camp. Indeed, the first enticing voice that Reilly heard early in 1925 was that of his former Moscow SIS station chief and trusted friend, Lieutenant (now Commander) Ernest Boyce. This made it far more difficult to reject the siren chorus as a whole and Sydney Reilly was no Odysseus who would tie himself to the mast to avoid steering for the deadly island. At heart, Reilly was always itching to jump on to the Bolshevik shore and refashion the course of history.

The precise role played by Commander Boyce in this final chapter of the Reilly saga has long proved difficult to determine. His personal file no longer exists in the SIS archives and, given the way these were maltreated over the years, its disappearance could as easily have been unmotivated (a victim of wholesale but random weeding) as deliberate (to remove an embarrassing episode from the files). The outline of his service record has, however, survived. This shows that from 1921 right down to 1928[1] he was in charge of SIS operations in Finland and the Baltic, under the normal post-war diplomatic cover of Passport Control Officer. He usually based himself in the Estonian capital, Tallinn. There are occasional references to him in the Reilly papers and these show that, even after the Moscow contract agent had fallen into disfavour with Whitehall, his old Moscow chief still valued both his friendship and his services. Thus, in early 1922, after Reilly's official links with SIS had been severed, Boyce asked London to forward him an invitation to 'make a trip to Finland before April'. Reilly's reply in a private letter passed on via the department much regrets that he cannot fit the visit in: 'I shall be very busy here in February and in March I want to watch how the cat will be jumping in Genoa.'[2] (What cat, why Genoa, and which jumps are not specified.)

Though the two men remained in friendly contact, Reilly must have been rather taken aback by a long private letter he received in New York from Boyce almost exactly three years later. In this, the commander, without taking the Trust entirely at face value, clearly believed that its credentials were worth an expert assessment and that Sydney Reilly was the man for the job: 'You would help me considerably by taking the matter up. The only thing I ask is that you keep our connection with this business from the knowledge of my department as, being a Government official, I am not supposed to be connected with any such enterprise.'

This letter and other written exchanges between the two men on the reconnaissance project survived in the hands of Reilly's family and have been published.[3] But in the story they present, some of the principal actors in the charade are still wearing their masks. Their real features are revealed only in the inside accounts given from the Russian side by Alexander Orlov and from the British side by Harry Carr. Thus the person who had done most to persuade Boyce of the Trust's validity and increasing strength was a 34-year-old Russian woman, Maria Zakhavchenko-Schulz,[4] who was already acting as a courier between Moscow and General Kutyepov in Paris. Both the general and, through him, Commander Boyce were convinced that she was a fanatical anti-Bolshevik and a dedicated servant of the White Russian cause.

The facts, as given to Orlov by the true leaders of the Trust operation, told a very different story. Maria was an OGPU agent who had been specially selected by Federov in 1924 for the task of luring Sydney Reilly to his doom.[5] Orlov calls her 'the most talented female operative Soviet Intelligence ever had; one who surpassed even Federov in the understanding of human nature and the power of persuasion'. Artuzov, who directed the great deception operation, dubbed her 'the Sorceress'. Who was this remarkable creature, now allotted such a key role in the Trust's game?

Orlov identifies her as the daughter of a Russianized Pole killed in the war when serving as a colonel in the Tsarist Army. She had herself held a commission in the White Army of the south and was among those evacuated to the West from the Crimea after General Denikin's defeat. In 1923 she settled in Belgrade where she was 'turned' by her lover at the time, himself an ex-Tsarist officer now working for the Bolsheviks. He persuaded her in an appeal to patriotism that they were the only force which could lift Russia back to power and greatness. The OGPU had recruited her for a very special reason. She was the niece of none other than General Kutyepov, the White Russian leader in Paris, and she changed sides only on the condition that she would never be required (as the OGPU had at first demanded) to lure her uncle into a Soviet trap.[6]

Orlov describes Maria as blonde and slightly built, 'a perfect actress with child-like blue eyes which seemed innocence itself'. This cloak of innocence protected her when, on more than one occasion over the next few years, the threads of treachery seemed to lead straight to her. Even then, she was able to persuade any doubters that she had merely been the unwitting tool of other traitors. Behind the blue eyes was a cool brain and a nerve of steel. But Orlov also mentions one vulnerable point. Federov once told him that 'the Sorceress', despite her many affairs, had a complex about the opposite sex and felt she had always been used by her lovers. This explained why she became so ruthless in deceiving and manipulating men in order to assert her dominance through this game of intrigue. Whether or not that were the case, a very feminine vulnerability was to surface at the end of her story. So much for the real face of the OGPU agent behind her White Russian mask. But some disguises had also been donned in the Allied camp.

One belonged to another key figure in the Reilly affair and the truth about him has now been revealed, this time in the Carr papers. The man whom Boyce asked to follow up his pressure on Reilly with further urgent letters was one Nikolai Nikolaivich Bunakov, who is described in later published versions of these events[7] as 'one of the Trust's more important agents in Helsinki'. In fact, Bunakov was an SIS agent, run in Finland by Boyce's chief lieutenant, Harry Carr, who was already using him to tap Trust sources for any intelligence items on offer about the Soviet Union.[8] After the first attempts to arrange a conference had failed (Reilly's suggestion that Trust spokesmen should come to New York to see him had, understandably, found no favour with the OGPU's master illusionists), Bunakov was made the principal go-between with Reilly. Carr records:

> Boyce decided to put Reilly in direct touch by correspondence with Nikolai Bunakov in Helsingfors [Helsinki] who thereafter played the role of intermediary between Reilly and the Moscow leaders of the Trust. Bunakov himself did not venture outside the frontiers of Finland, the exchange of subsequent correspondence and messages between him and the Trust concerning Reilly (who was given the pseudonym Zhelezny) being conveyed to and fro mainly by Maria Schulz. From the moment that Bunakov, who was under my direct control in Helsingfors, became the link between Sidney [sic] Reilly and the Trust, I was fully aware of the correspondence exchanged and the progress of the scheme.[9]

Carr goes on to describe how, from the first, the Trust had pressed for the decisive meeting to be held in Finland. Always ready with a plausible reason, the Moscow plotters explained that, if this country were chosen, then the Trust's secret envoys could make a lightning trip across the frontier. This would involve only a day or two's absence from their normal posts, and thus minimize the security risk they were running: Carr could find no fault with this argument.[10]

On 3 September, Reilly, having left a failed business and a mountain of debts behind him in New York, arrived in Paris for the first discussions with his well-wishers about his proposed mission. He had two conferences with the White Russian leader General Kutyepov who, according to Carr, 'while encouraging Reilly to take this step, made it abundantly clear ... that a journey into Russia would be very dangerous'. He should, therefore, stick to Finland. Pepita, the second of Reilly's bigamous wives, was also in Paris to greet him, as was Commander Boyce (accurately identified in Orlov's account of this conference as 'the British Intelligence Officer from Tallinn');[11] and, among others, his old comrade from the Petrograd days, the lawyer Grammatikov. All urged Reilly to go to Finland and meet up there with Maria Schulz, Bunakov and the 'special emissaries' from Moscow. Alexander Guchkov, a pre-revolution statesman who was reputed to have been the man who, in 1917, finally persuaded Nicholas II to abdicate, was also in Paris and he added his own voice to the chorus of encouragement.

Meanwhile, that ever-persuasive travelling salesman for the bogus Trust, Alexander Yakushev, had turned up in Finland to sniff out the ground for the impending rendezvous. The Carr papers describe a personal anecdote about his visit which makes a refreshing change from all these high-level hopes, calculations and trickery.

Yakushev had brought Maria Schulz, his fellow illusionist, with him to Helsinki and Bunakov invited them to a meal at his house. It was the first time that the British agent had met Yakushev as all previous communication had been via Maria or her so-called 'husband'. Bunakov later told Carr (who was eager to hear what his face-to-face impression had been) that while not excluding the possibility of provocation,[12] he thought that Yakushev was 'genuine enough'. But he went on to mention a little incident which had seemed trivial at the time but which was to prove prophetic.

The meal had been a family affair, with Bunakov's wife and teenage daughter present. Real business was not therefore discussed at table, where the conversation was purely social. But though Yakushev had only been exchanging small talk the young girl had intuitively seen through him. 'Father,' she had said to Bunakov afterwards, 'do not trust that man. He has got treacherous eyes.'[13] The experienced agent dismissed the idea as fanciful; so would the White Russian leadership in Paris have done, for they were entirely under Yakushev's charm. It was a pity that more teenage girls were not around to be consulted in the midsummer of 1925.

In the event, Yakushev managed to make the Trust's maze look even more inviting during this July meeting. Reilly, through a letter written in New York and displayed by Bunakov once they were out of the dining-room, was already expressing interest in establishing contact with Trust leaders. It was the host who now unwittingly helped the Moscow plotters to enhance still further the impression of their bona fides. Bunakov had a brother, Boris, still living near Moscow. Would it be possible, he asked Yakushev, to arrange for him to come out to Finland? A month later, Boris was duly smuggled out by Trust couriers to join his brother. Soon after that, Boris's precious violin was also brought out, to enable him to continue his work as a professional musician (and, in fact, for many years to come, Boris was to go on performing in Helsinki restaurants). Carr admits to another twinge of anxiety: was all this not just a touch too slick for any underground movement to pull off so quickly in a police state? Though not, of course, if this particular underground movement were really as powerful as projected, with contacts in the heart of the regime. So, yet again, doubt was stifled, and the 'Ace of Spies' moved on.

The mystery which has always shrouded Reilly's fateful trip can now be largely cleared up, thanks to two authoritative accounts of what happened at each of the final stages, in Helsinki and in Vyborg, the Finnish town close to the Russian border where the Trust had always planned to spring their trap. Harry Carr, the last British official – indeed, the last fellow countryman – to see Reilly alive, described what actually happened in Helsinki and the puzzling events which took place later on. Orlov's memoirs fill in the vital gaps about Vyborg.

Carr records that Reilly, who had travelled from Paris via Berlin and Stettin, arrived by boat at Helsinki on Monday, 21 September. He called in at the 'Passport Control Office' to meet Carr, who duly passed him on to Bunakov to handle all arrangements. However, before Reilly left the Finnish capital, he came to Carr's flat for a thorough discussion about his mission. Carr comments:

> Throughout our talk about the Trust ... it was understood that Reilly would not go beyond Vyborg and would be back in Helsingfors in time to catch the regular Saturday boat to Stettin, leaving in the afternoon of September 26th. In saying goodbye, I was naturally looking forward greatly to hearing from Reilly about his talks with the Trust's emissaries and what impression they and their claims had made on him. But I never saw him again. Nikolai Bunakov and Maria Schulz travelled to Vyborg for the conference with the Trust's emissaries, which was held in a 'safe-house' arranged by Captain Rosenström, the Finnish intelligence officer responsible for operations against Russia and, *inter alia*, for clandestine Trust affairs in the Finnish border zone bordering on the USSR. When Bunakov returned from Vyborg alone and told me that Reilly had gone clandestinely into Russia after all in order to confer with Trust leaders in Moscow, I was dumbfounded.[14]

And dumbfounded he remained. All Bunakov could tell him was that Reilly had suddenly changed his mind after asking for a private talk 'man to man' with Yakushev in the Vyborg villa. When Reilly rejoined Bunakov, it was to announce that he had decided to go to Moscow because nothing less than a summit gathering of the Trust's 'government-in-waiting' was about to be held there, and his presence was needed. The Trust, he said, had guaranteed to get him back to Finland after the crucial meeting in time to catch the boat back from Helsinki to Stettin on Wednesday, 30 September, only four days later than he had planned. But it was clear that Reilly had taken some persuading and had departed with a twinge of unease. He handed Bunakov a letter to his wife, Pepita, to be passed on to her 'only in the event of something going wrong'. Carr locked the envelope in his safe and manfully resisted the temptation to open it even after the storm over Reilly's fate had broken: 'How could I ... read a letter that might well have been the last one that a man had written to his wife?'[15]

The bait of attending, even perhaps presiding over, a meeting of Russia's 'Shadow Cabinet' in Moscow was obviously alluring to someone of Sydney Reilly's Napoleonic fixations. But how had he been tempted in Vyborg to swallow that bait, persuaded, almost against his instincts, that no vicious hook lay hidden underneath? The process is revealed by General Orlov who, on this matter as on others, had the unvarnished inside story; he was given the details by those of his colleagues who had done the persuading.

Maria Schulz clearly played the leading role in presenting the deception plan (though it was Artuzov and his cronies in Moscow who had devised it). There is no evidence that Reilly, the insatiable womanizer, had started an affair with her, to match Savinkov's fatal infatuation for Madame Derental. However, the conspirators promptly noticed that, like so many before him, Reilly had been captivated by her child-like charm; in short, the Sorceress had cast another spell, so she was the obvious choice to conjure up the final illusions. Two of these were related, with proud satisfaction, to Orlov.

The first allegedly involved one of Reilly's old British colleagues. A message was handed to him at Vyborg from a British intelligence officer 'whose handwriting Reilly knew well' reporting that 'bona fide anti-Kremlin groups' were seeking contacts with British statesmen. Any such feelers, it was suggested, 'should be taken seriously'.[16] The officer was not named and the OGPU had their own special departments for fabricating excellent forgeries. But in the eager and excited mood which was gripping Reilly, the message could easily have been read as Whitehall's tacit blessing for his mission. This was clever enough; but the second trick was vintage, rivalling even that Tiflis hospital charade performed the year before for the benefit of Savinkov's emissary.

On the journey to Vyborg, Maria had shown Reilly clippings of a photograph in *Pravda* depicting the revered Lenin in his glory days surrounded by thirty of his closest comrades of the revolution. She concealed the text but asked Reilly to fix in his mind's eye the features of one particular man at Lenin's shoulder. Reilly, she said, might soon come across him. Come across him he did, as one of the two Trust emissaries whom Yakushev had brought with him to the conference. But the man concerned was no former lieutenant of the great Bolshevik icon. His name was Deribass and he was yet another OGPU agent. The original *Pravda* picture, which was a genuine one from their files, had been doctored to insert the new face. So Reilly found himself receiving renewed assurances about the forthcoming insurrection from a man presenting himself as a former leader of the revolution who, along with so many others, had grown disenchanted with the turn it had taken.

It was this bogus anti-Bolshevik who produced for Reilly that final nudge which pushed him across the frontier. As Deribass later recounted to Orlov, he had first gone through the usual pre-rehearsed recital of the Trust's widespread power and idealistic motives; then he had mentioned that there would, of course, be huge profits to be made out of economic concessions. Whether or not the Trust knew that Reilly, always out to make a fortune, had just lost one in New York, is unclear. But the effect of the tacitly offered bribe was instantaneous.

'At those words,' Deribass related, 'Reilly's eyes began to glitter. This was the moment when I knew I had him in the bag.'

Indeed, by the following evening of 26 September, he was securely in the bag, or rather inside the Bolshevik's maze of iron. He travelled under the name of Nikolas Nikolaivich Sternberg (the last of his countless aliases), on a passport handed to him by Yakushev, and crossed over into the Soviet Union via the bogus Trust 'window', escorted by Deribass and the bogus Finnish border guard Toyvo Vayha.[17] Reilly's fate after that is described below, so far as it can be reconstructed on the common ground of half a dozen different accounts, old and new. All that is needed to round off this part of the story is to give the only official Soviet statement ever made which connects up with the affair. Like all that had gone before, this too was characteristically false.

An announcement in *Izvestia* a week later stated merely that 'on the night of 28/29 September, four smugglers attempted to cross from the Finnish frontier. Two were killed; one, a Finnish soldier, was taken prisoner and the fourth, mortally wounded, died on the way to Leningrad'. What were all those anxiously waiting for news in the West to make of this cryptic item: Bunakov in Vyborg; Carr in Helsinki and Boyce (who had conveniently disappeared 'on leave') in London? This was the very night on which Reilly was supposed to be making his promised return trip. An incident of some sort there had been – or so it seemed.

Carr records that, according to a Finnish military report, shots had been heard that night near the Russian border village of Allekul, which was slap in the middle of the famous 'secret window'. Moreover, an agent had reported seeing one individual carried away on a stretcher, wounded or killed; and, in the meantime, that trusted ferryman Vayha was nowhere to be found.[18] But the purveyor of all this 'supporting evidence' had been none other than Maria Schulz, who had remained in Finland to monitor developments there for Artuzov in Moscow, but whom Carr and Bunakov still believed to be a genuine member of a genuine underground. As we shall see, she had been ordered to stay behind to spread further disinformation about the Trust as and when required in the wake of Reilly's disappearance. This 'military report' was probably the first instalment.

In fact, Petrov (a.k.a. Vayha) was to be subsequently identified on the Estonian section of the Soviet Union's borders, still cheerfully functioning as an OGPU frontier guard. The 'mortally wounded man' on the stretcher was meant to be taken in the West for Sydney Reilly – as indeed it was, for the lack of any other scrap of evidence. This would ensure that the British government would have nothing immediately to protest about[19] because – unlike the American authorities in the case of the captured Kalamatiano – they had nothing solid to go on. As for the 'Ace of Spies' himself, Reilly was not a wounded man on a stretcher up on the northern border by the time of the 'Allekul incident' but a handcuffed prisoner in Cell No. 73 of the Moscow Lubyanka, and he would never see any frontier to freedom again.

19

The End of Sydney Reilly

Reilly's interrogation had in fact started in Vyborg while he was still a captive-to-be. This, at least, is the picture painted by the first detailed account of the affair from Soviet sources, which was not published until nearly seventy years later.[1] It takes the form of a report dated 2 October 1925, put together by the Estonian V.A. Styrne (then the assistant head of the OGPU's counter-intelligence section) and submitted to his immediate superior Roman Pilar, whom we have already met as one of Savinkov's captors. The report describes how 'Secret Agent A' (almost certainly Deribass) had held a wide exchange of views with Reilly when the two men first met at Vyborg on 24 September. 'Secret Agent A' was out to pump Reilly for his opinions on a variety of current topics in order to give the OGPU in Moscow some advance guidance. The voluble Reilly was only too happy to oblige.

Thus, he advised the government to take control of religion and the church, and profit from their influence instead of making the mistake of repudiating them. Another piece of advice – which came richly from the Jewish Rosenblum – concerned how to deal with the Jews of Russia. A pogrom could not be avoided but the new Trust regime (which Reilly fondly believed they were both talking about) should not dirty its own hands with persecution but should call any measures 'an expression of national feeling'. As for establishing the post-Bolshevik government at home, Reilly felt that the peasants and town-dwellers should be ignored and reliance placed instead on the factory workers and the Red Army. In its foreign relations, the Trust regime should on no account ally itself with the Poles, about whose future England was playing a double role. In another rich observation – this time in view of Reilly's Anglomania – 'C's' prize recruit affirmed that, though England was being obliged to play a leading role in European affairs, it was a task for which she was 'ill-equipped'.

Finally, he got round to the subject of money, and here Styrne's report runs parallel with that given by Orlov. The Trust obviously needed funds and Reilly now offered himself as its principal fund-raiser. He apologized for having no pile of cash to hand over on the spot but named a sure method by which it could be collected: Russia's museums should be relieved of their artistic treasures, those in the storerooms as well as those on display, and he, Reilly, would organize their sale abroad. At this, the OGPU man, playing his part to perfection, protested that surely the Trust should not sully itself with the methods of a gang of robbers. Reilly was unmoved. Such sentimentality had to be overcome 'for the sake of Russia'.

So, by the time Reilly and his 'fellow insurgents' reached Leningrad on 26 September (after a squelchy journey which began by wading across the Sister River), the OGPU had a fairly clear picture of their new victim. To fill in some more gaps, they continued to ply him with questions, still posing as fellow conspirators: Styrne, who met him for the first time that evening, presented himself in this guise. It was, therefore, a confident and excited Reilly who boarded the Moscow-bound train later that night, in the company of Yakushev and an unsuspecting White Russian hired, for stage effect, as a guard.

On the journey, the conversation was all about Savinkov, and once more Reilly seems to have been less than generous in his comments. While praising his erstwhile hero as brave and gifted, he pointed to the negative side of the great conspirator – his poor judgement of people and his inability to take quick decisions. There was also criticism of his personal life. Savinkov had been far too fond of comfort and of women (yet another rich statement, coming from

Reilly). Even worse: it was all too often the coarsest of creatures who took Savinkov's fancy. Madame Derental had been a prime example. In Reilly's book, she was just 'a dirty stinking Jewess, with a shiny face, fat hands and thighs'.

This contemporary Soviet account of Reilly's conversation sounds all too disconcertingly familiar. The onslaught against Madame Derental, mainly because of her appearance, is, for example, a faithful echo of his 'Dear Diary' indignation against General Poole's Russian mistresses in southern Russia four years before ('Never saw such ugly women in my life'). What Reilly might well have complained about was Madame Derental's duplicity rather than her dumpiness. But, of course, he had no idea of the prime role she had played in Savinkov's destruction, and the OGPU were not going to enlighten him.

The impression Yakushev must have had of his victim by the time they reached the capital was of a man prepared to be disparaging about his former colleagues (without actually betraying them) if only to inflate his own sense of importance. Of Reilly's egomania there could now be little doubt. He had declared himself to be 'Churchill's closest assistant' in the struggle against Bolshevism. It was a struggle to which he would devote all his own energy and resources, once he had settled his business affairs in America and could return to take charge of things on the Russian stage. Though the issue was not touched upon in Styrne's account, it should be noted that, at this point, the narrator simply did not know whether Sydney Reilly would be allowed to return to America or not. His fate was still in the balance, and it would not be the OGPU who took the final decision.

To begin with, as in the case of Savinkov a year before, the pretence of a genuine welcome extended by a genuine band of kindred spirits was kept up. Reilly and Yakushev were taken by car from Moscow railway station straight to a dacha in the nearby forests of Malukhava where a party of so-called Trust leaders had assembled to greet him. They all consumed a hearty meal together (an improvement on Madame Derental's omelette for Savinkov) and Reilly, in expansive mood, made pledges: he would send them $50,000 to launch the round-up of art treasures; moreover, he would introduce Yakushev to Winston Churchill if his supposed comrade-in-arms could get to England.

At this point a gap, and a fairly significant one, needs filling in the Soviet accounts, which present Reilly's eventual arrest as the preordained end of the story. In fact, unbeknown to him, an argument had been going on that day behind his back about his fate. Most of the OGPU team who had lured him over from Finland were in favour of letting him return unscathed and with all his illusions intact. That, they argued, was the only way to preserve the Trust's credibility. It was evidently Stalin who had ordained otherwise. This is stated or implied in two non-Soviet accounts made independently of each other with many years in between. The first was drawn up soon after the affair for the SIS by well-informed Russian émigré sources. On this point it states: 'The Trust began to take steps for his release, thinking that Reilly's arrest might draw suspicion on them and that they might be accused of it. But Stalin protested vigorously and the OGPU wanted either to make Reilly work for it, as Yakushev and Opperput had done, or, once and for all, to get rid of this man, whom they considered "dangerous".'[2] Orlov's memoirs are equally emphatic: 'The Trust agents wanted to let him return to safeguard their image. But Artuzov said "No. The order to arrest has come down and it is final".'[3]

It was dusk on 27 September before this unchallengeable order reached the gathering in the dacha. Even then, it was not carried out on the spot. When Reilly left with his escorts by car again for Moscow, he was, to all appearances, heading back to the railway station, to catch the night train for Leningrad, as per the programme laid down at Vyborg. No immediate attempt was made to disabuse him of the idea, and he was even allowed to stop off and write a message to his English contacts as proof that he had been in the Russian capital. The safe-house chosen by his OGPU guards for this unscheduled exercise was the Moscow apartment of the ubiquitous Opperput, whom Reilly still believed to be a soulmate of his, but whom the OGPU had long since known as one of them. By sending the message[4] Reilly had in fact unwittingly made one final contribution to the Trust's deception plan. But, once back in the car, the mask was abruptly dropped and the handcuffs clapped on. Instead of heading for the October railway station, the car made straight for the Lubyanka. Reilly was later said to have been the only person in the vehicle who remained perfectly calm.

The Soviet political police archives are, inevitably, the principal direct source for Reilly's presumed behaviour during the two months he spent inside the jail. Some of these reports have trickled out over recent years, but before quoting them it is worth giving the broad comments of General Orlov who talked in 1925 to the OGPU interrogators involved: Pilar, Federov, Artuzov and Styrne. (Dzerzhinsky seems never to have made a personal appearance.) Orlov writes:

> After his arrest Reilly was brought to the Lubyanka headquarters and ushered into Pilar's office. Pilar and Federov, two of the four men who manipulated the Trust, were the first to interrogate the famous prisoner. Pilar reminded Reilly that the Revolutionary Tribunal had in 1918 sentenced him to death and that his life was on the bargain counter ... He could still save himself if he agreed to supply the OGPU with the names of British spies in Russia and with other pertinent information about the personnel and operations of the British Secret Service. Reilly's responses were all negative and to the effect that under these circumstances, 'a British agent does not talk'. His behaviour under interrogation won him the respect of the OGPU chiefs.[5]

Orlov states that Reilly was later confined in the Inner Prison (the Butyrka) in the same comfortable living quarters which had been specially set up for Boris Savinkov. He was supplied ('for some unknown reason') with all possible conveniences and taken out for car trips in the countryside. The general's account concludes: 'Reilly was subjected to all kinds of psychological pressure but, according to what I was told by Federov and Puzitsky, no physical violence had ever been applied ... His interrogators got out of him whatever they could by the soft-glove treatment.'[6]

This account throws some doubt on the authenticity of the oft-quoted personal letter which Reilly is said to have written to Dzerzhinsky on 30 October agreeing to 'cooperate sincerely in providing full evidence and information to answer questions of interest to the OGPU'. (The questions specified concerned the British and American intelligence services and the Russian émigré organizations.) This letter was published in Moscow as early as 1967,[7] the first of a long string of documents on Reilly, Savinkov and the Trust operation to be leaked selectively over the following thirty years to the West. But there is, to put it mildly, a question mark over its authenticity. Orlov, who described in detail how the much more famous Marchand letter of 1918 had been personally outlined by Lenin and then either composed or edited by Dzerzhinsky, makes no reference to any direct communication between Reilly and the OGPU chairman, and the general never mentioned it when questioned privately in America on the affair. But, in an eerie twist to the tale, some doubt was also cast by the prisoner himself who, it is now known, left one last message to posterity in the form of a cryptic and disjointed diary written in pencil in his cell on scraps of cigarette paper.

It is easy to understand how he could compose these fragments (discovered later by the guards) for he was often left alone and undisturbed in well-equipped quarters which almost resembled a hotel room. The diary itself is harder to make sense of, both as to purpose and to contents. As there was precious little hope of it ever reaching the oustide world undetected (though Kalamatiano had indeed managed this feat) Reilly's aim may well have been to let the West know, some time in the future, what he had said and not said, and how long he had resisted saying anything. That day in the future did not begin to dawn until nearly thirty years later when parts of the diary appeared in the Western press and in joint Soviet–American publishing ventures, in which the Soviet side controlled what was being published.[8] By far the most authoritative version is a masterly reconstruction of the fragments identifying nearly all Reilly's coded references, which was first published in 1995[9] and further annotated two years later while this present work was in its final stages of preparation.

There are entries for five consecutive days, the first dated 30 October. It shows that even now, after nearly five weeks of pressure and continuous interrogation, Reilly was still displaying proud, almost contemptuous, defiance of his captors. The following extracts, with the decoding, give the flavour:

> 30 Oct. Additional inter[rogation]. Late afternoon ... When called from sleep was asked to take coat and cap – Room downstairs near bath – Always had premonition about this iron door. Present in room St[yrne], his colleague, assistant warder, 'executioner' and possibly someone else ... informed that ... unless I agree execution will take place nemedlenn [immediately]. Said that this does not surprise me, that my decision remains the same and that I am ready to die. Was asked by St[yrne] whether I wished time for reflection. Said that this is their business – given one hour ... Taken back to cell ... Prayed inwardly for Pita [Pepita, his second morganatic wife] made a little parcel of my personal things, smoked a couple of cigarettes ... Was kept in cell the full hour. Brought back to same room. St[yrne], his colleague and young fellow. In adjoining room executioner and assistant all heavily armed. Announced again my decision and asked [if I could] make written declaration [of it] ... to show them how an Eng[lish] Christian[10] understands his duty. Refused. Asked to have things sent to Pita. Refused. Told my death will never be known. Then began long rambling persuasion – same as usual ... Told them they are going to make greatest fools of themselves.

At this point Styrne and his colleagues evidently realized that their 'rambling persuasion' was not going to dent the prisoner's obduracy. So the process which Orlov had described as applying 'all kinds of psychological pressure' was set in motion. When Reilly remained silent after one final five-minute ultimatum had expired, Styrne left the room and called in the unnamed 'executioner'. Reilly was handcuffed and taken outside to a car in the courtyard already full of OGPU heavies. It was drizzling and very cold and the driver added to Reilly's discomfort by 'squeezing his filthy hand between handcuffs and my wrist'.[11] But the execution never took place. After further delays and attempts to jangle his nerves, the car left the Lubyanka heading for the woods (where Reilly imagined he would be finished off) only to turn back for the capital and re-enter the jail by another route from the north. There Styrne was awaiting him with the announcement that his execution had been postponed. Not surprisingly, Reilly's entry for the day ends: 'Terrible night. Nightmares.'

What does not appear in an otherwise fairly detailed account of events on 30 October is any mention of the letter of virtual submission supposedly penned to Dzerzhinsky on that very day. It is inconceivable that Reilly, who had throughout displayed defiance, would have failed to mention such a volte-face. It seems all the more probable therefore that the document was produced by the OGPU's diligent factory of lies and forgery to make things look neat and pretty in their files.

That being said, however, there seems little doubt that Reilly had by now reached an accommodation of sorts on the spot with Styrne, who had greeted him the following morning in a 'solicitous' mood. The solicitude could have been over Reilly's state of health, for the prisoner was given a thorough examination later that day by the Lubyanka's 'post-mortem' physician, Dr. N.G. Kushner, who was also a specialist on neurological problems. Reilly was known to suffer from migraines and even from a mild form of epilepsy.[12] The events of the preceding twenty-four hours were well calculated to induce either or both.

The OGPU now clearly became nervous about losing their famous prisoner before he had even submitted to a proper interrogation. In any case, it was time to try the traditional secret police technique of the abrupt switch from threats to blandishments. Accordingly, that same evening, having read the doctor's report, Styrne put on gloves which were not just soft but positively velvet. At eight o'clock that night, Reilly records how he was driven out for a walk in the countryside (dressed for the occasion in OGPU uniform to camouflage his identity) and then taken to a comfortable Moscow apartment for a good meal ('Great spread'). After that, having been assured that his death sentence had been stopped, he proposed his own 'programme' with Styrne, outlining the headings under which he was now prepared to talk. These included '1918', presumably covering the so-called 'Allied conspiracies'; the SIS and its American equivalent; the political situation in England and the United States and the Russian émigrés; above all the late Boris Savinkov.

His interrogations under these headings continued for the next four days, with regular intervals for rest and overnight sleep. There is no indication in his cigarette paper report for posterity that he had been broken down by his captors into a state where he was willingly blabbing about anything. He prepared several written reports, none of which was challenged and, quite apart from anything which he deliberately omitted (which would have been normal for any trained agent in control of his faculties), there was much that he simply did not know. The 'Ace of Spies' had been out of touch with his old department for more than four years and, in that period, SIS had been reduced in size and transformed in structure. In any case, as a one-time contract agent, Reilly had never sat behind a Whitehall desk, with access to the files.

It could therefore have been plain ignorance rather than dissimulation that lay behind Reilly's flat statement, made to Styrne on 2 November, that it was now impossible for the SIS to maintain any agent in Russia and that there had, in fact, been 'none since Dukes'. That, in the OGPU's view, was very wide of the mark, in the sense that intelligence operations had almost certainly been resumed under the cloak of the British Commercial Mission established in Moscow in 1921, and led by an old Russian hand, Sir

Robert Hodgson.[13] Reilly was repeatedly questioned on Hodgson's mission, about which he seems to have offered little, most probably because he knew little.

By a bizarre coincidence, the case of another person about whom Reilly was questioned that same day is dealt with in a document which has surfaced in his own personal SIS file. It concerns one Yaroslavski, an OGPU agent who had served with the Soviet Mission in Vienna and who seems to have been on very close personal terms with Reilly. This, at least, is stated in a letter marked 'Very Secret' sent on 1 October 1925 by Mikhail Trelisser, chief of the OGPU's Foreign Department, to his Vienna station.[14] Trelisser claims that Yaroslavski had given Reilly the task of bringing out of Russia the valuables he had stored in Leningrad and that 'Reilli [sic] was in possession of these when arrested'.

This is a mystery, for there is no reference to Reilly's carrying any such items when captured. But Trelisser had good reason to be probing, and with great urgency ('The above work must be put through at once, without awaiting its turn'), into any and all of Yaroslavski's connections. The agent in question had fled the Soviet coop, carrying OGPU secrets and OGPU cash with him. Initialled 'W.I.W.', a Whitehall minute on the intercepted letter[15] notes: 'Yaroslavski was a secretary in the Soviet Legation at Vienna. In June of last year he absconded after putting a considerable amount of Legation funds in his pocket. His disappearance led to a lot of enquiries into the Legation's methods.'

The last fragments of Reilly's prison diary are for 4 November. He was allowed to sleep until 11 a.m. but then wrote or talked until after midnight. The atmosphere was friendly and there were breaks for walks and meals. Hardly any attempt was made to re-examine him on anything of importance which he had previously volunteered, including his signed 'protocols' of his statements. This was an ominous sign that he was running out of usefulness for his interrogators. The last topics covered during these final sessions pointed in the same direction. They amounted to a pot pourri of disconnected odds and ends: the anti-Bolshevik work of Scotland

Yard; trade organizations and the possibilities of deals; questions on Persia and suspected right-wing émigré groups in Germany. For his part, Reilly dilated again on his vision of an Anglo-Soviet political and economic agreement involving both Churchill and the current Foreign Secretary, Austen Chamberlain. There was no argument and certainly no grilling. It was almost as though both captors and captive were now searching for things to ask and say. While Reilly may have sensed this mood himself, the last two sentences of his entry for 4 November – in effect his last words to the outside world – come as something of a shock: 'Feel at ease about my death. See great developments ahead.'

What developments he was thinking of remain obscure, unless he was feeling encouraged by the polite reception given to his ideas for a Soviet accommodation with the West. His premonition of death, on the other hand, was startlingly accurate, and it was to be realized earlier than he could have imagined.

Soon after 8 p.m. on the following evening, Reilly was taken out for what might well have seemed to him just another of his night-time relaxation trips into the countryside. The fact that one of the four OGPU officers in the car was Ibrahim, whom he had previously referred to as 'the executioner', would not have alarmed him unduly. Ibrahim had been the host at that convivial tea-time meal provided in a Moscow apartment only four days before. This time, however, Ibrahim was to be dealing out bullets, not lumps of sugar. The car stopped (feigning mechanical trouble) some forty-five minutes later near Bogorodsk in the woods north-east of Moscow. Feduleyev, the OGPU officer in charge, suggested they should all stretch their legs while the 'breakdown' was fixed. Ibrahim lagged behind the party and when they had all gone several paces ahead, fired a single shot into Reilly's back. He fell without a sound but was still alive when they turned him over. So, to finish him off, another bullet was put through his chest. The man who administered that *coup de grâce* was none other than Comrade Syroezhkin who, as 'Grisha' the bogus partisan fighter, had helped to lure Savinkov to his doom the year before.[16]

This last trick played on Reilly may appear cynical as well as brutal. Yet, in fact, the OGPU, by finishing him off in this fashion, were rendering tribute to the man whom General Orlov described, years later, as 'a hero in the true sense of the word' and 'a model for the standards by which intelligence personnel should be selected'.[17] His interrogators in 1925 are known to have shared that professional respect. Given their orders from on high, the only compliment they could pay Sydney Reilly was to shoot him unawares while strolling in the woods rather than execute him facing a firing squad in the Lubyanka courtyard, as the 1918 death sentence would have required. It was a rare, quite possibly a unique, salute to be sounded across this particular battlefield of intelligence. But then, Sydney Reilly had been a unique warrior in that conflict.

20

Fingerprints

They drove the body straight back to the Lubyanka. Here it was first laid on a table in the morgue to be photographed for the OGPU archives and then, four days later, buried in an unmarked plot in the graveyard of the inner prison. When they stripped the corpse and examined the clothes, they found, sewn in the coat lining, a small Union Jack. On the face of things, it might appear strange for a secret agent who had travelled under a profusion of false papers all his life, to carry about his person the clue to his real identity. Evidently, Reilly wanted to be recognized, *in extremis*, as an Englishman. This is perhaps the time to probe into the final unsolved mystery of mysteries surrounding Reilly's last adventures: to what extent was the British secret service involved in them? Emphatic denials of any such involvement, even quasi-official, were made down the years and have been repeated again in a qualified form to the present author. Yet, when this work was being researched, there emerged what can only be described as one or two sets of blurred and messy fingerprints seemingly left behind in Estonia and Finland by British intelligence, all of them connected with Reilly's doings.

For the first set of prints, we must go back twelve months before his death to the international uproar over the so-called Zinoviev letter,[1] whose publication in London on the eve of the October 1924 elections sealed the fate of Ramsay Macdonald's Labour government and ushered in the Conservatives under Stanley Baldwin to take its place. This was a rare example of a tremor in the intelligence world producing a positive earthquake in the field of high politics. Not surprisingly, therefore, Sydney Reilly has been presented as the instigator of the whole affair. According to this flattering account, it was Reilly who persuaded a well-known émigré forgery consortium operating in Berlin to fabricate the message on genuine Comintern stationery but with a forged signature.[2] But this tale is just another will-o'-the-wisp in the vapour trail of the *Ace of Spies* legend. In fact, Reilly was simply one of a chain of half a dozen persons, official and unofficial, who helped to guide the letter into the columns of the *Daily Mail* during the fortnight after its interception. The original was never produced then and never unearthed later, thus complicating the issue of whether it was genuine or not.[3] However, we now know from the papers of Harry Carr that translated copies were circulating in SIS stations abroad more than three weeks before its eventual publication in London. He writes of it in an oddly detached manner:

> SIS stations working on the Russian target, including Helsingfors, exchanged copies of the reports that each . . . sent regularly in the Legation's bag to London.
>
> For some time one of these stations had been sending home . . . copies of Soviet documents about what went on in the Politburo, the Sovinarkom (Council of People's Commissars) and the Comintern (Communist International). Amongst the usual batch of reports from this station that reached me at the end of September 1924 was a copy (English translation) of the Zinoviev letter. I read through the reports with great interest, as usual, but did not at the time attach any special significance to the Zinoviev letter report. We knew that the Comintern was doing in many countries just the sort of thing that the Zinoviev letter said was to be done in England, so there seemed nothing surprising in its contents.[4]

The writer of those lines was an experienced intelligence agent but, on this occasion, his political antennae were poorly adjusted. The dynamite in the letter lay in the fact that it was in England,

Carr's home ground, that Zinoviev was now urging what 'was to be done'. But was it the President of the Comintern or a forger writing in his name? At the time Carr seems to have shared the view, which he also attributes to Whitehall, that the letter was genuine: 'The Foreign Office learnt that the press had got a copy and, believing like SIS that the letter was genuine, decided to release their text first. Otherwise ... the Government would have laid themselves open to the accusation of suppressing important political information at a critical moment, for a general election was about to take place.'[5] Later, Carr added, it seemed 'abundantly clear that the letter was a forgery' and he attributed it, along with most other observers, to the counterfeiting gang headed by that one-time Tsarist Councillor of State and now émigré-on-the-make, Vladimir Orlov.[6]

The one point where the fantasy of Reilly's involvement touches reality is where he names Orlov and the Berlin gang of counterfeiters as the source of the fabrication. More substantial backing for Orlov as the author comes from those French intelligence archives of the period which are now available. A whole string of these *renseignements* running from December 1920 down to March 1929[7] deal not only with his prowess as a counterfeiter but also as a street merchant of intelligence wares, selling always to the highest bidder.

'He is currently,' says one Paris police report, 'supplying information to the French Mission in Berlin, the German government, the Poles, the Bolsheviks and others ... always demanding high prices.'[8] Later documents identify him as 'without doubt the forger of the false Zinoviev letter'.

But if the letter was one of Orlov's countless fabrications, and it was not Reilly who inspired it, then how did this particular forgery come to be on the market? A startling explanation is tucked away in that unpublished official history of the Soviet intelligence organization to which reference has already been made. Here it is flatly stated that the approach had come, by a devious but definable route, from an agent of the British secret service itself. The history names the actual forger as one Ivan Dimitrievich Pokrovsky (some-times called 'Lieutenant P.'), a member of Orlov's team who had genuine Comintern writing-paper in his possession. And the man who allegedly approached him in the late summer of 1924 (in Helsinki or Riga) was an operative of the SIS (though not an actual member) using the alias 'Captain Black'.[9] The captain is said to have asked Pokrovsky outright for 'material which could be used against the Labour government in Britain'. Orlov's man came up with various ideas, including a made-to-order inflammatory Zinoviev letter to be sent to the British comrades, and this was the suggestion adopted. It was agreed with Captain Black that the British police should be tipped off as to the addressee (the London headquarters of the British Communist Party) so that the mesage would be intercepted and passed on as genuine to the Foreign Office. The whole operation was allegedly run out of the British consulate in Riga.

Even by the convoluted standards of the intelligence war being waged at the time, an era when disbelief constantly has to be suspended, this sounds a very rum tale. It becomes ever more bizarre when these Soviet archives identify the mysterious Captain Black as 'a Russian officer with English origins' called General Korneyev.[10] Allegedly, both the forger and the SIS middleman were paid £500 for their services and advised, once the uproar devel-oped, to decamp to South America. This they duly did, traces of them later being found there, with British intelligence helping them to find work.

There are three factors which lend at least a measure of credence to this extraordinary story. The first is that Vladimir Orlov was widely reported to have also included British intelligence among his many regular contacts and clients (indeed French secret service reports sometimes describe him simply as 'a British agent'). The second, and more weighty, factor is the provenance of the story itself. It was not written or published to score a propaganda point against the West but contained in a sober history of Soviet intelli-gence several hundred pages long, which was never designed by its seemingly objective compilers to see the light of common day.[11] So what would be the sense in inventing this particular episode, which is recounted in the same factual style as the rest of the chronicle? It is perhaps worth adding that, at the few points on unrelated matters where the present author has been able to compare this 'in-house' history with other intelligence records, it has stood up perfectly.

The third factor, undocumented but not implausible, enshrouds the entire mystery of the Zinoviev letter and it concerns the reigning mood inside the British intelligence community itself. The organization as a whole was uneasy about its prospects under a re-elected Labour government (further budget cuts being the least it feared). Moreover, the service was widely held to contain a hard core of what would later be dubbed 'Cold War warriors', veterans of the revolution era opposed to any idea of political softening towards the Bolshevik regime, whose downfall they still ardently desired. Commander Ernest Boyce was reputed to be one of the hard core, and it is this which leads us on to the question of SIS involvement over the final and fatal escapade of Sydney Reilly.

We should begin by returning, in greater detail, to the account given by Harry Carr, Boyce's own lieutenant in the field, of the origins of the affair. The relevant passage in his unpublished memoirs reads:

> It was clearly important to establish whether the Trust was likely to develop into an underground organisation capable of staging a coup d'état against the Bolsheviks, as it claimed, with a view to providing advance information on such a momentous political development to H.M.G. It was in the hope of solving this riddle that Boyce had the idea of bringing his old friend Sydney Reilly, then engaged in private business affairs in New York, into our doings with the Trust. Who could have better claims than Reilly to get to the bottom of the matter?[12]

There is no record of any consultation which Boyce held with his department over the plan. Yet, to put it mildly, it is unlikely that they would have had no inkling of the idea to use such a controversial and high-profile figure as their one-time ST 1 to investigate a 'momentous political development' for the express enlightenment of His Majesty's Government. Boyce's plea, in his letter to Reilly (p. 284), to regard the whole matter as a private arrangement between themselves cannot in any case be taken at face value. It is fairly standard practice, in intelligence work as in diplomacy, for 'purely personal opinions' to be advanced in order to cloak official involvement, however slight, but to test the ground in case the omens look good.

In this context, Boyce's own movements during the critical period would have to have been cleared with his department and, presumably, explained. We find Boyce in Paris, 'on leave' at the time when the crucial council of war was held between Reilly and the White Russian leaders. Is it feasible to maintain that Boyce would have told his superiors nothing of the agreement for Reilly to meet with Trust leaders in Finland? Boyce had also arranged to be in London, once more 'on leave', during the precise period of that Finland meeting, in order not to be around when the talks took place. Again, would the reason for his deliberate absence not be known?

Boyce got back to his post rapidly enough once it transpired that Reilly, for reasons explained above, had decided to cross over into Russia, a journey from which he had not returned. After a frustrating stay in Helsinki where nothing could be discovered or explained, Boyce left for London (clearly to report), intending to go on to Paris to see, among others, the distraught Pepita. Carr's account continues: 'On arrival in London, however, Boyce found himself carpeted by the "Chief"[13] for the role he had played in this unfortunate affair and was ordered to remain in London and forbidden to go to Paris.'[14]

The most likely conclusion to be drawn from all this is that though the SIS may well have been at least aware that a reconnaissance meeting between Reilly and the Trust had been (unofficially) arranged in Finland, they – like Boyce, Carr, General Kutyepov and everyone else involved on the Western side – never contemplated and would never have approved of his journey across the border into the Soviet Union itself. In this respect, Whitehall's repeated denials that it had ever authorized such a journey can be accepted without reserve. However, evidence has survived in the SIS's own files that the service had resumed interest in their famous one-time agent at the very time, midsummer of 1925, when Boyce was trying to recruit his help again. On 20 July 1925, the department asked its New York station for an update on Reilly's current activities and reputation.[15]

The response was that Sydney G. Reilly was 'at present engaged in business under the name of Trading Ventures Inc. of which concern he is President ... at Room 549, Cunard Building, 25 Broadway'. His office, which had been visited, was found to be well furnished: 'He seems to be in a prosperous condition. The stenographers and other help seem to be of German and Jewish origin and the whole atmosphere ... is foreign.'

Reilly had also been interviewed personally 'under a suitable pretext' on London's behalf. He had made no reference to his career as an SIS contract agent, or even to the Soviet Union. He stated instead that he had once been attached to the British and Canadian Recruiting Mission in New York, a claim which had been investigated and found wanting. In general, the New York station delivered a very negative personal report on Reilly, referring right back to American official comments voiced in wartime that he was regarded as 'a suspicious character and a former German spy'. Cumming, it will be recalled, had ignored those warnings in 1918 and it seems that certain people in London were prepared to ignore them again now.

The mere existence of these CX exchanges could have been a pure coincidence, unconnected with the Boyce project. It could have been just another case of the right hand in intelligence work not knowing what the left hand was up to, the left in this case being the machinations of Boyce and his Cold War colleagues. But it could also have been that left and right were somehow linked, though both under a blanket. A mystery thus surrounds the launch of Reilly's last adventure, long before its brutal end.

That end remained itself a riddle to the people at Helsinki, who were fretting for any scrap of news which would confirm or reject that one cryptic Soviet statement about the shoot-up on the border. They were an oddly assorted bunch: Boyce, Carr and Bunakov of British intelligence; General Kutyepov, the White Russian leader from Paris; Pepita Bobadilla, Reilly's bigamous wife; and Maria Schulz, with her so-called husband. A report from Bunakov which appears in the Reilly papers gives the only inside account of what was going on.[16] According to Bunakov, Maria had been planning one last service for her Moscow masters before returning to the Soviet Union herself. This involved trying to clear them from blame for anything that had happened and, to achieve this, she had managed to ensnare Pepita, destined to become the widow of her own victim.

The distraught wife was anxious to pin responsibility on someone, somewhere, for what was looking more and more like a tragic blunder. She thus presented a vulnerable target for the ever plausible Maria who, in 'heart-to-heart' talks, persuaded her that the culprits were in London. The two women had decided (for very different reasons) that 'it was impossible to hush the matter up and that it must be made public'. A step-by-step programme, doubtless devised by Maria, was agreed between them to carry this out. A notice to the effect that Reilly had, so to say, died in action was to appear in *The Times* of London,[17] to provoke an official response from somewhere. If this met with silence (as it did) then an attempt would be made to have the question raised in Parliament. In the meantime, the incriminating letters which Boyce and Bunakov had written to Reilly were to be placed with other relevant papers in the hands of Pepita's London solicitors.

'It would seem clear,' Bunakov concluded, 'that, as a result of the conversations which have taken place between S.T.1's wife and Schulz, they have evolved a plan of making the matter public without involving either themselves or their organisation and putting the whole thing on SIS and in this way covering themselves.'

In fact, the SIS had already started to close up the hatches before this plan had even got off the ground. On leaving for London in mid-October, Boyce sent an advance message home which is the only report of his on the Reilly affair to survive.[18] In this, the commander makes no mention of his cardinal role in persuading Reilly to undertake the reconnaissance task, whose origin he describes as follows: 'ST1, introduced by me to ST/28, obtained letters of introduction to the representative in Finland of the Monarchist headquarters in Moscow *and against advice unexpectedly went illegally into Russia under an assumed name.*'[19]

The report accepts, more or less as read, the Soviet communiqué on the Allekul affray and adds (showing either dissimulation or naivety) that Reilly's identity was 'not yet discovered in Russia'. Boyce then adds: 'As Finnish Intelligence have secret connection with the Moscow Centre and at latter's request faced [?] illegal journey, *it is in everybody's interest, excepting wife, to hush up matter.*'[20]

It all amounts to a pretty cynical performance by Reilly's old colleague and personal friend. Cynical, but entirely professional. It looked as though ST 1 was either killed or doomed and could therefore be written off or disavowed. The priority now was damage limitation to preserve the SIS network in the Soviet target area. This meant above all keeping the identity of Bunakov as ST 28 hidden and maintaining smooth working relations with the Finns. Even Reilly might have approved. After all, he had already willingly embraced the dangerous role of fall guy once before, in midsummer of 1918, when trying to light the dodgy fuse of the 'Lockhart plot'.

21

Balance Sheets

The seizure and trial of Boris Savinkov, conducted in a blaze of publicity, contrasted with the blanket of silence which was thrown in Moscow over Sydney Reilly. No Soviet communiqué was ever to be issued on his fate. Yet both events had, between them, exposed that ingeniously constructed trap door through which the two men had fallen. Savinkov's gradual Damascene conversion while pacing the streets of Moscow, and its proclamation in his trial speech, sounded genuine enough to those, inside Russia and outside, who knew the mettle of this strange revolutionary. But the fact had to be faced, by those who believed in the Trust, that he had been tricked and betrayed and that their supposedly omnipresent friends had been unable to save him.

The case of Reilly posed even more troubling questions for the true believers. Savinkov's fate had at least been described for them, from capture to trial and death, in a series of official Soviet statements. But over Reilly the 'Trust' had been unable to secure one scrap of information, let alone a rescue or a release. For years the organization had been parading itself in the West as a network whose tentacles reached deep even into the OGPU. If this were so, how could it be that the weeks had gone by in Helsinki without anyone learning anything about what was clearly emerging as an OGPU plot? Reilly's unexplained disappearance had shaken the Trust's credibility in one of its key target areas – the Western intelligence community.[1]

However, by now both Yakushev, with his OGPU team of puppet-masters, and the Stalin regime which controlled them were beginning to lose interest in their grand deception game. The Trust was gradually running out of usefulness. One of its operational functions – the destruction of enemies abroad – had been partly fulfilled by the elimination of these two key adversaries, and less subtle methods were to be adopted for the others.[2] Moreover, the dire political climate in the Soviet Union which had given birth to the Trust concept was also changing in the regime's favour.

Lenin's much-vaunted New Economic Policy had been essentially just a ploy in the Bolshevik power game. When it was launched, in 1921, famine had threatened rebellion, and rebellion had threatened the regime. Five years later, though economic problems persisted, the twin spectres of mass hunger and popular unrest had, for the time being, at any rate, been banished. As Savinkov had been obliged to accept, Stalin was in the saddle and there was no force on the ground powerful enough to unseat him. The regime no longer felt vulnerable to White Russian threats, supported, as they had been on the battlefields, by Western governments. As a consequence, the strategic concept behind the Trust – lulling the whole imperialist camp into the passivity of 'wait and see' – had also run its course.[3] But how, exactly, was it to be wound up?

Soviet versions down the years have naturally tended to present the process as a carefully planned and controlled operation by which the OGPU disposed of its own creation at a time, and in a manner, of its own choosing. The truth, as given in objective unpublished Soviet accounts (and backed up at several points in Western archives), is very different. The Trust did have a whistle-blower, in the person of the ubiquitous and volatile Opperput. However, it seems clear that he blew that whistle not on orders but on an impulse of rage and jealousy, intensified by a love affair with, of all people, Maria Schulz. As with Savinkov and his Baroness Derental, the great survivor Opperput was to embrace his fate in a blaze of sexual passion.

The account of events as published in the West records that this unlikely couple had arrived in Finland on 14 April 1927, to put themselves in the hands of the local authorities.[4] Opperput came out with his own story in issues, between May and October, of the Russian language paper *Segodnya*, which was printed in Riga. In these articles, he presents himself as an OGPU agent working under duress (true, if the nature of his recruitment in Poland in 1920 is recalled). He then describes the mass deception operations of the Trust from beginning to end, including the capture of Reilly, which he had personally opposed at the time. His revelations were, in one sense, serving Moscow's ends, in that they revealed how thoroughly and how persistently Western governments and their intelligence had been bamboozled or, at the least, perplexed. But he was not performing this service at Moscow's behest,[5] as is shown by a curt reference to the affair in that in-house history of the OGPU/KGB cited several times above. This stated that, after the capture of Reilly, it was realized that the Trust was no longer needed to operate as before but the façade was preserved for a while. 'Then, early in 1927,' the history continues, 'the decision was taken to wind it all up – gradually letting it fade away by withdrawing agents and destroying case material. *The treachery of Opperput who fled to Finland on 12 April with Zakhavchenko interfered with those planned measures.*'[6] For a while, the chronicle adds, former close colleagues of Opperput's such as Styrne and Pilar feared for their lives and were given special guards. It is once more in the memoirs of General Orlov that we find not only confirmation of such a bald résumé, but elaboration, with the addition of much fascinating human detail.

His account begins with a description of the appearance and character of this double agent of many names and faces. The real Edward Opperput was a handsome strapping young man, then in his early thirties, a fitness fanatic with reddish hair and the build of a Tarzan. His main task, after he had been turned by the OGPU, was to function as the Trust's reception officer for duped White Russians as they crossed over at the Finnish border, seeking to make contact with the magical, but largely mythical, anti-Bolshevik underground. (Of these returnees, Orlov was told, only 10–15 per cent were executed; the great majority were allowed to return to the West, in order to preserve the Trust's credentials.)[7] Opperput's job was thus a fairly humdrum one and he became increasingly frustrated that he was given nothing better to do and was never admitted to the inner ring of the puppet-masters.

He had always been 'something of an odd-ball' who did not mix well with his OGPU colleagues but it was his feud with Federov which started to cause real friction. Opperput, who talked at conferences as though the Trust were his creation, grew more and more jealous of the man who had really put up the original concept and who argued for it so persuasively. This jealousy extended to their relative standings in the party: whereas Opperput had tried in vain to be accepted even as a humble member, Federov had been awarded the Order of the Red Banner, one of the highest Soviet decorations, for his role in Trust operations.

By the late autumn of 1926, Orlov relates, Artuzov had grown so concerned by the tension Opperput was creating in the group that he decided to carry out a special investigation into the troublemaker's grievances, and what, if anything, he could dare to do about them. The investigator chosen was Maria Schulz. The choice was to cause far greater turbulence all round than anything registered thus far. All that Artuzov had asked Maria to do was to find out why her colleague had isolated himself from all his former friends and, if he were indeed going through some sort of moral crisis, how this could be resolved in order to bring him back as an enthusiastic fellow-worker into the fold. But complications arose after Maria, in order to facilitate her task, was given her own apartment in the same Foreign Trade Community House where Opperput (who was divorced) lived alone under the name of Staunitz, the alias he most commonly used.

Whether Artuzov had calculated from the start that the two would end up in the same bed, as well as in the same building, is not clear. But even he could never have imagined the passion which would inflame the pair of them when this duly happened. This last love affair to feature in the chronicle of the Trust seems also to have been the most deeply felt, on the psychological as well as the physical plane. Maria, who could manipulate men almost at will yet still felt manipulated by them, had now found someone who needed her help as well as her body, a partner whom, at last, she could trust. The loner Opperput, whose splendid physique encased a coil of frail complexes, had found a woman whose iron will (behind those innocent blue eyes) gave him confidence as well as fellowship and the feeling that he could finally make his mark on events.

The mark they now chose to make together was to expose to the world the great Soviet scam of the Trust. Predictably, the infatuated Maria soon revealed to her lover the task that Artuzov had asked her to perform. Equally predictably, Opperput, already resentful at his treatment by the Trust, was enraged by the thought that his supervisors had resorted to spying against him. His revenge would be to bring down Artuzov's whole house of cards around him. Maria, not surprisingly, went with her lover. Apart from the bond which had developed between them, staying behind could have presented danger for herself. Moscow would no longer be a safe place for the person who, fairly obviously, had betrayed Artuzov's secret plan.

They thus turned up in Finland, out of the blue, as a couple of self-declared outcasts. What were their Western hosts to make of their story, and what was to be done about the pair of them? The second decision was left to the White Russian leader, General Kutyepov who once again had hurried to Helsinki to investigate as the tale of the Trust took this sensational new twist.[8] For what happened next, we can use a synthesis of unpublished accounts, none of them written for propaganda purposes;[9] taken together, they are more reliable, as well as far more detailed, than the brief communiqués over the affair issued at the time from Moscow.

General Kutyepov feared that Opperput's exposure sounded all too plausible (doubts about the Trust's credentials had, after all, been mounting steadily in the White Russian émigré camp).[10] Nonetheless, he was still groping for some further evidence of the trickery he had fallen victim to for so long. He decided that it was up to the whistle-blower himself to provide the final proof. He put it to Opperput that, in order to convince the doubters that he was not still acting as an OGPU agent but had genuinely turned against the regime, he should be prepared to return to the Soviet Union to help in a murder and sabotage operation. General Kutyepov had already launched such a terrorist campaign, substituting more active measures for the Trust's 'wait and see' doctrine which seemed to be bringing the émigrés such poor dividends.

Opperput, at heart a man of action and a one-time guerrilla fighter under Boris Savinkov, leaped at the challenge. So did his beloved Maria; not for nothing had she served as an anti-Red officer in the forces of Baron Wrangel seven years before. When they had still been part of the Trust conspiracy, each had argued with Artuzov, independently of one another, for a more aggressive stance against the émigré leadership instead of the passive policy of deception which was anyway becoming threadbare. Now, after their own change of heart, their targets had also been reversed: it was to be a terrorism levelled against the Bolsheviks, not executed on their behalf. According to one account,[11] it was the redoubtable Maria, rather than her White Russian uncle, who had taken the initiative in these debates, even to the point where he put her in charge of a new 'Military, National and Terrorist Society', seemingly stamped up out of the ground in Helsinki. Whether or not this last desperate charge of General Kutyepov was spurred on by his niece, she certainly moved up into the front line of the action.

On 30 May 1927, six terrorists in two groups of three boarded the night train from Helsinki to Vyborg, where they split up for separate assignments. The first group, led by the White Russian Captain V.A. Larianov, crossed the border and headed for Leningrad, where it accomplished its mission in style: a Communist assembly hall in the city was successfully bombed and all three attackers made their getaway through the mayhem and returned safely to Finland. It was to be a very different story with the second trio, made up of Schulz, Opperput and one Georghi N. Peters,[12] who made for Moscow.

Their first target here was the OGPU's community house on the Malaya Lubyanka, next to the jail itself. The group tried to blast the building on 3 June but the attack turned into a fiasco. The bomb failed and the three terrorists fled for their lives to the south, scattering for safety as they went. At this point Soviet communiqués take up the story and, not surprisingly, the picture soon becomes fuzzy. The first Tass statement, issued on 10 June, merely reported that an attempt had been made to blow up the headquarters [sic] of the OGPU in Moscow, no details being given. The official version of the end of the affair did not come out until nearly a month later.

On 5 July, Tass put out another statement naming all three members of the terrorist group and announcing their 'liquidation': that of Opperput on 19 June, followed by Maria Schulz and Peters shortly afterwards. At a press conference convened the day after the announcement, the OGPU's First Deputy Chairman, G.G. Yagoda,[13] described how a diary found on Opperput's body had proved that both the Leningrad and Moscow attacks had been planned largely by British intelligence in Estonia. This can only be regarded as a propaganda flourish designed to bring 'Western imperialists' on to the scene and so play down the key role of a renegade OGPU man in the operation. As is shown by the strict hands-off attitude Harry Carr had always adopted, on orders, towards the Trust, the last thing British intelligence wanted to do by 1927 was to get embroiled directly in any Moscow power game. And the last thing to be expected from an experienced agent like Opperput was that he should have kept an incriminating diary on his person when the hunters were hot on his trail.

Again basing his account on what his senior OGPU colleagues told him at the time, Orlov gives a more colourful as well as, in all probability, a more accurate version of the end of the chase. According to this, Opperput was cornered in Smolensk on 18 June by an OGPU pursuit team and died in an exchange of fire. Maria, who had fled separately into Byelorussia, shot it out with a cavalry unit near the village of Dretun five days later, on 23 June. She was said to have saved her last bullet for herself.

That sounds like a grimly decisive end to the tale, yet a smidgen of doubt was to be raised soon afterwards concerning Opperput. In 1928, another official Soviet announcement on the affair left out all mention of the former Trust agent and claimed that the Moscow terrorist attack had been launched by Maria Schulz and Peters (on whom the incriminating diary of the mission had allegedly been found). This version was echoed in subsequent Soviet intelligence literature.[14] It can be dismissed as a continuation of the OGPU campaign to cover up the betrayal committed by one of their key operators in the deception game.

Yet an intriguing if rather shaky question mark was to arise in Poland in the middle of Hitler's war.[15] A tall and powerfully built middle-aged man, with reddish hair, was trying in 1941 to ingratiate himself with the White Russian community in Warsaw, flourishing the visiting card of 'Baron Aleksander von Manteuffel'. He was prepared to admit that this was not his real name but that he had been born in the Soviet Union and was now running an antiques business in German-occupied Kiev. The 'Baron' was later identified by the White Russian office in Berlin as 'Edward Opperput, the man of the Trust' who had been arrested by the Germans as a Soviet spy and – presumably – shot. Though its foundations are slim, the tale provides a suitably mysterious finale for the man of so many aliases and for the game of deception which he had played for so long.

This narrative, which began in Bolshevik Russia in the spring of 1918, to be wound up there nearly ten years afterwards, traces the first round in that long battle of wits and wills between East and West which was to stretch down the century. How, briefly, can this opening phase be evaluated? Moreover, as it was also a game of consequences, what were its effects on later generations of contestants such as the Stalinist hardliners of the East and the Cold War warriors of the West?

If we first look back at that battle of wits, conducted mainly between the rival intelligence services, then there can be little doubt that it was won, almost hands down, by the Bolsheviks. Their political police (the most accurate label for the Cheka, GPU and the rest) admittedly enjoyed great operational advantages over their rivals. The secret services of the Western powers, like their governments, were all too often split by inter-departmental rivalries inside each state intelligence apparatus. These both reflected and magnified similar divisions within the alliance as a whole. Dzerzhinsky, on the other hand, was in unchallenged control of an organization which shared one faith and pursued one goal. To begin with, his experienced lieutenants were few in number, but even this had security advantages and made for swifter operations, especially as, like their master, they were all prepared to work eighteen hours a day for months on end. In the intelligence field, as on the battlefield, the Bolsheviks enjoyed the same advantages of unified command and compact inner lines of engagement.

Having said all that, however, the achievements of the Cheka, which was only a few months old when the tussle with the West started in earnest, were remarkable. Nor should too much be made of the fact that Dzerzhinsky had inherited the assets, in experience and manpower, of the Tsarist Okhrana, under which he had suffered so much himself. The Tsar's police numbered its informers and agents provocateurs by the scores of thousands and it had become adept at infiltrating the conspiracies of its opponents. Yet there was nothing in this inherited network (much of it to begin with of dubious loyalty) which provided the infant Cheka with a pattern for launching the complex deception campaign of the Trust, which was operated on an international scale and sustained somehow year after year. Even that great defector General Orlov, for all his hatred of the regime from which he had fled, always showed professional respect for, and even a certain pride in, that particular achievement of his one-time service: 'It was a cat-and-mouse game,' he once said to his closest American friend,[16] 'but an unusual one, for here it was the mouse, the Cheka, which was playing with the cat, and the cat, in this case, was the British imperial lion.'

Yet, though often outwitted, the Western secret services were not entirely outfought by the Bolsheviks, which is the impression sometimes given by academics who have had neither personal experience of intelligence work nor access to the key archives concerned. Even as distinguished an authority as Richard Ullman offends in this respect when he writes of British agents operating underground against the Bolsheviks: 'To judge from their own highly sensational accounts, they did nothing more useful than avoid arrest. In none of the many documents the author has seen is there even a hint that British information about Russia was derived from these sources.'[17] It is only a minor quibble to point out that escaping arrest while working against the regime of any police state when inside that police state is no mean achievement in itself. There are, however, two major flaws in his dismissive verdict. The first is that the four books of memoirs which the professor cited were commercially marketed tales which had little contact with reality. The second is that the 'many documents' he had seen (by 1961) excluded all of the factual evidence on British secret service work which later became available. Thus those despatches of Captain George Hill to London (both in 1918 to the War Office and in 1921 direct to Lord Curzon at the Foreign Office) constituted major intelligence sources of 'British information about Russia'. Even more so did the voluminous despatches which Reilly and Hill sent back from southern Russia during the winter of 1918–19.

As for the material which Paul Dukes, working alone, managed to smuggle out of Leningrad during the first eight months of 1919, this was quite literally the *only* first-hand secret intelligence information reaching London from any source inside Russia. As already described, its importance rated a special SIS naval operation to serve as the courier link, while its quality was to earn a unique field-service knighthood for the agent. It is worth noting here that though Dzerzhinsky apparently succeeded (in the case of Reilly's entrapment) in exploiting a dingy figure on the fringe of British intelligence, his service never matched the deep penetration, at the highest level, of the enemy camp, as achieved by Dukes. ST 25 had his man right inside Trotsky's 'Revolutionary Council of the

Northern Front', whose deliberations and decisions reached London almost verbatim.

Those are the plain facts. The scene immediately becomes obscure when one tries to assess what impact all this intelligence reporting had on policy. Very often, it merely reflected (or, at the most, enhanced) existing official views. Hill's prophecies, made in the summer of 1921, that it could be only a matter of weeks before the anti-Bolshevik armies of Denikin and Kolchak joined hands in Moscow merely echoed the over-optimism displayed throughout by the War Minister, Winston Churchill. On the other hand, gloomy professional judgements were often ignored, though some of them proved to be right in the end. Thus when General Franchet d'Espéry cautioned his government in 1920 against the folly of landing a large French expeditionary force in the Crimea (an operation which he ultimately was obliged to command), he was relying on assessments from his own and Allied intelligence services. A similar input lay behind the warning issued two years earlier, at the very onset of Allied intervention, by the Chief of the British General Staff, Sir Henry Wilson. The general foresaw a remorseless process ahead by which the Alliance, once it had dipped its toes into the Russian morass, could eventually be smothered up to its ankles, knees and neck, and find extrication both a difficult and a humiliating business. The truth is that there are precious few laurels for professionals whose advice is unwisely ignored by the politicians. On the other hand, when that advice is acted on successfully, it is the politicians who take the credit.

One final caveat needs to be entered against any critic (and there are some modern-day ones) who denigrates the contribution made by the three secret services as a whole to the Allied struggle against Bolshevism in the first years of Lenin's rule. All too often their work is viewed from the conventional perspectives as to how much information was supplied about the enemy and what the auguries were for his defeat. This ignores the fact that one of the chief roles (indeed, at times the overriding task) allotted to these services was not information-gathering but sabotage. In this they were consistently successful, and occasionally spectacularly so.

As we have seen, once the Bolsheviks had turned themselves into potential enemies of the West by making their separate peace with Germany, the priority of all three Allied missions in Russia was to prevent war material of any description abandoned or stockpiled in the country from falling into German hands. In the first instance, it was the Allied military missions and their intelligence services who were put on to this task. Throughout the spring and summer of 1918, Captain Hill was engaged in what he called this 'gentle sabotage' alongside the familiar intelligence-gathering of enemy battle order.[18] The 'stay-behind groups' which Lockhart, Boyce, Hill and Reilly were all involved in organizing (to continue underground resistance after any Allied withdrawal) all had sabotage as one of their main tasks. The aims of Sydney Reilly had always been political rather than military but the blowing up of key bridges was nonetheless a key feature of the so-called 'Lockhart plot'.

Sabotage, not intelligence gathering, had been the specific purpose of the French secret service unit sent out from Paris to Russia in June 1918 and the true identity of its commander, the naval officer de Verthamon, would have come as no surprise to the British, had they succeeded in discovering it at the time. Their own naval attaché, the ill-fated Captain Cromie, was no longer interested, from the spring of 1918 onwards, in keeping routine tabs on the dispositions and preparedness of the Russian fleets. His business, on increasingly urgent Admiralty orders, was to destroy or immobilize the ships of those fleets wherever they could be found and whatever state they were in, provided they were still afloat. The fully accredited diplomat had himself been turned into another 'special operations agent' (as they were later called); and it was a junior service colleague of his, the young submarine officer Lieutenant Agar, who later pulled off the most spectacular of these operations while an SIS man on SIS duties. If these early sabotage successes are entered on the credit side of the Allied intelligence tussle with the Bolsheviks, then the balance for the West begins to look more respectable.

To analyse the impact on East–West relations of this opening round in their long-term conflict would make a study in itself. All there is space for here is to note some of the major effects on each side of the divide. As regards the Bolsheviks, it is too simplistic to suggest that the 'Red Terror' itself was triggered off in response to the conspiracies of 1918. Terror was a birthmark of the infant Leninist regime, and Lenin himself took pride in it. Long before the attempt on his life he was striving to inject a more ruthless strain into Bolshevik rule which, he complained, 'was more like milk pudding than iron'. Apart from being the patron saint of the Cheka and all its doings, he was urging even this chosen arm of terrorism into greater violence, especially against rebellious kulaks, the wealthy peasant leaders whom he had ordered to be hung without trial. What the combating of Western and White Russian plots did lead on to was what one might call the nationalization of repression, turning it into state terrorism. It was legalized through special clauses (which Lenin helped to draft) in the Soviet criminal code and thus, by 1922, had become enshrined in the constitution.[19]

All this, like Lenin's New Economic Policy, served the same prime aim of preserving the regime in power. The same is at least partly true of that other image, fathered by the early struggles of the Bolsheviks for survival, namely the bogey-man of 'imperialist counter-revolutionary threats'. At the height of the civil war, when powerful Allied aid was flowing to all the White Russian armies and Lenin himself almost despaired of victory, that threat was real enough. But it was flourished as a propaganda weapon long after it had ceased to exist on the ground. Stalin knew perfectly well in the 1930s that the Western powers had not the slightest intention of invading his Russia. (Indeed, in May 1941, he even scoffed at warnings that the Germans were on the point of doing so.) But he also knew that the Russian people did *not* know and had to be persuaded that the old bogey-man was still alive and menacing. It was the folk memories of counter-revolutionary plots and the sufferings of the civil war which made this propaganda so effective among the masses in sustaining the Soviet empire of terror.

The impact of this first round of the East–West conflict on the Western mind runs along a whole gamut of effects. At the broad strategic end it re-established in the consciousness of the twentieth century the lesson that Napoleon had demonstrated in the nineteenth: Russia as a country was well-nigh unconquerable. Winston Churchill, as Minister of War in 1920, had seen all his hopes of defeating the Bolsheviks with White Russian armies dissipated by the sheer vastness of the landscape. Twenty-one years later, when Hitler invaded the Soviet Union and Churchill, now Prime Minister, promptly proclaimed it as an ally, he had sensed that the Second World War was won. Ironically, there had been many influential voices in Britain in the 1930s arguing for the opposite – namely an alliance with Nazi Germany to combat the worldwide anti-imperialist machinations of the Communist Comintern.

At the narrow end of the scale, the impact was much sharper, and this was felt especially within the Western intelligence community itself. The great scam of the Trust implanted in many minds – above all in those of the Americans – the sense that nothing which the Soviet Union said or did could be taken at face value. A two-way flux of defectors only added to the confusion, so that one powerful lobby in Washington grew convinced that the descendants of Artuzov and his puppet-masters still held sway in the Kremlin. No word or gesture which came out of Moscow could be believed. Even to consider conciliation was to walk into a pre-prepared trap. The debate over this fixation split the American intelligence services into two camps and the division spilled over into the administration at the very time of the Cold War when clear thinking to establish a unified policy was most needed in Washington.[20]

There were, of course, Allied leaders who kept their feet on the ground throughout the period we have dealt with. Lloyd George, for example, never shared Churchill's belief that the Bolshevik regime could be toppled, either by force or by intrigue. He went along with the intervention campaign but, rather like President Wilson, he set his hopes instead on its becoming 'liberalized'. Such was the British Prime Minister's message to Boris Savinkov. Nor were the White Russian commanders in the field, notably Admiral Kolchak and General Denikin, over-hopeful about their prospects. As we have seen, the latter, in a frank warning to the West transmitted via Sydney Reilly, as good as predicted the scenario for his ultimate failure: over-stretched lines of communication in the long march north to Moscow and a vast unstable hinterland to the rear of his army which he lacked the resources to control.

The real losers in the anti-Bolshevik struggle were those who, against all the odds, clung to visions which, in the end, betrayed them. The deluded Moscow conspirators of 1918 were ensnared by the very plots they had sought to weave. For the next three years, the Allies poured their treasures of money and material into the gamble that White Russian armies might succeed where conspiracy had failed (without, it seems, giving much thought as to how they would cope had the gamble come off). Then, when the military venture by proxy collapsed, the West placed what hopes it had left once more on the *coup d'état* alternative – this time encouraged by the siren songs of Artuzov and his men.

As for the two self-condemned martyrs of the conflict, Boris Savinkov had walked to his doom believing that he alone could restore liberty to his beloved Russian people, and that they were waiting with a great underground army to greet him. Sydney Reilly, though he had warned his friend and hero strongly about the peril he would face, took precisely the same step himself a year later, convinced in his case that he was about to make a fortune, as well as history.

Reilly's ensnarement rounded off a Bolshevik campaign of deception which had begun with the manipulation of the French journalist René Marchand in Moscow six years before. When asked by Orlov how to explain its success, Federov, one of its main operators, had replied simply: 'People believe what they want to believe.'

That verdict can well stand as the Trust's epitaph. However, it also applies to much more in the life of men and nations than the field of secret intelligence.

What Happened to Them

It seems best to deal first with the Cheka/OGPU figures who have featured in this narrative, since their fate is, almost without exception, swiftly recounted as well as uniformly sinister. Only the redoubtable founder and first head of Lenin's political police, Felix Dzerzhinsky, came to a peaceful end. He died, still in office, in July 1926, his reputation unchallenged.

Of his lieutenants whom we have met with, Artur Artuzov, the chief puppet-master of the Trust deception, became head of the NKVD's Foreign Administration in 1934 but was arrested and executed three years later in Stalin's mass purges. He was among those who were 'posthumously rehabilitated', a belated admission that Stalin had made a mistake.

I.K. Peters, Lockhart's indulgent jailer, who later interrogated both Savinkov and Reilly, rose to become first deputy chairman of the Moscow City Soviet before being arrested in the capital in December 1937 and perishing soon afterwards.

Roman Pilar, Dzerzhinsky's cousin who, as head of the Byelorussian Cheka, had seized the unsuspecting Savinkov in 1925, and helped to interrogate Reilly a year later, became deputy chief of the OGPU's counter-espionage department before also disappearing in Stalin's great purge. The same fate befell the ambitious young Estonian, V.A. Styrne, another stalwart of the Trust and interrogator of Reilly.

Iakov Blumkin, the assassin of Count Mirbach, did not even last that long. He was shot without trial in late 1929 on the direct orders of Stalin. His 'crime' was to have maintained secret contact with Stalin's defeated rival Trotsky, who was already in exile.

T.D. Deribass, who had applied the final touches in Vyborg to the Cheka's ensnarement of Reilly, rose up by 1934 to be a candidate-member of the party's Central Committee. He had evidently risen too high for Stalin's liking and he, too, disappeared in the 1937 round-ups. Colonel Edward Berzin, Lenin's prize decoy in the Lockhart conspiracy affair, was rewarded afterwards with a plum job in control of the Mogadan gold-fields before also falling victim to Stalin's executioners. And so with thousands of others, Chekists, party officials or Red Army officers, the revolution devoured its children.

We can turn next to those White Russian leaders who survived both the 'war after the war' and the Cheka's post-war attentions. General Denikin, despite his honorary British knighthood, which had been bestowed with an offer of asylum, left England for America, where he died at Ann Arbor in 1947. Baron Wrangel, the most dashing and determined of all the anti-Bolshevik commanders, had the most impressive send-off of all the émigrés. He had died on 24 April 1928 in Brussels aged forty-nine but, in accordance with his last wishes, his remains were laid to rest the following year in the Russian church at Belgrade. The church was known as the last refuge of the White Russian movement, and the local émigré community honoured it – and the dead man – as such. Detachments of White Russian army survivors, wearing their old Tsarist uniforms, provided a guard of honour, marching behind the imperial tri-coloured flag.[1] The demonstration was as stirring as it was forlorn, rather like Wrangel's life.

As for the fate of the Allied secret service men involved in the anti-Bolshevik struggle, the most dismal was that of the American agent Kalamatiano. As we have seen, this true hero of the conflict had returned home in the autumn of 1921 to something far short of a hero's welcome. His talents were out of fashion in an era which was accepting the stability, if not the morality, of the Bolshevik regime, and this acceptance made even his achievements an embarrassment. After a sixty-day leave of absence, he was informed, in early December 1921, that his services were no longer required by the State Department (who added insult to injury by back-dating his 'resignation' by two months). He did, however, receive a warm commendation for his services in Russia and was offered a post as a foreign language instructor at the Culver Military Academy where he had once served as a cadet.

This gave him and his family a congenial living but it was not the life he wanted; nor was it the life he was itching to tell the world about. Despite official dissuasion, he did write his memoirs but no publisher was prepared to take them on, perhaps because of official dissuasion. He sought distraction in hunting and fishing, only for the distraction to prove fatal. A frozen foot he suffered while out tracking in the winter of 1922–3 turned poisonous, and toes had to be amputated. 'I am departing the world in particles,' he wrote jocularly from hospital to his old mentor, Professor Samuel Harper.

But whatever had stricken him became less and less of a laughing matter as the months passed. The mysterious infection proved untreatable. By October, it was damaging his heart and then attacked his spleen and liver. He died on 9 November 1923 of a condition certified by the doctors as 'sub-acute septic endocarditis'.[2] He was only forty-one but had packed twice as much adventure into his few adult years as most people do in a full lifetime.

Turning now to the British, Bruce Lockhart's later life is well summed up by the title of his book, *Retreat from Glory*. As we have seen, he had fallen foul of the Whitehall mandarins and any glory he secured in Moscow looked well and truly tarnished after the fiasco of his eponymous plot. The best he could secure in the way of a new diplomatic opening was a job as commercial secretary (in those days a lowly post) and in 1920 he chose Prague instead of Warsaw because of the better shooting and fishing prospects in the new Czechoslovak republic. That said much about his feckless approach to the post-war challenge, and a life of dogged debauchery in the night-clubs of the Czech capital with, in his own words, 'a succession of Ilses, Kitties, Martinas and other international ladies' did the rest. After two years of this rakish existence, he was obliged to resign, laden with debts.

Five years followed on banking assignments in London and central Europe. All the time, the debts pursued him as he pursued the actresses and bar-girls (complaining, in 1928, that they were looking 'older and more jaded'). That same year brought him a lucky break into the dubious but well-paid world of the newspaper gossip columnist. Impressed by the tidbits he had contributed from time to time (and even more by a unique interview he had managed to secure with the deposed German Kaiser Wilhelm at Doorn, the castle of his Dutch asylum), Lord Beaverbrook, the proprietor of the *Evening Standard*, offered Lockhart the job of chief diary-writer on the 'Londoner' column. He was in congenial company here: the ex-diplomat Harold Nicolson, and Winston Churchill's rumbustious son, Randolph, were among those who scribbled alongside him. His work also opened the doors of London society – though the hostesses tended to be of the brash new-money type, avid to feature flatteringly in his columns. As before, he spent as much time (and far more money) in night-clubs as he did in drawing-rooms.

The outbreak of the Second World War lifted him out of this somewhat futile existence. He promptly returned to the Foreign Office as its East European and Balkan intelligence expert and eventually became Director-General of the enemy propaganda organization, the Political Warfare Executive. This carried the rank of a deputy under-secretary of state and that rank, in turn, brought him a knighthood. It was what he had once dreamed of getting as his country's ambassador to a major capital.

That was to be his only brief recapture of even a glimmer of glory. His post-war life became a repeat of those pre-war years of restless pleasure-seeking, though now dogged by bad health and a failing mind. He died, aged eighty-two, in February 1970 in the uninspiring setting of a Hove nursing home. It was a sad exit for the young Scotsman who had once felt, back in Moscow, that he might shift the axis of fate. Sadder when one reflects that, with better luck, less wily opponents, and more determination, he could even have succeeded. Instead, he was to go down in history as the author of a *coup d'état* conspiracy in which he never really believed and which led him, and British intelligence, into a trap actually devised by their intended victims.

The British agents who survived the dramas of Moscow in 1918 (and that meant almost everyone except Reilly) had very mixed post-war fortunes. Nothing, beyond a scanty record of service, has survived in the SIS archives about Ernest Boyce, the Moscow station chief who gave Reilly reluctant approval to go ahead with (and take all responsibility for) the projected Allied *coup d'état*. Nor, unlike Lockhart or Carr, did Boyce leave any memoirs behind, published or unpublished. Carr writes of him that he stayed on in the Baltic after the plot fiasco only to leave the service in 1928 'as the result of another unfortunate accident' (no details given).[3] It is known only that after ten years of trying his hand in business, he applied in 1938 to be taken on again by SIS, but was told that 'there was no post available'.[4] After that, his name simply disappears from the files.

The story of Paul Dukes is even more remarkable, inasmuch as the post-war SIS could not even find room for their prize performer in Russia, possessor of the unique knighthood bestowed for field operations. Again, there is little or nothing about this superb agent in the post-war archives, though a CX telegram in Reilly's file (of all places) tells when the parting of the ways occurred. Dukes was in Poland in 1920 on an assignment for the London *Times* and a message sent to Warsaw at the end of November contains the sentence: 'As regards ST.25, he can continue his work for the *Times* but must disconnect with us until further notice.'[5]

Dukes was never to be reconnected. One general reason was certainly the drastic slimming-down and restructuring imposed on the SIS by the slashing of its funds. But there were also personal reasons. Dukes was drifting more and more into mysticism (no great qualification for secret service work). In the process, he seems to have been losing contact with reality. Thus, when he proposed returning to Russia in the hope of resuming his old career there in the music world, he had to be brought to his senses with an emphatic veto. Instead, he took up a varied career as author, journalist and lecturer, without achieving the distinction to match his early fame. He died in 1967, an example of how wobbly the path of meteors can be in the fusty atmosphere of Whitehall.

George Hill seems to have had the most satisfactory life of all these veterans of the anti-Bolshevik struggle. Like the others, no place was found for him in the drastically reduced post-war service but he achieved some success in business and, as an author, with his memoirs (which were both sanitized and sensationalized). As with Lockhart, however, it was the outbreak of the Second World War which brought a recall to duty. He returned to Moscow on the British Mission there, with the task of liaising with his old opponents, the Soviet political police. He retired, adequately provided with honours, as Brigadier George Alexander Hill, DSO, OBE, MC and died in August 1970.

While in Moscow, Hill took the opportunity of pumping his Soviet intelligence colleagues about the fate of Sydney Reilly. The myth machine, which went on functioning long after the disappearance of the 'Ace of Spies', was seizing on rumours that he was, in fact, still alive – in the Middle East, in America and even in Russia itself. Not surprisingly, Hill drew a blank, for a blank was all there was to be drawn.

Reilly had, however, continued to preoccupy Whitehall for more than a decade after his death, though for very different reasons. The end of the saga is best introduced through the official files on another Bolshevik victim, the murdered naval attaché in Petrograd, Captain Cromie. Barely a fortnight after his death, the Foreign Office had had to deal with a proposal from his admirers that a memorial should be set up for him out of public funds. The department fended this off by declaring the idea to be 'somewhat invidious in view of the thousands of British officers who have met a heroic death without any such special action'.[6]

Concern about creating a very expensive precedent was probably not entirely absent in this. However, another request for money followed a few days later, and this proved much more tricky to settle. Josephine, the captain's widow, who declared herself 'in straitened circumstances', asked for special compensation on the grounds that, because of what she described as 'technical reasons', her late husband had not been merely a naval attaché.[7] Of this, of course, Whitehall was well aware for, as we have seen, ever since the spring of 1918, Cromie had been functioning as part saboteur and part spy/conspirator. Because he had been a naval officer, the Foreign Office tried to pass everything off on to the Admiralty. Their lordships, who could not deny having urged Cromie to drop everything apart from crippling the Soviet fleet, did their best. They voted the widow the absolute maximum for a fallen officer of his rank: a gratuity of £602.5.0 (£27,000 in today's money); an annual pension of £200, with an extra £24 as a compassionate supplement; and a gratuity of £200.15.0 for the couple's child.

This looked after the naval saboteur aspect of Cromie's official life. But what about the espionage side, which the widow also seems to have known something about? This was finally recognized by an additional special grant of £500 drawn from secret service funds, thus, as the file put it, 'avoiding any public comparison'.[8] Josephine had really done as well as she deserved.

It was to be a very different story for another widow of the Russia drama who later came to knock on Whitehall doors in search of money; or rather, as it concerned Sydney Reilly, a pair of widows.

The first supplicant was Margaret (Reilly's only legal wife) to whom he appears to have given hardly any support since he booted her out of his life to make room for the first of his bigamous brides, Nadine Massino. On 25 February 1926, three months after her husband's mysterious disappearance in Russia, Margaret approached the Foreign Office via the British Legation in Brussels, where she was living on the charity of Belgian friends. She claimed that Reilly had vanished with the then vast sum of £12,000 of her own money, which he had promised to pay back, and more, once he had used it to help overthrow the Bolshevik regime. The story sounds somewhat steep but Margaret's current situation was plain: she was on her beam ends, distraught and desperate to know to whom she might officially turn for succour. There is no minute or further comment on her letter, which appears without any reference number in Reilly's personal file. But the evidence that it came to nothing is contained in the plentiful documentation about a similar application for Whitehall's bounty which was put in twelve years later by Reilly's second bigamous wife, his precious Pepita. She, by now, had reverted to her former married name of Mrs Haddon Chambers.

It is somewhat ironic that here, for the first time in Reilly's copious file, the SIS and Foreign Office documents on his affairs are stamped with the supreme security marking of 'Most Secret'. Pepita had acted through a Mr Stuart Atherley, who (it later transpired) was her literary agent. Atherley, in turn, had gone a roundabout route via the then Minister of War, Major Hore-Belisha, whom he had known at Oxford. Could the minister not help 'in securing a pension ... for the widow of Captain Sydney Reilly M.C. of the Military Intelligence Department ... who, on 25 September 1925 entered Russia at the suggestion of a British official, Commander Eric [sic] Boyce, British Passport Officer at Reval and was captured and executed'.

The involvement of a government minister in the affair produced a vigorous if somewhat tardy reaction. The SIS response to Mr Atherley's approach (which had reached the department via the Foreign Office) is dated 14 April 1939. It sought to bury the question once and for all of official responsibility for Reilly's fate by repeating two of 'C's' previous pronouncements on the matter (one, dated 1 July 1927, being clearly in connection with Margaret Reilly's request). Two matters 'relevant to the present issue' were: '(a) All Reilly's activities after 1921 were his own private affair and those in Russia in 1925 had no connection in any shape or form with this organisation' and '(b) The allegation that Reilly entered Russia in September 1925 at the suggestion of the British P.C.O. at Reval is categorically denied by the latter.' The memorandum went on to claim that the SIS had, in fact, done all it could to discourage Reilly in 'his own, or White Russian activities' and ended, in tart fashion: 'There is no case whatever to justify re-opening this matter and, in view of the deceased's somewhat complicated matrimonial tangles ... it would be inexpedient to make any compassionate grant to Mrs. Haddon Chambers.'[9]

It was not quite all over, for the Pepita/Atherley camp then raised the matter of those incriminating letters (in their possession) which Boyce had sent to Reilly in August 1925. At this, an SIS man calling himself Mr 'C.E.S. Williams of the Foreign Office' was eventually sent to call on Atherley and persuade him that Boyce had acted 'against instructions'.

The SIS messenger added for good measure that Reilly, 'though a very gallant fellow was, like others of his type, a political adventurer. He was a fanatical anti-Bolshevik and, of course, in with the Whites. His intrigues were embarrassing to H.M. Government at a time when this country wished to establish better relations with the Russian government and it was this, coupled with some of Reilly's business transactions, which decided H.M. Government, at the close of 1921, to sever connections with him.'

The conversation closed with some talk about 'the other ladies in Reilly's life' and also – quite unnecessarily – about his possible illegitimacy and Jewish origins. Atherley, who 'seemed to be a very decent fellow' made no attempt 'to press matters further' and that was that. This, the last document in Reilly's copious file,[10] is dated 27 July 1939. So Sydney Reilly, having entered SIS life as a very special envoy at the climax of the First World War, did not leave Whitehall's files until the eve of the Second World War – though now in the guise of an unwelcome adventurer, a bigamist, and an illegitimate Russian Jew.

It was not an edifying envoi from his old department. Yet one suspects that the thought that it was his matrimonial tangles which had finally elevated him into the 'Most Secret' category of archives would have amused the 'Ace of Spies'. In which case, as with that much earlier European legend, the famous prankster and peasant folk hero Till Eulenspiegel, a ghostly chuckle might have been registered long after his execution.

Notes

First references to books and articles include the full publication details. For subsequent references, the chapter and note number of the first citation is given in square brackets.

1. The Man Carrying Diamonds

1 CX 2616, Reilly's SIS file.
2 Among other clauses in the treaty, the Bolsheviks had promised to recognize the independence of the Ukraine; to evacuate and relinquish all Russia's claims on her Baltic provinces; and to demobilize all her troops and lay up all her warships in their harbours.
3 Michael Kettle, *Sydney Reilly* (London, 1983), a short paperback stressing it did 'not purport to be a full biography'.
4 Robin Bruce Lockhart, *Ace of Spies* (London, 1967).
5 Reilly Papers, CX 2616. The document is sloppily undated though, as it is described as coming from 'a woman claiming to be the real Mrs. Reilly', the interview was presumably after she had been deserted some years later.
6 Robin Bruce Lockhart [1, 4], 31–60.
7 Reilly's story is that he was persuaded to go into Allied uniform by Sir William Wiseman, 'C's' influential station chief in Washington. A more likely version is that he acted on impulse after watching an air display put on by the Canadians in New York in the autumn of 1916.

8 Reilly Papers, CX 021744, CXM 188, received London 10 a.m., 4 March 1918.

9 Reilly Papers, CX 023996, sent from New York 6 p.m., 20 March 1918.

10 The story later spread around by Reilly that his appointment was directly due to Prime Minister Lloyd George, with whom he conferred in Downing Street, can be classed as another of his Baron Münchhausen tales. The name Reilly does not appear anywhere in Lloyd George's detailed war memoirs.

11 Up until then, the naval and military intelligence department of the Admiralty and War Office had shared responsibility for gathering information from abroad, with a political input from the Foreign Office. It had proven to be an inefficient as well as a cantankerous arrangement.

12 For a while, this became known as MIi(C) but, for simplicity's sake, I have used its eventual acronym, SIS (for Secret Intelligence Service), throughout.

13 Compton Mackenzie, *Greek Memories*, vol. III of the War Memoirs (London, 1932).

14 This had set off a game of diplomatic musical chairs. The Western consulate-generals, which had always functioned in Moscow, stayed on, acquiring an increasing operational significance. The embassies had left Petrograd after Lenin signed his separate peace, and set up shop in Vologda, some 350 miles north-east of the old Tsarist capital.

15 His predecessor, Major Alley, had been withdrawn as being too compromised with the old regime. He was the man who, at Murmansk while on his way back to England, had been able to remove suspicions about Reilly's bona fides.

16 It is interesting to speculate when Lockhart would have been let into the secret, had Reilly kept his head down. The newcomer was not being given diplomatic cover, so there was no need for his presence to be officially recognized or protected.

17 Robert Bruce Lockhart, *Memoirs of a British Agent* (London, 1932), 276–7.

18 Robert Bruce Lockhart [1, 17], 76.

2. Options

1 FO 371/3290, No. 50031.

2 Despite this firm tone, the façade was to be preserved, for the time being, that the Entente had 'no desire to take part in any way in the internal politics of Russia' and were 'in no way promoting a counter-revolution'.

3 It is interesting to note that, at this stage, the ideological argument for opposing Bolshevism as an evil in itself and a threat to the outside world was not even mentioned in top-level Allied assessments.

4 FO 371/3337, No. 2303. It was sent in the name of the War Cabinet.

5 CX 027753, despatched from Petrograd on 16 April 1918 and decoded in London two days later.

6 The equivalent of £45 million in today's terms.

7 CX 034025, despatched from Moscow on 28 May 1918. As it was basically a political survey and not an operational telegram, a copy was passed to the Foreign Office.

8 The plethora of parties which did exist at the time complicated any political assessment. They ranged from Anarchists on the extreme left to Nationalists on the far right. In between came, among others, the Socialist Revolutionaries (themselves split into three groups); the so-called Social Democrats or urban Socialists, whose radical wing were the Bolsheviks; then, as so-called 'Constitutional Parties', the middle-class Progressists; the Cadets, the party of the intelligentsia, whose main faction had a programme based on English radicalism; and the Octobrists, an almost defunct group formed to support the constitution of October 1905.

9 FO 371/3331, print dated 30 May 1918.

10 FO 371/3331, No. 44617, 12 March 1918.

11 The one type of agent Lockhart definitely was not was a secret agent, in its familiar connotation of a spy. He was never a member of 'C's' service and never worked for it, except in the sense of

providing its operators with an umbrella of official cover. Indeed, he professed a certain scepticism about their value – not surprisingly in view of the mess they inadvertently got him involved in.

12 See note 8.

13 Sir George Buchanan had been withdrawn because he was politically compromised as well as genuinely worn out. The French and American ambassadors, M. Noulens and Mr Francis, though equally anti-Bolshevik, remained at their posts.

14 Allied military missions had, of course, existed in Russia throughout the war, of which the largest by far was the French, under General Niessel in Petrograd. They had no authority, either before or after the Bolshevik revolution, to represent their countries in anything but military matters, though in the mayhem of 1918 ad hoc political contacts did take place.

3. 'Eyes and Ears'

1 FO 371/3330, Lockhart telegram of 1 May 1918.

2 Hicks, for example, was a poison gas expert.

3 The compromise eventually adopted was to keep secret service officers independent but to enjoin them to share information and 'collaborate in every way possible with the military'.

4 We know little or nothing of Lieutenant Reid beyond the fact that he was an RNVR officer who served for only about a year in Russia. The conditions of his assignment were set out in an FO 371/3326 telegram of 9 April 1918. In this message from London, Consul-General Wardrop was informed that Reid would be joining his staff from Petrograd for 'Military Control (Passport) work under the elaborate system centred in a branch of the War Office in London'. This system, already in operation in all neutral countries contiguous to Germany, enabled these officers 'to take advantage of the cover afforded by their passport work to keep a general control over the secret organizations responsible for the acquisition of naval and military intelligence'. The officer would

have the right 'to telegraph in his own cypher direct to his Chief in London'. Reid and his colleagues were the direct precursors of the civilian PCO (Passport Control Officer) system set up by SIS after the war.

5 No proper file on Ernest Boyce has survived in the SIS archives. Possible reasons for this will emerge later.

6 Hill's 26-page report on his intelligence activities in Russia is in FO 371/3350, memorandum dated 26 November 1918.

7 Hill was soon to be formally recruited into SIS.

8 FO 371/3329, No. 75985, 30 April 1918.

9 Nos 351 and 391 of Series Z, Box 607, File 6.

10 Not in April 1918, the date given in some books.

11 Telegrams 445 and 446, Series Z, Box 611, File 1.

12 This seems to be confirmed by the fact that when, as described below, the Cheka raided his hide-out, all that they found, apart from a small sum of money, was a hoard of high explosives.

13 In 1919, he was put on trial *in absentia* in Paris, charged with desertion and treason.

14 These include telegrams to Paris in September 1918 making it clear that Lavergne was resisting to the bitter end orders to leave Russia along with other Allied staff in Moscow.

15 Like the other Western powers, France had expanded its network of consular posts throughout Russia after the revolution. According to the *Annuaire Diplomatique* for 1918, in that year there were seven French consuls or consular agents based in Odessa (including outlying posts as well as offices at Kiev and Sebastopol); five in the Kharkov and Don regions; three in Georgia; one each at Omsk and Tashkent; and a headquarters staff at Moscow. Several unmarked papers in the intelligence archives (one on the bloody peasant riots in Byelorussia in the midsummer of 1918, for example) may well have originated from these consular missions.

Among other miscellaneous papers to survive is an excellent survey of the situation in the Volga region in August 1918, prepared by one Lieutenant-Colonel Bégou of the 33rd French Infantry Regiment. The colonel did his intelligence gathering over a twelve-month period while on detachment to a White Russian army, putting together a summary before returning to France. He seems to have acted entirely off his own bat.

16 The Central Intelligence Agency, or CIA, was established in 1947 and the author was in Washington on the occasion of its fiftieth birthday.

17 These were to prove protracted. The 'colonel' did not return to the Soviet Union until 1933, when he was received as an honoured tourist by the regime.

18 Unfortunately, despite an intensive search in the National Archives, only one example appears to have survived. This is marked 'No. 10' and dated 5 March 1918. It gives the situation on the ground after the signing of the Brest-Litovsk treaty as seen in Vologda, Tiflis and Vladivostok.

19 For the personal details of Kalamatiano's life and career I am indebted to the copious research of Harry Thayer Mahoney. He kindly provided me with all of his material, which was summarized in the *International Journal of Intelligence and Counter-Intelligence* (1995), vol. 8, no. 2. See also David S. Fogelson, *America's Secret War against Bolshevism* (University of North Carolina Press), ch.5.

20 They had seemed unimpressed to begin with. The stepfather who had left his new wife and stepson behind in Russia, started off as an unskilled worker in a barbed wire factory. Three years later, when he had advanced to the position of cashier of a grocery store in Bloomington, and then to that of a language teacher at Culver Military Academy, the family joined him.

21 This was on a par with the double-speak to be practised by all the Allies later on, when even armed intervention was deemed to be quite different from actual interference.

22 State Department, Consular Bureau, Microfilm Ref. RG59, M316, Roll 16, Frames 226–9. I am particularly indebted to Hayden Peake in Washington (see Foreword) and his researcher for unearthing these papers in the National Archives after several sorties up blind alleys.

23 He had succeeded his former chief, Maddin Summers, who had died in harness on 4 May. There were rumours that Summers

had been poisoned but the autopsy showed a brain haemorrhage, probably caused by overwork.

24 A monograph is clearly needed on the role played by the YMCA in Allied intelligence operations at the time. It served as a pool also for potential British agents.

25 His annual salary was fixed at $2,400, the same as the top rate for the 'Especially appointed Vice-Consuls'.

26 'Vecheka' is the acronym for the fuller title. This translates into English as the 'All-Russian Extraordinary Commission for Combating Counter-Revolution, Speculation, Sabotage and Misconduct in Office'.

27 For an exhaustively detailed account, see George Leggett, *The Cheka* (Oxford University Press, 1981), from which most of the following data has been extracted.

28 Leggett [3, 27], 257–8.

4. Maelstrom

1 FO 372/3290, No. 47823.

2 FO 371/3290, No. 51340 of 19 March 1918.

3 The best account of this episode is in George Kennan, *The Decision to Intervene* (London, 1958), 95–106.

4 At the time of the great German offensive of March 1918, nearly a year after the United States had entered the war, there were only four American divisions in France, and only one was fully trained.

5 London *Times*, 11 March 1918.

6 London *Times*, 20 March 1918.

7 If anyone had been setting the pace over Vladivostok, it was the British. The Russia Committee of the Foreign Office had suggested weeks before the landings that 'three warships and at least 2,000 men' should be sent to the port to secure Allied war supplies there, especially the stocks of tungsten, flax and tin. (FO 95/802: meeting of 8 February 1918.)

8 Quoted in Kennan [4, 3], 101.

9 *Pravda*, 24 April 1918.

10 FO 371/3286, No. 94955, 23 May 1918.

11 Not for the first time, there is a divergence between what Lockhart reported to London in 1918 and what he wrote in his *Memoirs* in 1932 ([1, 17], 282–3). In the latter he admitted that not only was he pushing at an open door with Noulens, but that the Frenchman was even more hawkish than he had just become over ignoring any Bolshevik objections to Allied landings.

12 Most of the Allied embassies had evacuated Petrograd in late February, when it seemed the city might fall to the German army. The provincial town of Vologda, some 300 miles to the northeast, was chosen because it was at the intersection of railway lines which ran both to the old Tsarist capital and to Moscow, soon to become the new Bolshevik one. Though the Petrograd embassy was left in the formal charge of the neutral Netherlands, a British consul, Mr Woodhouse, was left behind and, as we shall see, the building filled up again with British naval and intelligence personnel once the German military threat receded.

13 'Old Francis doesn't know a Left Socialist revolutionary from a potato,' Lockhart noted acerbically in his diary during the visit.

14 It is worth noting en passant that Masaryk was the only Czech nationalist who, from the first, worked without reservation for complete independence outside even a restructured Habsburg empire. Even within the ranks of the legion, there remained a minority with monarchist sympathies.

15 Only a handwritten copy exists in the secret service archives, bearing no CX number.

16 FO 371/3339, Telegram Nos 122 and 144.

17 Part of the money was raised from private individuals of Allied or Russian nationality, who were very happy to have the roubles in their local bank accounts converted into pounds sterling in London. It is worth noting that action on operational matters like these was left entirely to the consulates in Moscow and the embassy staff remaining in Petrograd. Vologda played no role.

18 FO 371/3286, No. 92955.

19 Trotsky did, however, organize the destruction of most of the Black Sea fleet at Odessa and other south Russian harbours, thus preventing it from being taken over by the Germans.

20 FO 371/3286, No. 108770.

21 FO 371/3286, No. 191, 10 June 1918. Characteristically, the Foreign Secretary softened the brusque tone of the message by himself adding an introductory paragraph stressing that Lockhart's difficulties were understood and that no personal criticism was intended. On reading that, Lockhart stayed at his post.

22 FO 371/3332, No. 92708.

23 The principal assassin was one Iakov Grigorevich Bliumkin, a twenty-year-old Jew from Odessa who had managed to get himself appointed head of the Cheka's new counter-intelligence section only two months before. It was thus a simple matter for him to arrive with forged official papers requesting an interview. The purpose of the interview, Bliumkin brazenly explained, was to warn the envoy that terrorists were plotting to kill him. At this, Mirbach enquired: 'And how exactly do they propose to do it?' 'Like this!' Bliumkin replied, suddenly producing and firing his weapon.

24 The three regiments hired by Lenin were among the forces first raised by the Tsar when Latvia was a Russian province.

25 Robert Bruce Lockhart [1, 17], 300–1.

26 Reilly's destruction of incriminating evidence was doubtless repeated at all moments of crisis. Moreover, both Boyce and Lockhart, in common with their Western colleagues, were to burn both cyphers and secret records when danger threatened. As early as 4 June, there is a curious telegram Lockhart sent to London (obviously in reply to a query from Whitehall) saying: 'I had already some days ago destroyed all my papers and documents' (FO 371/3332, No. 251). What London wanted destroyed at this point was probably papers on one sensitive issue of the time, such as links with Savinkov or plans to destroy the Russian Baltic Fleet. He had plenty more to be burnt.

27 Later Sir Thomas Preston, Bt of Beeston Hall, Norfolk. He and his family became close friends of the author, to whom he gave

frequent descriptions of the tragedy. He always protested his help-lessness to do anything to protect the imperial captives. Even persistent enquiries about their welfare had brought from the local Bolsheviks the threat of arrest. His requests for Foreign Office guidance reached London weeks after the murders had taken place.

28 FO 371/3229, No. 119, 3 May 1918. (By this date the family had already been moved further east to their eventual place of execution, Ekaterinburg.)

29 See *The Last Habsburg* (London, 1968) by the present author, pp. 222 *et seq.*

30 The landing duly took place on 2 August but with only a puny force of some 1,200 men (one sub-standard English infantry battalion, one French colonial battalion and 50 US Marines) under Major-General Poole's command. It had been preceded by a *coup d'état* against the local Soviet administration and the victors were to form the members of a 'North Russian Government' acknow-ledged by the Allies.

5. The Plot, As Presented Down the Years

1 The company of Marines, also commanded by Poole, which went ashore at Murmansk as early as 6 March, only three days after the Bolsheviks signed their separate peace, was too tiny to do anything except carry out its task: to guard the war supplies.

2 London *Times*, 10 September 1918.

3 Robert Bruce Lockhart [1, 17], 317–19.

4 They were coyly described as 'detectives' in the Soviet reports.

5 In FO 371/3336 (unnumbered), 1 September 1918.

6 *Izvestia*, 5 September 1918, for example.

7 The medal had been awarded to Cromie for his feat, as a subma-rine commander, in sinking the German cruiser *Undine* in 1915. He was given the DSO by his own government for the same action.

8 *Izvestia*, 3 September 1918.

9 See pp. 106–7 below.

10 What was less of a surprise, when Marchand's case was examined in the West, was why, assuming the letter was not a forgery, he might have written it. He harboured strong sympathies for the Bolsheviks and later joined the French Communists.

11 FO 371/3335, No. 15157, 3 September 1918. (The reassurance about documents was, at best, only partly true.)

12 War Cabinet, Minutes of Meeting 469, 4 September 1918.

13 FO 371/3335 (unnumbered), 4 September 1918.

14 FO 371/3340, No. 152653, 6 September 1918. (Ex-Viceroy Hardinge annotated primly: 'This seems a very good tel. to send.')

15 See below, p. 107.

16 FO 371/3336, No. 155127, London, 6 September 1918.

17 The episode is recounted at length in Robert Bruce Lockhart [1, 17], 314–16.

18 The fact that Reilly was able to get free at all was one factor in persuading his latest biographer that Reilly was himself a Bolshevik agent all along! (Edward van der Rhoer, *Master Spy*, New York, 1981.)

19 The nearest Lockhart came to one was when he took Moura on his staff, to be told by London that Countess Benckendorff and any other Russian nationals employed should be removed.

20 For example, A.L.P. Dennis, *The Foreign Policies of Soviet Russia* (New York, 1924).

21 *Go Spy the Land* (Cassell, London, 1932). (Pages 237–44 deal with the conspiracy.)

22 Robin Bruce Lockhart [1, 4]. Pages 74–81 deal spasmodically with the conspiracy; as usual, no sources are given.

23 Richard K. Debo, 'Lockhart Plot or Dzerzhinsky Plot?' *Journal of Modern History*, vol. XLIII, September 1971.

24 Reilly Papers, a 'Renseignement', 'Affaire Lockhart', marked 'Secret' and dated 2 November 1921. Both the security grading and the delayed production of this French document are puzzling.

25 She was the sister of Colonel Friede.

26 It is well summarized in an article by John W. Long which appeared in the journal *Intelligence and National Security*, vol. 10, no. 1, January 1995.

27 Reported in *The Times*, 9 May 1911.

28 Why this belated spate of Soviet claims should have appeared at this time is a little obscure. One suggestion is that it was intended to boost the image of the secret police in the post-Stalin era.

29 Richard Ullman, *Intervention and the War*, vol. 1 (Princeton, 1961). Page 291 first catalogues these discrepancies.

6. The Plot: What Really Happened

1 Called by him, in his certified English translation, 'The March of Time' (unpublished). Orlov's credentials for presenting an accurate and unbiased account, together with the author's personal knowledge of his record, are set out fully in the Foreword. The principal ones are, first, that he did not personally take part in the 1918 operation, and therefore had nothing to conceal or exaggerate; second, that though quietly proud of the 'Trust' as a professional operation, he was certainly not inclined to give the regime undue credit for anything; and third, that none of his revelations over the years was ever found to be false or distorted.

2 Interesting, inasmuch as Cromie's activities were always supposed to have been concerned with the Soviet Navy.

3 Almost certainly General Lavergne, though he is nowhere mentioned by name in these Orlov papers for 1918.

4 Author's italics.

5 Thus escaping the first round of Moscow arrests, though he was seized on his return to the Russian capital a few days later.

6 Though Hill had thus been quite accurately named as a major accomplice, he was not to be included in the subsequent indictment.

7 This drastic solution sounds much more likely than the comic scenario depicted in some Western accounts – namely that Reilly would merely ridicule the captured leaders by marching them

down the streets of Moscow without their trousers. It will be noted that, in the Marchand testimony as printed in the Soviet press, there was no mention that the French informer knew and passed on all the plans for the *coup d'état* in the capital. This omission was doubtless because the Cheka wanted to claim the entire credit for unmasking the 'Moscow plot' unaided.

8 Author's italics. Evidence of this 'editing' is all over the first four pages, devoted entirely to pained criticism of the French government's change of heart in opposing, instead of supporting, the Lenin regime.

9 How active a role was played in all this by de Verthamon is unclear but he was certainly up to his neck in the sabotage business. Orlov says simply: 'On 1 September, Soviet agents searched the French high school in Moscow where Colonel de Vertamont [*sic*], an intelligence officer from the Second Bureau of the French General Staff, had disguised himself as a teacher. The agents found in his room 18 lbs of pyroxiln packed in cans, a secret spy code and 28,000 roubles.'

10 His mistress, Trotsky's secretary, Evgenia Petrovina Shelyepina, proved a most valuable source of information. Because of this, Lockhart illegally gave her a British passport as 'Mrs Ransome' to leave Russia in 1918, though she did not marry the journalist until 1924.

11 FO 371/3342, No. 159609, 20 September 1918.

12 Author's italics.

13 FO 371/3336, No. 153837.

14 FO 371/3337, No. 171217, 11 October 1918.

15 FO 371/3337, No. 176527.

16 Robert Bruce Lockhart [5, 16], 47.

17 FO 371/3337, No. 185499, 8 November 1918.

18 Typically, the heavily edited *Diaries* [5, 16] show Lockhart discoursing in London at the time as though only the one memorandum existed.

19 Robert Bruce Lockhart [1, 17], 316.

20 FO 371/3348, No. 190442, 5 November 1918.

21 Confidential Memorandum to Secretary of State Lansing, Number 1302, dated 8 February 1919, and sent from Archangel, where Poole was acting as chargé d'affaires.

7. New Options: the Rethink

1 Received in Paris on 23 October and entered as No. 01129 in the files of the Sûreté Nationale.
2 CX 058652 (Cx 807), sent from Stockholm, 20 November 1918.
3 This was the so-called Northern Corps which had been set up a month earlier in Pskov, headed by extreme right-wing former Tsarist officers dedicated to restoring 'Greater Russia'. It numbered some 3,500 men and some of its officers were former prisoners-of-war smuggled back from Berlin. It became the nucleus of the expanded anti-Bolshevik North-Western Army.
4 CXM 877 sent, undated, to Stockholm via the Director of Military Intelligence, War Office.
5 'Notes on our Policy in Russia', 1 November 1918 (FO 371/3345, No. 198801).
6 Author's italics.
7 'Memorandum on our present and future military policy in Russia', War Office O. 1/180/517, 13 November 1918.
8 See FO 371/3344, No. 174439, 17 October 1918.
9 The Swedes and the Bolsheviks were already in contact before the Armistice was signed to sound out commercial prospects in the post-war world. An SIS report to London from the Stockholm station in October reported the arrival in the Swedish capital of Lenin's Minister of Finance, M. Gukovsky, carrying '40 million roubles in cash and a little platinum', to open up an account. Sweden would receive Russian metals, lubricants and flax in return for food and machinery. (CXE No. 055393, sent from Stockholm, 16 October 1918.)
10 CX 052684, received London, 8 October 1918.
11 He had succeeded General Alexeyev who had died in Rostov.

8. The Baltic: White Sea Heroics

1 The story of Agar's adventure is based largely on his own account in *Baltic Episode* (London, 1963). The naval side of the operation draws also on other works, notably G. Bennett, *Cowan's War* (London, 1964).

2 The head of the SIS Stockholm station at the time was Major Scale, but not all of the STs which he initially controlled remained under his wing. Those who were transferred to different stations still, confusingly, retained their original ST number throughout their careers in the field.

3 The name was changed to Kuibyshev in 1935.

4 In his book, *The Story of ST.25* (London, 1938), Dukes gives a carefully doctored version of the origin of these documents.

5 Appendix to Dukes [8, 4], 360–74.

6 See above, pp. 114–15.

7 Dukes was heavily involved with the so-called National Centre, a clandestine right-wing political movement which supported the Allies. He furnished it with funds and its members, in turn, were among his best intelligence informants. The centre was planning major uprisings in both Petrograd and Moscow for the autumn of 1919. The plot was betrayed, enabling the Cheka to smash the organization in mid-September, arresting hundreds of the conspirators. From that point, Dukes himself became a hunted man on the run.

8 When given a baronetcy for his services there he chose to be styled Baronet of the Baltic.

9 There were a few French warships in the Baltic to protect the small Allied forces on land but Cowan hesitated to call upon them, and with good reason. Their commander, Commodore Brisson, had warned him that sympathy for the Bolsheviks was so widespread among his crews that he dared not risk asking them to attack Russian vessels. (These same sympathies had brought the French Fleet in the Black Sea out in mutiny.)

10 CX 065263. From ST 25/S.N. 83. Sent from Stockholm, 25 January 1919.

11 Member of Petrograd's three-man Revolutionary Soviet of the Baltic Fleet.

12 Author's italics.

13 Trotsky had previously been Commissar for Foreign Affairs, in which capacity he had led the Soviet negotiating team at Brest-Litovsk. He resigned after criticism of the treaty as a sell-out at the Seventh Party Congress.

14 CX 066470 SN/92, forwarded from Stockholm, 13 February 1919.

15 CX 066471 SN/93, received Stockholm, also on 13 February 1919. The message was marked 'Translation from the Russian'.

16 The lady in question was the wife of Commissar Raskolnikov, mistakenly referred to as his widow. In fact, she was to be reunited with her husband the following June, when the British agreed to release him for no fewer than eighteen of their own officer prisoners in Soviet hands.

17 CX 066477, marked 'From ST.25(E) Translation', sent from Stockholm, 18 February 1919.

18 CX 073245 P/C 967 A/14 received in Stockholm on 29 June and telegraphed on to London the following day.

19 The seemingly omniscient Dukes had warned on 29 January of trouble brewing here for the regime, commenting, prophetically as it proved, that all the conspirators had to fear 'was the crew from the "Petropavlovsk", with its 12-inch guns'. (CX 066470, received Stockholm, 13 February 1919.)

20 This version is based on Agar's own story. It is likely that Cowan had given him a semi-official blessing for the action.

21 The Soviet authorities, as a token of respect for such professional daring, returned their bodies to Britain for burial.

9. Black Sea Hopes: Secret Service in the South

1 CX 2616, instruction from 'C', 10 December 1918.

2 Reilly Papers (unnumbered), letter of 'C' dated 12 December 1918, and collected by Reilly from 'C' just before he caught his boat train.

3 Reilly Papers (unnumbered), 25 December 1918.

4 The warning was passed on to London by the British Legation in Christiana, the Norwegian capital (renamed Oslo in 1925). FO 371/3319, No. 165188, 30 September 1918.

5 Kaledin received £10 million in British aid, equal to £4.5 billion in today's money, but achieved little with it and finally committed suicide in February 1918 as the Red Army closed in on Rostov, his headquarters.

6 Kornilov in April 1918, killed in action by a stray Red Army shell; and Alexeyev the following October of pneumonia and exhaustion.

7 The joint offensive by the Volunteer Army and the Cossacks in the Kuban had taken the key railway junction town of Ekaterinodar some eighty miles inland on 15 August, thus opening the way for the final drive to the coast.

8 In January 1930, he was kidnapped in broad daylight on the streets of Paris by Stalin's OGPU agents and taken back to an unknown but certainly murky fate in Russia.

9 This would have included the Cossacks. British military estimates made on the spot put Denikin's own field force at the time at little more than half of the total.

10 The two powers were still acting under the 'zones of influence' convention signed on 23 December 1917 purely with wartime strategic aims targeted at the Central Powers in mind. This had assigned to the British 'for operations against the Turks' the eastern half, i.e. the Cossack territories (a vague term), the Caucasus, Armenia, Georgia and Kurdistan. The French were to tackle 'enemy forces' in the area of southern Russia lying west of the River Don,

comprising the Ukraine, Bessarabia and the Crimea. All expenses were to be shared.

11 French woes were compounded a fortnight later when a major mutiny broke out in their Black Sea flotilla.

12 Reilly Papers, Despatch No. 4, sent from Ekaterinodar, 11 January 1919.

13 Air Ministry File No. 023893, 10 January 1919, and marked simply 'REILLY' in block capitals. (The composition of the letter and the handwriting are those of an educated woman, discounting the story that she had started life as a housemaid.)

14 Reilly Papers, CX 066117, sent from Odessa, 19 February 1919.

15 Reilly Papers, Despatch from Sevastopol, 28 December 1918.

16 Among the documents Reilly forwarded to London was a telegram from Major von Kochenhausen, the political officer of the German occupation army, warning that the Cossacks would receive no more German arms and equipment if Krasnov were not their leader.

17 Reilly Papers, Despatch No. 5, sent from Ekaterinodar, 21 January 1919.

18 Ibid.

19 The 'Tiger' had become so un-tigerish about the Bolsheviks that he was even against receiving them at the Paris peace talks, for fear that they would spread their baleful gospel to the French people.

20 War Office, O. 1/180/517, 13 November 1918.

10. Peace Flutters

1 FO 371, minuted note of 30 November 1918.

2 His influence on the Tsar during the supreme crisis of 1914 had been baleful both for his royal master and for Europe. It was Sazonov who, on the afternoon of Thursday 30 July, finally persuaded Nicholas to re-order general mobilization for his forces, thus rendering the outbreak of war almost inevitable.

3 Earlier that month, there had been a series of 'informal' meetings in Stockholm between Maxim Litvinov, Lenin's Deputy Commissar for Foreign Affairs, and a State Department official, W.H. Buckler, on possible peace terms. The British had followed the French lead in staying away – which hardly mattered as the talks came to nothing.

4 Lloyd George, detained in London to cope with an outbreak of civil and military unrest, had rashly sent Churchill as his spokesman. But the message Churchill wanted to deliver was his own.

5 Ten days later, Marshal Foch, the Allied Supreme Commander-in-Chief, produced an even more drastic plan: the moment a preliminary peace was imposed on Germany, a great arc of anti-Red armies, ranging from the Finns in the north, the Czechs and Poles in the centre, and the Greeks and Romanians in the south, was to move in to help the White Russian forces snuff out Bolshevism.

6 The details of the mission were given at length by Bullitt himself in his testimony to the Senate Committee on Foreign Relations, printed as Senate Document 106, 66th Congress, First Session, Washington 1919.

7 This was in marked contrast to the spartan hospitality being accorded to Arthur Ransome, the controversial left-wing correspondent of the *Manchester Guardian* who had been a useful member of Lockhart's old entourage. Ransome had returned to Petrograd on a fact-finding assignment of his own, and the city commissars had dined him on very basic fare beginning with soup flavoured with shreds of horsemeat. But then, compared with Bullitt, Ransome was a very scrawny dove of peace.

8 Henry Wickham Steed, then the paper's foreign editor and author of the article concerned, had been tipped off that peace talk was in the air by one of Colonel House's aides, his son-in-law Gordon Auchinloss.

11. The Siberian Tragedy

1 The standard source for his saga is E. Varneck and H.H. Fisher (eds), *The Testimony of Kolchak and other Siberian Materials* (Stanford University Press, 1935). It is based on an earlier Russian publication which included the transcript of his lengthy interrogation by the Bolsheviks in 1920.

2 Britain was to fall in right behind him, for that target figure exactly matched the eventual promise from London of 200,000 sets of British Army uniform and equipment, plus 132 field guns, 58 howitzers and half a million hand grenades – to name only the principal military supplies. In true Russian style, much of what did arrive was to be wasted in the field, sold on the black market or captured by the enemy; some 10,000 of whose troops went into attack wearing British khaki, webbing and puttees. (WO 32/5707, report of 7 June 1919.)

3 The Russian title was Verkhovny Pravitel which sounded too autocratic for comfort.

4 This was, to begin with, General Otani, the Japanese officer whom Tokyo had insisted should be the de facto Allied Commander-in-Chief. He was a full general, two ranks higher than Knox and his American counterpart, William Graves.

5 Ward, who continued to serve as an MP until 1929, wrote a vivid account of his experiences in *With the Die-Hards* (London, 1920).

6 *Report on the Work of the British Military Mission to Siberia 1918–1919.* WO 32/5707, dated Vladivostok, 10 December 1919.

7 FO 371/3341, No. 186244, 10 November 1918.

8 It was one of several set up in Siberia with a total establishment of 500 British officers and 75 NCOs. Their ambitious programme was to put 500 White Russian officers and 1,000 NCOs through a basic training course every two months.

9 WO 32/5707, report of 2 December 1919.

10 'It's all over,' commented Lord Curzon, the new Foreign Secretary, when the loss of this key rail centre became known.

11 Deuxième Bureau report, 27 October 1919 (Box 1358, File 2426 of Vladivostok Documents).

12 Ibid., reports all dated 15 December 1919.

13 It was circulated as a Cabinet paper (CP 1488 of 17 June 1920) though without naming the source.

14 At the same time Kolchak appointed Semenov, of whose intrigues he was totally unaware, to serve as temporary Commander-in-Chief until Denikin could take over.

15 To do the general justice, he may well have also been impatient to remove any complication which might hinder the final evacuation of his beloved Czechs, many of whom were still smarting under Gayda's dismissal.

16 WO 32/5720, minute of 26 March 1920.

17 General A. Denikin, *The White Army* (London, 1930), 314.

18 Documents on British Foreign Policy (DBFP), Series One, Vol. II, No. 694.

19 Ibid., No. 698.

12. Petrograd and the Baltic Tangle

1 Some two million tons had been delivered to the two ports during 1917 alone, most of which had never been cleared by the Russians.

2 General Staff paper of 4 February 1919, in WO 32/5677.

3 This called for a force of 30,000 Czechs from General Gayda's north Siberian army to fight their way forward to the key town of Kotlas on the River Drina where they would join hands with Allied forces based 250 miles away at Archangel.

4 These ranged from reports that the corpses of tortured Tsarist officers had been found with gramophone needles driven under their fingernails, to tales of respectable women being flogged for refusing to comply with Bolshevik edicts of free love.

5 Ironside formally took over from the egregious General Poole on 19 November 1918. His memoirs, *Archangel 1918–19* give a

vivid account of the campaign. General Charles Maynard's *The Murmansk Venture* (London, 1928), is its companion piece.

6 For example, the *Daily Herald* of 4 April 1919.

7 Admitted by Churchill in his *The World Crisis* (vol. IV: *The Aftermath*, London, 1929, 242). The evacuation of Archangel ended on 27 September 1919 and that of Murmansk on 12 October, with minimal casualties in both operations. Some 6,000 White Russians were evacuated, mostly to the new Baltic states. A White Russian force hung on desperately in Archangel, which was not taken by the Red Army until February 1920.

8 The Finnish leader, who became regent of his country, had demanded from the Allies, as the price of his participation, an Anglo-French mandate, substantial military aid and the promise of large territorial gains.

9 '*Renseignements au sujet du Front du General Iudenitch à la date du 17 Août*' (Box 7, n 364, Annexe 6). The information was part of a broad military survey drawn up by the French Deuxième Bureau in Poland.

10 WO 32/5748, No. 5703A, 18 March 1919.

11 *The Times*, 2 August 1919.

12 The deliveries noted by the French were only part of other consignments of guns, lorries and medical supplies drawn from the vast store of war material rendered surplus by the Armistice.

13 At this point, the dashing general is said to have declined an offer to examine the city through field-glasses, saying he hoped to be marching along its famous boulevards the next day.

14 When the bills for British intervention were totted up, they came close to £100 million (£4½ billion in today's money). Of that total, north Russia had taken £15 million; equipment for Kolchak more than £14.5 million; while £26 million had been spent on Denikin in the south.

15 Goltz had a distinguished career on the German General Staff before the war and served with distinction in it. His most recent exploit had been in command of a German division sent the year before to help Field-Marshal Mannerheim of Finland sup-

press the Bolsheviks, a task which he discharged with gusto and efficiency.

16 FO 371, Memorandum 198772, 2 December 1918.

17 Box 7, V 364 of the restituted documents, Deuxième Bureau, File No. 474.

18 Box 7, V 364, Deuxième Bureau, File No. 469.

19 It is worth recording that, at one of these discussions, Clemenceau actually referred to a secret report he had read about the reinforcements Goltz was receiving – a rare instance of intelligence input being cited by an Allied leader. Not surprisingly, the source he quoted was French (Minutes of Allied Supreme Council, 8 August 1919).

20 In March 1918, his Fifth Army had buckled under the immense pressure of the German spring offensive and he was removed from its command.

21 Both men wrote of their Baltic experience. *Soldiering On* (London, 1954) was the title of Gough's memoirs; Tallents's autobiography was called simply *Man and Boy* (London, 1943).

22 As a further complication, an extra layer of control was added on when a full-blown Inter-Allied Mission was set up in the Baltic under the French General Niessel, with senior Allied officers under him.

23 The German government was at the time reeling with angry shock at the peace terms just announced in Versailles, which included the notorious 'war guilt' clause. It was thus in no mood to comply with the formal demand for the general's recall.

24 Printed in DBFP Volume III, First Series, No. 22. The meeting was held at St Olai, a town between Riga and Mitau, and it was Colonel Tallents, one of the members of Gough's team, who drew up the report.

25 Ibid.

26 The man Gough chose to take over command was the young Irish Guards officer Lieutenant-Colonel the Hon. H.R.L.G. Alexander who had come out, first to Poland and then to the Baltic, in search of adventure. He was later to become far better known as Field-Marshal Lord Alexander of Tunis.

27 The time-table laid down that all German troops were to evacuate Riga within forty-eight hours, and the rest of the country 'as soon as possible'.

28 At one point, it was even proposed that France should refuse to ratify the Peace Treaty until German forces were withdrawn from the Baltic. (DBFP, Volume II, First Series, No. 136.) Marshal Foch suggested using the Polish army to kick them out.

29 Goltz continued his fulminations in his memoirs *Meine Sendung in Finnland und im Baltikum* (Leipzig, 1920). In the Foreword he warned that the West was doomed unless it vanquished the 'Asian tyranny' which was threatening it.

30 With Estonia on 2 February; Lithuania on 12 July; and Latvia on 11 August.

13. Denikin: 'One Last Packet'

1 London *Times* despatch from Ekaterinodar, Denikin's base headquarters, 5 June 1919.

2 H.E. Jones, MC, *Over the Balkans and South Russia* (London, 1923) gives a participant's account of these adventures. The British pilots even entertained hopes of bombing Moscow in support of what was expected to be Denikin's final autumn offensive to take the capital. The idea proved too extravagant for even Churchill to accept. However, Jones and his fellow pilots volunteered to a man to go on fighting under Denikin even after British official support was withdrawn.

3 The former Viceroy of India had already taken over as Acting Foreign Secretary from the exhausted Balfour, and was formally confirmed in the post on 29 October 1919.

4 See FO 371/4024, No. 97011 and others.

5 On 30 May 1919, Denikin, in a special Order of the Day, had recognized Admiral Kolchak as the 'Supreme Governor of the Nation' and Commander-in-Chief of the Russian Armies.

6 FO 371/4024, No. 102523, sent from Bucharest, 6 July 1919. It is

in this same report that Hill begins to get over-excited about his new role as 'the living link between South Russia and Europe'.

7 See below, pp. 225–6

8 Air Ministry Memo of 8 July 1919, Reference B 11305.

9 The black market in Ekaterinodar was so rampant that thousands of citizens were wearing army or nurses' uniforms designated for the front line.

10 Minutes of War Cabinet Meeting, 12 August 1919 (612 CAB 23/11).

11 It would be wrong, however, to classify Denikin personally as a right-wing monarchist in the mould of Kolchak. He seems to have been something of a liberal, the type the Bolsheviks feared most.

12 He was to win even greater fame in the Second World War when, as Marshal Budyenny, C-in-C of the South-Western Army, he played a leading role in the defeat of Hitler's Wehrmacht.

13 Denikin had earlier broken with Wrangel, whom he suspected of intriguing against him. In his memoirs, he claims that the recall was made at the insistence of the senior officers in the Volunteer Army and that he had merely given his name to the appointment. (*The White Army* [11, 17], 359).

14 WO 32/5710 (no file reference).

15 Extract from Minutes of Cabinet 17 (20) of 31 March 1920.

16 Denikin had been allowed to take with him the small son and daughter of the late General Kornilov, his mentor and predecessor as C-in-C of the Volunteer Army.

17 Cabinet 17 (20), Minutes of conference, 11 June 1920.

18 The British again refused to help with his final evacuation, leaving it to the French to cope with the flood of 80,000 soldiers and refugees trying to escape by sea. Again, Churchill registered his protest, but in vain.

19 Scheinmann, Orlov added, protested his innocence when challenged about the matter in Berlin. No attempt was made to kidnap him and he eventually settled in London, where he worked in a travel bureau. Curiously, the British intelligence authorities made nothing out of his defection.

20 Contained in WO 32/5748.

14. Transitions

1 This approach had been the brainchild of one E.F. Wise, an official of Britain's wartime Ministry of Food and subsequently chief British representative on the Allied Supreme Economic Council.

2 Bullitt seemed fated for delicate and ultimately doomed missions. During the Second World War, he served as American envoy to the Pétain regime in Vichy set up by the Germans during their occupation of France.

3 Poole, ironically, had left for Finland that same day, after trying in vain to warn Kalamatiano about the danger facing him.

4 For example, Harry Thayer Mahoney [3, 19]. The Orlov papers [6, 1] also refer briefly to the affair.

5 See Part Two, ch. 6.

6 Telegram from State Department to Stockholm, No. 1201, 11 October 1918.

7 Almost certainly Colonel Friede.

8 Message in National Archives R659 (1910–1929) 811.20212/7–811.20261/1494, Box 7460.

9 Ibid.

10 They are traced out, in hitherto unpublished details, in the files on 'American Military Activities in Russia' in the National Archives, RG59, M973, Roll 155, Frame 102–21. Of the 74 telegrams listed for 1919, more than half deal with attempts to secure Kalamatiano's release. Other efforts are recounted in the State Department's published documents under 'Foreign Relations' 1920 Volume III and 1921 Volume II.

11 Quoted in Mahoney [3, 19].

12 Reilly Papers, CX 2616, Minute from 'Production', 3 October 1919.

13 Reilly Papers, CX 2616. Memo to DMP at the War Office, dated, in writing, 7 September 1920.

14 Reilly Papers, CX 2616, typewritten copy of letter, unsigned, dated 4 January 1920. It is somewhat surprising that this casual glimpse

into Whitehall intrigues survived the attention of SIS weeders down the years. However, their techniques were often as random as they were ruthless (see Foreword).

15 Reilly Papers, CX 2616, paper marked 'Sec. V.', 3 September 1920. He also forwarded something of special interest to 'C' – thousands of genuine application forms for British, Swiss and Danish passports captured from the Reds by General Wrangel.

16 Reilly Papers, CX 2616, letter to Stanley Gall dated Prague, 19 November 1920. Rex Leeper was one of Reilly's few champions at the Foreign Office.

17 In 1920, the secret vote had been cut from £50,000 a month to some £120,000 a year. Finance was one reason why George Hill and even Sir Paul Dukes failed to be taken on to SIS post-war strength.

18 There is much anecdotal evidence of this. See, for example, p. 338.

19 Identified as Bertie Maw, then working in 'Production', i.e. Operations.

20 Reilly Papers, CX 2616, handwritten letter marked 'Austria 27.1.22'.

21 Ibid., telegram of 31 January 1922.

22 Ibid., letter to Vienna of 1 February 1922.

23 Robert Bruce Lockhart made the same point when referring to visits which Savinkov and Reilly paid to Prague in 1920–2, when Lockhart was commercial attaché at the British Legation: 'Reilly, who had always worshipped Savinkov, was now the real leader'. (*Retreat from Glory* (London, 1934), 99.)

24 Reilly Papers, CX 2616, G.7 message to New York, 24 July 1923. The message would have been addressed to the PCO, or Passport Control Office, the cover introduced after the war for all SIS staff stationed abroad. (See [3, 4].)

15. Spinning the Web

1 The GPU or State Political Directorate replaced the Cheka in name only in 1922. After a year, the world 'United' was prefixed to the title, making its acronym OGPU. That style survived until 1934.

2 Its Russian acronym; also sometimes abbreviated to MOTSR.

3 *The Trust*, the main CIA survey of the subject published by the American Security and Intelligence Foundation in 1989; a lecture by the agency's disinformation expert, the Polish-born Richard Wraga, delivered to British intelligence officers in the early 1950s; and various Soviet accounts.

4 He maintains in the book that the whole idea of the Trust had been first suggested by Federov. His real name, as recorded in unpublished Soviet intelligence archives (but not revealed by Orlov), was Andrei Paulovich Mukhin and he was yet another White Army officer turned Chekist.

5 The timing was opportune. Only a week after the Paris meeting, General Wrangel, ever the activist and organizer, founded his 'Russian Armed Services Union' (or ROVS, for short) which trained paramilitary combat groups for action inside Russia. The OGPU was able to monitor the entire process, and recruit a number of ROVS officers into the bargain.

6 The material which follows is drawn from his unpublished memoirs, to the relevant sections of which the author was given access.

7 Carr papers [15, 6], 54.

8 As Alexander Orlov was to reveal years later in his 'March of Time' [6, 1], there were often furious arguments within the OGPU when Federov pleaded for the release of a juicy piece of genuine military intelligence to be fed to the West and the Red Army spokesmen refused. A Politburo ruling was sometimes needed.

9 Carr papers [15, 6], 55. What Carr does not mention is that he and other Western agents were also receiving a lot of disinfor-

mation from Moscow, to ram home the message that further intervention was needless, as the Soviet regime was reforming itself.

16. The Entrapment of Savinkov

1 Orlov [6, 1], 122–7, gives a detailed account (drawn from Cheka files) of these earliest activities of Savinkov.

2 The enigmatic Edward Opperput, a man of many aliases and political persuasions, of whom much more will be heard later. He may have been a genuine Savinkov adherent at the time but was arrested by the Cheka a few months later and 'turned' into one of their leading agents.

3 Orlov [6, 1], 142 *et seq.* Like many of Orlov's disclosures, written in the 1960s, none of the details has been included in Soviet versions of the events released for publication thirty years later, notably *Deadly Illusions,* the co-production effort of John Costello and Oleg Tsarov (London, 1993).

4 Grisha used for his courier service other 'deserters' who had joined the guerrillas with him, and who now made trips to Warsaw as escorts for Savinkov's messengers.

5 Author's italics. The existence of Savinkov's two army corps in Poland as described by Orlov is confirmed by separate sources. The details of Savinkov's network and activities appear in Orlov [6, 1], 149 *et seq.*

6 Also recorded as 'Case 29' in the unpublished Soviet archives.

7 According to the CIA memorandum, which gives the fullest account of this operation, this special team, headed by Artuzov, consisted mainly of Roman Pilar (a Polish cousin of Dzerzhinsky, who sometimes used his *ancien régime* title of Baron Piliar von Pilhau); Federov, whom we have met already; Puzitsky, who was to play a key role in the deception; and Grisha himself. Orlov later quizzed all of them.

8 Orlov [6, 1], 158–75.

9 Savinkov was passing the gist of all these reports to the western Allies, via their grateful intelligence services, which served a parallel aim of the OGPU.

10 Lenin had died on 21 January 1924, with Stalin emerging victorious in a struggle with Trotsky for the succession. Fear of further instability at the Kremlin had persuaded Dzerzhinsky to step up his offensive against émigré and domestic anti-Bolshevik activity.

11 Orlov [6, 1], 173–5.

12 Nearly a quarter of a million dollars in today's money.

17. Inside the Web

1 Orlov [6, 1], 186 *et seq.*

2 Walter Duranty, *I Write As I Please* (New York, 1935), ch. 20.

3 Geoffrey Bailey, *The Conspirators* (London, 1961), 43–5. (See Foreword for author's real identity.)

4 They were all leading party or state officials. Neither Stalin nor Trotsky attended.

5 Orlov [6, 1], 190. He names the main people he quizzed on this particular point. They included Artuzov himself, Puzitsky, Grisha, and I.S. Agranov, something of a specialist on Savinkov, whose organization he had investigated in 1920.

6 Another ironic scenario indeed, in view of what lay ahead.

7 Letter published in the *Morning Post*, 8 September 1924.

8 The Reilly–Churchill exchange of letters is reproduced in Robin Bruce Lockhart [1, 4], 120–3.

9 *Pravda*, 12 May 1925. Again, the language has the authentic ring of Savinkov's voice. A forgery would have presented him in a far less sympathetic way, though the question might well be put: why was the letter published at all?

10 Winston Churchill, *Great Contemporaries* (London, 1937), 125 *et seq.* The one serious flaw in the Savinkov chapter is the woefully inaccurate assertion that it was Trotsky and other Bolshevik leaders who, in June 1924, had invited the famous émigré to return.

18. Trumping the 'Ace of Spies'

1 He was *not*, as is usually stated, dismissed in 1925, in the wake of the Reilly affair, but resigned after being 'blown' by the Russians.

2 CX 2616, letter written from Reilly's London address, Chambers D3, The Albany, and dated 23 January 1922.

3 Robin Bruce Lockhart [1, 4], 132–7.

4 Her fellow operator, Georgi Radevich, who posed as her husband, always played second fiddle.

5 Orlov [6, 1], 224 *et seq.* He devotes the whole of Chapter Six of his memoirs (65 pages) to 'Sydney Reilly, Britain's Intelligence Ace'.

6 One Western intelligence source has cautioned the author about accepting this particular part of Orlov's account, which is otherwise found unchallengeable. 'Niece' and 'Uncle' were also thought to be code-words exchanged between the two. But Orlov is emphatic about the blood relationship, which he refers to elsewhere.

7 For example, Robin Bruce Lockhart [1, 4], 134.

8 See above, p. 316–8.

9 Carr papers [15, 6], 56.

10 Unbeknown to him or to Bunakov, Boyce, Reilly *et al.*, the special 'window' on the Finnish–Russian border which the Trust claimed to have opened up for all these operations was itself part of the trap. It was supposed to be run by a Finn called Toyvo Vayha. His real name was Ivan Petrovich Petrov and he was an OGPU man. (CIA survey [15, 3], 9.)

11 Orlov [6, 1], 230. Boyce had taken special leave from his post to attend.

12 The word was obviously used here in the professional sense of agent provocateur.

13 Carr papers [15, 6], 58.

14 Carr papers [15, 6], 59.

15 It was indeed a touchingly intimate message, dated 'Vyborg, Friday 25 September 1925' and beginning 'My most beloved, my sweetheart'. He assured her that any delay in his return would be a

short one and that she should do absolutely nothing in the mean-time. (Text first given in Pepita's unfortunate book on Reilly published in London in 1931.)

16 Orlov [6, 1], 232.

17 As soon as he had made sure that Reilly was walking into the trap, Yakushev had gone on ahead, to prepare for his reception.

18 Carr papers [15, 6], 60.

19 As we shall see, the Kremlin had nothing to worry about on this score.

19. The End of Sydney Reilly

1 Article in the bi-monthly magazine of the FSB (the restyled KGB) in March 1993, entitled 'The Prisoner in Cell No. 73'. So far as it goes, it has credibility inasmuch as the essentials check with the story given by General Orlov twenty-five years before in Chapter Six of his secret memoirs. Further details from Soviet files – which the authors admit were treated selectively – are given in Costello and Tsarov [16, 3] 36–40. (See caution in Foreword.) Finally, there are some unpublished documents on the affair preserved in Reilly's own CX 2616 personal file. For once, there are no major discrepancies – only some gaps and a few unan-swered questions.

2 'The Murder of Sydney Reilly', a document without authorship, contained in the Reilly CX 2616 file. It is marked: 'Copy sent F.O. C/2858.'

3 Orlov [6, 1], 239–42 which deal with Reilly's arrest and interrogation.

4 It was on a postcard to Boyce, date-stamped 'Moscow, 27 October 1925' which the OGPU made sure was promptly despatched.

5 Orlov [6, 1], 240–2.

6 Ibid.

7 In the periodical *Literaturnaia Gazeta* on 20 December 1967. Such letters, extorted or forged, became almost a standard feature of OGPU practice.

8 For example, *Deadly Illusions* [16, 3], 38–9.

9 Richard B. Spence, 'Sydney Reilly's Lubianka Diary 30 October–4 November 1925', in *Revolutionary Russia*, vol. 8, no. 2, December 1995, 179–94.

10 Again, a rather rich Reillyism as he was neither English nor Christian in any proper sense. But, given his plight, any exaggeration can be readily excused.

11 This seems to have been the only occasion on which physical pressure, even of a mild and probably unpremeditated nature, was used against him.

12 Spence [19, 9], note 12.

13 By the time of Reilly's incarceration, he was functioning as British chargé d'affaires.

14 Intercepted by the British, translated and entered into Reilly's CX 2616 file without any reference. It is the only such document to survive which bears in any way on his capture.

15 Another oddity about the letter is that the 'Dear Comrade', to whom it was addressed in Vienna, was informed that the (fictitious) shooting incident at the Finnish–Soviet border took place on 24 September, whereas the official statement had placed it on 28 September. If this was not more deliberate obfuscation, then the OGPU was tripping over its own meshes.

16 One of several details not mentioned in the released Soviet documents on Reilly's end, selected from their voluminous Trust files. The decision to finish Reilly off, like the decision to arrest him, was probably taken by the Stalin-dominated Politburo, though there were now no operational gains in keeping him alive and even some possible hazards.

17 Orlov, in conversation with Edward P. Gazur (letter to the author, 6 December 1996).

20. Fingerprints

1 The letter, dated 15 September 1924, was supposedly signed by Gregory Zinoviev, President of the Soviet Comintern (the Third Communist International). Addressed to the British Communist Party, it called on them to further the Bolshevik cause by fomenting civil and military unrest in the country. Its publication was a lethal blow to a socialist party struggling to deny that it was shrugging off the shadow of a 'Red Menace'.

2 Robin Bruce Lockhart [1, 4], 126–9.

3 An enormous literature has developed over the years on the subject. Christopher Andrew in *Secret Service* (London, 1985), 302 *et seq.*, gives a characteristically thorough and balanced survey, based on such evidence as was available at the time. It leaves open the question of genuine versus forgery, though the balance of all later disclosures points to the latter.

4 Carr papers [15, 6], 50–3.

5 Ibid.

6 Not to be confused with the KGB defector, General Alexander Orlov, whose memoirs have often been quoted above.

7 The date when Vladimir Orlov was arrested by the Berlin police authorities when he finally overstepped the mark by forging documents supposedly showing that two American senators, Borah and Norris, had received $100,000 for services to Moscow. The police found in his quarters a collection of stamps and seals of all major Soviet organizations and facsimiles of the signatures of Soviet leaders.

8 PU 6109, 26 April 1922.

9 No 'Captain Black' has been traced in SIS archives either as a real person or as an alias. However, precious few archives of any nature on the Soviet target area during the period have survived.

10 The possibility cannot, of course, be ruled out that this was just another *nom de guerre.*

11 See, again, notes in Foreword. For this one episode only, the Soviet history does appear to have been drawn upon for the commercial

joint Soviet productions with Western collaborators. (See article in the *Daily Telegraph*, 15 January 1998.)

12 Carr papers [15, 6], 55.

13 Now Admiral Sir Hugh Sinclair. The first 'C' had died aged sixty-four on 14 June 1923, still at work after fourteen years at the helm.

14 Carr papers [15, 6], 61. The job of going to Paris to deliver Reilly's last letter to his wife was given to Bunakov.

15 CX 652 of 20 July 1925. The reference, and New York's reply, UN 1215 of 24 July, have incongruously survived in Reilly's personal file, CX 2616. There had been earlier exchanges about him during the previous November.

16 CX 2616. Report of ST 28 dated 17 November 1925 with no reference number and marked simply 'Translation of coded message'.

17 It was printed in the 'Deaths' column on 15 December 1925: 'REILLY: On the 28th Sept., killed near the village of ALLEKUL by GPU [*sic*] troops. Captain Sydney George Reilly, M.C. late R.A.F., beloved husband of Pepita N. Reilly.'

18 In CX 2616, No. CXG 948, Helsingfors, 13 October 1925. Marked 'Following from ST/0 to CSS'.

19 Author's italics.

20 Author's italics.

21. Balance Sheets

1 Harry Carr [15, 6], for example, writes of Reilly's disappearance: 'It convinced me that the GPU [*sic*] had played a big part in the affair, and my subsequent attitude towards anything to do with the "Trust" was tailored accordingly'. Carr had already unearthed evidence of Trust disinformation over supposed additions to the Kronstadt defences.

2 On 25 January 1930, General Kutyepov was kidnapped in broad daylight on the streets of Paris by an OGPU hit team but, due to a bungled operation by them, was dead by the time he reached

Moscow. Seven years later, his successor, General E.K. Miller, was also seized in Paris by OGPU agents and, this time, they were reported to have brought their captive back alive.

3 In June 1926 the so-called 'Eurasian Movement', which had always functioned as part of the Trust, was allowed to form its own 'Management Centre' for independent operations – a sure omen for the future.

4 The author has been told that, in addition to the in-depth debriefing of Opperput carried out by the Finnish Chief of Staff General Vallenlus, Captain A. Ross from the SIS station in Estonia also interrogated Opperput (whom British intelligence knew as Upelintz) in Helsinki. No copy of Ross's report appears to have survived.

5 This explanation, however, was accepted by Carr who regarded Opperput as 'Arch-villain No. 2' of the Trust operation (Yakushev being 'Arch-villain No. 1'). (Carr papers [15, 6], 64–5.)

6 Author's italics.

7 Orlov [6, 1], 245 (pp. 245–60 cover the saga of the Trust's demise).

8 According to Orlov [6, 1], Maria had already made an attempt in January 1927 to find refuge for Opperput in Paris with the White Russian community there. Without revealing to General Kutyepov the utterly bogus nature of the Trust, she told her uncle that one of its members had become disenchanted with the operation and was prepared to disclose its secrets to French or British intelligence, in return for asylum.

9 CIA survey [15, 3], 13–14; Carr papers [15, 6], 64–5; and Orlov [6, 1], 257–60.

10 In 1926, the Polish General Staff were ordered by the new military dictator of the country, Marshal Pilsudski, to carry out a special investigation of the Trust's credentials. They produced compelling evidence that these were bogus, and the marshal broke off all contact.

11 CIA survey [15, 3], 14. This does not feature in any other Western version of the story.

12 Also called, in some Western accounts, Voznesenky.

13 In 1934 he was to become head of the NKVD, as the political
police were then styled.

14 For example, in *The Memoirs of an Old Chekist* by F.T. Fomin
(Moscow, 1964). (The title has been translated.)

15 Geoffrey Bailey [17, 3], 268–9.

16 Edward P. Gazur, who told this anecdote, along with many others,
to the author during 15–18 September 1997.

17 Ullman [5, 29], op. cit. 134–35.

18 Or, as he phrased it elsewhere, 'combine identifications with
destruction and recruiting'.

19 For a modern and suitably rigorous exposition of this, see Dmitri
Volkogonov's *Lenin, Life and Legacy* (English trans., London,
1995), 233 *et seq.*

20 The author experienced this in several research visits to
Washington in the 1960s and 1970s. The feud between the rival
camps of opinion inside the CIA at the time is mirrored in the
controversy over the KGB defectors Golitsyn and Nosenko. (*The
Storm Birds*, (London, 1988), chs 11 and 12.)

Envoi: What Happened to Them

1 London *Times*, 7 October 1929.

2 For the details of Kalamatiano's final years, see Harry Thayer
Mahoney [3, 19].

3 Carr papers [15, 6], 67. Carr himself, it should be added, went on
to a distinguished career. He headed the Helsinki station right
down to 1940 and in 1945 was appointed SIS Controller of the
Northern Area, one of the four regions established in the post-
Second World War system for the SIS.

4 Private information.

5 CXC 177 telegram to Warsaw, dated 30 November 1920.

6 FO 371/4442, No. 157162, 14 September 1918.

7 FO 371/4442, No. 159461, 18 September 1918.

8 Ibid.

9 C/3014, also marked 'Most Secret', addressed to H.M.G. Jebb (later Lord Gladwyn Jebb) at the Foreign Office. The minute was written by the 'C' of the day in person and is in Reilly's CX 2616 file.

10 Minute to the Foreign Office, C/3397.

Note on Bibliography
(or, rather, the lack of it)

Several dozen books have been cited in my footnotes, illustrating various sequences of this narrative, and I do not propose to list them again now. So far as I am aware, this present volume is the only work in any language which recounts the first round in the East–West conflict from the standpoint of the rival intelligence services; thus there are no comparable studies to be cited. General histories of intelligence, such as Christopher Andrew's admirable *Secret Service*, devote only part of one chapter to the period, based almost entirely on published sources. Like all sparse surveys of the period, such accounts are in need of expansion, and often of correction.

Several of these academics have rightly identified their exclusion from sealed archives as a limitation on their work. In *Britain and the Russian Civil War*, the American Professor Richard Ullman, for example, produced thirty years ago what is still the best political survey of Anglo–Soviet relations during the first critical years of the Lenin regime. The bibliography, though described as selective, is, in fact, very comprehensive. Yet he was careful to point out that, on the secret intelligence aspect, he had little beyond a handful of sensationalized personal memoirs to go on. Similarly, the recently published history of the French Secret Services by Douglas Porch skips this early period almost entirely for the lack of anything informative to say. The reappearance of the *documents repatriés* referred to in the Foreword came just two years too late for him, for clearly he would have made good use of them.

The various personal memoirs and biographies I have cited were each of value in filling out the political or human interest sides of the story. However, their significance varied widely. Bruce Lockhart's *Memoirs of a British Agent*, together with his edited *Diaries*, remain the key works among the intelligence reminiscences. He stood at the epicentre of all the upheavals during the spring and summer of 1918 and for some episodes – Sydney Reilly's antics on arrival in Moscow, for example, or the collapse of the July *putsch* – he is the only major eyewitness. Yet, as detailed in Part Two, his accounts suffer from huge gaps and one serious flaw. The major gap in the *Diaries* is for the last three weeks of August 1918. Yet this was the height of the preparation and dismal failure of the plot which, mistakenly, bears his name. The serious flaw is his attempt to wriggle away from his own (admittedly limited) involvement in that plot.

As for the 'Ace of Spies' himself, the two familiar biographies of him (by Robin Bruce Lockhart and Michael Kettle) both suffer from being virtually unsourced from start to finish. The former clearly had the benefit of his father's help, among that from other 'fellow conspirators'. The latter, whose book is a brief paperback, appears also to have received family help, this time from Reilly's relatives. But neither indicates where this personal information came from, and both repeat great chunks of the suspect Reilly legend which his own secret service file now finally establishes as mythical.

On a very different plane of reliability are the modest but thrilling memoirs, *Baltic Episode*, of Augustus Agar, the young naval hero of the British triumph in the waters around Petrograd during the winter and summer of 1918/19. But even Agar never realized at the time the unique quality of the intelligence penetration he was supporting nor even the identity of the mystery SIS agent who was his co-hero ashore.

Of the books in English about Lenin's political police, the adversaries of Western intelligence, George Leggett's *The Cheka* proved exceptionally valuable both as a Who's Who of the Bolshevik intelligence hierarchy and as a sober assessment of their work. There are many military surveys and eyewitness accounts of the battles of the civil war, with General Denikin's *The White Army* at their head for the southern front and Peter Fleming's *The Fate of Admiral Kolchak* for the Siberian campaign.

By contrast I can find no work which describes and analyses the great Bolshevik deception scam which followed on the civil war (and wrought almost as much damage in the White Russian and Western camps). Again, we have had to make do so far with individual chapters in general histories or on selective and controlled releases from the Russian side, like some of the archives on 'the Trust' produced in 1993 for the first 'co-production' effort with the West, *Deadly Illusions*. This material was chosen from the old KGB files on General Alexander Orlov, the most senior Soviet intelligence officer ever to defect to the West. But twenty-five years before, Orlov had already written his own inside account of the Trust, in a book kept secret by his American hosts until now.

Hundreds of books exist on the closing phase of the Great War and on the accompanying collapse of the continental dynasties. With works like *November 1918*, *Royal Sunset* and *The Last Habsburg*, I have only added to their number (though venturing to do so in each case because of fresh material). Even if they added relatively little, researching and writing them has at least enabled me to place the 'Iron Maze' of this secret service battle in the context of the wider military, diplomatic and dynastic landscape which surrounded it.

Acknowledgements

In view of the fact that it was they who launched me out on what grew into a many-sided undertaking, it is somewhat ironic that the British secret service should have requested anonymity concerning their role. Ironic, but not surprising: no issues of national security arose over events lying so far back but there were reasons of what might be termed professional convenience which I have respected. My thanks must therefore go without names to that handful of intelligence officials, some active as well as retired, who have helped to steer things along over the past four years. It was some recompense for their help that, as stated in the Foreword, I was able to present material from French, American and Russian sources which was unknown to them.

By contrast, I am able to thank – and do so profusely – the one person who, above all, has led me through the maze of French intelligence archives, especially those untidy heaps of their own documents recently handed back to them by the Russians. Chantal Maurel, herself an historian in this field, was assigned to help me with my research, once political clearance had been given to allow me *carte blanche*. I could not have wished for a more charming and perceptive guide. Without her contacts and her perseverance on my behalf over the past year, the French role in this saga could never have been pieced together, even in the admittedly incomplete pattern we have managed to assemble.

A major problem we faced was the dispersal of much of the returned material among several centres. The Director of all the Archives of France, M. Alain Erlande-Brandenburg, was kind enough to lend his personal support to my research and to indicate where some half a dozen interesting files might be found. But despite such sponsorship from their 'Supremo', bureaucracy at lower levels occasionally blocked my path (lack of necessary *dérogation*, or special dispensation) when I ventured out solo, without my cicerone.

No problems were encountered, however, with the French General Staff's Historical Service at the Château de Vincennes, or with the 'Archives Contemporaines' at Fontainebleau and I am grateful to Clare Sibille and Christine Petillat respectively for their help at these two major centres. A smaller but nonetheless intriguing cache of intelligence material was found in the Museum of the Préfecture of Police in Paris and I must also thank M. Charlot for permission to consult those archives.

Two new helpers who appeared out of the blue in America (Edward Gazur for the invaluable Orlov papers and Harry Thayer Mahoney for his unique material on Kalamatiano) have been acknowledged already. I must also thank some familiar friends and helpers in Washington: notably Hayden Peake and Daniel Mulvenna. In addition to extending to me the hospitality of his Leesburgh home, Daniel passed on much interesting advice about Soviet disinformation. It is a subject to which he has devoted years of part-time research which I hope will eventually fructify into an authoritative book.

Away from special intelligence sources, I would like to thank, in Britain, the staff of our Public Record Office for their unfailing efficiency and friendliness (the latter is a quality which one would like to see transplanted into some of their French colleagues). The Imperial War Museum, both at Duxford and in London, have contributed many illustrations, some of them unfamiliar and my thanks go, in particular, to Peter Kent, the Curator of the Photographic Archive, and to Debbie Walters.

Once again, the person I have to thank above all for secretarial and administrative help is a dear friend, Susan Small, now Mrs

Stephen Bunker, and living with her husband in South Africa. The final text was, in fact, made ship-shape at their hospitable home in Constantia, Cape Town. It came as something of a culture shock to the fountain pen author to see all 150,000 words of his labours 'zipped' by e-mail direct to his London publishers in a matter of minutes. However, though this wizardry can transmit ideas it cannot, as yet, create them. Apropos publishers, it has proved a delight to return to the fold of Macmillan, after meandering among several other distinguished houses over the years. I was especially glad to see that the personal touch had not deserted them. A chat and a handshake with a senior executive was still enough to seal length, provisional title, publication date and price all in one go – without recourse to those 'acquisition committees' which plague so many of their competitors today. It is also, admittedly, a huge plus that they live only five minutes' walk from my London house.

There is one place, as opposed to one person, which needs to be specially acknowledged. For thirty years, I enjoyed peaceful retreats in the Chilterns from which to write (and shoot). The last of these bolt-holes was recently stopped up after yet another Oxfordshire family estate was taken over by big city money. A replacement soon turned up, however – also out of the blue.

Paziols is a fortified medieval village in the middle of the 'Pays Cathare' which does not even boast a hotel. Its 800-odd inhabitants are interested mainly in rugby football, hunting and wine. All are passions which I share, so there was no problem with local 'bonding'. The house I rent is built into the high ramparts, with one terrace looking out towards the Mediterranean and one towards the Pyrenees. The valley beneath is covered with the vineyards of Fitou, of which the commune is a registered producer. Even the cherished beech woods of the Chilterns cannot match the setting, nor its tranquillity as a workplace.

Appendices

Appendix 1. Reilly's personal 'shopping list' sent from Moscow in midsummer of 1918. Some of the items requested could be called professional 'props'. His chain of mistresses, who also served as couriers, needed the white cotton and crêpe de chine for their blouses. The recipient of the ladies' tailor-made suit ('rather full') is unknown.

Li'ndon for Cheviot
Black Satin
Cream "

3 yds Black Crêpe de Chine
  "   White "   " —
      for Blouses

Men's dark Tie.

M— me Paebcrand

No. 96

Evan E. Young, Esquire,   September 21, 1921
    American Commissioner,
            Riga.

Sir:

        The Department is in receipt of your despatch
No. 1168, dated August 23, 1921, with reference to
the so-called Lockhart case.

        In view of the extremely confidential nature
of the enclosure to this despatch, you are instructed
to forward all copies on file in your office to the
Department.

        I am, Sir,
                Your obedient servant,
                    For the Secretary of State:

                                    F. M. Dearing.

361.112K121/50

ELP:LSS   Alvey A. Adee
                    Sept.19 1921.

Appendix 2. Smothering the truth: Washington orders all copies to be
rounded up of a secret telegram for the American mission in Moscow which
admitted a degree of involvement in the misnamed 'Lockhart Plot' to
overthrow Lenin.

Any reference to the matter
contained in this communication
please quote date and number:-

8979

96

From S.T.25(E)

S/N.99.

C.X.066477

Translation

STOCKHOLM 16.2.19.

NAVAL.

Report sent to the Revolutionary Soviet of the Northern
Front.

~~In view of the political and military situation~~ it is to be
supposed that, in the sping when the seas are rid of ice, the
enemy will undertake the landing of troops in the districts of the
Finnish and Riga gulfs.

The most favourable places for the landing of troops are:

Finnish Gulf: Baltic Port
            Reval
            Mon-vik
            Papon-vik
            Kashper-vik
            Mouth of the Narova
            Mouth of the Luga
            Zoporsk bay

Riga Gulf: In the district Galsap – Rogge-kul
            Pernofi bay

As a safe-guard against forces being landed, all the places
named should be fortified, for which purpose it is necessary to
have ante-landing stations in each place.

These stations should consist of:

1) The mining of the seas in the neighbourhood of the station
2) Shore fortifications for the defence of the station and
   mine-fields.

For the following reason either of the above-named places
could be chosen for landing forces: Landing operations can only be
successfully carried out in places protected from wind and rough
sea. Besides, for successfully accomplishing the landing itself,
in the absence of fortified ports, it should be carried out in such
places where the ships carrying the troops can approach the shore
without danger. In this respect the places mentioned are especially
suitable thanks to the sloping sand shores and absence of rocks and
reefs. In addition to the above, the landing can be carried out on
a wide front at any of the places named, and thus contribute to the
rapid landing of forces and difficulty in repelling same.

This makes one believe that if the enemy seriously considers
landing forces that he will choose one or several of the places
named. It is necessary, therefore, to commence immediately to
fortify these places so that by the early spring they are completed
and we are not caught unawares by the enemy.

The ante-landing stations must be supplied with all necessary
materials and men.

In the technical supply for each station, besides the mines
the following should be included:

1) Motor boats of the type existing in the Mining Companies – 90
2) Rowing boats – 100
3) Motor boats for the commanding staff of the station – 10.
4) Projectors – 20
5) 3" field batteries – 20.

Appendix 3. A sample of the superb intelligence
material for which the lone British agent in Petrograd, Paul Dukes, was
later given his knighthood: part of a six page Bolshevik assessment of
where the Western allies would land and what detailed
anti-invasion measures were to be taken.

Index

INDEX

Cecil, Lord Robert: view of Lockhart, 113; memorandum on Bolshevik question, 28–30; reaction to Lockhart's recommendations, 58; reaction to Cromie's death, 89; reply to MPs' questions on 'Lockhart plot', 114

Central Intelligence Agency, 6

Chaivosky, Nikolai, 169

Chamberlain, Austen, 304

Chambers, Haddon see Bobadilla, Pepita

Charles, Emperor of Austria and King of Hungary, 77, 119

Chebyshev, Nikolai, 253

Cheka (OGPU): Orlov and, 6; formation of, 39, 53–5; rounds up French and British citizens, 81; reaction to shooting of Lenin, 84–6; Berzin, agent provocateur for, 91; gain evidence of Lockhart's complicity in plot, 104; and 'Lockhart plot', 108; raids, 115; Dukes poses as officer in, 132; violence under Iakov Peters, 141; capture Kalamatiano, 150, 233; raids on Western missions, 231; threat to American consulate-general, 232; deception, 249; following Lenin's orders, 251; contacts with MOR intercepted, 252; targets émigré centres, 253; control over Potapov, 254; as OGPU, 255; raid on hospital, 258; strike at Savinkov's underground movement, 262; invent Liberal Democratic organization, 263; put pressure on Pavlovsky, 265; plot for Savinkov, 266; elaborate deception of Savinkov, 267; trap for Savinkov, 268; employs Lioubov Derental as informant, 269; capture Savinkov, 270; preparations for Savinkov in prison, 272; effects on Savinkov, 276; reprimanded over Savinkov's death, 280; need to arrest Reilly, 283; agent Maria Zakhavchenko-Schulz, 285; forgeries, 290; interrogate Reilly, 294; luring Reilly to Russia, 294–7; undiscovered plot, 315; end of the Trust, 316; Opperput portrays self as agent for, 317; attitude toward Opperput, 318; target of Opperput & Schulz, 321; account of Opperput-Schulz terrorist actions, 322; as Bolshevik's political police, 323; under rule of Lenin, 327; figures featured in narrative, 330;

agents executed by Stalin, 331; ensnarement of Reilly, 331

Chekov, Anton, A Month in the Country, 64

Chelyabinsk, 52, 65

Chicherin, Georgi, 78, 175, 234

Chon, 258–9

Churchill, Winston: appointed Minister of War, 165; interventionist plans opposed by Lloyd George, 166; argues for Allied intervention in Russia, 167; delighted at collapse of Prinkipo project, 172; no comment on report on Kolchak, 194; plans to topple Bolshevik regime, 197; persuades Cabinet to send extra troops to Arctic, 198; plan to support White Russian assault on Petrograd, 199; raised British support for Yudenich, 203; urges award of Order of the Bath to Denikin, 214; pushes case for Allied intervention, 216–17; communications with Denikin, 218; enthusiasm for Denikin, 219; attempts to push intervention policy, 222; reluctantly telegrams Wrangel, 223; preference for grand attacks, 227; sends aid to Denikin, 228; Savinkov wishes to meet, 242; rebukes Reilly, 277; support for Savinkov, 278; tribute to Savinkov, 280; and Reilly's vision of Anglo-Soviet agreement, 304; over-optimism concerning Russian situation, 325; end of hopes of defeating Bolsheviks, 328

Churchill, Randolph, 333

CIA see Central Intelligence Agency

Clark, Sir William, 78

Clemenceau, Georges: approves policy on Bolsheviks, 29; on Czech Legion, 69; and Allied intervention in Russia, 166; vetoes Russian involvement in Paris peace conference, 168–9; softens attitude to Bolsheviks, 170; encourages dissent in anti-Soviet camp, 172; shot, 173; engineering peace treaty with Germany, 176; relations with British, 185; opposed to Churchill's plans, 197; insistent on ousting Goltz, 208; support for Poland, 224; celebrated, 280

Clive, Mr (British minister in Stockholm), 110

CMBs: origins, 129–30; operation against Baltic Fleet, 139–45; and Russian

[390]

INDEX

couriers, 140; attack on bombarding ships, 142; inaction to save Krasnaya Gorka, 143; return to courier duties, 144; sunk with losses, 145

Coates, Albert, 131

Congress of Soviets, 107

Cossacks *see under* Krasnov, General Peter

Cowan, Rear-Admiral Sir Walter: commander of British Baltic Fleet, 133, 137, 139; instructions regarding torpedoes, 140; lack of contact from Agar, 142; report from Agar concerning Terrioki operation, 144; in response to Terrioki action, 145; support for Yudenich, 202

Crimea, 157

Cromie, Captain: plans for destruction of Baltic fleet, 67–8; killed in Chekist raid, 84–6; British reaction to death, 88–90; Dzerzhinsky arranged contact with, 100; plot to entrap, 103; possession of his documents by Bolsheviks, 110; seen by Armour in Moscow, 111; Lockhart's statements on murder of, 112; sabotage attempts, 144; attacks on Russian fleets, 326; official files on, 335; function in Petrograd, 336

Cromie, Josephine, 336

Crowther Smith, H.F., 21–2

Culver Military Academy, 332

Cumming, George Mansfield Smith ('C'): GBS unable to draw on private diary, 4; sends telegram about Reilly's arrival in Russia, 13, 16; and Reilly's reputation, 19–20; appoints Reilly to Russian mission, 20–21; character, 21–4; influence on British involvement in Russia, 25; colleagues ST 30 &, 31, 140; receives first report from Reilly, 31–3; report from Boyce, 33–4; and independence of secret service, 40; as source for British decision-making, 43; and liaison with US State Department, 66; and Boyce, 71, 84; guidance sought from, 121; and 'unfinished business' in St Petersburg, 125; enrols Agar in secret naval mission, 130–31; recruits Dukes as secret agent in St Petersburg, 132; and Agar operation, 133; receives messages from Dukes, 134; concern over Agar, 139; in reaction to

Agar's actions, 142; operation to bring Dukes to safety, 143; in command, 144; summons to Dukes, 145; arranges meeting between Agar & Dukes, 146; presents Agar to King George, 147; sends Reilly on second mission, 148; recommends Reilly for Military Cross, 150; takes initiative, 151; Reilly reports on Denikin to, 158–9, 213; Reilly fulfills brief from, 165; official contact with Agar, 199; requires new assessment of White Russian position, 215; report from Hill, 225; communications with War Office concerning Reilly, 240; expresses confidence in Reilly, 241; backs Reilly's European mission, 242; rejects Reilly's application for full-time career, 243; enquiries from staff concerning Reilly, 244; as Reilly's superior, 295; ignores warnings on Reilly's character, 312; pronouncements concerning Reilly, 337

Curzon, George Nathaniel, Lord: withdraws British posts in Siberia, 195; view of Yudenich, 201; Hill reports to, 215–16; report from Hill concerning Denikin, 217; opposes Lloyd George's proposal, 229; opposes restoration of commercial ties with Russia, 230; despatches from Hill, 324

Czech Legion: formation of, 64–5; struggles to leave Russia, 65–6; Lockhart pleads for intervention on behalf of, 69–70; Wilson agrees to intervention in support of, 75; fighting for survival, 119; Wilson on, 124; morale in, 125

Czechoslovakia, 65, 119

Daily Mail (newspaper), 307

de Beers (company), 9

de Verthamon, Martial-Marie-Henri *see* Verthamon, Martial-Marie-Henri de

Denikin, General Anton Ivanovich: intelligence assessment of requested, 125; supports Kerensky, 152; headquarters in Ekaterinodor, 155; assessment of logistical needs, 156; Reilly's assessment of, 158–9, 162, 167; recognition of Kolchak as 'Supreme Ruler', 188; advance of Volunteer Army, 189; links with Cossack forces, 192;

INDEX

Kolchak transfers power to, 193; accuses Janin of betraying Kolchak, 194; observers press need to support, 213; British military units sent to support, 214; military successes, 214–15; British decide to support, 216–7; feared by Bolsheviks, 216; help from Churchill, 218; consolidating position, 219; defeat by Red Army, 220; holds on to Volunteer Army, 221; inadequate aid from Lloyd George, 222; weaker than Wrangel, 223; British economic mission fails to materialize, 225; Churchill acts through, 227; receives aid from Churchill, 228; Western hope for anti-Bolshevik crusade, 229; officially associated with United States, 236; associations with Reilly, 240; prevention of similar activists, 255; in relation to Maria Zakhavchenko-Schulz, 285; movements predicted by Hill, 325; assessment of prospects, 329; death in America, 331

Denmark, 89

Derental, Baron, 269, 274

Derental, Lioubov: object of Savinkov's affection, 269; after Savinkov's arrest, 270; betrayal of Savinkov, 270; protected by Savinkov, 274; visits to Savinkov in jail, 277; compared with Maria Schulz, 290; compared with Maria Zakhavchenko-Schulz, 316

Deribass, T.D., 291–2, 294, 331

d'Espery, General Franchet, 325

Deuxième Bureau: GBS access to archives, 7–8; archives catalogued, 8; files on Russian networks, 43; sections set up, 46

Dombrovský, Captain (Chief of Staff of Baltic fleet), 136

Don, the, 215

Donetz Basin, 157

Doolittle (American Vice-Consul), 52

Drogomirov, General, 159

Dukes, Paul (ps. Joseph Afirenko): recruited as agent in St Petersburg, 131–2; sends stream of reports, 133; assessment of Bolshevik fleet, 134–5, 137; reports to London, 139; description of pennant, 140; smuggled report, 141;

communications with Agar, 143; summons to return to London, 145; first meeting with Agar, 146; operating in Petrograd, 174; and stability of Petrograd, 199; teams up with Reilly, 242; material smuggled out of Leningrad, 324; post-War career, 334

Duranty, Walter: details of Savinkov's trial, 274; description of Savinkov, 275; report on Savinkov trial, 277; reports expanded on, 278

Dzerzhinsky, Felix Edmunovich: Orlov protege of, 6; and organization of Cheka, 53–5; captured by SR rebels, 72; Latsis, close colleague of, 98; investigates 'Lockhart plot', 99; arranges contact with Cromie, 100; allegedly behind 'Lockhart plot', 102; meeting with *Figaro* newspaper, 105; sends for Marchand, 106; and 'Lockhart plot', 107; and handling of 'Lockhart plot', 108; Karl Radek as spokesman, 110; appointment of Iakov Peters, 141; mental torture of Yakushev, 252; association with Artuzov, 253; involved in plans with Artuzov, 254; begins to target victims, 256; fear over Savinkov's guerrilla force, 258; maims Savinkov's organization, 262; plans for Savinkov, 272; preparations for Savinkov in prison, 273; treatment of Savinkov in jail, 274; proves Savinkov no threat, 276; attempts to honour promises to Savinkov, 279; possible murder of Savinkov, 280; Reilly writes to from Lubyanka, 301; extent of power, 323; success in service, 324; death in office, 330

Ekaterinburg, 52, 75, 77, 215

Ekaterinodor, 155, 156, 214

Emerson (of American Railway Commission), 191

England *see* Britain

Estonia, 122

Federov (Mukhin; Cheka agent): Orlov draws on accounts from, 6, 299; and the Trust, 254; reverts to real name, 263; selects Maria Zakhavchenko-Schulz to trap Reilly, 285; feud with Opperput,

INDEX

INDEX

Hindenburg, General Paul von
    Beneckendorff und von, 63, 121, 280
Historical Service of the French Army, 7
'History of Soviet State Security Organs', 9
Hitler, Adolf, 203, 212, 322
Hodgson, Sir Robert, 303
Holland, 89, 120
Holman, Major-General Herbert, 214, 217,
    222
Hoover, Herbert, 238
Hope-Carson, Lieutenant-Colonel, 201
Hore-Belisha, Leslie, First Baron, 337
Hughes, Charles Evans, 238
Huntingdon, Chapin, 51, 238

Ibrahim (Cheka agent), 304
Iogolevich, Michel, 192
Irkutsk, 52
Ironside, Major-General Edmond, 198, 199
Isaac, Captain (British Intelligence), 17–18
Isvestia (newspaper), 98
Italy, 29

Janin, General Maurice, 185, 193–4, 197
Japan, 59
Jellicoe, Admiral, First Sea Lord, 182
Jerram, Mr (acting British vice-
    consul), 152–4
Journal of Modern History, 95

Kalamatiano, Xenophon Dmitrivich: US
    station chief, 4; as American intelligence
    source, 49–50; recruited by Harper, 51;
    network controlled by, 52–3; at anti-
    Bolshevik meeting, 87; courier breaks
    down, 94; confined in Lubyanka, 97;
    tried in absentia, 97; involvement in
    'Lockhart plot', 105; Sergei Nikolayevich
    Serpukhovsky pseudonym of, 105, 231;
    head of American espionage operations,
    106; and 'Lockhart plot', 118; seized in
    Moscow, 150; State Department's
    master-spy, 231; seeks protection from
    Cheka, 232; betrayed by himself, 233; as
    bargaining chip for Lenin, 235; receives
    death sentence, 236; kept imprisoned,
    237; health in prison, 238; freed from
    prison, 239; in 'Butyrka', 272; compared
    with Reilly, 293; smuggles diary out of
    Lubyanka, 299; return to America, 331

Kaledin, A.M., 151
Kalmikov (Cossack commander), 187
Kanin, Admiral, 156
Kannegieser (assassin of Uritsky), 83
Kaplan, Dora, 83
Kato, Admiral, 59–60
Kerensky, Alexander, 14, 151, 152, 169, 181
Kerr, Philip, 174
Keyes, Brigadier-General Terence, 222
KGB, 9, 317
Khalifa, the, 133
Kharkov, 157, 216
Khartoum, 133
Kherson, 218
Kiev, 42, 162
King, Joseph, 70, 114
Kirpichinov (White Army Political
    Officer), 156
Kitchener, Horatio Herbert, 1st Earl of
    Khartoum, 133
Klimovich, General, Chief of
    Intelligence, 253
Knight, Admiral, 61
Knox, Major-General Sir Alfred: in
    Siberia, 58, 183–4, 193; control over
    Kolchak, 185; opinion of Kolchak, 186;
    and British Training School, 187; support
    for Kolchak's forces, 190
Kolchak, Alexander: file on, 8; leader of
    offensive in Siberia, 177, 215; career
    during World War I, 181; as a legend,
    182; accepts post as Minister of War,
    183; support from British officers, 184;
    official stance of British government, 185;
    championed by Knox, 186; tensions in
    camp, 187; political support, 188;
    successful offensive, 189; forced to
    retreat, 190; divisions within army, 191;
    prevents Gayda's attempted uprising in
    Vladivostok, 192; account of final weeks,
    193; betrayed by Janin, 194; death brings
    end of Allied involvement in Siberia, 195;
    exceptional Russian leader, 196; extent of
    Spring offensive, 197; plans to link up
    with Allied forces, 199; comparison with
    North-Western Army, 203; feared by
    Bolsheviks, 216; in retreat, 216;
    compared to Denikin, 217; in retreat in
    Siberia, 218; similarities with Denikin,
    220; ceases to pose threat to Lenin, 221;

INDEX

Japan, 29; backs Balfour, 30; and Lockhart, 36; on disunity in erstwhile Russian Empire, 71; argues against Allied military intervention in Russia, 166–7; suggests a Russian peace conference, 168; pledges financial aid, 151; convinces Clemenceau to soften attitude to Bolsheviks, 170; apprised of Bullitt's mission, 174; and peace deal with Soviets, 176; altered view of Denikin, 218; plans to reconcile Denikin and Lenin, 219; aim to use coal mines as bargaining tool, 221; fails to send adequate aid to Denikin, 222; decision not to support Wrangel, 224; struggle to get policy adopted, 229; hopes for 'liberalizing' Russia, 328; political message to Savinkov, 329

Lockhart, Robert Bruce:, 103 and 'Lockhart plot', 1, 81–118; involved in anti-Bolshevik activities, 3; character, 25–6; first impressions of Reilly, 25; Wardrop on, 36–8; sources available to, 39; as source for British decision-making, 42; powers as British representative, 46; recommends positive relationship with Bolsheviks, 57–9; recommends immediate Allied intervention, 63–4; ordered to support Cromie, 68; attends Fifth Congress of the Soviets, 73; and treatment of Romanovs, 76; isolated,78; arrested, 84; British reaction to arrest, 90; his account of 'Lockhart plot', 91–101; tried in absentia, 91; evidence of complicity in plot, 104; connection with Reilly, 107; alleged dupe, 109; Bolsheviks in possession of his documents, 110; arrival in Stockholm, 112; British reaction to, 113; report on experiences in Russia, 114; how and why 'fallen into Bolshevik hands', 115; attempt to buy Lettish regiments, 116; denial of truth, 116, 117; advice to intervene without interfering, 122; Dukes adds to intelligence gathering, 132; compromised by Reilly, 150; Major-General Knox's opinion of, 184; Kalamatiano learns of imprisonment, 231; interrogated by I.K. Peters, 232; compared with Savinkov, 277; involved in sabotage plans, 326;

relation with I.K. Peters, 330; Berzin's involvement in conspiracy, 331; publication of book, 332; career and death, 333; memoirs, 334; recall to duty, 335

'Lockhart plot', 81–101, 102–18, 121, 314

Lockhart, Robin Bruce, 95, 102

Lombard, Mr (British embassy chaplain), 85

Lubyanka, 6, 9, 97, 102

Ludendorff, General Erich, 63, 120

Lukomsky, General, 156

Lvov, Prince Georgi, 169

Macdonald, Ramsay, 306

McGrath, Captain, 77

Mackenzie, Compton, 22

Maclean, Donald, 7

Mahoney, Harry Thayer, 4

Maikop, 157

Maklakov, Vassily, 169

Mannerheim, General, 200

Marchand, René: and 'Marchand letter', 87–8, 92, 97, 99, 101, 105; secret conference in American Consulate-General, 106; describing Reilly's part in 'Lockhart plot', 107; question of publication, 108; as principal volunteer stooge, 109; publishing of letter, 111; and General Poole, 118; and composition of letter, 299; manipulation by Bolsheviks, 329

Masaryk, Dr Thomas, 65, 67, 173

Massino, Nadine, 19, 161, 336

'Memorandum in connection with Intelligence Work in Russia', 42–3

Menzies, Colonel, 240

Mexico, American spies in, 50

Mirbach, Count Wilhelm von, 62–3

Monarchist Association of Central Russia (MOR), 252, 254

Monarchist Council in Berlin, 252

MOR see Monarchist Association of Central Russia

Morens (director of French school), 97

Morning Post (newspaper), 277

Morton, Major, 240, 241

Moura see Zakrveskaia, Marie

Murmansk, Balfour, 24, 30, 32, 56

Mussolini, Benito, 268, 269

INDEX

INDEX

Trotsky, Leon: threats to regime, 1; Lockhart's assessment of, 57, 59; issues directive to disarm Czechs, 66; Lockhart acts as link with, 68; Reilly's alleged plans for, 98; and 'Lockhart plot', 107; pragatism of, 136; orders Baltic Fleet ready for action, 137; promises destruction of Black Fleet, 152; and annihilation of Soviet Eleventh Army, 158; Lenin voices fears to, 172; inspires resistance, 199; activity in Petrograd, 203; shows what Bolshevik forces can achieve, 226; celebrated, 280; penetrated by British Intelligence, 324; in exile, 331
Trust, the, 249–329
Tsaritsyn (*later* Stalingrad), 214, 216
Tsarev, Oleg, 8
Turkestan, 43

Ukraine, 71, 162, 215
Ullman, Richard, 324
'Union for the Defence of Fatherland and Freedom', 35
United States of America: supports White Russians, 1; sources for GBS, 4; and Brest-Litovsk treaty, 14; abandons alliance with Russia, 21; disagrees with British proposal on Russia, 29; lack of secret service, 47; Railway Delegation from, 48
Uritsky, M.S., 83, 108

Vassilchikov, George, 8
Vatsesis, General, 72–3
Vayha, Toyvo (alias of Petrov), 292
Vecheka, 234
Vermeille, Madame, 26
Vertement, Colonel Henri de *see* Verthamon, Martial-Marie-Henri de
Verthamon, Martial-Marie-Henri de: position of, 43–5; at anti-Bolshevik meeting, 87; escapes Chekist raid, 88; tried in absentia, 91; not mentioned in Bolshevik charges, 97; head of French espionage operations, 106; in General Poole's report, 118; sabotage in Russia, 326
Vienna, 303
Vilenkin, 257
Villa, Pancho, 50

Vinnichenko, Vladimir, 163
Vladivostok: British consulate in, 43; Japanese about to land in, 57; Allied landing in, 59–60; Lenin's reaction to landings in, 62; Wilson fails to support Allied action in, 62; Czech Legion attempts to break out of, 65–6
Vologda: Hill organizes courier links with, 42; Noulens sends telegrams from, 44; US consul ordered to, 52; Lockhart visits, 64; Allied envoys in, 77; Allied envoys leave, 78
Vologodsky, member of Directorate, 183
Volunteer Army *see* White Volunteer Army
von Manteuffel, Baron Aleksander, 322
Vorobiev, 227
Voronesh, 156

Waldegrave, William, 2
Ward, Lieutenant-Colonel John, 184
Wardrop, Oliver, 34, 36–8, 81–2, 112
Warsaw, Deuxième Bureau section in, 46
Wemyss, Admiral, 89, 147
White Volunteer Army: growing strength of, 151–2; in Novorossisk, 155; Reilly's assessment of, 156–7, 162; observers press need to support, 213; Hill's assessment of, 215–6; Allied hopes for, 218; successful campaign, 219; battle for Orel, 220; Bolshevik attempts to liquidate, 221; determined stands, 221; endure despite Denikin's defeat, 222
Wilhelm II, Kaiser of Germany, 120, 333
Williams, C.E.S., 338
Wilson, Sir Henry, 123–4, 167, 227, 325
Wilson, Woodrow: reluctance over intervention in Russia, 29–30; attitude to Bolshevik revolution, 50, 60–62; Bolsheviks reject overture from, 62; and Czech self-determination, 66–7; agrees to Allied intervention, 74–5; agrees to breakup of Habsburg Empire, 121; desire to discontinue Allied intervention in Russia, 166; suggests site for Russian peace conference, 170; collapse of Russian peace plan, 172; Bullitt represents at Paris peace conference, 173; informed of Bullitt's mission, 174; aiming to end US involvement in Russia, 177; doubts Tsarist loyalties, 185; official